Mirror

By the same author

Spiral

Mirror

Joseph Geary

London · New York · Sydney · Toronto · Dublin

A VIACOM COMPANY

First published in Great Britain by Simon & Schuster UK Ltd, 2004
A Viacom company

A CIP catalogue record for this book
is available from the British Library

ISBN 0-7432-3205 4 HB
ISBN 0-7432-3206 2 TPB

Typeset by M Rules
Printed and bound in Great Britain by
Mackays of Chatham plc

For Sylvie and Max

Acknowledgments

This book, while certainly inspired by the Museum of Modern Art, New York, is in no way meant as a journalistic exposé of that institution. However, I did feel that a minimal understanding of MoMA, especially in its handling of acquisitions, was essential to my story. Thanks are therefore due to Ellis Whitman, formerly assistant to MoMA curator Kynaston McShine, for her insights into that process. I would also like to thank Duane R. Chartier, president and CEO of The International Center for Art Intelligence Inc. for sharing his thoughts on the prevalence of art forgery, and the problems inherent in winnowing out post-war fakes in particular.

My sense of the queasy mix of American Cold War policies and Abstract Expressionism is derived pretty much entirely from Frances Stonor Saunders' terrific non-fiction account, 'Who Paid the Piper?' And I urge anyone interested in finding out more about this fascinating period to acquire a copy. The same goes for Eva Cockcroft's ground-breaking essay, 'Abstract Expressionism, Weapon of the Cold War', first published in 'Artforum' in June, 1974. The 'MAM' of my story rests squarely on the foundation stone of Russel Lynes' seminal, 'Good Old Modern: an Intimate Portrait of the Museum of Modern

Art', a book which was never far from my desk.

Thanks are due to Tina for taking me into the desert, and to Billy and David for their impressions on what it's like to live out there among the rattlesnakes and the retired hell's angels.

Finally, I'd like to thank my editor Kate Lyall Grant for her close reading and helpful comments, my agents Jim Rutman, and Simon Trewin for their constructive critiques, continued support and encouragement, and my wife for giving me just about everything a writer could wish for, starting with quiet and space in which to work.

Artists should have their tongues cut out

HENRI MATISSE

Under the city

That was the year that she gave up on art, swapped the galleries' blank inertia for the headlong rush of the subway car, the paintings' busy stillness for the zigzag jolting blur of fluttered windows and the scream of steel on steel. She was living on West 59th Street then, could walk the six blocks to the museum in fifteen minutes, but in the last week of February 1958 she rode the subway under the city, down to Coney or up to Inwood – sometimes two and even three times a day, hanging onto the porcelain straps as they clattered into the curves, reading faces and clothes, trying to imagine the lives behind the blank unseeing stares of other people, anything rather than think about what was going to happen next – because it *was* going to happen, she was sure of that, out there on the mud flats, out there on the eastern tip of Long Island where Franklin Koenig, her genius and Holy Fool, her visionary drunk was coming apart like summer road kill on the Queensborough Bridge.

He'd call her up in the middle of the night, his consonants mushy where his teeth had gone.

'I'm East of East Hampton. That's how far east I am. In the Land of Nod – of nothing doing.'

He blamed her for being stuck there – rightly, in so far as it was she who'd advised him to get out of Manhattan, she who'd told him to put some miles between himself and the Village with its bars and beery distractions. But he was the one who'd chosen Springs, partly because of Jackson, of course; Jackson who he liked to arm wrestle, Jackson who he'd match drink for drink until they were both crazy drooling blind. He'd gone out there to be closer to his friend, and then Jackson had crashed his Oldsmobile, leaving Koenig with nothing to look at but Lee and the lousy weather.

'I'm on the edge of the world, next stop Nova fucking Scotia.'

Wintry fronts rolled in from Canada and the first thing they hit was the farm, a creaky clapboard box that looked like a ship's wheelhouse dropped into the middle of a potato field.

'I'm looking at nothing,' he'd say in his toothless growl. 'No color nothing. Mud. Not even a goddamn horizon.'

Wrapped tight in her heavy winter coat, she rode the tunnels under the city, clinging to the strap or, on the craziest days, standing at the front of the first car like a kid, her fingers splayed against the buzzing glass. Anything rather than have to think.

He'd call her in the night, jerk her out of her deepest cold cream slumber.

'You've got no respect. That's the problem here. No idea what I'm going through, what I go through each and every day.'

He'd drink himself into a stupor in the early afternoon, so at night he was pretty chipper, ready to extemporize at length on the subject of the fairies at the Partisan Review or the Jesuitical sons of bitches scheming and plotting at the Modern.

'Be the artist you always wanted to be, you said.'

And it wasn't broad-brush polemic; he liked to get into detail. Three and four o'clock in the morning and he'd be picking apart Henry Kruger, the Modern's president from '39, or Ralph Buren, who'd taken over in '56.

She'd light a Chesterfield, lay the heavy black telephone on the burn-spotted pillow next to her head.

'Buren was on the Council for Foreign Relations. Did you know that? Sitting right next to Allen Dulles, right next to the head of the goddamn CIA. Kruger was in on it too. Conniving sons of bitches. Tell me what that says to you.'

His voice droned like a bug trapped in the receiver.

'And – *and* . . . Buren was with Kruger's intelligence outfit during the war. Did you know that? Did you know about Kruger's intelligence activities in South America? Oh, yeah. It's all wheels within wheels. Art and politics. Art and oil. Art and money. You know who did the first one-man show at the museum? Leslie Ann?'

Her name was always hook enough to snag her out of sleep. She'd come awake, the hot coal of her cigarette inches from her eyes.

'What?'

'Diego Rivera. Because Kruger was worried that the Mexican nationalists were going pull the plug on his oil interests.'

'Franklin . . . it's late . . .'

'Diego Rivera. The guy who used to stand outside the American Embassy yelling "Death to the Gringos!" You think I'm making this up? When Congress challenged Kruger for promoting Rivera you know what he said? He said the Reds wouldn't be so red if they were given artistic recognition.'

Like this for hours on end he'd ramble, the nutty spiel larded with establishment names – CEOs or chairmen or trustees who'd betrayed a trust or lied or ended in disgrace one way or another. There was Dick Pater, who he blamed for getting Alfred Faber fired as director of the museum back in '44. There was Samuel Bronfman, head of the Joseph E Seagram company, who'd started out selling frozen whitefish on the Canadian prairies, then made a fortune from bootleg liquor, and whose only crime as far as she could tell was to commission Mark Rothko to paint a mural. Koenig was enraged with Rothko for decorating Bronfman's goddamned restaurant. It was such a betrayal of everything they, meaning the New York School 'irascibles', had stood for.

She would drift into sleep, a cigarette burning between her

fingers, then jolt awake, the sharp smell of smoldering wool in her nostrils – hear his voice raging in the receiver, berating Rauschenberg and Johns, or Betty Pearson or Lewis Hartnal, director of the museum's International Program at that time. And if she tried to calm him down, tried to remind him how hard Hartnal had worked for him in Paris, how much they'd all done to put him where he was, he'd go nuts, fulminating, barely coherent. 'Be the artist you always wanted to be! That's what you said to me, you barren . . . you *cheating* bitch.'

So then she'd threaten to hang up, and he'd plead with her to stay on the line, start whining about his ailments: his teeth hurt; he'd had them pulled in Mexico City but they still hurt him. That was where he'd picked up the hepatitis, he was convinced of it. The hepatitis left him sluggish and depressed. A doctor on Fifth Avenue told him he was suffering from an iron deficiency. The doctor asked if he had blood in his stool. Either that or he wasn't making enough hemoglobin. At night his heart fluttered.

She asked him about the work.

'There is no work, you *cunt*!'

She'd hang up then.

She'd lie there looking at the window, waiting for the light to grow. There was work, of course. Plenty of work. It was stacked ten canvases deep all around the studio walls, some of it wrapped against the damp in oil cloth she'd bought at Dan Miller's store just down the road from Pollock's place. There was plenty of work, and there had never been a better time to show it, to sell it. In the five years since the Twelve Contemporaries show in Paris, Koenig's star had risen dramatically. Three months earlier his dealer, the poor long-suffering Becky Pearson, had sold two big pieces, one of which for $4,000, far more than Pollock ever got. Things had never been better for him, but now he wanted to tear it all down.

The tunnels ran for hundreds of miles. When the lights flickered dead, the blind roar and roll was like riding a rocket ship into the darkness. She clung on tight as though headlong movement offered some way forward.

'I hurt myself, Leslie Ann.'

It was at the end of February that he made his last call. Just after two in the morning. Rain seethed against the window.

'What did you do?'

'I hurt . . . myself. I'm bleeding. I'm my own . . .'

'Franklin?'

'So much blood.'

He sounded more than just drunk.

'Franklin, call Dan Miller.'

'They're coming for me, Leslie Ann. But late. They're too late. Hoover's guys. Those McCarthyite snot head . . . nitwits. I'm going to burn it all.'

She told him to sit tight, said she was coming straight out there. But he didn't hear her or he wasn't interested. He mumbled something she didn't catch, then started to sob, groaning in pain.

'My hand. My God, what happened to my *hand*.'

There was a noise. The sound of something hitting the floor. Metal on stone. It could have been a hammer. The line went dead. She called him straight back, broke a fingernail dialing his number, but the phone just rang and rang. And she knew the moment had come.

She called Hartnal. Hartnal was dumbstruck, thick-tongued and disoriented. Then angry. He'd been calling her all week, he said, had left notes at her building, had even sent a telegram.

'And *now* you call me? At two in the morning?'

'It's Franklin. I think there's a problem.'

She told him what had happened. He said he was going out there. He told her to stay put. He'd call her when he had news.

Thirty minutes later she was crossing the East River in her car, damned if she was going to be sidelined. The windshield wipers beat pie shapes in the streaming blur. It took her three and a half hours to get there. Once she passed East Hampton, she was driving in total darkness. The Ford bucked and shimmied as muck and stones kicked up under the body. She kept thinking about the noise she'd heard on the phone – the clank of something metal hitting the floor. Then out of nowhere she was crying, remembering the first time he'd touched her, pushing her back against the wall in his tiny kitchen. She'd bumped her head against a cabinet, making them both laugh. Then he'd lifted her skirt and put his paint covered fingers inside her and the laughing had stopped. He'd had a single room in the Bowery back then. The sag-belly ceiling was elaborately stained – a map of the underworld, he said it was. The drop leaf table he used as a desk was stacked with books. Spengler's *Decline of the West*, *Mein Kampf*, *Das Kapital*. He'd been trying to get a handle on the world historical individual.

Peering ahead through the streaming windshield, the first thing she saw was the cop. He was slouching along the side of the road, carrying a storm lantern, hunched inside a thick oilskin that hung down almost to his feet. It wasn't until the last moment that she saw the cars, and the sight of them lined up by the side of the road struck her stone cold.

'This isn't happening.'

She put the car into a ditch trying to park, had to climb out on the passenger side.

'Dear God, please.'

A heavy smell hung in the air. Burned wood and linoleum. And then the emotion hit. Realization. *I'm going to burn it all.* She staggered forward, the mud sucking at her city shoes.

Voices came out of the dark. Age-lined faces tilted up as she came along the path. There were deep gouges in the grass where a fire truck had gone through. A tangle of hoses. Hartnal was already there. He took her by the sleeve and turned her around, started walking her back towards the car, talking through his teeth.

'I thought I told you to wait by the phone.'

Even in the darkness and the rain she could see the doomed look on his smooth round face.

'Lewis.'

'He did it, Leslie Ann. The crazy bastard killed himself.'

She pulled free of him, staggered sideways, then went down into the mud.

'Liar! You goddamn liar!'

It was another man who helped her to her feet. A stocky character with hard hands. His face was smeared with soot, and the burnt smell was in his clothes. Detective Tillman. Hartnal told him that this was the young woman he'd been telling him about, the woman Koenig had called. Tillman started talking then. Leslie Ann could see his lips moving, but nothing was making sense. Then she realized he was asking her if her first name was Leslie Ann.

She had to clear her throat.

'Leslie Ann Benton. I'm an assistant curator at the—

'Modern Art Museum. Yeah, I got that.' Tillman nodded and looked over his shoulder at another man who was standing in the entrance to the house.

'Hey, Bob! Guess who's here?'

Leslie Ann shifted her weight from one foot to the other, her heels sinking into the ground.

'Leslie Ann,' said Tillman, his eyes searching her face. 'Maybe we should go inside, Leslie Ann.'

There were a couple of uniformed cops drinking coffee in the kitchen, standing under the oil lamp with an older man who looked like a local doctor doing duty as coroner. A wiry throwback to the depression era, the doctor had armbands that held his cuffs clear of his clean-scrubbed hands. She slipped crossing the threshold, saw it then, clamped a hand over her mouth.

At first glance it looked like mud, watery mud all over the kitchen floor. But where newspaper had been put down you could see liver-colored blotches. There was newspaper going out of the kitchen along the passageway to the back of the house. Tillman was scratching at his jowls.

'Did it in the bathroom,' he said reflectively.

'Took his right hand off with an axe,' said the doctor, nodding confirmation. 'Looks like the Chicago stockyards back there.'

The room began to turn. Leslie Ann asked for a cigarette. A match flared in front of her face, and she sucked smoke. *I hurt myself, Leslie Ann.* Through the buzz of the nicotine she was aware of the men talking.

'Knocked a chunk out of the sink doing it.'

She thought she was going to throw up, turned her head, met Hartnal's frozen stare.

'Can I talk to you alone, Miss Benton?'

The detective was talking to her. She focused on his soot smeared face.

'Why did you ask about my name?' she said.

'Koenig left a note.'

The last thing she saw before Tillman closed the living room door was Hartnal's face, gray as pigeon feathers under the kitchen's sickly light.

It was raining again. The cup she was holding was the only warm thing in the room. He wanted to know how well she had known the deceased.

Leslie Ann gazed down at the steaming coffee.

'Miss Benton?'

She gave a start, frowned, forcing herself to focus on this man in his terrible brown suit.

'I'm sorry,' she said. 'I'm a little upset. This is all very . . .'

Tillman repeated his question.

'I was the first person to notice his work,' she said softly. 'This is going back ten years or so. I was writing for a magazine then. *The Partisan Review*. I discovered him really.'

She drew her freezing feet tight against the couch, shook her head.

'What did he say?' she said. 'In the note.'

'Something about someone called Matisse. Something about HUAC. Is that the . . .?'

'The House Un-American Activities Committee. Yes.'

'I thought they were all washed up. With McCarthy and so forth.'

'No. They're still in business.'

'What does this committee have to do with Mr Koenig?'

'Franklin thinks – *thought* . . .' She shook her head at that, took a moment to let it sink in. 'He believed that there was a HUAC file on him, initiated when he joined the Communist Party of America.'

'This guy was a commie?'

She drew on her cigarette, fixed him with a straight look.

'After the war – like a lot of people in this country, he was pro-Stalin. We called him Uncle Joe. Those were different times, detective.'

Tillman made a stir in his seat. It was clear he didn't remember them being *that* different.

'Most of the New York School people – Pollock, de Kooning, Koenig, Gorky – most of them worked for the Federal Arts Project under the New Deal. Coming out of the depression, socialism, left-wing politics . . . well it was in the air.'

Tillman was shaking his head, a look of cold distaste on his blunt features.

'Anyway, he's been very crazy lately. He thinks – *thought* – that someone was following him. A man in a gray hat.' She registered the skeptical look on Tillman's face, and raised her eyebrows. 'I know. It sounds very Philip Marlowe. But Franklin claimed to see this character in the street all the time. Even out here. He thought this man had maybe gotten into the house. He thought maybe he was with HUAC or the FBI or maybe one of the right wing groups.'

'Such as?'

'Oh I don't know. The Patriotic Council in Dallas. The Minute Man Foundation. I think they're in Boston.'

'And? What do you think? About this guy in the hat.'

'I don't know.'

'You don't think that tonight – what happened here had anything to do with—?'

'No. No, I don't.' She looked at the cigarette stub in her fingers, took a breath. 'When Franklin called me, he said he'd hurt himself. He said . . .'

Tears brimmed, and for a moment she couldn't talk. Tillman handed her a soot-smeared handkerchief still folded in a square.

She opened it up, dabbed at her eyes, looked around the sad little room. Koenig had been there three years but had hardly made any kind of impression, hadn't even bothered to paint over the wallpaper which still carried a frieze of gloomy art deco roses dating back to the thirties. The furniture was scabbed with clots of paint, and, around the walls, at waist height, there was a smeary band where he'd wiped his hands or cleaned a brush. It looked like the ring in a dirty bath. And this wasn't even the studio.

Tillman shifted in the chair. He was watching her intently, fat fingers pushing up at his nose.

'He said he'd hurt himself,' she managed after a while. 'He said he'd hurt his hand. He said he was going to burn the paintings.'

Tillman made notes.

'What did he say about Matisse?' said Leslie Ann.

Tillman reached into a pocket and came up with a greasy scrap of paper, squinted at the penciled scrawl.

'Yeah, Matisse. Who is that? A friend?'

'A painter. Famous. He died a few years ago. Franklin never met him.'

She reached for the note, and Tillman let her take it.

'HUAC won't stop until they've nailed me to their cross. Matisse was right, Leslie Ann.'

'"Matisse was right",' said Tillman. 'What's that about?'

The paper fluttered in her fingers. Koenig's black scrawl.

'It was something we talked about. A kind of joke.'

'Yeah?'

'Franklin liked to talk. He was a big talker. Matisse said that artists should have their tongues cut out. Meaning they should paint rather than talk about painting.'

Out in the kitchen someone dropped what sounded like a metal basin. Tillman shuffled his feet, then was still for a moment, nodding. He cleared his throat, looked a little embarrassed.

'Miss Benton, I hope you don't mind my asking. But were you and Mr Koenig lovers?'

For a moment all she could do was sit there, her hands clutching the warming cup.

'Why do you ask?'

'Curiosity,' said Tillman. 'Why? Is this a difficult subject?'

'Not difficult, but . . .'

'But?'

'Potentially embarrassing. I was . . . the general perception is that I was instrumental in bringing Franklin to the attention of . . . the Museum but also Becky Pearson, his dealer. If it got out that he and I were . . .' She met Tillman's steady gaze. 'It might seem unprofessional. Mixing business and pleasure.' Tillman nodded but she wasn't sure he understood. 'I hope I can count on your discretion.'

Tillman shrugged.

'Sure. I'd appreciate it if you could tell me a little more, though.'

She put her cup aside, took her time lighting another cigarette.

'In the beginning,' she said, softly exhaling. 'In the very beginning, yes. Franklin was a very attractive man, and I was . . . young.'

'This is ten years ago you said.'

'Yes, but it feels like a hundred.'

'But more recently?'

'I can assure you that for many years now Franklin Koenig lived only for his art.'

'That right?' Tillman pulled a little bundle from his jacket pocket. Letters held together with a thick rubber band. 'I found these in his bedroom. From a lady by the name of Linda Carey. You know her?'

'No.' Leslie Ann brushed ash from her coat.

'No?'

'He mentioned her. Some girl, I think. That's all.'

He nodded at that, setting his jaw.

'Pretty girl,' he said. 'There's a couple of photographs. Looks like he was pretty taken with her.'

'Could I . . .?'

She was reaching again.

This time Tillman shook his head.

'Sorry, Miss Benton. They're his private papers. I'll level with you though. This Linda Carey comes across like a real fruitcake.'

He tapped the letters on his chunky thigh.

'Some pretty sick stuff in here. I'm gonna be getting in touch with Miss Carey.'

Leslie Ann shook her head. Koenig had barely talked to her about Carey. She was one of several bones of contention. She became aware of her breath condensing in the frozen air. He is gone, she said to herself. She couldn't quite believe it.

'He was very unhappy,' she said. 'He had health problems. An iron deficiency. Hepatitis. He had his teeth taken out in Mexico last year, and . . . well that's where he thinks he – where he thought he picked it up.'

'He had his teeth pulled?'

Leslie Ann put a hand to her mouth.

'There was a long history of things going wrong. Abscesses. Decay. Of pain.' She drew on the cigarette, exhaled.

'Who's his doctor?'

'I don't know. He was seeing a man in Manhattan.'

'So you think that's what made him do this? He was depressed about his health.'

'No,' she said. 'It was the work. He was going through a crisis with his work.'

He'd lost faith. It was the fire in the studio that snuffed him out, scorched his lungs and lined his mouth with soot, but he had hacked off his hand in the bathroom. The doctor said he must have stayed in there for quite a while given the quantities of blood they'd found. There was a possibility that he'd blacked out with the pain.

The fire had been reported by one of the residents of Springs just after three a.m. The East Hampton fire truck had arrived about thirty minutes later by which time the studio was ablaze. With all the paint and wood and solvents it had burned like a torch despite the rain. The blackened body had been recovered next to the little pot belly stove, the severed right hand clutched in the left.

Koenig had lost consciousness in the bathroom, then come to, staggered through the house, and across to the studio which was in a converted potato barn fifty feet from the back door. It was amazing that he'd made it at all. But that was what he had done. Apparently, torching the studio had been important enough to stay conscious for.

When Leslie Ann emerged from the living room, she found Hartnal in conversation with the cops in the kitchen. Gray light was coming up outside and they were discussing *Lust for Life* which had made it to the East Hampton picture palace the previous summer. The cops didn't see how Anthony Quinn could get the Oscar for best supporting actor for eight minutes' work and Kirk Douglas come away with nothing.

The conversation died.

The plan was to take a look at what was left of the studio in daylight, see if there was anything that could be salvaged. They ventured out onto the muddy lawn under a sky the color of zinc. Splashed over the mud, still visible despite the churning of the fire truck's wheels and the firemen's heavy boots, was the bloody track Koenig had left on his last walk to the studio.

'I never understood why he did the thing with the ear,' mumbled the younger of the two cops as they made their way towards the smoking ruin. 'Van Gogh, I'm talking about.'

'It was the ear lobe, actually,' said Hartnal, coming to a halt. 'There was a prostitute he was obsessed with, and he wanted to give her something. A token of his love.'

'I thought it was the whole ear,' said the young cop, sounding disappointed.

Leslie Ann kept walking, the men's voices fading behind her. Her feet were soaked through by the time she reached the burnt shell of the building, but she was so lost in thought she barely saw what she was stepping in.

I

Ellen

Thursday lunchtime in mid-July. The oyster bar in Grand Central Station. Just the sea-food-tangy air worth the six blocks you had to walk from the museum.

They were perched on stools, tearing the heads off shrimp and sipping Sauvignon Blanc, talking about the painting. Everyone was talking about the painting, even the chat shows and the tabloid press, churning their usual mix of outrage and bemusement: twenty million dollars for a childish daub! Twenty million dollars for fifteen feet of orange emulsion! The media talked about it as though the Acquisitions Committee had already committed the funds.

'Besides,' said Ellen, leaning forward to fluff at the other woman's hair. 'It's twenty-three million.'

For a seventy-three-year-old, Leslie Ann was holding up pretty well, but her hair had a tendency to wilt in the summer's dizzying heat, her Parisian bob showing pale streaks of scalp, and gray white roots.

'Am I looking disreputable?' she said, mildly submitting to Ellen's touch.

'You look great. Which is more than I can say for me.'

It was true. Glancing at herself in the mirror behind the bar, Ellen pushed at the lopsided clump of her own arrangement. There was a kink in her dark hair which became curls in the humid weather. On the stickiest days she piled it into a knot and fixed the whole mess with drugstore barrettes, which meant exposing the little bud of flesh-color plastic in her right ear. But she was okay about that, thought of her hearing aid in the same way Dylan Thomas regarded his cigarette, as a badge of iniquity, a badge she wore with a kind of nostalgia for the wild child she'd been up to and including the summer of '85 when she'd blown her eardrum at a rock concert in London.

'It's all Bissel, of course,' she said, looking back at Leslie Ann. 'Leaking to the press, trying to pile on the pressure.'

Taylor Bissel was a Soho dealer specializing in post-war abstraction. He'd called the previous Friday to give the Modern an opportunity to put together an offer for the painting. In the absence of Bruce Perry, the Chief Curator of the Department of Sculpture and Painting, out of the country on some sort of dialectical materialist boondoggle, Ellen had gone down to Soho to check out the painting, accompanied by Lewis Hartnal, the Modern's venerable, cigar-smoking chairman.

Koenigs were always a big deal. There were so few of them out there for one thing, but for Ellen it was more than just a question of rarity, or the tragic history they carried with them, or the personal associations that attached her own life to a number of the paintings, it was the works themselves; even the smallest drawing was a source of intense pleasure to her. But the thing she saw in Bissel's showing room had come as a complete surprise nevertheless. She'd been blown away. That was certainly how Ben, her six-year-old would have put it. She'd had to sit down. Man-high and spanning just over fifteen feet, *Mirror* unfurled in a series of dark ovoids that were suspended in a deep orange-red. Somewhere between the boldest Klines and Motherwells in style, it was anchored in deeper, darker waters by something which could only be termed Koenigness. It was *sui generis*, undoubtedly authentic. And she had an eye for these things. Was known for it.

The only thing more impressive than the painting was the asking price. When Bissel had said how much he was expecting to get for it, she'd done her best to look cool, while struggling to mask her disappointment. Hartnal had been more candid, had said that in the current economic climate, the trustees' appetite for setting records was noticeably diminished. But Bissel wouldn't budge. He knew he could get that much for it, already had a number of private collectors expressing interest. He'd only come to the museum in the first place because of their long-standing relationship. So then she'd found herself selling the idea to Hartnal, and to her surprise he'd gone along. They could at least *try* to get the trustees on board, and in the meantime they'd be buying themselves a little wiggle room pending Perry's return. Bissel had agreed to a five-day loan, and the picture had been crated up and transferred to the museum basement.

On Saturday morning she'd fired off an email to Paris, half-hoping that Perry wouldn't get it, and then engaged the services of an expensive upstate firm to put together a conservation report for presentation to the trustees. Spectrum Analytical had turned the assignment around in two days, concluding that the painting was executed in oil on primed linen, measured 72″ × 180″, and that nothing in the canvas thread count, stretcher type, paint, ground, or patina indicated a post 1957 origin. That didn't mean it couldn't have been painted post-1957 (it could have been painted six months ago) but there was nothing in it that positively *negated* the story that Linda Carey, the seller, had told Taylor Bissel. In other words it wasn't daubed in emulsion mixed with K-Y Jelly (a combination which had been used before, *and* passed the scrutiny of so-called experts) or any other substance that hadn't existed when it was supposed to have come into being.

Of course as soon as Perry had returned from Europe (he'd come straight to the museum from the airport on Tuesday evening) he'd gone on the attack. He didn't like the painting itself, said that it was 'overcooked', and 'slow' (slowness of execution was sure sign of fakery), that the colors were wrong. He was furious with her for initiating the acquisition process without first getting his approval. When she told him that there were other parties interested, and that Bissel had given her only five days to decide, he'd laughed in her face. Of course! That was how these scams were worked. She couldn't believe that he was accusing Bissel of fraud, and when she challenged him he backed down. He'd been dealing with Bissel for years. In fact he was as near as Perry got to being a friend.

As for the technical analysis, he said that, as she ought to know, it was basically worthless, part of the game dealers played to persuade buyers of what they wanted to believe anyway. When it came down to it the market in big ticket art was based on a simple fact: there was too much money chasing too few masterpieces. Billionaires wanted stellar product, and if that meant that they had to convince themselves that brilliant copies were the real thing, then they'd proved again and again their readiness to do so. Technical analysis was the tool of choice in the process of self-delusion.

But his real problem was the provenance, the chain of ownership linking the present owner, Bissel, to the painter. Given the kinks and twists of history, world wars, pogroms, holocausts – the record of ownership was rarely clear, but in the case of *Mirror,* Perry felt that the narrative was particularly suspect.

The painting had supposedly come into existence in the fall of 1957 at Koenig's house on Long Island. 'Supposedly', because there was no evidence, and no witnesses. The only really solid documentary corroboration had been provided by the person who'd sold it to Bissel, which of course raised questions itself. It was a letter, dated December 12th 1957, in which Koenig thanked Linda Carey for '*taking the pain away*', and said that he was sending a painting: – '*I'm calling it* Mirror. *It's about fifteen feet across and I thought it would look nice there in the main entrance of the motel under the mountain lion. If Earl agrees.*'

The woman who had shown Bissel the letter, claimed to be no lesser person than Linda Carey herself. She'd told Bissel that she had gone to Spain in 1963, and stayed there, only recently returning to the US since her Spanish husband's death.

The year before Koenig's suicide, he had made a trip to Mexico City where he had undergone extensive dental surgery, putting an end to years of suffering. It wasn't too much of a stretch to see the pain referred to in the letter as the likely aftermath of that ordeal. As to how Linda Carey might have taken the pain away, the woman who approached Taylor Bissel, had been categorical: while Koenig had been a guest at the Rio Rancho motel she ran with her first husband Earl Sears, a man forty years her senior, they had become lovers. She'd hung onto the painting all these years for sentimental reasons and had decided to sell it partly because she thought it should be in a major collection and partly as a way of putting her affairs in order. All requests for an interview with Carey had been blocked by Bissel, who took the view that he was being extremely generous, not to say indiscreet, by even letting them know who the seller was. For his part, he was convinced the woman was who she said she was, and that she was telling the truth. Whether or not they did was a matter for them, but he was not going to help them expose Linda Carey to unwanted public scrutiny, not to mention investigation by the IRS. It was the standard dealer's position, but Perry found the whole thing very fishy, and had demanded that the work be withdrawn from Friday's trustee lunch.

But then Wednesday had rolled in, and stories started appearing in the press, and the whole situation had become more and more politicized (as was so often the way at the museum) and Ellen came to feel that she couldn't back down on the painting without losing face. It wasn't as if she was forcing the acquisition. She simply wanted the trustees to take a look. And she had gone back to Perry, and let him understand that not only she, but Hartnal, and other members of the administration, would be very put out if he didn't at least let the painting go on show. At the mention of Hartnal's name, Perry had gone white, and in a voice that was tight with suppressed rage, he'd warned her that she was playing a very dangerous game.

Leslie Ann was rubbing a frayed wedge of lemon onto her wrinkled finger ends. She caught Ellen's look and frowned.

'What?'

Ellen raised her eyebrows, pretending not to understand.

'You're smiling, Ellen,' said Leslie Ann, dropping the lemon among the pink scraps on her plate. 'You're not supposed to be smiling. You're supposed to be bitching about what an a-hole Bruce Perry is.'

'A-hole.' Ellen smiled. 'That is so *you*, Leslie Ann.'

The old woman made a little give-it-up gesture with her left hand.

'Twenty-three million,' said Ellen, nodding, smiling, still not coming clean. 'What would Koenig have said?'

Leslie Ann twinkled, scrunching up inside her ancient black Chanel two piece. She loved to be teased.

'He'd have said thank you very much,' she said. 'Not that he would have expressed it that way, of course. There would have been an expletive. There always was.' She fumbled in her ratty, silk-lined purse, coming up with a small bottle of pills. 'Of course, twenty three million dollars was a lot of money back then.'

They were both smiling now. Twenty-three million was still a lot of money, in fact more than anyone had ever paid for a post-war painting, and in a deal, if the deal went through, that wasn't going to be driven by Japanese real estate as when the big De Kooning sold back in '89.

'So?' said Leslie Ann. 'Are you going to tell me?'

'I found something, Leslie Ann. Last night. In the archive.' She leaned forward and touched her old friend on the arm. 'I found a little document that changes everything.'

2

When Ellen had first started working at the museum, she'd attended the monthly trustee lunches as Perry's mute factotum, handing out presentation dossiers, and making sure everyone was on the right page. She wasn't allowed a seat at the table, couldn't partake of the food, and wasn't expected to speak unless spoken to. It was also understood that she should wear a skirt, the shorter the better. Thirty-one years old, a graduate of Oxford University and recipient of a Busch Reisinger curatorial internship at Harvard, she'd found herself being deferred to as the person who knew how to change the toner in the photocopy machine.

But, while playing the corporate Geisha had been humiliating, it had also been an extraordinary education, an opportunity to watch up close as the museum sought to excite the trustees into an act of pollination. The Modern, per se, had a comically small budget (twenty thousand dollars per month to spend on new works) and was therefore entirely dependent on the generosity of the trustees to keep the collection moving forward. A disparate and colorful bunch comprising studio heads, real estate tycoons, aristocrats, corporate raiders, industrialists, media moguls and fashion designers, the Acquisitions

Committee, as it was soberly referred to was, united only by its passion for the prestige that art ownership conferred, and a certain vagueness about matters of art historical detail.

The lunches took place in the museum's penthouse restaurant which looked out onto the leafy greenery of the garden occupying the strip of land between the museum building and West 52nd Street, and were in fact the second part of an event that began in one of the downstairs galleries where the trustees were shown the works up for consideration. It was at the lunch that they were invited to consider details of provenance etc., and to be reminded of how the Chief Curator felt – 'reminded' because every lunch, particularly where significant or controversial acquisitions were being mooted, was preceded by several days of strenuous lobbying by the Chief Curator and his supporters.

Just to watch the whole process unfold had been fascinating, but then, after a couple of years, she had been given a little more freedom. With Leslie Ann pushing from the sidelines (she had retired from the museum in 1978, having been passed over for promotion to Chief Curator), and Lewis Hartnal making no secret of his affection for her, Ellen had been allowed to walk the trustees around the downstairs show, and even make the occasional presentation. Now she took her place next to Perry at the table, and it wasn't always the most comfortable spot.

The Friday *Mirror* was up for consideration, he was being particularly difficult. She hadn't seen him since their heated exchange on Wednesday evening, and he'd spent the whole of the lunch pointedly ignoring her. In the show downstairs he'd made a couple of cutting remarks about the quality of the picture, and since then had been dragging his feet over the few relatively insignificant works that were on offer.

In contrast to most people at the museum who tended to follow Lewis Hartnal's lead by dressing up, Perry favored T-shirts and jeans in various shades of black, and shuffled around in a pair of cowboy boots – scuffed, black, pointy-toed, things with herniated seams over the two inch heels – that with his shaggy gray hair and whipcord leanness made him look like a superannuated Country and Western star. For the lunches, he put on a black velvet jacket, and weirdly enough the whole thing worked.

He'd obviously decided that the best way to deal with *Mirror* was to ignore it. There were only two other paintings that were of real interest, but he managed to drag things out so that in the end it was with only ten minutes remaining, and some of the trustees taking sly glances at their stellar timepieces, that he turned to Ellen and fixing her with his cold stare told her she was on.

'Thank you, Bruce.'

The room fell silent. Everybody there knew that this was her big moment. Just to be presenting a painting valued at more than a couple of million dollars was a first.

'We come to the last item on list,' she said, glancing around the table as the billionaires turned to the dossier she'd put together. '*Mirror*. There's been an awful lot in the press this week, a lot of it inaccurate, so I'd ask you to clear your mind of that, and focus on the facts.'

The presentation went badly.

She started in with the technical analysis while Perry held his head in his hands, sighing. As before in their private conversation, he dismissed the Spectrum Analytical report as irrelevant, pointing out that there were too many good forgeries out there to be able to rely on scientific analysis. As for the provenance issue, he said he found it very hard to believe that a work of this size and significance could just disappear for forty-odd years.

'It was in Spain,' said Ellen. 'In a village outside Valladolid. Linda Carey—'

'The person who *says* she's Linda Carey.'

'—said she kept it rolled in the attic. No-one knew about it.'

Perry chuckled, and glanced around the table. People were shaking their heads, some, taking their lead from Perry, smirked.

'Would it be possible to interview Linda Carey?' said Tilda Kraft, a slender woman in her late forties, heiress to the Gold Coast shopping mall fortune. 'She was obviously very convincing.'

'Convinced Bissel anyway,' said the man to her right.

'Taylor Bissel is protecting his client,' said Lewis Hartnal. 'It isn't unusual for clients to request anonymity, and—'

'But in a sale of this importance, I think the vendor might have made an exception,' said Perry, cutting him off.

'We *are* talking about a record-breaking amount,' said Art Freeland, a retired music industry mogul.

Ellen squared the papers in front of her.

'I realize that,' she said, 'and I certainly wouldn't be presenting it to you if I didn't have complete faith in its authenticity.'

'*Complete* faith?' said Perry. 'Goodness me, that sounds almost mystical.'

'Well if it comes to that, I do . . . I did—'

'Pick up a vibration?' said Perry.

A soft chuckle went round the table.

Perry shook his head, obviously convinced that she was finished.

'So . . .?' he said 'Perhaps we could have a show of hands.'

'Actually, there is one more thing,' said Ellen. She turned to the back of the presentation dossier. 'I refer you to appendix a. The San Diego catalog.'

3

Lewis Hartnal had the big corner suite with windows looking onto 53rd Street, but even so it felt pretty cramped with everyone jamming in there after the lunch. Ellen stood with her back against a filing cabinet, accepting a steady stream of congratulations, while talking half-humorously with Hartnal about where she thought the painting should hang, when a micro-cassette suddenly appeared in front of her mouth. A smooth faced character with a shaved head – he said he was a reporter with the *Times* – wanted to know what it felt like to have brought one of the most significant post war paintings into the collection.

It was the catalog that had clinched it. She'd found it in the museum library on Wednesday night; a badly printed brochure tucked away among scraps of ephemera, obviously considered too flimsy to be stored with the Koenig catalogs. Ten by eight inches wide and printed on fragile yellowing paper, it was a simple folio publication, stapled twice in the fold. On the front cover there was a reproduction of *Parabola II* one of the paintings lost in the fire at the Long Island studio. Like the rest of the reproductions, *Parabola II* was rendered monochrome in fading blue black ink. She'd found *Mirror* at the back, two pages from the end.

In the summer before his death, Koenig had organized a one-man show of his work at a chapel on the coast north of San Diego. For exactly one month, twenty-three works had hung on the simple plaster walls, and been viewed by maybe a hundred people, many of them bemused locals. Leslie Ann had made the trip from Manhattan with Betty Stack of *Time* magazine in the hope of cooking up a splashy illustrated feature, but Koenig had quashed it, refusing to go the route Pollock had taken just a few years earlier on the cover of *Life*. On the other hand he'd been fine about allowing a local printer, a first generation Italian more used to producing menus and business cards, to put together the catalog.

The bald-headed journalist was nodding as she spoke, an earnest expression on his face, and Ellen realized that she was talking without knowing what she was saying. Her feet weren't quite touching the ground, and it was only partly the champagne.

'What do you think?' said the reporter.

Ellen blinked, caught a glimpse of Perry moving through the crowd. He was sipping what looked like scotch, and had removed his velvet jacket. He caught her eye and looked away.

'What do I think of what?' she said, refocusing on the reporter.

'Of the fact that in a museum that was founded by women, there has never been a woman at the head of the flagship department.'

Ellen took a moment to consider the reporter's face. He was perspiring slightly, looked a little desperate. It occurred to her that he might have blagged his way into the room, and was trying to get as much as he could before Janice Piat, MAM's PR person chased him off.

'I didn't know we had any flagships in the collection,' she said smiling, looking around the room, hoping to be saved. Hartnal had abandoned her. She couldn't imagine how a journalist had gotten in there. Certainly, the trustee lunches were out of bounds to the press. He leaned in towards her.

'I meant the Department of Sculpture and Painting.'

Ellen nodded. He was right, of course. The museum had been founded by a woman. Mrs John D. Kruger (nee Rachel McCray of the Boston McCray's, founders of the Standard Life Insurance Company) had come up with the idea while on a cruise in Egypt with two of her socialite friends, and in the seventy-four years of its existence the closest any woman had ever come to running the Department of Sculpture and Painting was Leslie Ann.

'What do you want me to say?' said Ellen, getting jostled in the crush. 'The four men who have held the position have all been remarkable.'

The reporter sniggered at that, his red eyes going complicit, wanting her to know that he knew she was just being diplomatic.

'You don't think it's time for a change?' he said.

He was starting to annoy her. It was all very well wanting to work up a critical piece on the museum, but he had to be completely ignorant of the way the place was run to think that anyone would be going on record with controversial statements.

'People are saying that *Mirror* has brought a lot of tensions to the surface,' he said, not even waiting for an answer now. 'Do you have anything to say about that?'

Ellen shook her head, turning away, and someone grabbed her hand. It was Michael Pauling, a distinguished seventy-year-old, one of the museum's five vice chairmen. A vein on the inside of his lower lip showed moistly dark as he came up against her to say something complimentary. *Mark my words,* swam up out of his tainted breath.

'Thank you, Michael. That's very sweet of you.'

The journalist was pushing a business card at her.

'Perhaps I can call you tomorrow,' he said. 'I'm writing a piece on women in the museum.'

Ellen nodded, but she was moving on now, accepting handshakes, feeling more like a politician than a curator. Hartnal intercepted her by the door. Generally very restrained, he was beaming, his round, finely lined face, slightly flushed from the drink.

'Ellen, you can't possibly being going back to work,' he said, putting his hand on her waist. 'There are some people I want you to meet.'

She didn't get out of Hartnal's office until well after three, and found museum people still wondering around the corridors in the company of trustees. Tilda Kraft cornered her in the staff bathroom and told her that she was very proud of her for having stood up so wonderfully well to Perry's bullying.

'I swear, that man is the original sexist throwback.'

Ellen looked at herself in the mirror. Her hair had slipped sideways out of its knot, and her dark eyes were pinched and tired. It only took a couple of bad nights for her to look like a groupie from a heavy metal band.

'Look at me. You'd think I'd been drinking all afternoon.'

'You look great,' said Kraft. 'You always do.'

Ellen turned.

'Really,' said Kraft, blinking. She swiveled her hips then, disco-style. 'Edgy. Punky. At least you would if you cut your hair.'

Ellen smiled.

'Thanks. I think.'

'Where do your eyes come from?'

'What?'

'They're so dark. There's Jewish blood somewhere. I mean with a name like Lindz.'

Ellen frowned at her own reflection.

'Some,' she said. 'Russian Jews going back a couple of generations. But it was my mother who had the dark eyes, and she got those from Ireland.'

Kraft went back to looking at her own surgically-enhanced face in the mirror.

'Strutting around in those high heels.' She shot Ellen a look. 'Perry I'm talking about, not you. You're never out of those flatties.'

Ellen glanced at her pumps. At 5′ 10″ she was as tall if not taller than most of the men in the museum, certainly the older ones. She was a good two inches taller than Perry.

'Perry!' said Kraft, flashing her eyes. 'It's gone on long enough.'

'What has?'

'He thinks *we're* all idiots.'

'Bruce is very serious about his art,' said Ellen.

'Oh, don't be so English,' said Kraft.

Ellen shrugged, applying some color to her mouth now. She *was* English. There was nothing she could do about that even if she'd wanted to, which she didn't, since, within the confines of the museum, it had always seemed to work in her favor. There was an expectation of integrity and good manners that she was conscious, at times, of playing up to.

'I'm sorry,' said Kraft. 'That came out a little . . .'

Ellen smiled, shook her head.

'Did you read his book?' said Kraft.

Perry had published a short study of the art world three years earlier. *Know What I Like* was very funny in a biting highbrow way.

'Making fun, twisting everything in knots. He's writing another one, you know. Anyway, who cares?' She put a hand on Ellen's wrist. 'I think *Mirror* is *magnificent*,' she said. 'I think you've been very bold, and we're lucky to have you.'

She couldn't work. People kept coming into her dingy little office at the back of the building. At five o'clock, she decided to call it a day. She was heading for the door when the phone rang.

'A minute.' There was a sharp clack of plastic, then a softer knock as the phone at the other end, dangling from its knotted cord bumped against the kitchen wall. Sounds of home. Ellen smiled. She could hear Sandra, her Salvadorian nanny, tearing paper off the big roll that Ben used for painting. He'd be working at the kitchen table, tongue jammed in the side of his mouth as he applied the color. Sandra came back to the phone, breathing hard.

'There is groun' beef.'

'On the sink, yes. I took it out of the freezer this morning. Could you do it for him with the little peas?'

'He say you goin' eat with him.'

'Yes. Yes, that's right. I'm about to leave. I'll be with you in thirty minutes.'

'Okay.'

'Forty. Around six.'

'Mr Gregory call.'

'When?'

'*Ahora*. Ten minutes. He arrive from the airport.'

Greg was in New York for the weekend. He was taking Ben back to LA with him on Monday evening. This was a first, and something she was very uneasy about.

'He don' like the peas.'

'What's that?'

'Ben. Last time he spit them. I give him corn.'

'Okay, corn. Sandra, can you put him on?'

There was another thump and then Ben was there, telling the story of his day. The facts came thick and fast with lots of backing up to explain and elaborate. He had been telling everyone about the trip to LA.

'Did you talk to your father?'

'When are you coming home?'

'I'll be there in about thirty minutes.'

'You sound funny.'

'Funny ha-ha?'

'You sound drunk.'

Ellen laughed.

'What do you know about drunk?'

'What are you doing?'

'Working.'

'You have to pack my suitcase.'

Ellen brought a hand to her mouth.

'Mommy?'

'I'm here, sweetheart.'

She found her way back to her seat, and for a second she couldn't speak. It was the suitcase. The thought of his things in it. The thought of his little socks and undershirts crammed into the cargo hold of the plane. Crammed into the freezing dark. Her heart was pounding. She took a breath, reached for the bottle of mineral water on her desk. Everything was going to be okay. She was going out to LA herself at the end of August, was going to stay in a hotel at Venice Beach.

'Mommy?'

'We'll pack it together,' she said. 'We'll make sure we don't forget anything.'

She hung up. Anxiety attacks now. Ben's trip out west had seemed like such a simple sunny insignificant plan back in March when Greg had first suggested it, but since then it had accumulated mass somehow, become onerous. It was because of Abigale, of course.

Abby, as she preferred to be called apparently, had two children of her own from a previous marriage, the youngest a couple of months older than Ben, the eldest nearly ten. These boys had the run of two acres of steeply sloping terrain landscaped into a kind of Japanese adventure playground complete with giant boulders and bamboo. She knew all this because Greg went on about it every time she saw him.

A production assistant for a while, two years earlier Greg had taken a job on a project that brought him to New York at least twice a month, and so little by little he had come back into their lives. They'd muddled along in this transcontinental way until the previous winter when his luck had changed. He'd always said he was lucky, even back at Oxford where he'd been a Rhodes Scholar, he'd talked about his luck as though it were a little trust fund he had tucked away. But the truth was in LA he had been struggling, not quite connecting socially, spending most of what he earned on rent and his ridiculous German car. And then he'd met Abigale.

When Ben's trip had first been mooted, Greg had still been living in his Santa Monica condo. It had never occurred to Ellen that he might be moving in with her, and that Ben would be staying in her big white house in the Hollywood Hills. Now she was worried about him having too good a time, coming back to New York in September and finding the apartment and their lifestyle a little lacking in glamor.

She had the presentation dossier for *Mirror* in her hand. Had picked it up from the desk while talking to Ben. There was a sticky note on the cover from Jerry Lloyd, one of her favorite people in the museum, an assistant curator in the Department of Film and Media. *Who's the fairest of them all? You are!! Congratulations!*

She hefted her leather shoulder bag, and headed for the door.

Standing by the elevator, she noticed the door to Perry's office. He had one of the big suites facing the street. Looking through the crack, she could see him walking up and down in front of his big windows. He was talking to someone on the phone, sounding depressed. He turned and caught her watching him. She raised a hand. Without the slightest acknowledgment, Perry came across the room, and for a second stood there looking at her through the gap. She thought he was going to close it without saying a word, but then he offered a nod.

'I was just leaving,' said Ellen.

Perry nodded again, did his best to smile. The elevator arrived.

'Have a good weekend,' said Ellen, stepping inside.

'Ellen.'

She paused between the doors. He was still in his doorway, looking lost, looking as though he wanted to say something, but couldn't find the words. There was a stain on his T-shirt from the crème brulée they'd had for dessert.

'How's your boy?' he said. 'Ben, is it?'

Ellen blocked the doors with her foot.

'He's fine, thanks. Very well. He's going away next week. For the vacation. He's going to spend some time with his dad.'

'Where is he? The dad.'

'Los Angeles.'

Perry sighed, pushing stray hair back from his forehead. Twice divorced, he knew all about broken families. Ellen had seen the way his children, two girls from the first marriage, a boy from the second, treated him when they came into the museum. He was a stranger to them. He was nodding now.

'You know, I love this place,' he said.

Ellen stepped out of the elevator. The doors came together behind her.

'That might sound corny, but it's true. I was teaching at Princeton when they offered me the job. And . . .' He smiled, shaking his head. 'I couldn't believe it. I mean, can you imagine? All this . . . all this . . .'

He clutched at the air, museum air.

'Art?'

'Ghosts. *Lives*. All these people, crazy bastards who lived their lives to paint or to sculpt or print or whatever. It's an incredible thing. Don't you think? Wanting to make beautiful things. That being the point of your life.'

Ellen nodded. This was all very weird. In ten years of working there, she'd never seen Perry like this. Suddenly the euphoria, if that was what it was, dissipated. The somberness returned.

'We never talked about this stuff, Ellen.'

Ellen shook her head. The truth was they hadn't talked alone together in a long time. About anything. The truth was he kept her at a distance.

'I'm sounding valedictory,' he said with a dark look. 'And I don't mean to. I just wanted . . .' He came out his office into the corridor, got up close enough for her to smell the whiskey on his breath. 'I just wanted to say that, whatever differences we may have had, I think you'd make a wonderful chief curator. I think you'd do a wonderful job.'

4

Saturday morning was pottery, then judo. Saturday afternoon was swimming class at the 'Y'. Sunday morning was baseball. The weekend blurred with Ben's activities and dealing with Greg, and trying to cope with all the phone calls and emails congratulating her on the *Mirror* acquisition. Greg pretended to be pleased for her, although it was always difficult for him to hide his feelings about the museum and the art world in general. He thought it ridiculous that anyone would pay twenty-three million dollars for a piece of canvas 'smeared with paint'. For her part, Ellen found herself watching him as he talked about the pilot season and syndication and the problem posed by unscripted TV and wondering how she could ever have deluded herself about loving him. Of course it wasn't just about his conversion to the church of the mass media; there was a past to deal with, a history which included Greg walking out on her in the middle of Ben's first year.

She still couldn't think about any of that without dark stuff welling out of her depths, so she did her best not to think about it, knew that it was essential not to in fact. Being angry at him had made her ill for a time, depressed enough to require medication, and if it hadn't have been for the support she'd had from Leslie Ann and the museum, she might have given up on the States altogether, and gone back to England – decisions that would have made a bad year even worse. Since that awful year, Greg had prostrated himself before her a number of times (he was a ready weeper, and had a terrific line in self-flagellation), and had developed a theory in which his behavior was explained as 'a kind of nervous breakdown'. Now he was better. Now he was ready to shoulder some of the responsibility.

They'd agreed to be civil with each other for the sake of Ben, but it wasn't easy.

On Sunday morning they were in Central Park watching Ben play baseball, which seemed to involve him standing in the outfield most of the time, picking at loose threads on his uniform and struggling to keep his catcher's mitt from dragging in the dirt. He was short for his age, and had Greg's turf-thick blondness. From her he'd gotten the pallor, and the dark eyes. He had her feet too, narrow and bony with toes that barely touched the ground when he was standing straight. In the first months after his birth these details, like the little pleat that appeared in his top lip when he smiled, had been capable of fixing her in rapt wonderment for minutes at a time. When people had said how much he looked like Greg (they'd said it less after he'd abandoned them) she'd accepted it with a nod, but never failed to point out how much of Ben was her.

She looked down at the newspaper in her lap, and tried to focus.

'You know it'd be much better if you stayed up at the house.'

Greg was sitting a couple of feet away from her on the same bench, eyes on the game. He'd lost weight since she'd last seen him. He'd also gotten rid of a terrible mid-life crisis pony tail which had come as a huge relief.

'Better?' she said. 'How's that?'

'Well, you're going to be down there at Venice Beach. That's an hour away if the traffic's bad.'

'An hour away from what?'

He turned and did the thing with his mouth, pushing it up on one side in a smile that was supposed to make him look like a good-natured chump. There was a time when she'd found it attractive.

'I'm only out there for two weeks, Greg. I have a big room. A king-size bed. Ben can stay with me down at the beach. You can come down to us.'

He put up his hands.

'Okay. But I think you'll find that's not the way it's going to work.'

He shook his head, then cupped his hands to his mouth, yelled something at Ben who was jogging in from the outfield now, getting ready to bat.

Ellen looked back at the paper, and the headline she'd been staring at for the past two minutes suddenly snapped into focus.

Koenig Mirror Shows Cracks

The acquisition of a recently discovered Franklin Koenig is at the heart of a growing rift between Modern Art Museum grandees and controversial Chief Curator, Bruce Perry.

MAM's Acquisition Committee voted to buy Mirror from Taylor Bissel, a SOHO based art dealer, on Friday for a whopping $23 million, the highest price yet for a Post War work. The acquisition has been hailed as a considerable coup given the scarcity of Koenig's work by all except the Chief Curator of the Department of Sculpture and Painting, who opposed the deal from the beginning. Now insiders are complaining that Perry's crusade to change MAM's collection to reflect his view of mid-twentieth century art has put him out of touch with the museum and its all-important trustees. 'Mirror is precisely the kind of high-profile acquisition that MAM should be making,' said a trustee who requested anonymity, 'rather than the penny ante deals that typified the earlier part of the year.'

Some are even calling for Perry to step aside in favor of curatorial assistant Ellen Lindz, who is credited for bringing Mirror to the museum.

(Perry under fire, see section A2)

'Way to go, Benny!'

Greg was yelling again. Ellen looked up, saw Ben sprinting for second base and sliding in a cloud of red dust.

'Did you see that?' said Greg, eyes dancing. 'Neat little bunt, then he took off like a rocket.' He stood up, cupping his hands to his mouth. 'Way to go, son!'

'Greg.'

Other parents were turning around on the benches, smiling mostly, Ellen had to admit. She squinted out at the diamond. Ben was patting his clothes down now, sending out little puffs of dust.

She ducked back into the paper, turning the pages of the arts section, then found herself staring into Perry's eyes. He had struck a statesman-like pose for the camera that made him look even more arrogant than he was. The caption underneath was lifted from the body of the text: '*Perry has taken us into revisionist backwaters, making a nonsense of everything MAM represents.*'

At the bottom of the page was a section bemoaning the lack of women in a museum created by women. Ellen read on.

> Leslie Ann Benton, who played such a crucial role in the development of the museum's collection in the fifties, came closest to occupying the position, but was passed over in 1978 in favor of Theodor Els. Benton resigned shortly afterwards. She believes that when the time comes, there will be no shortage of female candidates for the top curatorial position. It was Benton who brought Lindz into the museum, and the two women are known to be close. Was Lindz a possible successor? 'Ellen Lindz has shown herself more than capable of running the department,' said Benton. 'She is very much in tune with the spirit of the place and has a feeling for the work that I personally have rarely encountered.'

There was another photograph, this one of Leslie Ann standing in front of one of her three Koenigs, holding a candle in her bony hands.

When they got back to the apartment, Ellen found the answering machine full. She got Ben out of his uniform into the bath, and left him with Greg while she returned calls in the kitchen. They ate dinner together with the window open, Ben and Greg talking baseball, Ellen tuning out, thinking about the article in the *Times*. She had checked the byline, but hadn't recognized the name, thought perhaps it had been written by the journalist who'd cornered her in Hartnal's office.

They packed Ben's suitcase in his bedroom. Greg had explained all about how Abby's youngest had mounds of stuff, and how Ben wouldn't need to bring very much in the way of clothes. So, naturally, she'd gone out and more or less replaced his entire wardrobe. Every item in the suitcase, excepting the sweaters her mother had knitted for him, was new, including several snappy Hawaiian shirts that they both agreed were very LA.

They put him to bed at eight o'clock and Greg kissed him goodnight. He said he'd pick him up from the apartment the following afternoon. Ellen said that wasn't going to be necessary. She was going to take him to the airport. They'd meet Greg there.

'Okaaay,' he said, giving her his crooked smile. 'Need to be there at two o'clock, though. Two hours before take off.'

Ellen looked down at Ben, and gave him a wink.

'I think we can manage that, can't we?'

Ben frowned.

'What about your job?'

Betrayal. Ellen smiled.

'They'll just have to do without me.'

The phone started up in the kitchen, and this time Ellen ignored it.

She waited for Greg to leave the room before kneeling down next to the pillow, sat there for a while, stroking her baby's hair in the near-darkness.

'Why is everyone calling you?' he said.

'The museum bought a painting,' she said. 'Everybody's very excited.'

Ben frowned.

'I was the one who found it,' said Ellen.

Ben's eyelids drooped. He was drifting into sleep now, his gentle breath smelling faintly of toothpaste.

'You found it?'

'Sort of.'

'What kind of painting is it?'

'Abstract.'

'Squiggly.'

'Yes, squiggly. Big squiggles by a man called Franklin Koenig.'

Ben rolled over and looked at the wall.

'Is he the one in the den?'

She had a number of Koenig photographs on the wall in the study. They were mostly from his last summer on Long Island.

'That's right.'

'Daddy doesn't like him.'

'Really?'

'He says he's desperate.'

'Desperate?' Ellen thought about it, then smiled. 'You mean Dan.'

There was a picture of an old boyfriend in the study too. Dan. He had died a long time ago. Greg had met him once when Dan came up to Oxford from London where he was attending art school. Since that visit, Greg had always referred to him as Desperate Dan.

'Why do you like it?' said Ben.

'Like what?'

'Squiggles.'

'It's like music,' she said. 'But for your eyes.'

He thought about that for a moment.

'Is he the one in the book you did?'

'Koenig? Yes.'

The book had been published by the Museum. An evocative biography complete with sumptuous color plates of the works and photographs. Leslie Ann had encouraged her to write it, wanting her to get at Franklin Koenig, the man. No more than a hundred pages long it had nevertheless been incredibly hard to write, mainly because Leslie Ann had been breathing down her neck most of the time. She'd been incredibly generous with her time, and given unprecedented access to the letters still in her possession, but she had wanted her version in print, a version which Ellen, reading between the lines, had often felt was a little roseate, to say the least. When she'd suggested going into Koenig's final fling with Linda Carey, Leslie Ann had become cold and remote. She hadn't wanted 'that piece of ass' memorialized in any way. It was the one time they'd ever had anything like a serious argument.

Ben stirred in the sheets.

'Mommy?'

'Yes.'

'Why did you and daddy stop living together?'

She continued to stroke his hair.

'We were unhappy,' she said.

'Why?'

Because your father was a selfish bastard.

'I don't know, baby. We just were.'

Greg was waiting for her in the kitchen, looking old under the ceiling light.

'Would they let an English woman run the museum?'

Ellen moved past him and started to put the dinner things in the dish washer.

'They probably think it's kind of classy,' he said, watching her do the work as usual.

'They've had non-US nationals in the job before. The museum's a pretty cosmopolitan place.'

She twisted the dial to 'wash'.

'Are you sure about tomorrow?' he said.

'Sure I'm sure. Why wouldn't I be?'

'I don't know, you seem to be really busy. All this business with the painting.'

She stood up straight, a dirty fork in her hand. Greg looked at it, looked at her, smiling, shaking his head.

'What? I'm just saying . . . things are obviously going very well for you. You might not want to be taking your eye off the ball to –'

'Screw the ball, Greg. I've been juggling the ball for a while now. Quite successfully, I might add. It's decided. I'm taking Ben to the airport.'

He gathered up his wallet and keys.

'I'm not trying to take him from you,' he said.

Ellen decided to ignore that and walked him to the front door. He turned to say goodnight. They were no more than a foot apart. Ten years earlier it was the kind of situation that would have suggested a kiss.

'You know, Greg. It's been pretty hard these past six years. I think I've really held it together.'

Greg kept his eyes on hers, nodded. Then he did kiss her. Just leaned forward and pecked her on the mouth. She drew back shaking her head.

'I feel sorry for her,' she said.

He did the crooked smile again.

'Is it my fault I still have feelings?'

She started to close the door.

'It's going to get a lot harder for Ben, isn't it?'

Ellen froze.

'What is?'

'If they give you this fucking job.'

Billy in Soho

Billy Kovich always knew Manhattan was bad for her. It only took a few days in a place where there were faggots holding hands like it was okay, for her to start brooding, looking back, regretting all the stupid things she'd ever done, starting with taking the money in Baltimore. Or, rather, getting *caught* taking the money. That was what she regretted – not looking over her shoulder before she'd made her move. Then she'd get to wondering what the hell she was doing wherever she happened to be stuck – staring up at the ceiling in a franchise hotel room, or unwrapping the tiniest soap in the city while the cheapest shower curtain in the *world* worked its way into the crack of her ass instead of selling her house in White Plains and moving down to Miami like she'd planned to all those years ago.

She was brooding on it now, standing in front of the big metal desk, waiting for the dealer to wriggle out of his jacket.

Miami was the reason Baltimore had happened, of course. She'd thought it would be kind of nice to get out of the Lafayette Projects where she'd seemed to be spending most of her life – stuck in shitty vans running surveillance, listening to the rain on the roof, her ATF duds getting stunk up with takeout noodles and sweat and the other guys' farts. Alcohol Tobacco and Firearms had a field office in Miami. That was the simple fact that set her off. She'd had visions of herself riding around in a Jeep Wrangler, her hair going white in the sun, had even started making enquiries about real estate, and then the Lafayette Boys thing had happened and her ATF career was suddenly over – all for ten thousand dollars, a little wad of hundreds still crisp in their paper band.

It had slipped into her jacket pocket so easy. She hadn't even planned on doing it unless you counted being very aware that other people did it all the time and thinking it wasn't such a bad thing given the risks they all took, and what they were paid. Working ATF cases, cash was always falling out of bags, or lockers, or ice boxes, and it didn't always find its way into the evidence log. But the wrong person had seen her, and that was that. No job, no pension. Dishonorably flushed down the shitter like a used tampon. She'd always felt they'd been harder on her for being a woman.

The dealer was having trouble getting his arm out of the sleeve.

'You got your . . .' She pointed a manicured finger. 'The cuff thing, it's . . .'

The dealer gave a dainty tuck to his French cuff and pulled his arm through. He was what you'd call silver-tongued, keeping up the patter all the time he was struggling with his clothes: it wasn't every day he met an FBI agent of *either* sex; his usual clients were rather less worldly; why didn't she take a seat and tell him how he could be of service, etc.

She watched him make his way around to the other side of his desk, pausing at a corner to take a breath. Evidently, walking was a problem, involved hitching a hip then shooting a tasseled loafer through while the weight was off. He was at the swivel chair now. Taylor Bissel. The Pilsbury Dough Boy in a Cerruti suit. She figured he was worth at least thirty million. Her quick eyes registered the Patek Philippe, the chunky seal ring, the gold buckle on the alligator skin belt. She wondered at what point a person decided to fasten their pants *above* the gut instead of just letting the fucker hang. A fine brush of silver hair topped a head that was the shape and color of a dinner roll. It was the eyes that told you the real story. They came straight at you, hot and quick like a strip search at Bogota airport.

She winced at the sound his chair made.

'Please,' he huffed, twirling a dimpled hand, indicating a swivel chair shaped like half a cantaloupe. Everything was like that in the office – over-beautiful, over-designed. And there was expensive looking art everywhere, big-ticket daubs she wouldn't have put in her downstairs john. The one behind the dealer's head was vaguely familiar. Big scratchy flowers in pinks and yellows.

'So . . .? Agent Rissoli? In what way can I . . .?'

'Quite a place,' said Billy. 'Lots of light.'

Bissel shrugged.

'The rents are outrageous, but where else in the world . . .'

'Right. Where else in the world?' Billy pointed at the picture. 'Here's where I show myself up. Is that . . .?'

'An Andy Warhol.'

'Get out of town.'

'Pop.'

Billy tilted her head.

'Pop Art,' said Bissel. 'He was a pop artist.'

Billy nodded, smiling. In the acne-scarred face, the mouth was a surprise, the full lips coming together in a perfect cupid's bow. Her eyes were hard. The color of wet slate.

'Just out of curiosity, what's a picture like that worth?'

'You don't want to know.'

Billy pushed manicured fingers into her perm-damaged yellow hair. Waited.

'Six hundred thousand,' said Bissel. 'Six hundred and fifty.'

'What did you pay for it? Be honest now.'

Bissel gave a little swivel to his swivel chair.

'Well, I'd rather not . . .'

'Come on. I'm curious.'

'I got it for four hundred.'

Billy let out a low whistle.

'I'm in the wrong line of work, Mr Bissel.'

She took out her cigarettes.

'I'm sorry.' Bissel made a face: sympathy and regret. As much as she wanted. 'I don't allow smoking in here.'

Billy gave him a wink like they both knew he was kidding. Then flipped open the cap on her clunky Zippo, put a flame to the tip of a Marlboro, sucked smoke with a great show of relish.

'It's okay,' she said, brushing ash from her pants. 'I won't exhale.'

She chuckled then, sending smoke across the desk.

Bissel got a choked look, grabbed at the phone.

'While you're fumbling at those keys,' said Billy, 'maybe you can raise the guy who set up the North Shore Trust.'

That slowed him down.

'What's his name?' she said. 'Gottlieb? Damned if I could reach him.'

She wedged the cigarette between her lips, and leaned forward, tweaking her left eye against climbing smoke, took a notebook from the back of her pants.

'Can of worms, that trust. Set up in '96. Revocable. Inter vivos. Paintings, drawings, jewelry, bearer bonds. Hard to put a value on some of the stuff, but the IRS has its ways.'

Bissel put the phone down. His mouth was open.

'You used it to acquire the property in the south of France. Wife's the trustee, inscribed under her maiden name. It's not registered anywhere. No city, county, state or federal records. There are only two documents that prove it exists. One of them's in Gottlieb's safe.'

Billy's pretty mouth pursed around the filter.

'Don't look so guilty,' she said. 'Lookit, you're an art dealer. A painting here, some cash there. The IRS can't expect you to declare everything!'

'What do you want?'

Billy exhaled, unclenching a little, coming down from the hardness. She was good at this, specific in the way she presented herself, in the way she applied pressure.

'I'll tell you what it is,' she said. 'I'll tell you the thing that bothers me.' She put the cigarette in the side of her mouth, returned the notebook to its pocket. '*Mirror*.'

'The Koenig?'

The slate color eyes went flat and dead.

'No, Taylor. The one in your bathroom.'

'I don't understand.'

'Hey, I don't understand why you crunch Tylenol instead of getting a hip replacement, or why you carry so much cash around with you, or why you insist on cramming your ass into that stupid fucking Porsche, but who cares, right?'

Bissel made a little quarter turn in his chair, re-setting his feet.

'Who?' he said. 'Who's concerned?'

Billy shook her head, exhaling. It wasn't going to be like that, apparently.

'We're concerned about the vendor, Mr Bissel. We're very concerned about Linda Carey.'

6

The question kept Ellen awake until the early hours of Monday morning. Greg was right, of course. It would be harder for Ben is she was offered the job. It would be harder for them both except materially, where it would become an awful lot easier. In salary terms, the step up from assistant, at $50,000 a year (MAM was notorious for miserable remuneration) to chief curator was considerable. Perry took home something like $150,000 annually, on top of the money he could earn speaking at conferences, making TV appearances, and writing introductions for publications both inside and outside the museum. Similarly, publishers were always proposing book projects; he just never took them up on it.

But all that was pie in the sky, since there was no question of her being offered the job. Chief Curator of the Department of Sculpture and Painting was a celebrity appointment, and no amount of in-house support, particularly from the anti-Perry camp, was going to change the fact that she wasn't a celebrity, not even in narrow art world terms.

With the exception of the legendary Alfred Faber, the first (one was tempted to say ur-curator, the person responsible for making the Modern what it was) all of the men who had held the position were profoundly of the establishment, celebrities in their own way, known for their connoisseurship but also moneyed, connected, close to the Kruger family. Even Perry, in his iconoclastic way was a part of it, having been adopted by David Kruger after the publication of *Know What I Like* as a dauntingly articulate, court jester type. What was she in comparison? Her little Koenig book had been very favorably reviewed, but no one was begging to snap up the paperback rights. She was just a thirty-six-year-old single mother who was pretty good at her job. Her reputation didn't spread much further than 53rd Street.

The sound of jackhammers filled the air. A road crew was ripping up a section of the sidewalk to lay cable, and she had to cross the street in front of the brooding mass of St Thomas' Church. In the shadowless morning light, the museum hung above the smoke and noise, looking insubstantial, like an architectural drawing almost. She remembered the first time she'd seen it, back in 1986, when she and Dan had made their epic voyage across America, starting in Manhattan and ending up in San Francisco. She had been disappointed by the shoe-box stark plainness – Frank Lloyd Wright termed it the 'flat-chested style', a sexist epithet that she nevertheless thought about right. It was only much later that she came to understand just how quirky and ingrown this shining monument to function really was.

The problems had begun with Alfred Faber's wanting Thermolux for the façade instead of the white marble the architect originally envisaged. Faber had dreamed of open spaces suffused with natural light, but what the Thermolux (a layer of spun glass sandwiched between two sheets of glass plate) actually delivered was eye-pinching dazzle. In the end it had been necessary to line the façade with a second wall just to protect the paintings, and to light the galleries with electricity. Likewise, the original concept of free-flowing spaces sectioned by mobile hanging walls had quickly been abandoned in favor of a layout that became increasingly labyrinthine, and rigid as the collection grew. To the street, the museum presented the severest of simple lines, but inside it was full of kinks and compromise, blind walls and cul de sacs.

Learning just how much this was true of the institution as a whole had constituted a large part of the education she had received there. Getting a handle on how it all worked – who you trusted, who you *always* deferred to, who you could occasionally ignore – had not been easy. Back in '29 when Mrs John D. Kruger Jr appointed the first president, and director, she'd established the basic organizational paradigm, comprising a functionless but ultra-connected plutocrat supported by a couple of trusted (preferably male) billionaires.

These days the functionless plutocrat was Chairman Emeritus David Kruger, and his right and left hand men were Chairman of the Board, Lewis Hartnal, and President, Glen Schaeffer. Below these three, everyone else was on salary, and that included the Director and the Chief Curators of each of the five curatorial departments. The trustees added a final layer of complexity, and with them you had to tread very carefully.

She went in through the main entrance on West 53rd and made her way through the tourists and students already milling in the lobby. Most of the museum employees went around to the back and took the elevator, but Ellen preferred this route, riding the brushed steel escalators as though still a student herself back in the summer of '86, coming in to see the Rothkos and the Pollocks for the first time. Back then a large part of the excitement had come from being with Dan, then newly-graduated from art school in London. They'd spent two whole days there in a state of ecstatic dilation, absorbing painting after painting, sculpture after sculpture, getting high on all the beauty, wandering out into the sculpture garden to smoke a cigarette every couple of hours and unpeel the pages in their rain-warped guide book.

She still got a twinge of nostalgia when she saw the students.

Since then, she'd come to love the museum in a more rounded less intense way, but she still got a visceral buzz from the sacramental silence, the brimming light, the sensorial thump of a masterpiece blazing on a white wall. *I love this place*. Perry's words came back to her as she rose through the building, catching glimpses of Picasso and Matisse – pinks and blues and greens – beauty, beauty, beauty. She kept thinking about their conversation. He'd said he didn't mean to sound valedictory, but the more she thought about it, the more that was how he'd seemed. He had been saying goodbye. He was leaving.

On the fourth floor, she punched numbers on a keypad and went through into the offices. The museum changed here. The proportions had been skewed by false floors and ceilings that permitted the introduction of cable and modern air-conditioning. Industrial-looking carpet replaced the hard wood of the gallery floors and instead of masterpieces, ratty posters from past exhibitions hung in cheap frames on the scuffed and blotchy walls.

But above all it was the atmosphere that changed. There was an air of intrigue at the Modern; the place was known for it. People tended to lower their voices when expressing opinions, closed their doors to have serious conversations. The conventional wisdom was that it had been this way since Alfred Faber, who was known as the Cardinal for his Jesuitical, not to say Machiavellian, ways. But after five years of working there, Ellen had come to the view that it was the institution itself that generated intrigue. Structured like a corporation (if you cast the trustees as the stockholders), it was actually more like a court with a difficult mix of those people who owned things but knew little about them, and those who owned little but knew a lot. Powerful ignorance came face to face with impotent expertise on a daily basis.

Which didn't make it an easy place to work, but, as Leslie Ann, who knew the museum better than anyone except maybe Lewis Hartnal, often pointed out, if you wanted to handle Twentieth Century art, there was no other place on the planet to be. The Modern had started earlier and with more acquisitive purpose than any comparable institution. Having made the bulk of its important acquisitions before the art price hike of the 1970s, it had assembled a collection that could not be rivaled now. Everything the Modern had, it had either in the finest examples or in dizzying depth. That was the term employed: we have Picasso *in depth*; we have Matisse *in depth*; we have Rothko *in depth*. The collection of Abstract Expressionists, in particular, was unmatchably deep and broad. This meant that any given exhibition they decided to put together started out well furnished, but also exerted a kind of planetary pull on other institutions. Everyone in the art world wanted to loan his best works, because that was the only way he stood a chance of having the Modern return the favor. Masterpieces arrived from all over. Every month brought the unwrapping of something extraordinary. You could take a certain amount of courtly shenanigans for that kind of excitement.

I think you'd make a wonderful chief curator.

She tried to shut it out, but the thought was there at the back of her mind. She couldn't believe it – couldn't believe *in* it. But then again, neither had Bruce. He had been teaching Princeton when they'd offered him the position. *I couldn't believe it. I mean, can you imagine?*

She looked in on Lewis Hartnal and was surprised to find his office empty. Nor was his assistant there.

The phone rang as soon as she entered her cupboard of an office.

'Ellen?'

It was Lewis Hartnal.

'I wonder if you'd mind coming up to the boardroom? There's something we'd like to put to you.'

7

The men were sitting around the big Art Deco conference table, glanced up as she came into the room. Lewis Hartnal, looking very dapper and pink, was at the head of the table next to Glen Schaeffer, the Museum's septuagenarian president. Opposite, were vice chairmen Michael Pauling and Simon Klimt-Heuer. Roland Staunton, the museum's cost-cutting director, a jogging fanatic who looked a good deal younger than his forty years, was sitting directly under the air conditioning next to a man Ellen had never seen before, a white-faced character in a rumpled linen suit, who frowned as she crossed the room.

Bruce Perry was also there, slumped in a chair, looking if anything worse than he had on Friday afternoon.

'Ellen,' said Hartnal, half smiling, rising in his seat, gesturing for her to take a place near to him. 'Perhaps you'd like some coffee?'

She didn't notice David Kruger at first. He was over by the windows that offered a sweeping view of 53rd Street and Midtown, wearing an immaculate blue suit, and looking every inch the founding family scion. He was said to spend most of his time in Paris at his Sixth *Arrondissement hôtel particulier*, and when in the States, was either up in Maine where he was building a house, or down in Florida at Strands, the estate his family had owned since the middle of the nineteenth century. He was looking out at the street, talking softly into his cellphone, pushing the hair back from his forehead. If he'd seen her enter the room, he gave no sign of it.

Everyone was drinking coffee except for Staunton who had some sort of power drink that needed to be slurped directly from the squat plastic bottle. Schaeffer asked if she'd had a pleasant weekend, listened to her reply with an exaggerated expression of interest on his spreading, soft-jowled face.

Ellen glanced over at Perry, but he was engaged in examining the edge of the table now. Staunton, who was keeping half an eye on Kruger, slopped cold coffee into her cup, and managed to detach his gaze long enough to introduce the man in the linen suit as Porter French. He didn't say who French was or what he was doing there. Neither did anyone else.

Kruger wrapped up his call, flipped his cell phone shut and came over to the table, reaching for the coffee pot.

'*David*,' said Staunton in a hurt voice. 'That's *cold*.'

He got to his feet and went to order some more as Kruger took a seat at the other end of the table, smiling, but still oblivious to Ellen's presence, apparently. Ellen frowned. They had met several times, and he had always noticed her before. Unbuttoning his jacket, he hiked a shoe up onto his knee, looking very tan and slim and pleased with himself.

'I think of Nassau as next door,' he murmured to no one in particular. 'But by the time you're cleared for take-off and whatnot . . .'

'We're all very grateful to you for coming back, David,' said Hartnal. 'And at such short notice.'

There was appreciative muttering around the table. Everyone was grateful, apparently.

Coffee arrived. Kruger got it hot and fresh.

The air conditioning surged with a muffled roar.

'I'm sure you're all aware why this meeting was called,' said Hartnal, leaning forward and opposing wrinkled finger ends over a stack of documents. 'But just so that everyone is on the same page – we're here to discuss *Mirror*.'

Ellen could feel the a/c on the backs of her hands, but her face was suddenly very warm.

Hartnal summarized the circumstances in which the painting had been brought into the museum.

'Bruce was in Paris when Bissel called notifying us of the opportunity, which is why it was Ellen and I who went to look at it.'

Kruger nodded. The man called French was scribbling notes.

'I have to say I was very impressed by the painting. As was Ellen. In fact, Ellen . . . I think we can say . . .' Hartnal opened his hands.

'I loved it,' said Ellen, looking around at the somber faces. 'I thought it was very special. Is there . . . Is there something wrong?'

'Bruce was pretty much opposed,' said Kruger, ignoring her.

'I think it's probably fair to say that had Bruce been here, the painting would never have made it into the building,' said Hartnal. 'Is that right, Bruce?'

Perry shrugged, his eyes fixed on the table.

'Bruce,' said Kruger mildly. 'We all understand this is difficult for you, but your help would really be appreciated.'

'I didn't like it,' said Perry gruffly. 'Too big, too good. Old lady finds it in the attic after all these years.'

Ellen opened her mouth, but Hartnal was moving on.

'But Taylor Bissel,' he said, addressing himself to Perry now. 'He's a man whose word carries some weight.'

'Taylor's good,' said Perry. 'But he has bills to pay like everyone else. His judgment can be clouded on occasion by wishful thinking.'

'So,' said Hartnal, addressing himself to Ellen again. 'Bruce was against it, and you—'

'We both liked it,' said Ellen. 'You and I. A lot of people liked it. And anyway, it's a wonderful painting. I don't see the—'

'Let's *try* to stay focused,' said Kruger, still not looking at her.

'You were concerned to establish provenance,' said Hartnal, forging ahead, 'and you searched the archive and you found the catalog.'

'Yes,' said Ellen, clearing her throat. 'That's right.'

Hartnal removed the catalog from his pile of papers, and pushed it into the middle of the table.

'Just so that we're all clear on this,' said the stranger in the linen suit. 'Miss Lindz, and Miss Lindz alone is responsible for what went into the presentation document? Is that right?'

It was the first time he had spoken, and the effect of his clipped inquiry was to make everyone around the table sit up a little straighter.

Ellen drew a hand across her mouth.

'Ellen?' said Hartnal.

'Yes. I put it together. I did the photocopying, and the binding. I always do.'

'The catalog,' said the stranger. 'When did you first come across it?'

Ellen looked at Kruger, then at Hartnal. Then refocused on the character in the suit.

'I'm sorry, who are you again?'

'Porter French.'

'A friend,' said Kruger, examining his fingernails. 'A trusted friend of the family.'

A lawyer, thought Ellen. Something like that.

Perry was raking at his hair.

'We're interested in the catalog,' said French, giving Ellen a hard stare. 'We'd like to know how and when you first came across it.'

'Wednesday,' said Ellen. 'The Wednesday after Taylor Bissel called me.'

'Wednesday sixteenth?' said French.

'If you say so. The Wednesday before the lunch.'

'Bissel contacted you . . .'

'On the Saturday. I expressed an interest, went in to take a look at it with Lewis on Monday. I felt it was good. In fact—' She looked straight at Perry, '—it's the finest example of Koenig's work I've seen. I asked Bissel to release it to me so that I could start the process of putting together support for the acquisition.'

'Then you started on the documentation,' said French.

'I had the Koenig letter to Linda Carey. Then, on Wednesday night, I found the catalog.'

French was scribbling notes.

'I remember because I was late getting home. I had to ask my nanny to give dinner to my little boy. I found this thing in the library – in the Koenig file, and I was . . . It was exciting. I stayed late making copies and so forth.' She looked around the table. 'Is anyone going to tell me what this is about?'

The question was met with stony silence. They were all staring at her.

'Do you recall having an argument with Mr Perry on Wednesday afternoon?' said French.

Perry was shaking his head, looking more and more depressed.

Ellen cleared her throat. Her cell phone started up. She fumbled for it, frowned at the number, switched it off.

'We had words, yes.'

'Do you recall what about?'

'Does it *have* to be the Spanish Inquisition?' said Perry.

French looked at Kruger who returned his questioning gaze with a nod.

'We argued about the picture,' said Ellen. 'Bruce was against even showing it to the trustees. I said there were a lot of people who thought it was good. That I wasn't the only one.'

'What was the impression you took away from that conversation?' said French.

'What do you mean?'

'Did you think the painting was going to be presented to the trustees?'

Ellen shook her head.

'No. No, I didn't.'

'And then, on Wednesday evening you found the catalog.'

Ellen stared at the catalog in the middle of the table.

'The catalog was in a file?' said French.

Ellen looked up.

'The catalogs are stored alphabetically by artist. But flimsier material – ephemera like flyers, invitations, posters and so forth gets stored in files. There's a file for each artist. Some of them have two or three. The San Diego catalog is more a brochure than a real . . .'

She watched French turn the catalog around so that it was facing her.

'Is this it?' he said.

Ellen looked around at the stern faces, then picked it up. She leafed through it.

'It looks like it.'

'For goodness' sake,' said Perry.

The a/c cut out, and suddenly it was silent. Noises filtered in from outside. Car horns, a distant police siren.

'There's a problem,' said Kruger. He was staring straight at her now. 'It appears that the catalog has been tampered with.'

Ellen put the catalog down. French said something to her, and she had to have it repeated.

'A folio has been replaced,' he said. 'There are rust marks from the staples on all the folios except for the folio that was inserted. The print on the doctored folio is wrong. Whoever did this went to the trouble of finding period paper. They probably got hold of a book printed around the same time, removed the end papers etc, but beyond that there's no real attempt to reproduce the . . .' He seemed to become aware of the gravity of the situation, of the serious faces turned in his direction. 'It's not the same ink,' he said simply. 'Or even the same process. This looks like it came from a bubble jet printer. If you can believe that.'

Ellen reached for the glass of water in front of her, took a good mouthful. At least she knew what they were talking about now.

'We checked it against the examples held by the Smithsonian and the Whitney,' said French. 'Neither contains any reference to a painting by the name of *Mirror*.'

'I don't . . .' Ellen fumbled in her pocket and came up with a Kleenex. 'I don't understand. Am I . . .' Her voice was dying. She couldn't get her breath. 'Am I being accused of something?'

'How long have you known Bissel?' said French.

'That's *enough*!' said Perry, slamming his hand on the table. 'For goodness' sake.'

'Bruce,' snapped Kruger, 'this may come as a surprise to you, but this investigation—'

'Investigation?' said Ellen, weakly. She was on her feet. 'This is . . . this is . . .'

'Ellen,' said Hartnal softly. 'Please don't make this any worse.'

'Worse?' she choked, going cold. 'How could it be worse? You're accusing me of some sort of fraud. It's . . . it's ridiculous, defamatory nonsense.'

The old men were staring up at her as though she were a dangerous criminal.

'There will be no defamation,' said Kruger, giving her a steely look. 'Certainly the museum will not be bringing any charges.'

He stood up, and faced her, his mouth set in a grim line.

'What you do is, of course, your own business.'

8

She found herself on 53rd Street in the heat and noise. Didn't even know how she'd gotten down there, she was so angry. The road crew was pouring asphalt. Black scabbed machinery clattered in the tainted air. Choking on acrid fumes, she pulled against the weight of her shoulder bag, dazed, sick, furious for allowing herself to be ushered from the room like a lackey. It was Hartnal who had guided her out, his hand in the crook of her elbow. *I'm sure no one's really accusing you*. He'd ushered her towards the door speaking softly, saying that it was all very unfortunate, but that she had to understand how serious the situation was. And then she was outside, and the door was closed.

She needed a lawyer.

She stumbled forward, stricken, her eyes stinging in the smoke, heading for the blur of traffic on Broadway.

The Bissel Gallery occupied the first and second floors of 103 Spring Street, and was fronted with unbreakable glass. A quarter of an hour later she was pushing in through the front door where she was immediately confronted by Javier, Bissel's assistant. They had met a couple of times, but at first he didn't recognize her as if her distress had changed her physical appearance. Then he was apologizing, showing her through to the offices at the back of the gallery.

Bissel's door was closed. Ellen could see him on the phone through a window in the door. Buttoned up in a beautiful gray suit, he was sweating profusely, shaking his head as he talked. When he saw her, he frowned. Ellen knocked, opened up.

'I can't talk to you.'

She wasn't even in through the door.

'I just had Sam Brokaw on the line,' said Bissel.

Brokaw worked for the firm of attorneys used by MAM. Ellen waited for more, but Bissel just stood there staring as though he expected her to start smashing the place up.

'Taylor, I'm . . . I'm being accused of . . . *tampering* with a document – a catalog. They're accusing me of—'

'I can't talk to you.'

He lowered himself into his seat.

'I've been advised not to talk.'

'Taylor?'

'I'm sorry, Ellen. I don't know what's going on, but I do know it's very serious.'

'Taylor, I need to talk to Linda Carey. You have to—'

The phone started up. Bissel answered, swiveled, giving her his thick back. At the other end of the line, someone was shouting. When Bissel turned back to face her he was white. He hung up the phone.

'I'm sorry, Ellen. I'm going to have to ask you to leave.'

'Taylor, I swear to you, I don't know what's going on at the museum, but I have absolutely nothing to do with it.'

He stared, perspiration beading on his forehead.

'I'm going to ask you once more, Ellen. Please.'

It was only when she was back out in the heat and noise of the street that she remembered Ben. It was nearly one-thirty. She was supposed to have picked him up at the apartment at midday. She took out her cellphone. It was switched off. She'd switched it off in the meeting.

She fumbled at the tiny keys, did something wrong, then had to scroll back to get the right function. There were three messages. She stuck a hand out for a cab, the phone pressed to her ear. The first message had come in at 11.05: *Ellen, it's me, Greg. I'm just calling to remind you that you need to be at JFK at two o'clock.* The second was from Sandra, at twelve-thirty. It sounded like she was crying: *Mr Gregory call me. He want to know where you are – if you pick up Ben. I say no and he yell at me.* Y yo no puedo – *I say him call you.* A battered yellow cab came swerving out of the traffic and pulled to a halt at the curb. Ellen opened the back door and tossed in her shoulder bag. Then climbed in herself, the cell still clamped to her ear. The last message was Greg again: *Where the hell are you? You're supposed to be on your way here by now. I can't believe you're screwing this up for him.*

It seemed to take forever to get back up town. Every light was against them. Then the cab got stuck in traffic at the end of the street. Craning her neck, Ellen saw Greg putting Ben into the back of a cab in front of her building. She jammed a bill through the window at the driver, and opened the door.

'Hey! Lady. Be careful.'

They'd come to a halt against a parked car. The door wouldn't open more than a couple of inches. She called out through the gap, then got back in and closed the door. She could just see Greg walking around to the other side of the car. The driver inched forward and this time she clambered out, dragging her bag with her. She started to run.

'*Greg! Greg, wait*!'

He was ducking into the car.

'*Greg*!'

He looked up, saw her, froze. He was standing there open-mouthed as she came pounding along the sidewalk.

Sandra was standing in the street door, tears streaming down her face.

'What the *hell's* going on?' she yelled.

'We're missing the fucking plane is what's going on.'

He remembered Ben inside the car, and slammed the door shut. Ellen ducked down, looking in through the window. Ben gave a timid wave.

'You were supposed to be here at twelve,' said Greg.

'I know, I'm sorry I got . . . I got . . .'

'Caught up at work. Yeah, I guessed.' He shook his head and put his hand on the door handle.

'I was in a meeting. I . . .'

For a second she thought she was going to lose it. Her vision blurred. Greg let go of the handle, stood there shaking his head, waiting to hear what she had to say. She knew that if she tried to explain she'd start crying, and she was not going to cry.

'This isn't really working, Ellen.'

Something snapped then. She was blind for a second. Her throat seemed to thicken. Greg's words came to her muffled by the roar of blood in her ears.

'You're never with him. You fob him off with whatever her name is, and—'

Ellen grabbed at the door handle, but Greg ripped her fingers away. He was panting, staring at her with wild eyes.

'No,' he said, 'you're going to hear this.'

'There's nothing you can tell me about what is and isn't working!' She was yelling, out of control. She didn't want to be yelling in front of Ben, but she couldn't help herself. 'You were the one who—'

'I fucked up. I *fucked up*. I know that.' He put a hand against his chest. 'But I was . . . that was a long time ago and you . . . you're his *mother*, Ellen. You're his mother and you don't . . .'

'Don't what, Greg?' She pulled in a shuddering breath. '*Don't what?*'

'You farm him out to the help or to pottery or judo or whatever fucking thing. You fill his life with all this *stuff* so he won't notice there's nothing in the middle. There's nothing there. *You're* not there.

All you think about is your stupid museum and your stupid meetings and what they're saying about you in the press.'

He seemed to realize how far he'd gone, took a step back, setting his jaw.

She couldn't speak.

'So we're going to LA now,' he said in a small voice. 'I'm going to get us on a later flight, and we're going to LA.'

He walked around to the other side of the car, and got in. The driver started the engine.

Ellen looked in through the window. Ben was looking out at her his face pale and rigid in the gloomy interior. She opened the door, squatted down.

'I'm sorry, baby.'

His chin puckered.

'It's okay,' he said. Her big boy, being brave. It was the worst thing, of course. The tears were streaming down her face now.

'It's okay, Mommy.'

He was stroking her hand – a clumsy, childish caress.

'It's okay.'

Greg leaned across him, clutching for the door handle, and for a second he stared up at her, a look of pure hatred in his eyes.

'You done now?' he said.

And she was. She stood up on rubbery legs, and let him close the door, watched the cab pull into the traffic.

Billy in Queens

The magazine said Lindz had been educated at Oxford before going on to Harvard. Billy's eyes tracked across to the photograph, saw a snotty-looking woman who obviously had some kind of eating disorder.

'Let's drive around,' said Jay, climbing into the Beemer.

'Isn't somebody getting fucked over?' said Billy.

Jay turned to look at her, looked at the magazine.

'I mean all this modern art,' she said. 'All this money.'

She became aware of him then. His smell. A kind of old-fashioned cologne like her dad used to wear. She looked up from the page.

'Doesn't it piss you off?'

'The art?'

'Yeah, Picasso all that stuff. Women with noses on the back of their heads. People taking a dump in a can and selling it for millions.'

Jay just stared. Nothing bothered Jay. He had a thing about not getting mad. He was fifty-eight years old and in better condition than she was. He had the old-man hair, though – thin and gray. He had the old-man eyes.

'There's a camera,' he said.

Billy tossed the magazine, and eased out into the Monday afternoon traffic, wondering why it was Jay didn't want her coming into his office. He ran his business out of a three-room suite at the mall on Roosevelt Avenue, had a secretary called Melanie, and a P.I. certificate on the wall behind his desk. There'd never been any problem with her going in there before.

'In his office,' he said. 'He's got it hidden in a picture or something like that.'

The Warhol. Billy closed her eyes.

'*Then* would have been the time to talk about this, Jay. Before I went in there.'

Jay pushed the seat back. A couple of inches shy of six foot, and 160 pounds tops, he never seemed to have enough room.

'I didn't know then, Billy. The client didn't know then. It's the dealer's big secret.'

The client. He had a way of talking about it. Like he was still a spook.

'So how come the client knows now?'

Jay shot her a look, and for a second she saw her dad – the way he used to look at her when she came home from school with the smell of cigarettes in her clothes. Jay and her dad had worked together in Washington for twelve years, bugging embassies and setting up wire-taps. They'd been together the night her dad took a header down a stairwell and broke his neck. The first time Jay had touched her was at the funeral. She was seventeen years old. But for a long time now he'd been more of an uncle. He'd relocated to New York in '94, about the time of the big Rick Ames shake out at Langley. She'd heard he was dropped just because he'd done some work for Ames, but he never talked about it. The nearest he'd ever come to it was to say he'd had a problem with a polygraph test. Whatever the whys and wherefores, he'd been forced into the private sector, and done pretty well there. And when things had gone wrong for her in Baltimore, he was the one who'd helped her out, starting with getting her off the booze.

'So now he's got me on tape,' said Billy.

Jay went back to watching the traffic.

'He's not going to do anything with it.' He dropped his window a couple of inches. Street noise blasted in. 'He sold this painting. He took his cut. He knows you know about the Trust. So . . .'

'So?'

'So he's hoping you went away.'

'He's not worried about me taking the paperwork? He doesn't think this is all going to unravel?'

Jay sighed.

'These guys, these dealers, they're used to squeezing through gaps.'

'I thought electronics was your thing, Jay. Since when are you an expert on the art market?'

Billy saw an amber light, and put her foot down. The Beemer went *whoosh* as they flashed across the intersection. Jay was shaking his head now. Billy checked her mirror.

'What?'

'You drive like a teenager.'

'Thanks.'

'And you brake too hard.'

'If you don't like the way I drive, how come we're having this conversation in my car?'

Jay was watching the street on his side. There was something about this job. Even for Jay this was pretty tight-lipped.

'I want you to go talk to him, Billy.'

'To Bissel? I thought I didn't need to worry.'

'You don't, but if he taped you, the chances are he taped the vendor.'

Billy nodded, seeing it now, and seeing beyond it into something she didn't much like.

'The client, your client, wants to see Carey on tape,' she said.

Jay gave a nod.

'You can pick up the film he made of you at the same time.'

'Why is it I feel like I'm being incentivized here?'

'Pull in here. This is okay.'

Billy turned, rolled into the parking lot of a Home Depot. She found a space, and sat there for a moment considering her options.

'Don't think I'm not grateful, Uncle Jay.'

'Don't call me that, Billy.'

'Why not?'

'Makes me feel old.'

She turned to look at him. He was fucking old.

'If it's the money . . .' he said.

Billy nodded, half smiling. It was *always* the money.

'Okay,' she said. 'Let's talk about that.'

'You get the tape, I can double your normal fee.'

Her normal fee was a thousand a day plus expenses. The client had deep pockets.

'This painting,' she said after a moment. 'Bissel sold it for twenty-three million.'

Jay was smiling now, shaking his head.

'What?' said Billy. 'You telling me that isn't what this is about?'

'Next thing, you're going to be talking about your cut.' He shifted in the seat, trying to get comfortable. 'This is just another job, Billy. I could ask someone else, but they might not be so concerned about the tape Bissel's got of you impersonating an FBI agent.'

'Jay.'

His eyes did a little shimmy, checking out her mouth. He liked her mouth.

'You didn't know about the camera *before* I went in there, did you?'

The skin bunched between his non-existent eyebrows.

'I wouldn't do that, Billy.'

He held her gaze. Honest Jay Tolson.

She looked away, lowered her window.

'Where am I supposed to find it?'

'He's got this house in Forest Hills. His wife's in Europe with the kids. Vacation. You go out there, tell him you want to talk to him about the Trust. Then, when you're inside, you ask him for the tapes.'

'They're at the house? I mean, you know that for a fact?'

'It's the assumption. He's got this safe in his study.'

'The client knows all about him.' She glanced across. 'Who is it, Jay? The museum?'

'What difference does it make?'

'I just want to know what I'm getting involved in.'

'You're not getting involved in anything.'

He wasn't going to tell her. Billy looked out at the parking lot. A couple of honest citizens were trying to load some fiber board into the back of a Volkswagen Jetta. Two thousand a day plus expenses.

'So I'm telling him to open the safe?'

Jay shrugged.

'You're just asking for a couple of tapes. What's he going to do?'

'Shoot me?'

'Billy, the guy deals in art, not drugs.'

10

She'd cried the first time she'd met Leslie Ann. It was in the fall of 1987, the beginning of her last year at Oxford, and Leslie Ann was there as a guest of her tutor. She'd been placed next to her at dinner one evening, and was talking in an earnest, self-conscious way about Joyce, when, in the middle of comparing Michael Fury's flung stones to the tap of snow against the window at the end of *The Dead*, she'd burst into tears, and proceeded to tell her how her boyfriend had killed himself the week before by jumping from the second floor window of his digs in Paddington. They'd ended up in Leslie Ann's rooms, drinking cognac, Ellen talking about the phone conversation she'd had with Dan a couple of hours before he'd done it, and Leslie Ann telling her about her last talk with Koenig, also telephonic – how she had never been able to forget the sound of the axe hitting the stone floor of the bathroom where he'd cut off his hand.

It was Leslie Ann who had encouraged her to consider a career as a curator, Leslie Ann who had parlayed her into the two year curator's course at Harvard, partly by talking up the art school foundation year she'd completed prior to going to Oxford. By the time she went to Harvard in 1993, she had already been living in New York for three years, unhappily married to Greg, drifting, haunted by thoughts of Dan, so depressed she had taken Prozac for a while. Leslie Ann had taken her in hand, and when she came out of Harvard, renewed – redefined in a way – her self-confidence at an all time high (undaunted even by the unplanned pregnancy which eventually resulted in Ben) it was Leslie Ann who had opened the doors of the Modern.

And now they had closed.

That was the way it seemed to her anyway, sitting in the living room of Leslie Ann's east side brownstone, staring stupidly at the photographs on the wall behind the big velour couch. It was raining outside, a summer storm going some way to clearing the tainted city air. The room was crammed with furniture, art, memorabilia – everything impregnated with a stale smoky smell. The photographs dated from the fifties for the most part, Leslie Ann looking very young next to Alfred Faber, for example, at the opening of the Rachel Kruger sculpture garden in 1953, or standing in the wreckage caused by the fire that gutted the second floor of the museum in 1958, or with Pollock and Koenig at the house Pollock and Lee Krasner shared on Long Island – the picture taken just before Koenig decided to move out there.

Ali, Leslie Ann's Siamese came in through the half open door and jumped up onto the back of the couch, and then Leslie Ann was there, a little hunched inside her loose fitting black clothes, smoking one of the colored Russian cigarettes that she referred to as her 'Mata Haris'. Seeing the drawn, wooden look on her narrow face, it came to Ellen that she had arrived in the middle of one of her friend's debilitating migraines.

She got to her feet.

'Leslie Ann . . . I'm sorry, I—'

The old woman pulled her into a hard embrace, and just like that Ellen was crying.

'I'm sorry, I—'

'Stop saying you're sorry. *I'm* sorry. I'm sorry I wasn't there at this ridiculous town council meeting.'

Ellen pulled back, and looked into her friend's tired eyes.

'You heard, then.'

'Lewis called me just after lunch. I've been with him all afternoon.'

She sat Ellen down, and went over to a drinks cabinet, poured a good three fingers of bourbon into a squat crystal glass.

'Drink me,' she said, handing it to Ellen.

Ellen took a mouthful and winced, then asked her what Hartnal had said. Leslie Ann took a seat on the couch opposite.

'They're talking about going through every document in the building. Every piece of paper. Every letter. Every bill of sale.'

Ellen leaned back, closing her eyes.

'It's unprecedented,' said Leslie Ann. 'Unprecedented. The integrity of the museum's archive . . .'

The archive was the memory, the basis of authentication. Without the archive, much of the museum's collection would be indistinguishable from the sea of fakes beyond its walls.

'And this catalog . . .' said Leslie Ann. 'If this could happen once, perhaps it has already happened. That's what they're thinking. Perhaps it has happened a thousand times.'

'I didn't do anything.'

Leslie Ann shifted on the couch, sending Ali to the floor.

'Leslie Ann. I didn't do anything.'

'Ellen. Please. I know you didn't.'

Ellen opened her eyes. Leslie Ann was batting away smoke.

'Unfortunately, this is so serious that . . . I mean, quite apart from the integrity of the museum, there's the small question of the twenty-three million dollars. Lewis is hoping that Taylor Bissel will eventually come around to the view that at least part of the asking price should be reimbursed, but . . .'

'But what?'

'Well, Bissel, understandably perhaps, is standing behind the painting. He says it's good.'

'He does?' Ellen tucked in her chin, considering this piece of news. 'Good. Good, because, so do I.'

She looked up. Leslie Ann was watching her, a compassionate frown puckering her deeply lined forehead. Her small regular features had changed little over the years, but five decades of smoking had given her a cured, leathery look.

'Leslie Ann,' said Ellen, 'you know how I am about these things.'

'Clairvoyant,' said her friend, her eyes deadly serious.

Ellen blushed. They had often talked about her 'eye'. Some people just had it – a visceral response to the genuine article, an instinctive bridling in the presence of fakes.

'Let's call it a powerful instinct then,' said Leslie Ann. 'And with this painting you're saying . . .?'

'I swear, I've never . . . It's why I did what I did. Why I brought it into the museum in the first place. It's good, Leslie Ann. It's a Koenig.'

They were quiet for a moment.

'What does Bissel say about the catalog?' said Ellen.

'As far as I can gather from Lewis, he hinted that the catalog might have been introduced into the archive by someone who wanted to *discredit* rather than confirm the painting's authenticity.'

'*What*?'

Leslie Ann was shaking her head.

'I know. Much as I dislike Bruce Perry, I can't quite see him going to those lengths.'

Ellen pushed back against the couch, and took a good long pull on the bourbon.

'It doesn't make sense,' she said. 'If I hadn't found the catalog, I would have probably backed down. Bruce told me he didn't want it in the show. That was what we were arguing about on Wednesday afternoon, and I pretty much . . . I mean, he was really angry about it, so I . . .'

'You wouldn't have shown it?'

'No, probably not. He is my boss, after all. But then . . . well, I did find the catalog, and so . . .'

They were both shaking their heads now.

'Who found it?' said Ellen. 'I mean, who was it that noticed the problem?' She hadn't thought to ask at the meeting.

'Perry. Apparently, the dimensions are wrong. The painting Bissel sent to the museum had lost an inch—'

'In the re-stretching,' said Ellen. 'Yes, that's right. The Spectrum Analytical report picked up on that. The original painted surface was an inch wider than the stretcher which they thought was probably quite recent.'

'So the painting that was exhibited in San Diego should have been an inch wider. But the entry for the catalog shows . . . well, it's the same as the painting Bissel was offering.'

'Seventy-one inches by one hundred eighty.' Ellen sipped her drink. 'So Bruce noticed this, and took a closer look.' It sort of made sense. She drew a hand across her face. 'Jesus Christ.'

'It's terrible,' said Leslie Ann. 'A terrible thing. Kruger's got this lackey – some sort of reconverted attorney.'

'Mr. French. I met him this morning.'

'You'll be hearing from him.'

'Do I need a lawyer?'

Leslie Ann frowned, drawing on her cigarette. Then she was shaking her head, shrugging.

'I can't believe this,' said Ellen, covering her eyes with her hand. 'I can't believe any of it.'

Leslie Ann came and sat beside her, and for a moment they were still, Leslie Ann holding her hand.

'Ellen, you will get through this,' she said softly. 'Your friends will help you. I will help you.'

Ellen nodded, holding back the tears. Leslie Ann put an arm around her shoulders.

'They threw me out, Leslie Ann. Kruger showed me the door. He said what you do now is your own business.'

She turned to look Leslie Ann in the eye.

'Is that . . . does that constitute a dismissal? I don't even know.'

Leslie Ann took her hand away, and her face settled into a new sternness.

'What?'

Leslie Ann winced.

'Ellen, please. My head.'

She reached over to the lamp next to her, and flipped it off.

'They're very angry,' she said after a while.

Ellen hitched herself sideways on the couch so that she could see the other woman's face.

'Perry is very angry at you for bringing the thing into the collection, and Kruger takes his lead from Perry. There's going to be media attention. It's the kind of thing . . .'

She shook her head, and took a pull on her cigarette.

'What?'

Leslie Ann turned to look at her.

'It's the kind of thing Kruger hates.' She was still for a moment. Then she put her hand on Ellen's. 'They're not going to dismiss you, Ellen.'

Ellen nodded, wanting to believe that this was a good thing, but she could see by the look on Leslie Ann's face that it wasn't.

'They won't dismiss you over this because they won't want to risk litigation. They won't want any of the details in the press.'

'But . . .'

'But they'll want you out.'

Ellen couldn't speak. It was disastrous.

'They will write you references,' said Leslie Ann. 'Even Kruger.'

Ellen stood up and went over to the window. The lights were coming on in the street.

'Do you remember when the Duchamp was stolen?' said Leslie Ann.

Ellen watched a car go by down in the street. She got a flash of Ben sitting in the car, being brave, wondered if he'd arrived in LA yet. She shook her head.

'Actually, now that I think of it, this was just before you joined the museum,' said Leslie Ann. '*The Bicycle Wheel*. A Dadaist icon. One of the keystones of the collection.'

'Yes.'

'In the summer before you joined the museum this character, a young man, walked into the museum and took it. He just went up to the second floor and took it off the stand. It's there, as you know, in the middle of the room surrounded by other rooms and corridors and doorways. You know how the museum is. So this person had to put the sculpture under his arm, I mean a wooden stool with a bicycle wheel attached, and walk past a half dozen guards. He got to the second floor landing, and went down the escalator, then out through the lobby into the street carrying this icon of modern art under his arm.'

Ellen turned from the window.

'I don't understand. I mean, the Duchamp is still there.'

Leslie Ann nodded, exhaling.

'He went out through the revolving doors, carrying the thing in his arms. By this time people were beginning to notice. A couple of guards went after him. The young man broke into a trot, heading for Fifth Avenue. On Fifth Avenue he hailed a cab.'

Ellen was shaking her head.

'He *hailed* a cab,' said Leslie Ann. 'There was no getaway car. Nothing like that. He hailed a cab, and by incredible good fortune got one. He bundled the Duchamp into the back and disappeared.'

'Unbelievable.'

'But true. And here's the point. No one said a word. Not the director, not the Chief Curator not PR not anyone. Silence. A day later, according to legend as it were, the sculpture was thrown over the wall of the sculpture garden, breaking the legs of the stool and bending the bicycle wheel. No-one saw it happen. It was just found there.'

'So they never . . .'

'The perpetrator was never captured.'

'I can't believe I never heard about it.'

'No one talked. The Duchamp was restored. It is now on display back among the Picassos and the Van Goghs. The incident was forgotten. This is the museum, Ellen. Nothing gets out.'

'This will get out,' said Ellen. 'If I go to the press.'

'If you go to the press, they will smear you.'

'How? I haven't . . .'

Leslie Ann was shaking her head. She stood up, came and joined Ellen at the window.

'They'll say you doctored the catalog to make sure *Mirror* was bought. They'll say you wanted to prove Perry wrong, that you wanted his job.'

She was nodding now.

'Just remember, they don't know what happened here, Ellen. That's why Kruger brought French in. They don't know what happened or who to trust. You're the one who brought the painting in. You're the one who found the catalog. You're the one they are looking at.'

'But I didn't . . .'

Leslie Ann put a hand on her arm.

'All Kruger wants is to settle this affair *intra muros*,' she said softly. 'And my advice, my advice as your friend, is to cooperate.'

11

The paintings were protected but the library wasn't. It was as simple as that. The documents contained in the library could be ascribed a monetary value, but nobody thought about them in those terms, certainly not the museum's insurers. There were things in there that were irreplaceable, as unique as the Matisse *Dancers* down on the second floor, but only a handful of academics even knew of their existence, and they were not intrinsically valuable. The cameras and the alarms, the steel gates and the automatically locking doors were reserved for the paintings.

'What you have up here is a sprinkler system which hasn't been tested in eight months, some smoke alarms and a broken camera,' said Porter French.

Lewis Hartnal looked at the back of French's head and stifled a sigh. They had been reviewing security all afternoon. Bob Gifford, who was responsible for those matters, Staunton, himself, and French. They had started on the ground floor as per David Kruger's instructions, and had worked their way up through the building. Gill Bryant, the chief librarian had been asked to stay after work and was now part of the posse following French around. French was incredible.

Meticulous wasn't really the word for it. He could stand looking at a security camera or secure door for minutes at a time, thinking apparently, but about what, it was hard to say. He had a video cassette in his hands, kept slapping it against his thigh.

'The one in the reception area is working,' said Gifford.

They had come to the elevator. French stepped in and held the door for the others.

'You have students coming in here,' he said. 'Visiting academics. You let them handle the documents without any kind of supervision.'

'Not all the documents,' said Staunton. 'We restrict access to the more valuable items.'

'And things that are fragile,' said Gill Bryant.

'But that's the lesson here, isn't it?' French turned and looked from one to the other. 'Everything's valuable.'

They got out in the basement and French led the way through to the room where the monitors were stacked. There were nine of them, producing images from twenty three cameras. Every couple of seconds the screens twitched and a new perspective was offered. French slotted in the tape, and fiddled with buttons until he was looking at an image recorded from Wednesday 16th, the evening Ellen Lindz was supposed to have found the catalog.

'Where's the date?' said French, stabbing a finger at the line of flashing blanks in the bottom left of the screen. 'You haven't even got it set up properly.'

They all crowded into the small space, looking at the screen. It was true, the digital clock was running, but the date didn't show.

Gifford mumbled something about his assistant, and took the cassette out of the slot. It was clearly labeled in marker pen: 08/16/03. 16:00–19:00.

'It's all here on the tape, Mr. French.'

French gave him a withering look.

Finally, at ten o'clock, he was finished. He said he'd make sure they saw a copy of his report. As of the following day, the library was to be closed to the public. The official story would be that maintenance work was being carried out. Rewiring – something of that nature.

'What about the documents?' said Gill Bryant. 'Are we going to go through them? Look for . . . signs of tampering.'

French scratched at his throat.

'We're going to have to think about that,' he said. 'Meanwhile I want to see the video tape taken from camera 6/23.' He shot Gifford a look. 'That's the one in the reception area of the library. The one that's working, but isn't set up properly.'

Gifford blushed a deep rose color.

'They only go back three months,' he said. 'The tapes, I mean. I keep them three months and then destroy them.'

'Really.' French said it as though he couldn't be less surprised.

Gifford looked from Staunton to Hartnal.

'We decided that about a year ago. There just isn't room in the basement to store them. And they're a fire hazard.'

Hartnal touched Gifford on the sleeve.

'That's okay, Bob.'

French shook his head.

'We'll just have to hope that whoever did this, did it in the last three months,' he said.

12

Everyone knew. That was the feeling she got as she pushed in through the big revolving doors at the 53rd Street entrance on Tuesday morning, trying to look businesslike, trying to look like everything was fine. People who normally smiled or said 'hi', had their heads bent to their work, were apparently very occupied.

Passing through the secure door into the fourth-floor offices, she found Jerry Lloyd lurking by the coffee machine. A hundred and forty pounds of nervous energy, Jerry was a dead ringer for the Woody Allen of Annie Hall. He was also one of the most conflicted intellectuals she knew, a gay star-struck maverick in a family of eggheads. His elder brother was a tenured professor in Twentieth Century history at Columbia, while his sister, three years his junior, was something grand in bio-tech at MIT. He grabbed her as soon as she came through the door.

'What the hell's going on?'

Ellen walked on past him.

'Hey, Jer. Fine thanks. How are you?'

'Not fine,' he said, following her now, spilling coffee on the blotchy carpet. 'I'm feeling shut out.'

She shot him a look as she opened the door to her office.

'One minute, you're the MAM cover girl,' he said, following her in, 'the next everyone's saying . . .'

Ellen turned.

'What? What are they saying?'

Jerry closed the door.

'Everyone's talking about this meeting.'

She found her way to the seat behind her desk, and sat there shaking her head.

'Come on, Ellen. This is me. Jerry. Your friend?'

Normally just the sight of him standing there in his terrible corduroy pants and frayed bowling shirt was enough to make Ellen smile, but not today. His state of gossip-arousal modulated into something more sympathetic.

'It's the painting, isn't it?'

Ellen lifted her hair from the nape of her neck. Then took a look at her desk. There were no summonses or sinister memos from French.

'Jerry, I can't talk about it. I'm in enough trouble as it is.'

'I knew something was going down when I heard about Bissel.'

He watched her expression change, pushed his glasses tight against the bridge of his nose.

'You haven't heard?'

'No.'

'Yesterday morning this woman, this FBI agent was in there, asking questions about the painting.'

'*What*?' She was shaking her head now. 'Who told you this?'

'I heard it on the fruitvine.'

Film and Media was Gossip Central for some reason, a magnet for gay men who seemed to spend their whole time trading scandal while sifting through Clarence Sinclair Bull glamour portraits of Greta Garbo.

Ellen tilted her head.

'The fruits in question being . . .'

'Kevin, who heard it through Cissy Vara, you know the woman who works at The Corliss.'

The Corliss Gallery was a couple of doors up from the Bissel. Cissy Vara, was a very intense, very buttoned-up cross-dressing Brazilian who Ellen was always meeting at museum functions. Vara prowled the gallery trying to get people to buy Frank Corliss's seemingly endless supply of shock art much of which seemed to involve people urinating on each other.

'And Vara got it from?'

'Bissel's assistant. Javier, is it?'

'Who said, specifically . . .?'

'That this butch woman came in flashing her ID.'

'FBI.'

'FBI. Bissel took her into his office.'

'The conversation happened in his office?'

Jerry gave a nod, then removed his glasses and started polishing them on his shirt.

'So how does Javier know she was there to talk about the painting?' said Ellen.

'She *seized* all the paperwork from the transaction.'

'Bissel told Javier about this?'

'What? No. This is the thing, and I'm swearing you to secrecy here, okay?'

Ellen gave a nod, but then Jerry seemed to have second thoughts. He put his glasses back on, blinked at her from behind the thick lenses.

'No, I can't tell you. Seriously. Because Javier could get into trouble.'

'*Jerry*. What did he do?'

'You didn't hear it from me, Ellen.'

'Okay.'

He leaned forward and tapped her phone with a fingernail.

'Bissel's got this office system and he's always getting Javier to set up conference calls with clients, and Javier *always* listens in.'

'I don't understand.'

'He puts Bissel on hold, dials up the other party and then hits 'conference'. He just sits there lapping up all this classified stuff.'

'No I mean I don't understand how . . . you said this FBI person came into the office.'

Jerry frowned, then shook his head. 'Oh I see what you . . . No. No, he made a call to his wife after the FBI woman had gone, and Javier picked up. I'm just saying about Javier. Apparently he's all over Bissel's personal dealings. Bissel called his wife, and Javier pressed the button, you know, to get the line, and just listened in. So Bissel told his wife what had happened, and Javier went to look for the *Mirror* paperwork because, like I say, he's basically this *spy*, and it was all gone. Bissel stayed in his office all afternoon. He wouldn't come out.'

Ellen stood up.

'Ellen?'

'Yes.'

'You okay?'

She went across to her filing cabinet.

'No. Not really. I'm angry, Jer. I'm very pissed off.'

She found the *Mirror* presentation dossier, and pulled it out.

'Jerry?'

'Yeah?'

She turned to look at him.

'Can you . . . could you?' He was already standing up. 'Thanks for this. This may be a big help. But I need to make some calls.'

He gave her a hug at the door, and she went back to her desk. She sat there for a long time holding her head in her hands. There really was a problem with the painting. Because why else would the FBI be taking an interest? It was a disaster. A twenty-three-million-dollar disaster.

It was nearly eleven o'clock. Eight a.m. in Los Angeles. She picked up the phone and called the number Greg had given her. The machine came on, and a woman's voice asked her to leave a message. For a moment she froze.

'Oh . . . yes, hi. This is Ellen. Ben's mother. I . . . I just wanted to make sure he arrived safely. Thanks.'

She hung up, then cursed herself for being so stiff.

Beyond the window, the day was cooking up hot and humid.

She called Bruce Perry. Grace Hartigan, his assistant, picked up.

'Is he in?'

'He's with Mr French.' Grace said the name with a certain distaste.

'Do you know when he's going to be done?'

'He's got a lunch at twelve-thirty, so . . .'

'I need to talk to him.'

'I'll give him the message.'

Ellen hung up, and sat there turning the pages of her desk diary. She had two meetings scheduled for the afternoon, both of them with Perry, one to discuss a Hopper retrospective coming up in the fall, one to discuss a problem that had arisen with some Chagalls which were to be part of an émigrés and immigrants show that was very dear to Bruce's heart.

She stood up.

Perry had one of the six big suites facing 53rd Street. With a single loud rap, she opened the door.

Porter French was sitting in front of the huge Frank Lloyd Wright desk. His head snapped around as Ellen walked into the room, closely followed by Grace Hartigan.

'I'm sorry, Bruce, she . . .'

Perry scowled from the depths of his fat leather chair.

'It's okay, Grace. I'm sure there's a good reason for Ellen to be running into my office like a maenad.'

Porter French chuckled at that. Ellen touched at her hair, fixing him with what she hoped was a withering look.

'I'm sorry Mr French, but there's something I need to say to Mr Perry in private.'

French looked across the expanse of waxed oak at Perry, who was now holding up his hands in mock submission.

'I'll be in with Lewis,' said French, rising. He gave Ellen a stern glance, then left the room.

Perry lowered his hands.

'Well?'

'I just heard that Taylor Bissel is under investigation by the FBI.'

Perry settled deeper into his chair. If the news came as a surprise, he didn't show it.

'They seized documents,' said Ellen. 'Pertaining to the—'

'Ellen.' The hands came up again. 'Believe it or not, Taylor and I *are* still on speaking terms. I know all this.'

'So . . .'

'So what?'

'So I'm thinking, if the FBI thinks Taylor Bissel is worth investigating, perhaps he *is* worth investigating, because perhaps he . . . he's somehow *involved* in whatever is going on here.'

'Nicely put,' said Perry. Then, seeing the look on her face: 'Ellen, you may well be right, but I still don't understand why you came barging in here. French is the last person you want to be rubbing up the wrong way at the moment.'

'I came in here because *you* are the one who's accusing me of—'

'I'm not accusing you of anything.' Perry set his jaw. 'I noticed a little discrepancy in the evidence you presented to the trustees, a little discrepancy *you* should have noticed, and I brought it to the attention of the board. That's all.'

Ellen looked down at the carpet.

'Ellen. Why don't you sit down.'

She found her way to a seat, took a breath, looked up to meet Perry's steady gaze, and saw something she didn't expect to see: compassion, pity.

'You do believe me?'

'I do believe you about what?'

'When I say I had nothing to do with this catalog.'

Perry shook his head, and pushed out an irritable sigh.

'Ellen, I believe that you committed a colossal, career-ending fuck-up. And yes, for the record, I do believe you about the catalog. I don't think that even you are so mad or so deluded as to think that you could advance your career by faking an important document.'

Ellen felt the blood rise in her cheeks.

'So . . .' She clutched at the air. 'French – this whole investigation . . .'

'Will run its course. And by the end of it Mr Porter French may have a slightly less superficial understanding of how this place works. He will go back to David Kruger and report that you brought a twenty-three million dollar piece of shit into the collection. *Against* my advice. *Against* my repeated requests for you to drop it. That's why you're in this situation, Ellen. Not because of this ridiculous catalog. They don't know *what* to think about that. They'd *like* to think you planted it, and that's why French was brought in: to try to prove that you did. But that's just so they can legitimize doing what they are going to do to you anyway.'

He paused, and she saw the look again. Pity.

'They're upset at you, Ellen. The museum is angry. Kruger is angry. For some strange reason he doesn't like to have the collection put in doubt.'

'The picture is good,' she said into the silence. 'Authentic. I'm sure of it.'

Perry drew a hand across his face.

'Ellen, Ellen, Ellen.'

'Bruce, with all due respect—'

A finger came up. He was staring at his desk, too angry to look at her.

'Please don't talk to me about your instincts,' he said softly.

'You only say that because . . .'

His eyes snapped up to meet hers, and Ellen bit her tongue.

She looked up at the drawings hanging on the wall behind his head. Edward Hoppers. Simple sketches of diners. Lovely. Sad.

Perry softened a little.

'Ellen, I know you have a special affinity with Koenig's work. Don't think I'm blind to that. I know you also have an affinity with Leslie Ann Benton. And if you don't mind me saying so – with all due respect as you put it – this affinity, this friendship, has served you well. It would be a shame if you were to let it spoil things for you at this sensitive juncture.'

Ellen met his warning look, and shrugged, shook her head.

'What does that mean?'

'It means be guided by your own lights. Don't let yourself be someone else's . . .' He seemed to think better of it, was shaking his head now. 'If I'm saying anything, I'm saying this is time for objectivity. For the cold hard light of day.'

'I couldn't agree more. That's why I want you to talk to Taylor Bissel. On my behalf.'

He was looking uncomfortable now.

'He won't talk to me,' said Ellen.

'And what do you want me to say?'

'I want you to ask him where Linda Carey is.'

Perry stared.

'I want to talk to Linda Carey,' said Ellen. 'I mean, if anybody knows the truth about this, she does.'

Perry leaned forward and put his elbows on the desk. For a long time he said nothing. Ellen watched as he pulled the elastic band from his grizzled hair, and shook it loose.

'Ellen,' he said eventually. 'There's a problem with Linda Carey.'

'What problem?'

He raised a hand, slowing her down, wanting her to remain calm. It was one of his patronizing habits – this directing of emotional traffic, one of the things she hated.

'Taylor called me, yesterday,' he said. 'This was after he'd been savaged by Brokaw. He was shaken up, you understand. Brokaw's been instructed by Kruger to do his barracuda numero, threatening him with this and that, basically demanding that Taylor return the money to the museum. A mistake in my view, but I won't go into that. Taylor told me that he wired the money, half the money, to Linda Carey's account – a corporate account at a bank in Wyoming.'

He fixed Ellen with his dark eyes, obviously hoping for a response.

Ellen shrugged. It didn't mean anything to her.

'Okay,' he said. 'It turns out that the state of Wyoming allows you to open a corporate account without an identifying tag like "Inc." or "Co.". You can open a corporate account and give the *impression* that it's a personal checking account.'

Ellen shook her head

'I still don't understand what you're telling me.'

Perry sucked in an exasperated breath.

'Well let's say you're *not* Linda Carey, but you want to give the impression that you are. You have to come up with some ID, a social security number, and when it comes to the actual payment details, it kind of helps if you have an account in your name. I mean, Taylor makes wire transfers to numbered accounts in Geneva from time to time, lots of clients demand anonymity, but if you're not Linda Carey and you don't want to arouse any suspicion at all, you might feel more comfortable saying, "Here's a personal account in my name. Onshore. Nothing suspicious about it. You can wire the money there".'

'So Linda Carey . . .?'

Perry gave a nod.

'Is no more Linda Carey than I am.'

It was getting worse and worse.

'But . . . but she can still be *found*,' said Ellen. 'This person. She can still be made to own up, to . . . to clear my name of any wrong-doing.'

Perry drew a hand across his mouth with a rasping sound of bristle. For a moment it looked like he was going to say something harsh. He took a calming breath.

'Taylor paid someone to check it out,' he said. 'They contacted the local Chamber of Commerce in Cheyenne yesterday afternoon, looking for the paperwork. But guess what? The company directors don't have to be listed in the articles of incorporation in Wyoming.'

'So there's no name.'

'No, there's a name. I mean, I'm paraphrasing Taylor here so don't hold me to the details, but as I understand it there is a legal obligation to have what they call a resident agent in the state. He or she has to have a real address. Linda Carey's resident agent is some other person – Sandra or Sara Green. She's registered with an address in Cheyenne. Taylor's PI went there, and it turns out it's a motel. The PI asked about Mrs Green, and learns that Green is this elderly woman who took a room, and asked if she could use the motel address to receive mail. She said she was moving to the area and needed an address while she was looking for a house. Something like that. Oh and she paid cash. Taylor's guy ran a check for Sandra or Sara Green using Carey's date of birth, and came up with . . . well, nothing. He thinks this Carey person used Green to make it impossible to track. It's like calling yourself Smith.'

Ellen was nodding, a hand clamped to her forehead.

'I'm sorry, Ellen. It's all smoke and mirrors.'

It took him a second to realize what he'd said. Neither of them laughed.

13

Lewis Hartnal had a little closet in his office where a wash basin had been installed. There was also a hanger for a suit, shelves, toiletries. He could freshen up without going to the staff bathroom at the end of the corridor, could change a shirt, put on a tux if he had to, which was the case at least three times a month, could check his thinning hair and the ruin of his once perfectly acceptable face. In his head, he was still hovering somewhere in his mid-forties, but when he turned on the little light over the mirror he was confronted with a different self, a self he'd yet to grow into, a very, very old man.

The phone started up, and he set his jaw, his eyes on the wrinkled fingers that fiddled ineffectually with the buttons of the clean shirt he'd just put on.

It had been a grueling couple of days. The San Diego catalog couldn't have weighed more than a couple of ounces, but it had hit the museum like a wrecking ball, throwing out shock waves in every direction. He'd been on the phone all day, talking to French, talking to Kruger, fielding inquiries from worried trustees, even getting queries from insurers, and dealers. In the late afternoon there had been a call from a journalist, some character from the *Post* who appeared to have gotten wind of something about an FBI investigation into Taylor Bissel, all of which was very disturbing. And then there had been the call from Leslie Ann. The conversation couldn't have lasted more than ten minutes, but it had shaken him. Leslie Ann was convinced *Mirror* was genuine, and she had convinced him. Which left the niggling question of why someone would want to put a tampered catalog in the library.

There was a soft knock at the door. Hartnal finished buttoning his shirt and turned.

'Yes?'

Bob Gifford's long face appeared in the gap. He was flushed and sweating and there was something – it looked like a strand of spider web – snagged in his lank white hair.

Hartnal attempted a smile.

'I did call,' said Gifford, 'but . . .'

'I was probably on the other line. What is it, Bob?'

'I think I found something for Mr French, Doctor Hartnal. And I wanted to show it you first.'

Hartnal watched him come into the room, registering the cardboard box he was carrying. It looked like video cassettes stacked in neat rows. Gifford had been going through the recordings taken from camera 6/23. French had asked him to report anything 'unusual'.

'I know there's a TV in here somewhere . . .'

Hartnal pointed to the battered old thing in the corner of the room.

'Do you mind if I . . .'

'Go ahead, Bob. Go ahead. Did you find something?'

'Mr French asked me to start from last Wednesday evening, and go backwards.' He pushed the tape into the slot and turned on the TV. 'So that's what I was doing. But I . . . I ran into a problem.'

'You did?'

Gifford was scratching at his throat, obviously quite excited by what he'd found.

'The tapes run three hours,' he said. 'Anyway, I'm watching midnight to three a.m. for Tuesday July fifteenth and I get this.'

Hartnal approached the television screen, blinking sore eyes. The picture was grainy black and white. At first he couldn't work out what the rectangular mass at the bottom of the picture was. Then he recognized the reception desk in the library. There was a computer screen, a potted plant. An expanse of gray carpet. Nothing. The digital clock was running, but as before, a line of flashing blanks instead of a date.

'Do you see it?' said Gifford.

'No, Bob. I'll be honest, I don't.'

Gifford grinned, then pointed at the computer screen, partially visible in the bottom right of the picture.

And now that Hartnal was looking, he could see it. It was a screen saver. A piece of what looked like tortellini bounced into view then disappeared to be followed by an identical piece in another shade.

'Pasta,' said Gifford.

'Pasta, Bob?'

Gifford's grin went even wider. His eyes were shining.

'The union,' he said. 'The Professional and Administrative Staff Association. People had the screen saver running before the strike which was back in May. Some people just didn't take it off.'

Hartnal nodded, watching the pasta bounce into view, then drift away again. The strike had lasted four days. It had been about a reduction in health benefits. Usually it was about pay.

'You obviously don't remember, Doctor Hartnal.'

He was starting to be annoying.

'Mr Staunton sent around a memo,' he said, 'telling everyone to get rid of the screen savers.'

This was news to Hartnal, but it sounded like Staunton's sort of approach. Staunton referred to the union representative, a combative red-faced woman in the film stills archive, as the 'chief noodle'.

'Yes, Bob. Now that you remind me, I do vaguely remember something of that sort.'

'He said it wasn't conducive to a harmonious working environment. The memo went out around June fifteenth, I checked with his secretary. Now, I'd bet my bottom dollar there wasn't a single piece of digital pasta bouncing around after that. You know how seriously Mr Staunton takes these—'

'Yes, Bob. Yes, I do.'

'So I'm asking myself, how come there's a chunk of pasta on the screen on July sixteenth?'

'I think I can see where you're going with this, Bob.'

'So then I look at the little serial number on the side of the tape, and its out of sequence. The label says July sixteenth, but the serial number looks like it came from another box. Maybe back in June. I'm particular about using tapes as we unwrap them, just to keep things tidy down there. The serial numbers aren't exactly in sequence, but when I open a pack I run through them before I open another. Anyway, so now I'm looking at serial numbers prior to June fifteenth. And guess what?'

Hartnal did his best to smile.

'June fourteenth looked wrong. The label was good but the serial number was wrong. So I put in the tape that's labeled June fourteenth – midnight to three a.m. for camera twenty-three. And guess what?'

'You got a blank screen.'

Gifford's smile died on his lips. He was thrown for a moment. Then he was nodding, eyes dancing.

'Exactly. A blank screen. Nothing. Nothing recorded at all. And guess what else?'

'Lay it all out for me, Bob.'

'I looked at the tapes for every other camera. All twenty-three. They're all blank.'

'So . . . where did they go? The original tapes?'

'They've all been relabeled. The tapes for July sixteenth, the tapes recording midnight to three a.m., are all wrong. The serial numbers come from June fourteenth. They were switched.'

Hartnal clapped him on the shoulder.

'I think Mr Porter French is going to be very impressed. Where are the tapes now?'

'Downstairs in security.'

'Can you bring them up, Bob? The blanks too. Bring them all up here.'

14

Dan said he never wanted kids. He said he wanted to work out who he was before he started building someone else. It was the kind of thing you did say when you were just getting started as a grown up – when it looked like you could plan things.

Gazing at the photograph in the den, Ellen wondered if he'd have ever changed his mind as he got older. She was kneeling on the floor, surrounded by notebooks and papers. Even stripped to her underwear, she was way too hot. The den was the only room in the apartment where the a/c didn't work properly, the only room where you really needed it. If you opened the little window above the desk, a garbage smell drifted up from the back of the building.

In the picture she was wearing a man's suit, a heavy double-breasted thing she'd bought for a couple of pounds in a thrift shop. Her hair was chopped short. She'd been going through her Frida Kahlo phase, and if she'd been able to pencil in the space between her eyebrows without being laughed at she would have. Dan was just Dan, wiry, blond, T-shirt-and-jeans Dan. There was something of the young Truman Capote about him, a sly catamite smoothness that had been an incredible turn on back then. He was standing behind her, his beautiful hands on her square be-suited shoulders, whispering something into her at that time still functional ear.

He'd been twenty-four when he'd killed himself. In the photograph that terrible night was still two years away. He'd come up to see her in Banbury in the spring of '85. She'd just started the third semester at the art school where she had elected the fine art option. For six whole weeks she had been a painter.

He'd told her that she should never have children either. He had a theory. It was childbirth and child-rearing that explained the absence of great women painters. When she'd tried to stand up for her sex, citing all the wonderful women painters there were, starting with her beloved Frida, he'd ask her where the Picasso was – the Leonardo, the Vermeer, the Goya, the Matisse, the Velazquez, the Van Gogh. He'd believed in her, though; never tired of telling her how talented she was. All she had to do was embrace the life as he was embracing it in his squalid Paddington house. That was what he'd told her. And she had embraced it. Eighty-five was the year she'd gone crazy, smoking heroin, trashing herself at all night parties, bursting an eardrum and not even caring and getting an infection that had made her want to die. She'd learned that she'd been accepted at Oxford while she was recovering in the hospital. And then she'd met wholesome but ironic Greg. Not straight away, though. She and Dan had their perfect summer in '86. Their perfect American summer.

The phone was ringing. It had been ringing for a while.

'Ellen?'

It was Greg, finally calling back. He'd just returned from the beach. They'd been down at the beach until five, had just gotten back in. Ben, apparently, was loving it.

'You could have called me before.'

'I'm sorry, Ellen. Like I said—'

'Can you put him on?'

'Sure.'

There was a muffled clunk and then some laughter, then *screams* of laughter. It came to Ellen that she was holding her breath. Then Greg was back.

'Sorry, they're just getting hosed down. We're all covered with sand. Are you okay?'

A woman's voice came through from the background: 'Can't she call back?'

Abigale. Bright and cheery. Ellen pressed her teeth together.

'Ellen?'

'I didn't hear from you. I was worried.'

'Yeah, I can see. You left, like, four messages.'

'I was worried.'

'Did you think they'd blown us up?'

She closed her eyes. The sweat came out along her hairline as her heart started a tight, bopping palpitation. In the jumble of confused feelings, she saw Ben's things in his little suitcase, then the photograph on the wall – Dan whispering in her ear.

The suitcase in the freezing dark. A premonition.

'Ellen?'

'Don't joke about things like that.'

He said something about it only being two weeks before she was out there herself. Then he went quiet, thoughtful.

'Ellen, I'm sorry for what I said yesterday. I know how hard it's been.'

She tuned out, her eyes on Dan's eyes.

'Ellen, are you still there?'

He'd been talking to her.

'What?'

'I was asking – do you want us to pick you up at the airport? Because if you do, it's no problem.'

Us. A sourness came into her mouth.

'In fact we'd be delighted,' said Greg.

'We?'

'Me and the boys.'

'I don't want *her* boys,' she spat. 'I want *mine*.'

She blinked. She was shaking.

'Your boy is here,' said Greg, 'and if you saw him . . . My God, Ellen, if you saw him here in the sun.' There was swallowing noise, Greg choking up in his Shinto theme park.

'Fuck you, Greg.'

'Oookay.'

'Fuck you.'

For a long time he said nothing. Ellen could hear Abby in the background. Then Greg was back.

'You've got to get past the resentment, baby. For him if not for yourself.'

'I am past the resentment. I'm into the loathing.'

There was a beep on her phone.

'There's a call I've got to take. I'll call you back.'

'Okay. I'll—'

She pressed the button on him, and got Perry. She'd called him earlier, asked him to call her back. She apologized for having called him at home, said she wouldn't have done it if she didn't think it was important.

'I didn't want to wait until tomorrow.'

Something fell to the floor. She could hear him fumbling around, cursing. She heard the snap of a light switch, another muttered curse.

'So? What is it?'

'I've been thinking about what you said today. About Bissel trying to find Carey, and I think I can help.'

'Help?' There was a harsh rasping sound – Perry raking stubble.

'I think I can help clear up this mess.' Ellen massaged her eyes with the heel of her palm. 'All I need is for you to set up the meeting.'

'With Taylor.'

'Yes.'

'Ellen . . . Don't think I don't understand.'

'If you put in a word, told him you know I didn't have anything to do with the catalog, he might open up.'

'Ellen?' There was more rasping. A jaw-cracking yawn. 'Did I miss something? Because you're not making any sense.'

'What if this *were* Carey?' she said, pulling a photograph from the pile of papers on the floor; a battered snapshot showing two women standing on the edge of the Grand Canyon: one, middle-aged, pleasant-looking in a big-hipped, floral-print-dress kind of way, the other, in her mid-forties, lean, wearing jeans and a denim shirt. She'd moved her head just as the camera clicked, but you could still see who it was. Ellen squinted. 'This person who sold the painting.'

'It isn't.'

'You don't know that. All you know is that she was careful about covering her tracks. But she might have other reasons for doing that.'

'Look—'

'Bruce, there's an easy way to find out. There are cameras in the Bissel gallery. I've seen them. This woman, she walked in through the front door, right? He's probably got her on tape. If I can get a look at her, I'll know. I mean, I'll probably be able to say.'

Silence. Perry breathing against the mouthpiece.

'I've got photographs of Carey,' said Ellen. 'It shouldn't be—'

'Ellen, this woman – according to Taylor – this woman was old, maybe in her seventies.'

'Carey would be sixty-four, sixty-five this coming December.'

'That's not my point. I'm saying you're not going to be able to recognize her from some photograph taken forty-something years ago.'

'No, but I might from a photograph taken twenty-something years ago.'

'What?'

'The thing is, when I was writing the Koenig book—'

'That godawful coffee table thing.'

Ellen sucked in a breath. He was incredible.

'Yes,' she said, calmly. 'That's the one. Well, godawful or not, I worked really hard at it. I wanted to do justice to the—'

'Can we get to the point? Because I'm sitting here in my shorts thinking that what I really need now is—'

'I wanted to research Linda Carey. Koenig had a fling with her at the motel, and even if it was no big deal – which I think you'd have to question now in the light of this picture—'

'The picture's a fake, Ellen. Christ. A. Fake. How many times do I have to say that?'

'Well, anyway, I wanted to find out who she was. What became of her. So I went to the state archive in Santa Fe, and—'

'You did *what*?'

'I flew down to Santa Fe.'

'For your little book?'

'My little book was fifty thousand words long, and I probably wrote twice that amount. But . . . yes, okay, I admit I probably went a little overboard. What can I say? It was fun. I went to the state archive and I found the names of Carey's neighbors in land registry documents dating back to fifty-seven. I then checked those names against entries in the current Albuquerque phone book which led me to Constance Martin, a lady who'd been a friend of Carey's back in the day.'

She brought the photograph up into the light. Constance Martin was smiling broadly at the camera, delighted to have found her old friend. A chance meeting. Martin had been touring Arizona with her husband, and had recognized Carey in the crowd at one of the lookout points. Carey had claimed to be on her own.

Ellen had interviewed Martin on her front porch. Seventy years old by then, and very sick, she'd only been back a couple of months. She'd moved up to Portland in the sixties. Her husband had died a couple of years earlier and she had returned to Albuquerque to die herself, something she'd talked about in very matter-of-fact terms.

'She gave me a lot of insights, talked about how wild and star struck Carey was, how she hated being stuck at the motel with the old man who she'd only married to escape her—'

'Motel? Which motel?'

'Bruce, I went through all this at the trustees' lunch.'

Silence. He obviously hadn't been listening to the presentation.

'Carey ran the Rio Rancho motel with her husband, Earl Sears. That was where she and Koenig met in fifty-seven.'

'Okay. So . . . this old woman . . .'

'Constance Martin – she remembered Carey leaving town in the spring of fifty-eight, *really* shaken up by Koenig's death. She showed me a photograph of her and Carey in 1981. She ran into her on vacation. It's not a great photograph, but to be honest Carey doesn't look that much different to what she did when she was a young woman. She kept her figure, and she still had the hair.'

'This is all great, Ellen. What the hell difference does it make? Whether it's Carey or not, this woman disappeared. Taylor's got a professional searching for her, and so far he's turned up nothing.'

'But that's where I can help. You see, Carey left town pregnant.'

Silence.

'Bruce?'

'Wait a second.'

He put down the phone. Then she was hearing rustling sounds. He came back.

'Constance Martin was pretty sure of that. She said she had a feeling Carey went to Phoenix to get rid of the baby. So I went to the Office of Vital Records in Phoenix. I was in Albuquerque anyway. I just rented a car, and drove down there. I checked out the births registered in the State of Arizona in July and August of 1958.'

'Wait, wait. Back up. You just said Carey went to Phoenix to have an abortion.'

'Constance Martin *thought* she did. Abortion wasn't legalized until 1973. So even if she did have one, there weren't going to be any records anywhere. On the other hand, if she'd changed her mind . . .'

'*If* she was pregnant, *if* she went to Phoenix, *if* she changed her mind.'

'I know, but by this time I was really intrigued. I had this theory –

just wishful thinking really: a star-struck girl gets herself knocked up by a celebrated painter. I mean, he's on the cover of magazines. His death was national news. Does she really let that go?'

'Who the hell knows?'

'I guess I just loved the idea that there was this person walking around. Koenig's child. Maybe completely unaware of who his or her father was . . .'

'Yeah, well.'

'Koenig was at the motel in November of 'fifty-seven, and that gave me my window – something to aim at. I went into Vital Records in Phoenix and *bam*!'

'Bam what? You found something?'

'There weren't any births registered for Koenig, but there was one for King. August fourth, 1958.'

Perry was laughing now.

'Jesus Christ, Ellen. That was the best you could do?'

'Bruce, 'Koenig' is German for 'King'.'

'And 'knockwurst' is German for 'baloney'.'

Ellen pulled out another scrap of paper from her pile.

'Rosa May King,' she said, reading from her copy of the birth certificate. 'Mother registered as Linda King. Linda, Bruce. Linda King with a Phoenix address. And guess what it says for 'father'?'

'What?'

'Unknown.'

'That proves it then.'

'Bruce, Taylor Bissel needs to know about all this. At least his PI does. If that's what he's using. That's how they catch these people.'

'What are you talking about?'

'Well, let's say Linda Carey is still in touch with her daughter. You find the daughter, you find the mother.'

'Ellen?'

'What?'

'How come none of this made it into the book?'

Ellen eased at her bra. It was too tight across her ribs, made it hard to breathe when she was doubled up. The truth was, after her arguments with Leslie Ann over Linda Carey, she'd decided to shelve the research.

'Well you know, the book was only fifty thousand words long, so . . . I couldn't include *everything*.'

'Benton didn't want to hear about Linda Carey.'

Ellen gave a nod, said nothing.

'Did you tell her about your trip?' he said.

'I was going to, but when I raised the whole issue of Carey, she flared up at me. She said Carey was very bad news. Dysfunctional.'

'Dysfunctional? In what way?'

'I don't know. Leslie Ann won't talk about it.'

There was a long silence.

'Okay,' said Bruce, finally.

'What?'

'Okay, I'll talk to Bissel.'

'I'd appreciate it.'

'In the meantime . . . it would be better if you didn't say anything about this. To anyone.'

Ellen sat up straight.

'Why not?'

'Just take it from me. You don't want to be drawing any more attention to yourself.'

15

The phone started up just after seven. Ellen let the machine take it, listened to the messages from under the bedclothes. A reporter from the *Post* wanted some sort of comment about the '*Mirror* situation'. Janice Piat, the PR person at the museum, called instructing her to refuse all media requests for interviews. Then Tilda Kraft weighed in, wanting to know what the hell was going on at the museum. Were there doubts about *Mirror*? Was she really leaving? Was Perry pushing her out? Porter French left a message when she was in the shower, asking if she wouldn't mind giving him a call at the museum.

She went down to the street, half-expecting to be mobbed by the press at the front door, but the news wasn't that hot, apparently. The story *had* made it out of the arts section of the *Times*, however. She read it, riding the subway down to 50th Street.

Mirror – Cause For Reflection?

Speculation is growing that Abstract Expressionist masterpiece 'Mirror', recently purchased by the Modern Art Museum for the record-breaking sum of $23 million, is a forgery. Janice Piat, spokesperson for the museum, sought to scotch rumors yesterday, stating that 'Mirror', the last work of deceased artist Franklin Koenig, is unquestionably authentic and will be hanging on the second floor, once restoration work is complete.

When asked why Ellen Lindz, the assistant curator responsible for bringing the painting into the museum, was ejected from a Monday morning meeting of top management, Piat offered no comment. The emergency meeting was chaired by founding-family scion David Kruger III, who flew in from Nassau by private jet, and has not been seen in Manhattan since last year's 9/11 fund-raiser at the Metropolitan Museum.

Museum watchers noted with interest that Lindz brought the painting into the collection despite vigorous opposition by chief curator of the Department of Sculpture and Painting, Bruce Perry. Have Perry's doubts proved justified? Art world insiders are inclined to think so, especially given similar signs of strain at the Bissel Gallery, through which 'Mirror' was originally sold.

According to a source close to the gallery, Taylor Bissel, the gallery owner, recently received a visit from an unnamed female FBI agent, who allegedly seized papers pertaining to the 'Mirror' purchase from Linda Carey, a friend of the artist's in his last troubled years. As this paper went to press, the Manhattan Field Office of the FBI was unable to confirm any such action, or give details of any supposed investigation into the 'Mirror' sale.

As for Linda Carey, efforts to locate her, have resulted in a series of dead ends. Ms. Carey appears to have disappeared from public databases in 1963, despite the fact that the Social Security Death Index carries no record of her passing – facts which the museum's trustees will find cause for reflection.

When she walked into her office just after nine, she found a stranger sitting behind her desk. He jumped up as she came in through the door, and shot out a hand. He was a tall, awkward-looking character in a sports jacket and gray pants. He said his name was Adam Straub, and that he'd worked as an assistant curator at the Whitney under Gill Pellegrini, one of Ellen's colleagues at Harvard. He was researching a book about the Ashcan School artists on a Guggenheim grant and had been asked to come in to work on the upcoming Hopper retrospective. All this came tumbling out, as Ellen, skirting around him, installed herself in her chair.

She sat there shaking her head.

'I don't really . . .'

Straub smiled.

'Oh boy,' he said, rolling his eyes. 'I don't think anyone told you I was coming in.'

'That's right, I . . .'

At that moment Roland Staunton arrived, looking flustered. He invited Straub to use the conference room at the end of the corridor, and as soon as the door was closed, asked Ellen if she'd seen the report in the *Times*.

'I just read it.'

'It's really not good,' he said, staring at her, dead-eyed, his lips pressed into a line.

'Roland, it has absolutely nothing to do with me. I haven't even spoken to the press to say 'no comment'.'

Staunton nodded, but he didn't look entirely convinced. Ellen set her jaw, indicated the door through which Straub had just passed.

'Do you think you can tell me what that was about?'

Staunton lowered himself into the seat opposite. He said he wasn't going to insult her intelligence.

'That's good of you,' said Ellen, wondering what the hell was coming now.

'Ellen I'm sure I don't need to tell you that the museum is . . . well it's *complex*. Complicated. There are all sorts of people, and—'

'Roland. This Straub character – he said he's been asked to work on the Hopper project. Can you tell me in what capacity?'

Staunton grinned, but his eyes were deadly serious.

'Bruce felt that, given your workload, it might be better if—'

'What workload? Hopper *is* my workload.'

Staunton stood up.

'You should probably have this conversation with Bruce.'

'I'm having it with you. Are you telling me you don't know what's going on?'

He didn't like that. The expression went out of his face.

'There's going to be a review of the acquisition process,' he said dryly. 'What has happened with the Koenig has raised a number of doubts about the soundness of our procedures: criteria for initial selection of works to be presented to the trustees; the establishing of the chain of provenance. David wants a full report with case studies by the end of August. We had a meeting yesterday afternoon and it was decided that you're the best person to produce it. You won't be working alone obviously. You'll be spending a lot of time in the archive reviewing past acquisitions.'

Staunton allowed himself a tight little smile.

'Locking the stable door after the horse has bolted if you ask me. But I suppose it's understandable after something this traumatic.'

They wanted rid of her. For some reason it hadn't really hit home until that moment. They were going to bury her in a tedious and futile assignment. And when that was finished, they would find her another. They were taking the Hopper out of her hands. They were taking the art out of her hands.

'Bruce did this?'

'Ellen, I know you and Bruce have had your differences, but, well, this really isn't a time for petty in-fighting.'

She must have looked distraught, because something like compassion came into Staunton's eyes.

'Bruce is Bruce, Ellen. And, speaking very plainly, more plainly than I should, we're stuck with him. There are plenty of people who wish that weren't the case, but it is the case. If you knew the convulsions we went through the last time we had to appoint someone to run the department, you'd understand, and the man . . . well, he has a following. He has his *supporters*.'

He nodded, giving her a significant look.

'Meanwhile, any support, any references you might have been hoping for, will be forthcoming. I *personally* will write anything you ask.'

It was like a physical blow.

'What are you *talking* about?' Ellen gasped. 'If you think . . .' She started to choke up, forced herself to get a grip. 'If you think I'm going to resign . . .'

Staunton was shaking his head.

'Ellen,' he said softly. 'You'll receive every support in looking for your next position.'

She found that she was on her feet.

'*Fire* me,' she said, and a fleck of spittle arced across the space between them. 'Fire me and we'll see how it plays out in court.'

Staunton wiped his face.

'You don't want to make this any uglier than it already is.'

'But I . . . I didn't do anything *wrong*.'

Dark blotches appeared under Staunton's blank gray eyes.

'You brought this *fucking* thing in,' he said calmly, and he walked out.

She was so angry, felt so desperate, she almost refused to talk to French, but the thought of burning up whatever goodwill was left for her, made her reconsider.

The interview took place in a windowless room on the fifth floor. There was a broken overhead projector on the floor in one corner, a stack of stationery. It was obvious from his questions that French was getting nowhere with his so-called investigation. He started by trying to get her to admit to some sort of relationship with Bissel. Not an intimate relationship, but some sort of association that could be construed as a basis for complicity. It was ridiculous.

'I understand you went to see Bissel after Monday's meeting,' he said, blinking pink lash-less eyes at her. He was in his linen suit again, a terrible chain store thing that stood up from his shoulders like a football uniform.

'So what if I did?' said Ellen.

'What did you want to talk to him about?'

'Linda Carey.'

'Why?'

'Because I think that whoever it was who sold this painting to Bissel, would be able to explain about the catalog.' She flashed her eyes at him. 'It's just a crazy hunch I have.'

As soon as she was out, she went looking for Perry. He was in the basement, supervising the unpacking of some works that had arrived from the State Museum in Moscow. She found him in the restoration department workshop, holding a small red and gray Rodchenko in his hands. He didn't hear her come into the room, was too absorbed, examining the surface of the painting in the natural light that filtered down from glass bricks set in the ceiling. He had a faint smile on his lips.

'They're burying me, Bruce.'

The smile died.

One of Perry's helpers came into the doorway, an attractive young woman with a red headscarf. She had a query about some paperwork, but when she saw the looks on their faces, backed off. Perry closed the door.

'I just had a chat with Staunton,' said Ellen, trying to keep the anger out of her voice.

'Ellen.'

'He said I'm going to be rather busy for the next month. I'm going to have to cancel my trip to LA.'

Perry grimly nodded.

'Ellen, I told you they were angry.'

'You're saying you had no part in—'

'The decision was taken at a meeting yesterday afternoon. There have been a *lot* of meetings. It wasn't for me to decide one way or the other.'

'But you didn't feel you should stand up for me? You didn't feel you could repeat what you said to me last night – that in your opinion I had nothing to do with the catalog.'

He put the painting down on a work bench.

'Ellen, I—'

She snapped up her hands.

'You know what?' she said, backing away, reaching for the door handle. 'I don't want to hear it. But I'll tell you this: I'm not just going to roll over. With or without your help, I'm going to find Linda Carey. I'm going to get whoever is behind this to own up. I'm going to find Rosa May King and I'm going to—'

He took a step toward her, his face clenching in a look of absolute fury. It cut her off mid-sentence. Just as suddenly, the look was gone. He was unsteady on his feet, blinking, looking around the room.

'Rosa May King is a stupid fantasy,' he said softly. 'She's just an idea of yours.'

'Maybe she is,' said Ellen.

She turned the handle, but then Perry blocked the door with his foot. He was trying to smile, but she could see that he was beside himself – furious.

'I'm talking to Bissel,' he said, under his breath. 'I'm going to talk to him later today. I'll get any tape he might have of this person. I'm trying . . .' He sucked in a breath, let it out in a trembling sigh. 'I'm trying to help you, Ellen. I want to help you.'

She didn't know what to think now, but she knew there was something deeply wrong. Something bad, hanging just below the surface. She took a breath to speak, but he put a hand on her arm.

'Don't talk to Benton,' he said. 'What you told me last night. You keep it to yourself.'

He was completely crazy.

'What? Why?'

He stepped away from her, dropping his hands to his sides.

'Because I think she's involved.'

A bird landed with a spidery click of claws up on the glass bricks. A pigeon or maybe a crow. The shadow moved over Perry's face. For a long time neither of them spoke.

'You're going to have to explain that, Bruce.'

But he was shaking his head, raking at his scalp, a grim smile on his face. He turned away, went across to the other side of the room. Ellen stayed where she was, her hand on the door handle. Then she saw something new, and it frightened her. *He* was afraid.

'Bruce . . .'

'Look,' he said, trying to hide it. '*Look*. There's—'

The handle turned in her fingers, and the door came open.

Lewis Hartnal was there. For a split second he looked startled to see them there together, then recovered his usual smoothness. He greeted Ellen warmly, told her that he thought she'd make a wonderful job of the report Kruger had requested. There was a kind of insanity in the way he said it – as though he was completely oblivious to the tectonics at work. He said she must come to him if she needed help or advice of any kind. Then, having dealt with her, he turned to Perry, said he'd been looking for him for the past half hour.

16

She walked south along Fifth Avenue, entered Madison Square pretty much oblivious to what was going on around her. Muffled sunlight slanted into browning leaves that hung motionless in the heat. Pigeons stirred and clumped, ruffling in the dust. She found a bench, and sat down.

Perry was crazy. That was as close as she could get to a clear thought. Crazy. The notion that Leslie Ann might be in some way involved with the painting, with the catalog, with any of what was going on at the museum was too bizarre even to get a handle on. Of course, years of familiarity and friendship made it difficult for her to see Leslie Ann doing anything to compromise or taint Koenig's memory, but even forcing herself into some sort of objective view, she couldn't see it. Leslie Ann's whole life had been an act of curatorial worship. She had discovered Koenig. She had supported and promoted him, had gone on doing so after his death. Koenig was largely what he was because of her. And she was the only person to have hung onto her paintings, kept them despite the trouble it gave her. She felt tremendous guilt about not handing them over to a museum. She felt guilty holding on, but couldn't let go. They were too important to her. Koenig was too important to her. So for that person to do this thing was unimaginable.

She called the museum in the late afternoon. On the phone, Perry was tight-lipped, curt almost. He said he couldn't talk. He said he'd call Bissel. That much he promised. He'd set up the meeting, and get back to her. But he didn't get back. He left her dangling. Wednesday night she cancelled a dinner engagement, had a long talk with Ben on the phone, then went to bed early, lay awake listening to the phone ring. People called. Friends. Museum people. Jerry Lloyd. Leslie Ann left a message saying that she'd heard about her being taken off the Hopper show. She said she hoped she was all right.

Thursday dawned gray and humid with the threat of heat behind soiled-looking clouds. On the news all the talk was of tropical storms heading for the Carolinas.

She had a whole day of waiting for the call from Perry, doubting everything, questioning everything until finally the person she doubted most was Perry himself. One image kept coming back to her: Perry emerging from his office after the trustee lunch, going into his spiel about loving the museum so much. She saw his bloodshot dark eyes, saw his sadness. *I'm sounding valedictory.* At the time she'd thought he was teetering on the brink of resignation, but now she saw it differently, and seeing it differently felt like seeing it clearly for the first time. It was her he'd been saying goodbye to.

'Me,' she said, staring at herself in the bathroom mirror late on Thursday afternoon. Dripping from her second shower of the day – it was the only way she could cool down – she gazed into her own eyes, looking directly into the black rounds of her pupils, and saw it all. The only way it made sense: Perry had already known about the catalog when he'd come out to the elevator.

'He was saying goodbye to me,' she whispered, holding the towel to her mouth, breathing its soapy smell, staring and staring, her neck and shoulders going tight as the idea bloomed. She had only found the catalog on Wednesday night, had only talked about it to Leslie Ann on

Thursday. The first time Perry saw it had been in the presentation she'd made at the Friday lunch, and even then he'd only been looking at a *photocopy* of a page from the brochure. There was no way he could have known about the tampering. There was no way he could have known. You had to look at the original and look very closely to see what was wrong. He couldn't have known, but he must have. *I just wanted to say that, whatever differences we may have had, I think you'd make a wonderful chief curator.* He'd looked into her eyes as he'd said it, and now she saw it for what it was. Consolation. She'd have made a great chief curator if she hadn't fallen into his trap. Because the catalog was a trap: not a clumsy attempt to authenticate a painting, but a subtle plan to discredit one. To discredit her. He'd known she was going to seize on it. He'd known she'd make it central to her presentation. He didn't want the painting in the collection. He didn't want her challenging his position in the museum. So he'd found a way to kill two birds with one stone.

Unless she was wrong, of course. Wrong about the whole thing. And there were good reasons for doubt. There was something else behind it, beneath it. If she was right about the catalog, he'd already gotten what he wanted on Monday so why had he been so ready to talk in his office on Tuesday morning? She was already screwed. But he'd wanted to talk, to tell her all about how Linda Carey wasn't Linda Carey. There'd been all the stuff about the bank account. Detail. Thinking about it now, still gazing into the mirror, it all seemed bogus to her – scripted, like part of a sales pitch. He didn't want her looking for the seller. Why? Because he knew something about her? Knew something about the painting? There were layers here. She couldn't see them, but she knew they were there. He didn't want her looking for Carey, and he didn't even want her to *talk* about Rosa May King. Not to Leslie Ann, anyway. Why? Did he know about Rosa May King too? A person whose existence he didn't even believe in. Or was he just scared she'd find something out?

The questions went round and round. She walked up and down

the stifling apartment, stopping to stare at the telephone, willing it to ring. She drank iron-tasting tap water from a thick-bottomed glass, stopping in front of mirrors to push at her tangled hair, to mutter and curse.

And then she called him.

She made the call on Thursday afternoon. She called him at the museum, and got Grace. Perry came on the line, sounding wired. He said he'd been about to call her, had been on the point of picking up the phone. He asked her how she was doing, hoped he hadn't freaked her out too much the day before.

'Bruce.'

'Yes?'

'Did you talk to Bissel?'

'I did. Absolutely. I had some trouble getting hold of him which is why I haven't gotten back to you before now.'

'You didn't get back to me. I just called you.'

'Yeah, but I was about to call you.'

'What did he say?'

'To be honest, it didn't go very well. He's upset. He's been having a rather difficult time.'

'You told him I had nothing to do with the catalog?'

'Yes. Yes, of course. But as I say—'

'Did you tell him about my idea?'

'Yes.'

'About identifying Linda Carey, going after Rosa May King.'

'Ellen.'

She nodded. Here it was again.

'What's wrong, Bruce?'

'I told you about that. About talking about that.'

'Yes you did. I've been thinking about it, trying to understand.'

'We should talk. We should get together.'

Stalling. Manipulating her, trying to keep her in the dark. She felt unsteady on her feet. He was saying something to her, his voice going soft, complicit, talking about getting together at the beginning of next week, stringing her along.

'Bruce,' she said, cutting him off mid-sentence. 'You're a fucking liar.'

And she hung up. She walked out of the kitchen, through the apartment to the den where she flipped her rolodex to 'B'.

She grabbed up the phone, punched keys, the receiver trapped against her shoulder.

It was Bissel himself who picked up.

'Mister Bissel?'

'This is he.'

'Hi, my name's Rosa May King.'

A pause. She could hear him breathing through his open mouth.

'What can I do for you, Ms King?'

Oblivious. He had no idea.

'Did Bruce Perry mention me to you?'

'I'm afraid not. Perhaps you could—'

She hung up, hit the speed dialer, got Leslie Ann's machine.

'Leslie Ann, I need to talk to you about Perry.'

17

It was raining again. Slumped in the back of the cab, Ellen gazed, unseeing, as droplets tracked zigzag paths across the partially opened window. She felt suspended, dazed. They were crossing the park when her cell phone started up. She fumbled for it in her shoulder bag, pressed it to her ear, half-expecting Leslie Ann.

'Ellen, Bruce. I just got a call from Bissel. I know what you did.'

She pulled herself upright on the seat, saw the rain, and beyond the rain, clumped foliage and twisted tree limbs.

'I think I know what you must be thinking,' said Perry, 'but you're wrong.'

The traffic slowed. Up ahead the light turned amber then red.

'Ellen, we need to talk. We need to sit down and talk. Ellen?'

He was almost yelling into the phone.

'Yes.'

'Are you in a car?'

The lights changed to green.

'I don't understand it, Bruce. I don't understand. I worked hard for you. For the department.'

'I know you did, Ellen. But listen to me, this isn't what you think. This isn't about you.'

'It isn't?' She set her jaw at that, got a raw jolt of anger that made her head throb. 'That's funny, because it feels like it is. It feels like it's me who's in the sewer pipe.'

They crossed Fifth at 86th Street.

He sucked in a breath.

'I tried to warn you, Ellen. I did everything I could. But you're so . . . you're so goddamn stupid, and . . . and *blind*, and you . . . you talk about your fucking instincts when all it is, is Benton brainwashing you into thinking what *she* thinks and . . . I told you not to touch the painting. I told you it was bad.' He was raving, barely coherent. 'Well now, I'm telling you again, I'm warning you again. If you go to Benton or any of—'

'You're threatening me. That's what you're doing. You're threatening me, and I won't be threatened, so you can—'

'No! I'm trying to help. Can't you *see* that? I'm trying to stop you getting . . . I mean it, Ellen. You have to listen this time. I'm trying to stop you getting hurt.'

This was so crazy it made her laugh. She looked at the phone in her hand, and laughed. The cab jolted to a halt in the middle of an intersection as a bus surged past. The driver cursed in a language she didn't understand, then jammed his foot down.

Perry was still talking.

'Ellen, I swear to god, if you talk to anyone about this . . . about Linda Carey, or Rosa May King, or any of this business with the Koenig.'

They turned into East 92nd Street. Ellen leaned forward.

'Just here on the left is good,' she said, saying it as though everything were fine.

'If you talk to – to Benton, Hartnal, Pauling – any of those lying octogenarian parasitical *fucks*, you will fuck things up so totally, and . . . look, listen to me – listen to me.' He took a breath, struggling to calm himself down. 'You will be putting us both in danger.'

The last words came out calm, matter-of-fact.

Ellen peered out through the streaming window at Leslie Ann's front door. Her hands were shaking.

'What the hell are you talking about?'

'Ellen?' He groaned. 'The Koenig?'

The street door came open, and Ellen saw Leslie Ann standing there, holding an umbrella. It flared blackly open as she came down the steps.

'What about it?'

'It's real.'

The car door came open.

'Are you okay?' said Leslie Ann, peering in at her. Ellen killed the signal.

'What?'

'Are you all right?'

'Fine. I'm fine.'

Leslie Ann frowned at her face, then looked at the cell-phone in her hand.

'Just now on the phone, you sounded . . .'

'Yes. Yes that's right.'

'Well? Are you coming in?'

She stood back, and beyond her Ellen saw Lewis Hartnal standing in the doorway. They were like a couple. Brother and sister maybe. Leslie Ann extended a wrinkled hand.

'Come in out of the rain,' she said.

The study was at the back of the building. Ellen stood at the tall sash window, looking out onto gardens. Two houses along, she saw a white marquee. People were huddled under the canvas, holding plates of food and looking out at the weather.

Behind her, Lewis Hartnal, wearing a moth-eaten cardigan, and holding a glass of red wine, was talking about the upheaval at the museum. Porter French was starting to get on everyone's nerves. Ellen knew that she should be listening, taking an interest, but Perry's voice kept spiking through. The painting was real. *Mirror* was real. She couldn't understand why that didn't make her feel good.

She became aware of the silence.

'Ellen?'

She turned.

Leslie Ann was sitting in a battered leather chair, a frown on her withered face.

'You said you wanted to talk about Bruce.'

18

Taylor Bissel eased his legs out of the Boxter, took a moment to get his breath, then heaved himself to his feet. The four-story Victorian loomed above him, empty and a little forbidding without Irene and the kids. Then again, with everything that had been going on at the gallery, he was glad they were away in Europe, and nurtured the faint hope that, by the time they got back at the end of August, the whole *Mirror* situation would have blown over.

– Hi, my name's Rosa May King.

The call had spooked him. He'd recognized Lindz's voice immediately, and as soon as she'd hung up, he'd called Perry. Perry said he'd never heard of Rosa May King, and couldn't begin to imagine what Lindz was playing at. They'd both agreed that what it looked like most of all was a nervous breakdown. Ellen Lindz was cracking up.

Unpeeling damp cotton from his back, he reached into the car for his suit jacket, then started across the gravel driveway.

It had been a terrible week so far, most of it spent in the company of attorneys whose sole aim seemed to be to make matters more complicated. There had also been some very frustrating conversations with the Manhattan-based firm of private investigators that he'd been using for years to do background credit and asset checks, or to trace people who needed tracing. Ever since he'd first heard about the San Diego catalog, that was what he'd been trying to do – track down the woman who'd come into the gallery claiming to be Linda Carey. The minute he'd heard that the Wyoming bank account was actually corporate, he'd known he was in trouble. Since then, the expensive and elaborate inquiries that he was having to fund pretty much out of petty cash (the PI seemed to prefer it) had yielded nothing.

As for the Modern, their initial suspicion and belligerence had given way to persistent calls requesting information. David Kruger had settled on a character called Porter French to head up the investigation – a clinically charmless person who behaved as though he owned him and the gallery too, and didn't think much of either. The truth of it was that Bissel was as much a victim as the museum, especially if Kruger compelled him to hand back what he'd made on the deal.

The one source of comfort in the whole confusing mess was that no one seemed to want the story to get out, except for Javier who he'd fired as soon as he'd the read the article in the *Times* (it hadn't taken much to work out who the 'source close to the gallery' was). And then there was Agent Rissoli. It turned out that the FBI had never sent any such person – at least that was the word from the Manhattan field office. He didn't know who she was, or why she knew so much about his personal affairs, or why she was interested in Linda Carey or *Mirror* and it gave him such a headache just thinking about it that it was almost easier not to think about it at all.

He pushed his key into the lock and turned it. The door came open with a wash of cooler air, and a faint but unmistakable smell of cigarette smoke. Entering the gloomy hallway, he checked his slender wrist watch. It was nearly eight o'clock. Rosa, the cleaning lady, came by in the morning, should have gone home hours ago.

He checked the alarm system. It was disarmed. So she was still there. She had been noticeably less effective since Irene had left, obviously thinking that, as a man, he paid less attention to the state of the toilet bowl or the windows. He pushed open the kitchen door.

'Oh!'

It looked like he was having a heart attack.

Billy half-rose in her seat, watching the dealer reach out to steady himself, watching him send over the vase on top of the big commode. He didn't go down though. There was a sound of trickling water.

'Don't you die on me now, Taylor.'

Bissel gave a nod, his bulging eyes fixed on the tiny gun in her hand. She was wearing surgical gloves.

'My heart,' he gasped.

'Are you surprised? Be honest.'

Without moving from the chair, Billy beckoned with her free hand, watched him shuffle over to the table and slump down. He reached inside his jacket.

'Taylor.'

He froze, blinking sweat out of his eyes.

Billy smiled.

'Everything's okay, Taylor. Really. This gun is for my protection as much as anything. You have medication, right? Beta-blockers? Something like that.'

'In my pocket.'

Billy let him take a little pill. Gave him a moment to calm down. The water from the vase was dripping now – *tap, tap, tap*.

'So, Taylor, tell me. What the fuck is going on? I mean is this *Mirror* picture a fake or what?'

He blinked at that, pinched the sweat out of his eyes with chubby fingers. Shook his head.

'No?' said Billy. 'Yes? Come on Taylor, don't make me beg.'

'It's authentic. In . . . in my opinion.'

'So . . . what's all the fuss about?'

He told her. About the museum. About the forged catalog.

'Didn't see anything about this in the paper.'

'They're not talking about it.'

'They're talking to you.'

'Yes. Unfortunately. I'm involved.'

'So who did it? Who forged the catalog?'

Bissel shook his head.

'They don't know. Ellen Lindz, the assistant curator – maybe it was her.'

'Really? I can see her faking an orgasm, but apart from that . . .'

He shrugged.

Billy watched him for a moment, trying to see how it was.

'Don't hold out on me, Taylor.'

'I'm not. I really don't know what's going on over there. The museum – it's like a closed order. Like a monastery.'

'They asking for their money back?'

He nodded.

'The chief curator thinks it's a fake. He's threatening to resign.'

'Ouch,' said Billy, wrinkling her nose. 'You give back the whole twenty-three mil?'

'No. It won't . . . it won't work like that. They don't want a fuss.'

'How they gonna avoid it?'

'Officially, they'll stand by the painting. That's my guess.'

'What about the curator guy?'

'I think they'd rather lose him than lose face. Any other way they're going to look bad. And they'll be out of pocket.'

'Explain that to me.'

'They can't give the twenty-three million back to the trustees, because I don't have it to give them.'

'You spend it already?'

'I paid nine million to Linda Carey. It looks like I'm not going to be able to recover that.'

'Because?'

He looked at the gun.

'Come on, Taylor. We're just talking here.'

'I don't know where she is.'

'What about the other fourteen mil?'

'They're going to want that back.'

Billy jutted her bottom lip.

'What do you get to keep?'

Bissel shrugged.

'My reputation.'

Billy smiled, nodded.

'This Linda Carey,' she said. 'She's one slick senior.'

He dabbed at his forehead with his shirt cuff.

Billy rose.

'So anyway, I'm gonna need those tapes,' she said.

Bissel looked up at her.

'You made a tape of me.' Billy narrowed her eyes at him. 'You do that with all your clients? Tape their private conversations?'

'The cameras are there for security.'

'I'm not talking about the gallery. I'm talking about the camera in your office.'

That gave him a jolt. For a second she thought he was going to start with the gasping again.

'Don't worry,' she said. 'I'm not gonna tell. I know you have your reputation to consider.'

He was chewing, working at something in the back of his mouth, as though his teeth didn't fit right.

'I want the tape you made of me, and the one you made of Linda Carey.'

Bissel's forehead bunched moist and seamy.

'This is that no good son of a bitch, Javier.'

Billy shrugged.

'They're for my protection,' said Bissel. 'I only keep the tapes if I have reason to doubt.'

'Well, then, I guess you kept the tape of Carey. And I *know* you kept the one of me.'

She came around the table and stood over him.

'I just want the tapes, Taylor. And then I'll be out of your hair.'

He made little whimpering noises as he walked through the house. Billy followed him, keeping the gun against the back of his neck. They went into a study on the ground floor. Billy saw books, pictures. Bissel liked his art big and sloppy. He knelt down and moved some cartons. Billy saw dull steel. A dial. There was a little safe down there. Bissel twisted his great head, looking up at her.

'Don't worry, Taylor. I'm not here to rob you.'

He turned back to the safe door, hunching his sweaty shoulders. There was a soft clunk, and the door came open. Billy ducked down a little, trying to see past his head. He had a lot of stuff in there. Papers, cash, a little bottle of something blue. A tremor went through him.

'Taylor?'

He clenched, convulsed, made a retching noise, tucking his head into his shoulders.

'Taylor.' She grabbed his shoulder, didn't see the pepper spray until it was too late.

19

Leslie Ann insisted on holding her hand, and it was all she could do not to pull it away.

'Ellen, you're trembling.'

She forced herself to look into her old friend's puzzled eyes, then found herself describing the conversation she'd had in Perry's office on Tuesday afternoon. Hartnal and Leslie Ann looked on as she told them how Perry seemed to know an awful lot about Linda Carey, including the fact that her Wyoming bank account was in fact a bogus corporate cover that made it impossible to trace her – all the time thinking that *Mirror* was real and that Perry *himself* had said so, to *her*; that he'd been willing to expose himself as a liar rather than have her talk about Rosa May to Leslie Ann or any of 'those lying parasitical octogenarian fucks', all of which seemed crazy – these thoughts going round and round in her head as her mouth worked at making sense, and Hartnal and Leslie Ann frowned, looking more and more puzzled, while beneath it all, behind it all, Perry's threat of danger seemed, despite all his lies, to snag her like something founded, anchored, solid. It was his fear. The fear she'd seen in Harold Rosenau's workshop. The fear was real.

'I don't understand,' said Leslie Ann.

Ellen looked up, meeting the old woman's gaze head on.

'What? What don't you understand?'

Hartnal got to his feet and walked away across the room to stand by the desk.

'When you called, you said you wanted to talk about Perry.'

'That's right.'

'So . . .'

'It was Perry that told me about Carey.'

Leslie Ann looked across at Hartnal.

'And?'

'Well, isn't it odd that Perry should be doing all this research into Linda Carey?'

Leslie Ann leaned back, letting go of her hand.

'He isn't.'

'What do you mean?'

'We employed some people,' said Hartnal. 'The museum. We're looking into Carey and Bissel and so forth. The whole transaction.'

'Perry was just repeating what was aired in Tuesday's meeting,' said Leslie Ann.

'But why did he tell you all this?' said Hartnal.

Ellen turned.

'I don't know. I went into his office. I suppose . . . I challenged him. I said I was going to find Carey myself. He told me I'd be wasting my time.'

'Why would you want to find Carey?' said Hartnal.

'To clear her name,' said Leslie Ann in an irritable undertone.

Ellen nodded in agreement.

'If I could find Carey, maybe I could get to the bottom of this business with the catalog, and then—'

'This "business with the catalog" as you call it,' said Hartnal, cutting her off. But then he seemed to think better of what he'd been about to say. He came back to his chair, sat down heavily.

There was a heavy silence. Ellen looked from one to the other.

'Ellen?' said Leslie Ann. 'He didn't call you, did he?'

'What?'

'Just before you arrived you were talking on the cellphone. That wasn't Perry?'

Ellen shook her head.

'He didn't threaten you in some way?' said Hartnal.

'No.' She felt like she were drowning. 'No it was just . . . a friend.'

They exchanged a look. Then Leslie Ann seemed to remember her cigarette. She drew on it and sent a plume of smoke up at the ceiling.

'Ellen. This situation . . . the situation with the catalog, the painting . . .'

'Porter French is going to be making a presentation to David Kruger,' said Hartnal. 'Sooner rather than later.'

'In the meantime . . .,' said Leslie Ann, turning her gaze on Ellen now, 'you should steer clear of Perry.'

'You think—?'

'I think, in your position, I'd know when someone didn't have my best interests at heart,' said Leslie Ann, her wrinkled lips pinching the filter. 'I'd keep away from him.'

It was over.

Ellen was coming down the front steps when Leslie Ann called her back. Standing in the doorway, she looked frail and tired. The light coming from behind gave her hair the look of a wispy cocoon over the smooth roundness of her skull. She extended her hand.

'It must have fallen out of your bag in the study,' she said, holding out the cellphone.

Ellen froze halfway down the steps, then came back up. She took the phone from her, doing her best to smile.

'Are you sure you don't want me to call a cab?' said Leslie Ann.

Ellen shook her head, backing away.

'Haven't you forgotten something else?' said Leslie Ann.

Again Ellen froze, and this time Leslie Ann held out her arms. Ellen came back up the steps, and allowed herself to be pulled into a firm embrace.

'My dear Ellen,' said Leslie Ann. 'My dear friend.'

She pulled back, looking up at her with her tired lusterless eyes.

'This will soon be over,' she said.

She didn't unclench until she was on Park Avenue. Then she stood in the middle of the sidewalk, breathing hard, looking at the cellphone in her hand as though it were a bomb. They had taken it from her bag. Leslie Ann had taken it to check the number of the last caller. A cab smacked the curb with a squeal of worn brakes. It took Ellen a moment to realize that it had stopped for her. The window came down with a shuddering sound.

'Need a ride, lady?'

The perspiring face was lit green by the dashboard, and out of nowhere Ellen got a hard jolt of fear. Irrational. Instinctive. She backed away, tripped on a flagstone, then hurried off along the sidewalk.

She didn't get back to her place until nine, walked into her street, spooked, tautly alert to the silences and shadows. She couldn't shake the image of Leslie Ann holding out the phone. She looked up and down the street, then punched the code to enter her building. There was no light in the lobby. She didn't notice it until she was halfway through the door.

The only light was coming from the elevator. It was at the back of the echoing marble space, past the rows of mail boxes. There was just enough light to see by. She heard footsteps coming along the sidewalk behind her, and stepped inside. The door swung closed behind her.

She was being ridiculous. She took a step. There was a thump of heavy machinery and the elevator doors came together with a geriatric shudder. The car rose up through the building. It was really dark now.

Call the elevator. That was all she had to do. Press the button, and wait for it to come back down. She held her breath and crossed the darkness to the illuminated call button. Pressed it. Pressed it again. There was another thump, and the cables started to whine.

'Tell me you didn't talk to Hartnal.'

She span around with a yelp.

Perry was there, his face streaked by shadow as the elevator car came back down. He looked scared, rigid with fear.

She slapped him. She hadn't planned on doing it. It just happened. Perry staggered back.

She hit him again, harder this time, tears coming in a hot wave. Perry just stared, made no attempt to defend himself. There was blood on his nose now. Her hand throbbed from the blow.

The elevator doors came open. An old woman was standing there blinking, obviously startled to see them. Then she saw the blood on Perry's face. She hurried out, dragging a dachshund behind her.

'When are they going to fix the goddamn lights?' she yelled.

The street door came open. Closed.

Perry smeared blood with the back of his fist.

Ellen raised her hand again, but this time he put up an arm.

'You abject, miserable, abject, fucking *liar*.'

'Not *here*.'

He abruptly turned away, came to a halt in the entrance, waiting for her.

'Why?' she said in a strangled voice.

Perry shook his head.

'You did this to me,' she said. 'You let them . . .'

'I had no choice.'

'You had no choice! You had no *choice*!'

She blinked, startled by the sound of her own voice in the marble lobby. Her heart was pounding thickly.

'Tell me you didn't say anything,' said Perry. 'About Rosa May.'

When she didn't reply, he came back across the lobby until he was standing up close enough for her to smell his breath.

'In a way you deserve it,' he spat. 'For being so fucking blind and stupid all these years.'

20

It took Billy an hour to get the shit out of her face. She stumbled around for a while completely blind, cursing, trying to find her way to a bathroom or the kitchen, anywhere she could get some cold water on her face – ended up back in the kitchen, standing at the sink with her head under the open faucet, gasping with the cold of it, blinking her burning eyes.

She was standing in a pool of water. She leaned on the sink, barely able to see. A dog came into the kitchen. She heard the claws ticking on the tile floor. She squinted, made out a very ancient mutt with a plastic sleeve around his head to stop him scratching at the raw patch behind his left ear.

'The fuck did you come from?'

He hadn't barked once, not even when Bissel started yelling.

'Hey?'

The dog just stared. Deaf, she figured.

'You hungry?'

Blinking, cursing, she made her way over to the refrigerator, and found a slab of paté in greaseproof paper. She dropped it into a bowl by the back door. She sat down at the kitchen table, massaging her eyes, listening to the dog scarf paté. Then she checked her hands. The gloves were intact. There were no rips or scratches. Nothing like that. Nobody was going to be finding anything under his fingernails except some talc maybe.

'Motherfucker,' she said under her breath. 'Fat motherfucker.'

A coronary. That was what she figured. He'd hit her with the spray. Blindsided her. They'd waltzed around a little, Bissel trying to get a hold of the gun, and then he'd let out a groan, and gone down, dragging her with him. She'd stayed on top of him, blind, listening to him struggle for breath. It seemed to take an awfully long time for him to go slack.

'Fucking fat fuckhead.'

The dog was chasing the bowl now, making little scraping noises on the floor. She looked over at the open refrigerator. There were other packages in there. Neat little white bundles with the Whole Foods sticker. Bissel liked his cold cuts.

She went back to the sink, seeing better now, drank water from the faucet, then walked through to the front of the house. The front door was locked. Out front there was a big gate with cables running up the side into what she guessed was a security camera. No one was going to be bothering them.

She went through to the study.

He was lying face down in some black dirt. He'd hit a pot plant going down, flipped the thing over. She was about to pick up the pot, then stopped herself. One of Bissel's eyes was open. His face looked twisted and dark. The end of his tongue showed between his teeth and there was some blood. Myocardial Infarction. Happened all the time. A guy his age, and his size. He'd been opening his safe, and he'd had a heart attack.

Jay was going to freak out.

She squatted down in front of the safe. Cash. Used notes in an elastic band. She took it out, riffled hundred dollar bills. A four-inch stack. The wife probably knew all about it. It was a possibility anyway.

She put it back. She wasn't going to make the same mistake twice. She saw bearer bonds in a manila envelope, a skinny little Patek Philippe wristwatch. A bottle of cheap cologne.

The tapes were tucked away in back. A stack of nine. No identifying labels. No nothing.

She slotted one into a little VCR which was set up on a book shelf. She took a minute messing with the remote. The screen came to life. No sound. She fiddled with the remote some more, got a guy with a thick accent, talking about a picture. A date and time showed bottom left. The tape had been made three years earlier. A memento, then. Like he said. Tapes of interviews that had given him reason to doubt. She yanked it.

It took ten minutes to find the tape with the right date, and then she was looking at an old woman with big spray work hair. A hard, intelligent face, hollowed out by illness. Cancer, if she'd had to guess.

She boosted the sound.

'*– not a well person, not for a long time.*'

A southern accent. Texan maybe.

She rolled back to the beginning, saw Carey sit in the chair. When she got to the part about not being well, she put a hand on her breastbone. The woman was seriously skinny. Bissel was his fruity self.

'*I understand, and let me say once more how much I appreciate the opportunity to look at the work.*'

Billy looked at the corpse.

'*I heard you're the best person for Franklin's work.*'

'*Well, yes. This period, this school is something of an obsession for me. Forgive me for asking—*'

'*You want to know where I went.*'

She had gaps in her teeth when she smiled.

'*Where I've been all these years.*' She sighed.

'*After Franklin died. I was depressed for a time. My doctor recommended a trip. A cruise he said. But I didn't want to be stuck on a ship with a bunch of people I didn't know so . . . I just got on a plane to Spain. I always wanted to see Spain. My mother was from there, and we always had Mexicans working at the motel. So . . .'*

'Yes.'

'Have you been to Spain, Mr Bissel?'

Bissel moved his big shoulders. He talked about Madrid. He said 'Puerta del Sol' with an accent. He said 'Prado'.

She watched the tape to the end. Carey had married in Spain, had made her life there, living in Valladolid with her husband, a military man. He'd died a year ago. And now she had come home to die herself.

She worked the remote, rewinding, looking for highlights.

'And the painting?'

'Was with me in Spain. It looked wonderful there. I was always careful about the dust and the humidity.'

'The humidity?'

'I didn't let it dry out. But you'll see for yourself. You'll see how wonderful it is.'

There was a soft farting sound. Billy looked at the corpse, and shook her head, then went back to the screen.

'You bought this, Taylor?' she said. 'You bought this lady coming back from Spain?'

There was a smell. Billy shook her head some more, then rewound.

'Fat pig.'

She watched the video two more times. She didn't believe a word.

21

Back at his place, Perry went straight to the drinks cabinet and poured himself a whiskey, then stood there in the gloom, holding out the bottle. Ellen shook her head, watched him cross the living room and collapse into a broken arm chair. The apartment was a three bedroom place overlooking the Armory on Madison and 94th. He'd moved into it after his second marriage fell apart. She'd heard from other people about his books, had envisaged floor-to-ceiling shelves, reading lamps, couches. The reality was more like a depository, and a disorganized one at that.

The books were everywhere. There *were* shelves lining the walls, but they were crammed two and in some places three layers deep, the lower tiers hidden by teetering stacks. Unopened packages blocked access to cabinets and doorways, some ripped and showing the glossy spines of yet more books. Bound collections of newspapers stood plinth-like under manuscripts, some of which were held together with elastic bands, others spilling sideways in dog-eared wads, heavily marked with Perry's black scrawl. There were photocopies, color reproductions, art magazines, unopened mail.

Perry saw the look on her face, and shrugged.

'Bibliophilia,' he said. 'It's not illegal.'

She had to step over stuff to get into the living room. An answering machine blinked in the gloom.

'Why did you do it, Bruce?'

He eased off his cowboy boots, then rose and pushed through a partially blocked door into what looked like a study. There was some rummaging around, a muttered curse. Then a light came on. He reemerged, carrying a wad of papers, tossed them onto a coffee table.

'Take a look for yourself.'

Ellen gathered them up, cleared herself a space on one of the couches. They were type-written documents. Or rather photocopies of what looked like smeary carbons of type-written reports. Some were stamped, 'TOP SECRET'. Some had serial numbers. Ellen squinted at a couple of lines then put them aside.

'I need you to explain why you had to destroy my career, Bruce.'

Perry poured himself another drink.

'You went to see her, didn't you? When I called you, you were on the way over to see her.'

'I didn't tell her anything. About you. About Rosa May.'

That seemed to help. She watched him relax back into his chair. He closed his eyes.

'A year ago I received a letter,' he said. 'Through the mail. There was a Montreal postmark. I don't know how he got my home address, but I guess it's not too hard. There was a key to a post office box in a mail receiving agency in Manhattan. That's where he sends the documents.'

Ellen looked at the smeary typewritten papers.

'Reports,' said Perry. 'Mostly House Un-American Activities Committee.'

'The McCarthy thing.'

'It was up and running long before McCarthy. They set it up back in 'thirty-eight. They were going after the reds under the bed long before Stalin got the bomb – monitoring everyone, especially members of the Communist Party of America.'

'Bruce.'

He opened his eyes, gave her a look that was full of contempt.

'Ellen, I know you like to take a more intuitive approach to these things, but bear with me. I think you'll find the detail interesting.'

He took a drink, settled back into the chair, shading his eyes with his hand.

'In 1945 the CPA numbered thirty thousand, and—'

'What is it with you, Bruce?' He looked at her from under his hand. Ellen shook her head. 'Why do you have to be such a prick all the time?'

He smiled, but it wasn't a warm smile.

'Listen, Ellen, I really don't care about your opinion of me.'

Ellen looked at the cut on his mouth, wished she'd hit him harder.

'Communist Party of America,' he said. 'Thirty thousand strong in 1945. Not a lot in a population of two hundred and fifty million or whatever it was back then. And the joke was that most of those so-called communists were undercover FBI. It was practically a branch of the Justice Department.' He chuckled, sipped his drink. 'A young man joined the CPA that year. A clerk with a shipping company. Troubled, dirty, a disillusioned idealist. He'd studied painting under Hans Hoffman for a while.'

He shot her a look.

'That's right, Ellen. You knew about this right? The whole communist party thing.'

Ellen flared up.

'I wrote a book about this, Bruce.'

Perry smiled under his hand.

'Yes. "Martyr King". What a great story that was. You know what? I actually read some of it. It wasn't half bad given the material you were working with.'

'You're too kind.'

'Anyway, we both agree. He was a commie. They were all pretty communistic, of course. Pollock, Rothko, Reinhardt, Gorky. Different shades of red, but pinkos, definitely, and Koenig *very* red. Pro-Stalin, at least to begin with. He came to New York wanting to be a painter, went through the Regionalist thing, took a look in the Ashcan, sucked up the Mexican muralists. Then he met Hoffman. Went abstract. He managed to get by as long as the Public Works of Art Project kept paying twenty dollars a week. But then Roosevelt put an end to that in 1942, and he starved. He starved for quite a while and then he went looking for a job, ended up in the shipping company, joined the union, and then the party. The House Un-American Activities Committee started monitoring him in 1946, and guess what? They monitored him right up until the night he died.'

'The man in the gray hat,' said Ellen.

Perry sat up in the chair, and finished the drink.

'That's right,' he said. 'The man in the gray hat. You ever read Detective Tillman's report?'

Ellen gave a nod.

'Tillman got it all down,' said Perry. 'He canvassed the area, thought maybe this guy in the hat had something to do with Koenig's death. He asked the good people of Springs if they'd seen anyone like that. Nobody had. So he dismissed it as delusion.'

Perry gave her a straight look.

'You think he was wrong,' said Ellen.

He nodded at the reports that were next to her on the couch.

'Who do you think wrote those? Who do you think sent them to me?'

Ellen watched him stand, watched him go over to the drinks cabinet. This time she joined him. They sat in silence for a while drinking.

'He's very angry,' said Perry eventually. 'Every couple of months I get a call. He usually blocks the ID function, but a couple of times I've picked up a number. Different numbers. He's out west somewhere. Arizona. Nevada. When *Mirror* showed up I was in Paris. He left a message on my machine.'

He was on his feet again.

Ellen settled back into the couch, resting her elbows on sliding piles of books and papers. Perry flipped on the hi-fi. Slotted in a tape.

'The quality's not good,' he said over his shoulder. 'I recorded off my answering machine which is digital so . . .'

He pressed the button, boosted the sound. Now Ellen was hearing what could have been breathing, but could have been the sea, a hard-to-identify rushing sound that faded and swelled. Then an old man's voice, booming, ragged, incoherent.

'*—as free when what it was, was just lies and manipulation and . . .*'

Perry hit 'fast forward'.

'That's just ranting. I'll get to the . . .'

He hit 'play'.

'*—stop it. That's all. I don't care how. Stop the sale. She will not fill her pockets. She lied to him. She cheated him. She's no better than the rest, no better than Benton. She's worse. They sacrificed him, and they dipped their . . . their dirty beaks and now she . . . she wants to do it all over again. If you want the truth, Mr Curator, you'll stop it.*'

Perry hit 'stop', and turned to face her.

'That's why,' he said, simply. 'That's why I did what I did.'

Ellen struggled out of the books and papers, stood up. The whiskey had left her feeling a little woozy.

'You flushed me down the toilet,' she said. 'You destroyed my career, so that this . . .' She gestured at the documents on the couch. 'This old . . . cold warrior would . . .'

'Tell me the truth,' said Perry. 'Give me the true history of American art.'

He said it with such a look in his eye, all she could do was shake her head.

'And it's almost done. Almost finished.'

'Almost?'

'There's something he's been holding back. Something he's been struggling with.'

Ellen started to back away.

'Sometimes . . . when he talks to me, I think he's going to let it all come out, but then he . . . something makes him clam up. For a year he's been sending me . . . material – things you wouldn't *believe*. Things you would *not* believe about Koenig and Benton and Hartnal and Kruger – the museum, the OPC, *kulturkampf*, everything.'

Ellen stumbled on a pile of books, almost fell.

He grabbed her arm. 'Ellen. I'm sorry. For what I did. I would have done anything to avoid it. But I couldn't let the picture come into the collection. Not knowing what I know.'

'But it did come in. It was the catalog that . . . that swung it. If it hadn't been for the goddamn catalog—'

'No. No, you have to understand. It was the only way I could be sure. You weren't listening to me. You were so hopped up on your own sense of . . . your *deluded* sense of your own importance at the museum – talking about how much "Lewis" liked it, and hinting at other supporters, and I could see you were working yourself up to taking a stand against me, staking your ridiculous claim to the department.'

He let go of her arm, and stepped back, registering the stunned look on her face.

Ellen put a hand to her cheek, and swallowed hard. She took a step back, and did fall this time. She went down in the books and papers. Perry was reaching for her, trying to help her up.

'Don't touch me.'

She got to her feet.

'I knew you'd want to establish provenance,' said Perry, still trying to explain. 'I knew you'd find the catalog. It was the only way I could think of that would guarantee the painting would be discredited. I thought you'd notice the problem with the dimensions straight away. I fully expected you to come to me saying that someone had been messing with the library. At that point the picture would have been dead. But you didn't. You didn't see it. It was one detail too many. And you only saw what you wanted to see. Then at the lunch . . . I'm sitting there thinking, someone's going to see it, someone's going to see it.'

Her vision blurred as she turned for the door.

'*I* couldn't say anything,' he said, coming after her. 'It would have looked suspicious. I *had* to let a couple of days go by.'

She turned to face him, her eyes glittering.

'I *knew* it was real,' she said, striking herself in the chest. 'I *knew* it was real. That was the detail that caught *my* attention. The authenticity.'

22

He listened to his messages while she was in the bathroom, and when she came back out, he was searching for something.

'You think the museum is this building with white walls where someone decided to hang some great art,' he said.

They were in his study, surrounded by books and papers. It was worse in here. The floor was covered with screwed up balls of paper that had obviously fallen from the overflowing waste paper basket. A single reading lamp burned, throwing shadows over the walls and ceiling.

Perry was rummaging around in his drawers, lifting wads of paper, shoving books aside. He'd removed the elastic band that kept his hair in place, and now it stood out on one side in a clump. His mouth was puffy where she'd hit him.

'There's all this great art, and the founders, Rachel Kruger and her friends, decided to put some of it together so that the great American public would know what great art is, and be able to sit and look at it, and maybe buy a few postcards afterwards.'

He was laying the groundwork for their collaboration. That was how he was going to repay her for trashing her career. He wanted her to help him finish the book he'd started.

Ellen watched him search for whatever it was, and sipped what was probably her third glass of whiskey. She felt drained, lost. All she wanted to do was sleep, but going down to the street, and finding a cab was too much effort to even contemplate.

Perry stood up, and went through a door on the other side of the study into a corridor. Ellen saw white walls, paintings under lights, more doors. A light came on. She heard faucets open, water filling a basin.

'Did you ever wonder why the second one-man show the museum put together was for Diego Rivera?' he called out.

After a moment his head came round the doorway.

'Bruce, just tell me about Koenig.'

'Okay, let me ask you another question,' he said, disappearing again. 'An easy one. Back in the forties, who was it that ran the museum? I mean, who was the president?'

'It's always been a Kruger. Henry Kruger took over from his mother in 'thirty-nine. Stepped down in 1956, I think. So he was actually at the helm for two decades.'

'Not bad,' said Perry, coming back into the study. 'Not quite true, but pretty close.'

Ellen just stared. She was beyond being annoyed.

'You're forgetting what happened in 1940,' said Perry, looking under the desk now.

Ellen took a sip of her drink. She hadn't forgotten. She didn't know. Perry ducked out of sight.

'A year after becoming president, Kruger went to run the Office of Inter-American Affairs for President Roosevelt. He then went on to become secretary of state for Latin American affairs.'

'He was an establishment figure,' said Ellen with a shrug.

His head came up from behind the desk.

'One minute he's running his mom's museum, the next he's at the heart of Roosevelt's administration – where he stayed until 1946, by the way. How come?'

'I have a feeling you're going to tell me.'

'Because he had influence and connections in Latin America. Petroleum interests. Continental Petroleum in Venezuela, particularly. And he knew about commies, a growing concern for this fair land at that time. And this wasn't just about Kruger working his connections. The museum itself was in play. The Modern organized nineteen exhibitions of contemporary American painting for the Inter-American Affairs Office. It was – *art* was a kind of blunt, fluffy instrument, mostly used for schmoozing, you know – fancy openings at the ambassador's residence where the local dignitaries could put on a sash etc. etc., but sometimes it could be a little more pointed like when the museum helped Dwight Morrow cultivate the Mexican muralists.'

He paused for a drink. Then ducked back out of sight.

'Bruce, what are you looking for?'

'It's okay. It must have just . . . Diego Rivera,' he said. 'Communist. Do you think he would have gotten that one-man show if it hadn't been for the threat Mexican nationalism posed to Kruger family oil interests? Do you think he would have been hired to paint the mural at the foot of the Kruger Tower if it hadn't been for those same oil interests?'

Ellen frowned. She'd been to Kruger Tower a hundred times, and never noticed any mural by Diego Rivera.

'Kruger had it removed,' said Perry, coming back up to check out the look on her face. 'Story goes, Rivera was almost finished, and Kruger came to have a look. There was a little problem. Vladimir Ilich Lenin was on there. Unmistakable. Kruger asked Rivera if he wouldn't mind taking him off. When Rivera refused, Kruger paid him his twenty-one-thousand-dollar fee and got a bunch of guys to chisel Lenin out. With jackhammers! And while they were at it, they removed the rest.'

He looked down at the papers strewn on the floor. Ellen was shaking her head.

'I don't see what this has to do with—'

'The point I'm trying to make is that the Kruger family was at the heart of the political establishment. Kruger returned to the museum in 1946, but his interest in government dealing continued, deepened in fact. The Kruger Foundation, for example, was subcontracted by the government to study foreign affairs, and Kruger attended meetings where the most influential thinkers of the period worked out US foreign policy. Then Eisenhower appointed Kruger special adviser on Cold War strategy in 1954. He was chairman of the Planning Coordination Group which oversaw all National Security Council decisions, *including*—'

A buzzer sounded.

Perry froze. The noise came again – whoever was downstairs really leaning on the button. Ellen returned Perry's frozen look, then slowly shook her head.

'Bruce, I didn't say a word.'

He stood up straight, listening. It was quiet now.

'Probably just a mistake,' he said softly.

The phone jolted them upright. It was ringing right there in the study. Perry pushed aside a bundle of photocopies as the machine kicked in. Now they were listening to the recorded message, then a beep, then Hartnal.

'Bruce. Lewis here. I'm sorry to come by unannounced, but, well, I'm down here with David and we really need to talk.'

'David?' said Perry, smoothing grizzled hair back from his forehead. 'Kruger?'

The machine was still running.

'Bruce, I know you're up there.'

There was a soft click, and the line went dead.

'Kruger?' said Perry.

He looked around the room as though considering hiding places.

The buzzer in the hallway started up again.

He stalked out of the room.

Ellen stayed put, straining to listen.

'Lewis?'

Perry, sounding strained as he talked into the intercom.

'Bruce! Hello!' Hartnal's voice buzzed big and bogus. 'I thought you must have gone out. Did you get my message? I left a message on the machine, and—'

'Yes. Yes, I just caught the tail end of it. I was . . . I was in the bathroom.'

'Oh . . . oh I see. I wonder – do you think you could come down?'

Ellen rose.

'It's late, Lewis. I was just about to—'

'It's not so late really. It's just that . . . I don't know if you heard me before, but I've got David down here and—'

'He's in Manhattan?'

'He's here with me. He's anxious to avoid seven years of bad luck.'

He laughed, and it was a big bogus laugh.

Ellen was in the living room now, the hair coming up on the back of her neck as she tiptoed over piled books to the window. She looked down at the street. A black Town Car was double parked, hazard lights flashing.

'Well, he should have called me if he wanted to talk about it.'

'He's been rather busy.'

Ellen went through to the hallway. Perry was standing there with his eyes closed. He turned, gave her a look. There was a stillness in it, a candid deadness that frightened her. He shook his head.

'He's worried that the press are going to be all over this tomorrow,' said Hartnal, 'and . . . look Bruce, I feel silly talking into this microphone thing.'

Perry was shaking his head again, obviously trying to think.

'Bruce? Are you still there?'

'Okay.' Perry closed his eyes, and leaned forward, resting his head against the wall. 'Okay, come on up.' He pressed the buzzer, and stood back. Turned to look at Ellen.

'You'd better leave. Just go up to the next floor landing, and wait a couple of minutes.'

She shook her head.

'Ellen.'

'I want you to tell them.'

'*What?*'

'*What* you did. And *why* you did it.'

In two strides he was up against her, eyes blazing, grabbing her by the arm, pushing her backwards into the living room.

'For Christ's sake, Ellen. For once in your life *listen*. You have no *fucking* idea what you are dealing with here.'

There was a muffled knock at the door.

Perry froze, his face rigid, slick with sweat. Then he walked her backwards into the study. She stumbled on papers, had to hold on to him to stay on her feet.

'Stay here,' he hissed. 'And don't touch *anything*.'

He turned off the light. Then, taking a last look around at the scattered papers, closed the door.

She could barely breathe.

She heard Perry open up. Hartnal came in, mumbling something she couldn't catch as they came through into the living room. She couldn't hear Kruger. Slipping off her shoes, she moved closer to the door.

'He's in the car,' said Hartnal, his voice coming to her muffled through the thick door. 'On the phone. The man is always on the phone.' He laughed then, the same false laugh as before. 'I'm sorry, Bruce, you're going to have to come down.'

'I thought David was back in the Caribbean.'

'He postponed. Like the rest of us, he's very worried about you leaving the museum.'

'I didn't say I was leaving. I said I'd resign if *Mirror* stayed in the collection.'

'Quite. Personally, I think it's very laudable, Bruce, you sticking to your guns like this. But . . . well, this is a discussion we should probably have with David. Shall we?'

Ellen inched closer to the door, her heart beating in her throat. She heard a grunt, sounds of straining, Perry putting his boots on.

Receding footfalls on carpet, then floorboards. The front door opened. Closed.

She waited in the dark like that for maybe a minute before opening the study door. Perry had turned off the light. She moved over to the window, stepping on books and papers. Down on the street the limousine was pulling away.

She looked around the room, then went over to the couch, and picked up the photocopied sheets. Then she went back into the study, and turned on the desk lamp. There were no windows in here. No-one would see the light from the street. If anyone happened to be watching.

Some of the documents looked like reports. Some appeared to be transcripts of conversations. She took in place names, dates, times. The earliest started in February of 1949. Some of the documents had sections blanked out.

She sat down in Perry's armchair. It was very dull reading. There were names, times of day, people stopping for a drink in a bar, people buying a magazine, then walking back to their apartments. She put them aside, saw a notebook under a couple of magazines. Perry's scrawl was unmistakable. She flipped back to the beginning, read. *He has links to the House Un-American Activities Committee – HUAC established in 1938 to investigate disloyalty and subversive organizations – when Benton went to his apartment in 1949 they were watching.*

She knew all about the meeting with Benton, of course. The encounter was a matter of legend. Benton, newly-graduated from Harvard, a writer with the Partisan Review, walking in to this filthy apartment where a number of long 'mural-like' canvases were stacked, the fruit of Koenig's labors under the PWAP scheme. The article she had written about that encounter had marked the beginning of Koenig's ascension.

She turned the pages, engrossed, oblivious to the noises around her – the hum of air conditioning, the creak of floorboards overhead, sirens down in the street. Perry's scrawl was minute, at times impenetrable, bristling with obscure names and initials: – *started with Braden's article in the Saturday Evening Post (20 May 1967). After that, a steady leaking of information, some intentional (*all *intentional?) – how the Congress, the fulcrum for OPC's extraordinary leverage had offices in thirty-five countries, published over twenty prestigious magazines, arranged and funded art exhibitions, owned a news and features service, organized and funded high profile international conferences, and rewarded musicians and artists with prizes and public performances . . . Congress everywhere and into everything, the basic idea: the Russians were running a cultural Cold War in Europe – spreading the word, particularly in France, that maybe America was the new economic superpower, but culturally it was a desert.*

She flipped pages, saw block capitals double underlined. *HIS ANGER* and beneath that: *FEARS ASSASSINATION. PARANOID?* Then there was another long passage. It was a torrent, an avalanche: *—the Modern, at the heart of Kruger's empire, a cultural counterweight to the Kruger Trust and Banking Corporation with roots that went deep into the intelligence community. Ralph Buren, who first joined the museum in 1940, formerly Secretary of State for Air, worked for Kruger in Inter-American Affairs, and ran the CIA-sponsored Farfield foundation, then went on to become president of the museum in 1956. Under him, director Louis Guilbaut, who believed that modern art was the 'foremost symbol' of democracy, openly lobbied Congress to finance a cultural campaign against communism, and held regular meetings with the National Security Council's Operations Coordinating Board and the State Department.*

It went on and on, some passages were underlined, others crossed out. She shaded her eyes against the light, leaned forward until she was just a few inches from the page: *—within the Congress the most* *effective kind of propaganda was defined as the kind where the subject moves in the direction you desire for reasons which he believes to be his own.*

More capitals: *HOLDING SOMETHING BACK. SOMETHING IMPORTANT.*

At eleven o'clock, beginning to get a little antsy at the thought of Perry returning and finding her there going through his stuff, she came across a smudged mimeograph marked 'CONFIDENTIAL/HAND POUCH DELIVER'. It was short. Terse.

> 11/09/57. FBI Memorandum: Phoenix Special Agent-in-Charge John Leahy to Director Manhattan SAC Charles Webber. Charles: Per your request for Linda Carey medical history. Carey entered the care of Doctor Miles Stanton, a psychoanalyst registered to practice in the state of Arizona, 06/15/54, after an unsuccessful suicide attempt. She is being treated for a compulsion to mutilate herself. Details to follow.

Ellen sat back in the chair. It was just as Leslie Ann had said. Carey had serious problems. She picked up the sheaf of documents, and a key dropped out. It was a small silver key with a round flat head. A plastic tag was tied to it marked with a Broadway address. It came to her that this was what Perry had been looking for. He'd started looking after he'd listened to his messages. She went out into the living room, still holding the sheaf of papers, and picked her way across the rubble to the machine.

There was only one message, and it was very short. The voice was the voice she'd heard on Perry's tapes: – *It's in the mail.*

It was the sound of the key being pushed into the lock that brought her head up.

Perry.

She rose, and moved swiftly through the living room and back into the study where she turned off the light. She heard the front door come open, then softly close. Now she was looking at the gap under the door. Whoever it was, they hadn't put the light on. She heard a footstep. Another. Soft, stealthy, coming towards the door.

She backed out of the study, and into the passage on the other side. The handle to the study door was turning. She stepped into the bathroom as the door came open, saw the tub, saw the shower curtain. Holding her breath, she stepped in behind the shower curtain, and stood there, heart pounding, the papers fluttering in her hand, listening to the sounds of someone opening drawers, searching . . .

II

Linda

The woman stood in the middle of the aisle, shaking her head at the banked greetings cards. She held herself very straight, wore slacks, a sleeveless white blouse, scuffed loafers that were cracked and parched-looking under their coating of desert dust. She was in her late sixties, and had the hollowed-out look of the terminally ill. She had the kind of big spray-work hair that went out with the tail fins on Cadillacs.

Her burnt out eyes wandered, looking for something to like. The cards were terrible, inspirational shots of sunlight in redwood forest glades or cartoons with smutty gags. Behind her, the plate glass window shuddered every time a truck boomed past, and every time that happened she gave a start. Her nerves were shot. She was all nerves. Part of it was coming off the lithium. But it was being on the edge of the desert too. It was being so close to home.

She picked out a card, a bouquet of roses with gilding on the edge; an old-fashioned card, the sort of card she remembered from when she was a girl. Not the right kind of card for a modern young woman. She dropped it back, then, cursing under her breath, snatched it up again, and limped over to the check out.

She paid cash, watched the young girl's bitten fingernails on the grimy plastic keys. The girl's name tag said 'Melanie'. There was the faint shadow of a hickey on her throat. Linda nodded. There'd be a tattoo somewhere, she was sure, the kind of thing you regretted later on. She herself still carried a burn on the inside of her right calf courtesy of the '53 Harley her first boyfriend rode. From time to time she saw the same mark on other girls, and thought that everyone had to make their own mistakes, and that it was no good trying to warn people or give advice. You learned by your mistakes, and moved on. Unless, of course, they were big mistakes. The kind she'd always made.

The card went into a plastic bag, and the till receipt went into her wadded billfold. Earl didn't like her keeping them, but how else was she supposed to keep track of what they spent? And anyway, it wasn't as if they left a trail of any kind.

When she'd bought the first card (it had been for Rosa May's twentieth birthday back in August of '78) Roy had gone nuts, had said that she was just torturing herself. The past was the past. She'd done what she'd done. And for good reasons. He'd put the fear of God into her, saying that if she ever mailed it, they'd find her. That was the one thing she could be sure of. If they knew about Rosa May, they'd be watching. Especially around birthdays. Birthdays, Christmas, Thanksgiving. All the times the heart strings got a tug. At the time she couldn't believe there was any way they could know about Rosa May, but she'd been scared enough to listen. He told her that the fact she'd changed her name in Phoenix didn't make any difference. She might have left a little something behind. A nothing. A conversation in an elevator, a parking ticket she never saw because some kid ripped it out, a fender bender she might not even have noticed, especially the way she drove, something that was on record, something that was sitting in an archive somewhere waiting to be picked up. Roy had a thing about archives.

Of course, he was nuts about that sort of thing in general. Surveillance. Invisibility. When she'd bought Rosa May's first card, they'd been living in a camper. He'd bought it under an assumed name, not even licensing it for the road, had told the dealer he was buying it as a personal residence. Whenever they'd moved, which they'd done a lot up until they got the house, he'd get a fifteen day permit to move it to a location in another state. They'd find some farmer, or struggling campsite owner, pay a week in advance, always cash, and be happy until someone asked a question or Roy got the urge to cover his tracks again. They'd had five years of Formica and foam rubber before she'd finally put her foot down.

That first card had set him off, and so she'd put it aside, thinking that one day maybe she'd get a chance to send it. And the following year she'd gotten drunk, and forgetting all caution, had written a letter, a lying stupid letter explaining about the Hoffa trial and witness protection. She'd mailed it from Portland, kissing it before she put it into the box, and said nothing to Roy, of course – making it just one more little secret. And the year after that she'd almost done it again, but she wasn't that stupid, and so she'd gone back to cards – buying them, filling them with her terrible writing, and her love and pain and longing. And now they were in a little bundle in a suitcase. They'd been tucked away in the dark like the painting was until she'd pulled the damned thing out.

She walked out into the heat and across the parking lot, squinting in the dazzle, breathing whatever filthy thing it was they put on the fields up here. She opened the doors of the Mercury to let it air for a minute, resisted the urge to look in the trunk. The Mercury was a rental. She'd picked it up at San Francisco airport, and was supposed to be able to return it in Palm Springs. It was a change after the Corolla. She'd chosen it mainly because of the trunk, had assumed that four million dollars was going to take a lot of space. But in the end it wasn't so much. A million in hundred dollar bills made a stack about four feet high if you could keep it from toppling over.

That was what she'd done for the first few nights at the hotel, sat in her room stacking ten thousand dollar wads. Carefully packed, the big

Samsonite took three million dollars in two layers. The rest she'd wrapped in plastic and put in her little battered carry-on with the squeaky wheels. The remainder was in the bank. Different banks. In different countries. It had taken a long time to set it all up. It was Roy who had taught her about hiding assets. Roy could hide anything. You only had to look at what he'd done with the swimming pool to know that.

Originally, the idea behind the money had been to get some help. She'd never talked to Roy about it, hadn't even told him she was sick (and anyway she could be dead in front of the TV for a week before he'd notice). But then the specialist had told her that her blood was bad and that no amount of money could change that. He'd given her a year. Maybe not even. But here she was, a year later, feeling not too bad, and the painting was finally sold for more than she'd ever expected.

She tested the seat with her hand, before lowering herself into it. She put the birthday card on the passenger seat. She'd write something in it – best wishes to her little girl. Rosa May was going to be forty-five – twenty-five years older than she had been when she'd first met Koenig. It was quite a thought. Rosa May. Probably married herself, by now. Probably with children of her own. She was going to wrap the money in a parcel. She was going to put a ribbon on it.

24

Something bad had happened. That was the thought that kept her from sleep until the early hours. Friday morning she was awoken by the sound of a garbage truck down in the street. She rolled over in the bed, sending papers to the floor, then pushed herself upright, blinking tired eyes, the whole of the previous night coming back in a rush – hearing the sound of the key, thinking in that first split second that it was Perry, then deciding almost simultaneously that she was wrong.

She thought about it now, came to the same conclusion she'd reached at three o'clock in the morning: if it had been Perry, he'd have put on the lights.

Something bad had happened.

She'd taken the key with her, almost hadn't, then thought she couldn't not. Whatever was going on, she had a right to know.

The key was in her desk drawer. The papers were all over the floor. Classified information. Ten years of detailed reports, memoranda and phone transcripts. For what? The FBI had kept files on all the Abstract Expressionist people, but even for the period this kind of surveillance seemed excessive.

She looked at her watch. It was nearly nine, and she was going to be late. She scrambled out of bed, and dragged herself through to the shower. Leaning back in the stream of cool water, she got a flash of Perry's scared face, the way he'd looked when Hartnal knocked at the door. She had no idea what she was dealing with. That was the last thing he'd said to her. She had no idea. She needed to call him to make sure he was all right. She turned off the faucet and stood there in the dripping silence, remembering sounds of stealth, the creak of a floorboard – whoever it was, making their way through the living room in the dark. She'd hidden in the bathroom, stood there in the bathtub scared rigid, a sheaf of papers fluttering in her hand – had stood there for what had felt like forever, listening to boxes and files being moved around. Then whoever it was had gone back out, closing the door softly behind him.

'It was Perry,' she said softly, really wanting to believe it. He hadn't called out because he hadn't expected to find her still there. He hadn't put on the light because he didn't want anyone to know he'd returned. He knew he was being watched and so . . . She looked down at her feet, saw soapy water twisting into the drain. She had to call him. It was the only way to be sure.

She was pulling on clothes when the phone started up. She stood there with an arm pushed into her shirt, listening to Hartnal. His voice sounded grainy with fatigue.

'Ellen, it's Lewis. I'm calling to say . . . well there's been a development which . . . well it has a direct bearing on your situation. I think . . . Ellen? Perhaps it would be better if you came straight in to the museum . . . There's going to be some media interest. So, please, not a word to *anyone*.'

She called Perry as soon as Hartnal had hung up. Got his machine. She left a message, gave him her home and cellphone numbers.

Back in the bedroom, she gathered up the strewn documents, and shuffled them into some sort of order. They needed to be somewhere safe. She walked through to the den and the first thing she saw was Dan, whispering into her ear. She paused for a moment in front of the photograph, wondering what he would have said about her missing the problem with the dimensions in the catalog. Perry had said that it had been one detail too many and that was so close to something Dan had once said to her that out of nowhere she was remembering their last conversation on the phone in all its bitterness and resentment.

The fall of '87. The telephone in the porter's lodge.

He'd said she was giving up on him because she couldn't stand the life, by which he'd meant the artistic life, by which he'd meant a life where you really didn't give a damn about anything or anyone except your thing whatever that happened to be – in her case, as he'd conceived it, her quirky portraits. '*You talk about commitment, but you're the one who can't commit,*' he'd said. '*You never once committed to the things you tried to build.*' He'd said she was seeing Greg because he was easy-going and cynical, and that underneath she was the same. She was headed for consumerism and suburbia and a baby – for him the worst possible outcomes, especially the last. It was babies that had stifled female creativity through the millennia. It was a baby that would stifle her. He'd been angry, of course; she'd just told him that she wanted out, couldn't handle it any more – the lack of structure, the dirty sheets, the craziness, and the drugs, but standing there with the documents in her hand and looking into his eyes, she knew that, had he been standing there next to her, he would have said the same or similar things about her current situation. She'd missed the problem with the dimensions because she wasn't invested. It had been one detail too many.

The phone was ringing again. The press this time, some character who said he was with the *Times*. Her number was ex-directory, but he'd gotten hold of it somehow.

'I don't know if you remember me, but we met at the museum last Friday. I hope you don't mind me calling you at home, but . . . well,

I'm very anxious to talk to you about Taylor Bissel – what happened to him. You can reach me on—'

She didn't hear the rest of it, went straight through to the living room, and flipped on the TV. Then she called Jerry Lloyd on his cell. He was already in the museum.

'Jerry? Did you get the *Daily News* this morning?'

'No.'

'Something happened to Taylor Bissel,' she said, flipping channels.

'Like what?'

'I don't know. That's why I'm calling.' She hit New York 1. A heavily-made-up anchor was frowning at the camera. 'I thought you might have heard something.'

'No, I—'

'Wait!'

She saw it, then. The glass façade of the Bissel Gallery. She boosted the sound. The screen jumped to an image of Bissel's house in Forest Hills. A young woman was standing in front of the gate.

'What is it?' said Jerry.

'Shit.'

'Ellen?'

'Taylor Bissel's dead.'

She rang off, called Perry, then hung up as soon as his machine kicked in. Then her phone was ringing again. It didn't stop. People were leaving messages. Word was spreading about Bissel.

She was on her way out of the apartment when she noticed the documents. They were still on the kitchen table – stacked there in plain view next to the key. She grabbed them up, and almost stuffed them into her shoulder bag, getting a little frantic now.

She saw the refrigerator, yanked open the door of the icebox, and just like that the feeling came – the same ballooning anxiety she'd felt when Ben had said they had to pack his clothes. It shook her, rooted her to the spot. For a moment she couldn't move at all, stood there with the door open, the cold air drifting out to meet her in an icy smoke. Then she was grabbing at boxes of lean cuisine and frozen pizza, jamming the papers into the back where the ice was thickest.

25

She had never known Hartnal come into the museum unshaven. Standing at his window, wincing each time the telephone started up in the office next door, he looked like he hadn't slept in a week.

'Jackals,' he muttered, touching at the knot in his dark silk tie. 'You didn't talk to any of them?'

He turned to look at her, squinting a little as though having trouble focusing. Ellen shook her head. A small posse of reporters had taken up temporary residence in front of the main entrance of the museum. There was even a cable TV crew down there, a guy in denim pushing a microphone at anyone going in or out who looked like museum staff, asking for comment on Taylor Bissel's death. Hartnal came back to his desk.

'The cleaning lady found him, apparently.'

Ellen nodded.

'I saw the reports on New York 1.'

'Of course, everyone's trying to link it to *Mirror*,' he said, sitting down. 'Talking about this phony FBI agent going in there the other day.'

They had been running a loop taken from the camera over the

main entrance in the Bissel gallery. You could see it was a woman but that was about all. A black baseball cap, blond hair that looked like a wig. Nothing.

Next door the phone started up again, and this time the call was put through. Hartnal touched wrinkled finger ends to his eyelids, and pushed out an exasperated sigh, then stabbing a button, he turned away from Ellen to answer the call.

'David,' he said warmly, his shoulders taking a more relaxed slant. Kruger was talking at the other end, airing what sounded like complicated issues. Five minutes into it, Hartnal propped his head on his hand.

'No,' he said, eventually. 'No news yet.' He listened for a moment, shaking his head. 'Yes, yes I know. Completely unrelated, I'm sure . . . The unfortunate man was three hundred pounds. It could have happened at any time. Yes . . . yes. I will.'

He hung up, looked lost for a moment.

'Your message,' said Ellen. 'You said something had happened. Something that had a bearing on my—'

'Yes,' said Hartnal, lowering his head a little, 'I believe I may have mentioned to you last night that we were making some progress in our investigation. That French was going to make a report to the board. I didn't want to talk to you about it before hearing what Perry had to say, but . . . well, to cut a long story short, Bob Gifford came to me with some pretty compelling evidence pointing to Perry as the person who tampered with the San Diego catalog.'

Ellen did her best to look astonished. Perturbed came easier. For the next ten minutes she watched Hartnal talk, barely able to follow what he was saying, catching the odd word or phrase – video tape, security cameras, a screen saver that shouldn't have been there.

'Last night, after our conversation, I went to see Perry at his apartment. I wanted to confront him with the evidence.'

Untrue. She'd heard the whole conversation. Or perhaps he'd raised the question of the catalog in the car.

She realized that he was staring at her.

'This is terrible,' she managed. 'I can't . . . I can't believe it.'

'When I say evidence, there's nothing that would stand up in court, of course, but there are a number of indications that . . . well, they left *me* in no doubt.' He nodded, a stern look on his face. 'To cut a long story short, I shared my thoughts with him, and he became very . . . agitated. And now . . . well, Bruce seems to have disappeared.'

He just came out with it. Ellen sat back in her chair.

'I know,' said Hartnal, producing a pristine handkerchief from his jacket pocket. He gave it a shake. 'Wait until the press gets hold of *that* little nugget.'

'Disappeared?'

Hartnal shrugged. There was a smell of lavender now.

'All I can say is he was supposed to be here at nine o'clock this morning, and it is now ten. He isn't answering his phone, and he isn't answering the door. I sent Staunton over to try to find him.'

Ellen felt sick.

'Perhaps he had to go out,' she said weakly.

'Normally, I'd take the same view, but in this case . . .'

'He owned up?' said Ellen, conscious of a nerve tweaking under her left eye.

'Not exactly, but . . . as good as. He offered his resignation.'

'Does Kruger know about it?'

'He does.'

Then Ellen remembered: Kruger was supposed to have been in the car.

'What did he say?'

Hartnal looked at his manicured nails, thoughtful for a moment.

'David . . . obviously David is very upset. About all of this. Every aspect.' He glanced up at her, crimping his eyes. 'Needless to say, *you* can expect a call from him, Ellen. He wants to give you a personal apology.'

Ellen was looking at the handkerchief in Hartnal's fingers.

'But why?'

'Well, I think he feels that—'

'No, I mean, why would Bruce do it? Plant the catalog?'

Hartnal opened his arms as if to display the full range of available deceits.

Ellen was shaking her head. She wanted to hear it from him. At least get his take on it.

'I can only imagine he wanted to discredit the painting,' he said. Then he leaned forward, and put his elbows on the desk. 'To discredit . . . *you*.' He nodded soberly. 'This will doubtless all become much clearer when he decides to show his face. Unless of course . . .'

'What?'

Hartnal smiled, shaking his head.

'Ellen, if this is what it appears to be, it would be understandable if the man felt at least just a *little* ashamed. He might not want to explain. Certainly, he'll be counting on David to keep it all very quiet. No, I'm afraid that this will not play out in a particularly edifying manner. Bruce will resign because of the painting. That will be the official story. The museum will stand by the work that Ellen Lindz brought before the trustees. We will all move on.'

Ellen looked down at her hands.

'Ellen?'

She looked up.

'Some good will come out of it,' said Hartnal, offering a rueful smile. 'Not wanting to be too crass about it, I'd say it left you in a very strong position here.'

The color came into her face. Shame. She knew what it was without being entirely clear why she was feeling it. Somehow Perry's judgment had stuck with her. *It was one detail too many.* She became aware of Hartnal's expression. There was a tightening in his wrinkled brows that wasn't quite a frown.

'Ellen, last night, when Leslie Ann asked you if Bruce had called you, just before you arrived . . .'

He was smiling now, his pale tongue resting against his stained lower teeth.

If they'd taken her phone, they knew perfectly well who she had been talking to. Her face was burning.

'Ellen,' he said gently. 'It's all right. I hope it won't seem too patronizing to say that I think you've handled yourself with remarkable maturity these past few days.'

She couldn't breathe, found herself shaking her head.

'Did he threaten you in some way?' said Hartnal in the same soft voice.

'Yes,' she said, exhaling. 'I mean no, he didn't threaten me, but yes it was Bruce.' She took a breath, another, tried to think. 'We'd had that conversation about Linda Carey in his office, her bank account and so forth, and . . . well, I think he was worried about me repeating what he'd told me; things which he'd been told in confidence.'

There was a long listening moment, both of them trying to see if this made sense. Hartnal was quite still, suspended, holding her with his unblinking gaze.

'Yes,' he said. 'Things he'd been apprised of *intra muros*, as it were. That makes perfect sense to me.'

He smoothed strands of white hair against his scalp.

'I hope you don't mind me asking.'

'Of course not,' she said. 'You're right to.'

'I don't *feel* right doing it, but – to be honest – I've felt a bit lost recently. You know how it is here. Eddies, undercurrents. Sometimes one has an urge to take a breath of air at the surface.'

Ellen nodded, took a gulp herself.

'I'm embarrassed,' she said. 'I . . . I don't know why I lied. I—'

'You were being loyal,' he said. 'Which is admirable. You were being loyal to someone who had no right to expect it.'

The past tense hung there for a moment, but he was already flowing on.

'Did you see the *Post* this morning? They're offering a thousand-dollar reward for anyone with information on the whereabouts of Linda Carey. They've got this dreadful computer-generated image of her on the front page. Some sort of composite based on what Bissel's assistant remembers, and what they could get from the security camera.'

'A thousand dollars doesn't seem like much.'

'That's what I thought. Perhaps Rosa May would see it differently.'

Seeing his smile, the hair came up on the back of Ellen's neck. Then he was laughing, leaning back in his chair.

'I'm sorry,' he said, dabbing at his left eye. Then, seeing the look on her face, he reached out to her. 'Really, Ellen. It was silly of me. It wasn't meant to sound quite so sinister.'

He shook his head.

'One of our lawyers was with Taylor Bissel yesterday afternoon when he received a call from a young woman named Rosa May King. She asked him if Perry had mentioned her to him, and when he said no, she hung up. Bissel has caller ID. He had a feeling he recognized the voice. It wasn't very difficult for him to put the number and the name together.'

Ellen stared. In her irritation with Perry, she'd made the call from home.

'Ellen?

'Yes,' she said, her face flaming now. 'Yes it was me. I was . . . it was stupid. But I really was annoyed with Bruce.'

Hartnal opened his hands, inviting her to go on.

'After the *Mirror* situation blew up, Bissel wouldn't talk to me. So I asked Bruce to intervene. He said he would, but then I got the impression he was deceiving me.'

'And this Rosa May? Does she have something to do with the painting?'

Things were moving way too fast. She had no idea what Hartnal knew and what he didn't. He was smiling at her, a puzzled look on his face.

'Ellen?'

'I don't . . .' She started then stopped. Took a breath: 'I thought . . . I *thought* there might be a possibility that she was Linda Carey's daughter.'

'Daughter?'

He sat back in his chair, making it crack.

Ellen gave a tight nod.

'It's just an idea I had.'

Hartnal was watching her now, immobile, his age-spotted hands tucked in against his narrow, slightly concave chest. Next door the phone continued to ring, but he seemed oblivious, had ears only for her as she explained about her visit to Albuquerque and the interview she'd conducted with Constance Martin, Carey's friend from her days at the Rio Rancho Motel. When she was finished Hartnal placed a hand flat against his breastbone.

'You know . . . Ellen, this – it would have been helpful, if you had mentioned this possibility to the board.'

She set her chin at that.

'I was *extra muros* so quickly, Lewis.'

'To Leslie Ann, then.'

'I tried to at the time. When I was researching my Koenig book. Leslie Ann didn't want to know. Just the mention of Carey made her angry.'

Hartnal was nodding again.

'And, 'King'?' he said. 'You assumed that Carey had Americanized the father's name. Is that it?'

'It was just wishful thinking, really.'

'What was the date of birth?'

'I don't remember.'

'You didn't make a note?'

'Probably somewhere. I probably have it written down somewhere, but . . .'

Hartnal took out a pen and started making notes himself.

'Of course if it were Koenig's child, conceived when he was at that motel, the birthday would have to be sometime around . . . now,' he said.

'If there is any connection at all. But . . . if you don't mind me asking. Why is it of such interest?'

Hartnal put the cap back on his pen.

'Ellen, like you, the museum is very concerned to find Linda Carey. Preferably before the readers of the *Post*.'

He nodded, giving her a moment to dwell on that, then struggled to his feet. He came around the desk, and reached out for her hands. Ellen rose too. For a moment, he said nothing, gazing into her eyes, and when he spoke, his voice was hoarse with emotion.

'I know I speak for David Kruger when I say how much I regret what happened here, Ellen. When I think how unfairly you've been treated, it makes me sick to the stomach. I'd understand it perfectly if you were to express a desire to go after Perry in a court of law. But . . . well, all I ask is that you think about it, and think about your place here. Loyalty means a great deal to David Kruger, and he knows how to repay it.'

26

Jay came along the sidewalk looking pretty good in his black T-shirt and jeans, a Yankees baseball cap covering the white hair today. Billy tapped the glass of the diner with her Zippo, and without checking his stride, Jay gave a little lift to his chin, letting her know he'd already seen her, that his spook's eyes saw it all, and that he wasn't in the mood for bonhomie. Shouldering his way in through the street door, he made his way between the chairs, looking like someone who wanted his unhappiness to be seen and noted.

Billy wedged herself deeper into the booth, watched him drop a copy of the *Daily News* on the table, watched him put a finger on the picture of Taylor Bissel.

'Infarct,' she said, dipping to sip her burnt coffee.

Jay took a seat, and pulled off his cap, looked instantly ten years older.

'Local PD already forgot about it,' said Billy.

A waitress came over. Jay ordered coffee.

'It's interesting you should say that,' he said when the woman had gone away again. Then he drew a hand across his face, shaking his head.

'What?' said Billy.

He fixed her with his small colorless eyes.

'You know, your dad was a great guy,' he said.

'What's my dad got to do with anything?'

'Listen,' he said, holding out a hand. 'Just give me the tapes.'

'Wait. What? What's this about?'

'Did you even *get* the tapes?' he said, his lips barely moving.

Billy's face went hot.

'Hey! *Hey*!'

Heads were turning in their direction. Billy returned stares, then went back to shaking her head. She didn't understand it.

'What's your problem, Jay?'

The expression went out of Jay's face, but he was white-lipped, more angry than she'd ever seen him.

'Billy, I *know* about the money.'

'What money?'

Jay just stared.

'Just give me the fucking tapes.'

'Jay, I swear to God. I don't know what you're talking about.'

He leaned in towards the table.

'Bissel's wife says there was three hundred thousand dollars in the safe.'

'You're talking to his *wife*? *She's* the client?'

His eyes got a pinched look. He pushed sideways in the booth, taking the paper with him. On his way.

'Look,' said Billy. 'I saw the money, and I swear to you I didn't touch it. No . . . no, I tell a lie. I picked it up.' She looked around, leaned forward to whisper. 'I picked it up and I put it back.' She pushed back in her seat, reached for a cigarette, remembered she couldn't smoke. 'Now if it wasn't there when the police came in, either the . . . this cleaning lady took it, or, God forbid, the cops. Okay?'

Jay looked out through the grimy window. Traffic was at a standstill on Jackson Avenue.

'I swear on my father's grave,' said Billy. Then, leaning in again: 'You don't think I learned my lesson in Baltimore?'

Jay shook his head, looking sad now.

'Billy. This money goes missing, and suddenly the cops are thinking homicide. So now the forensics people say there's pepper spray residue on the body.'

Billy was wagging her finger at him.

'No, no, no, no, no. He sprayed *me*.'

She told him how it had gone down. Jay watched her, deadpan. There was no way of knowing if he believed her or not. His eyes tracked down to the yellow envelope that was under her car keys. Swing doors thumped open in the back of the room.

'He's opening this safe,' said Billy, 'and he tries to jump me. Sprays me. Then – I don't know – maybe the pressure, the stress . . . He just keeled over.'

'That looks like one tape,' said Jay.

'I burned the other one.'

She pushed the envelope across the table.

'Did you look at this?' he said.

'Had to make sure I got the right one.'

People came in from the street. Kids. A boy and a girl. Jay watched them walk over to a booth.

Billy narrowed her eyes as a character in a wheelchair rolled past the window. No legs and a little placard: Navy Seal. Please Help.

'Maybe she went back to Spain,' she said.

Jay said nothing.

'Did you see the *Post* is offering a reward?' she said.

But Jay was getting up. The meeting was over.

'Whatever,' said Billy, hitching herself sideways. 'You owe me four grand.'

He pointed at the copy of the *Daily News* he'd left on the table. There was an envelope in the fold.

'See you around, Billy.'

And he walked out of the diner.

27

'*The pie guy*,' someone yelled, and heads rolled back in laughter. Ellen blinked in the strobing flash of a camera, saw bridgework and bicuspids, ribbed palates, tongues, gums – everything caught for posterity. A mouth came close to her ear. She felt the breath of it. A broken voice murmured congratulations, but by the time she turned whoever it was had already moved on. The red eye of a video camera was roving around in the dark beyond the candlelight. She tried to concentrate on the conversation she was in, became aware of the food on her fork. Something pink and raw. She was supposed to be eating, but it was impossible to eat. '*When I told Wayne, he started yelling*.' She'd been in meetings all afternoon, chugging caffeine, watching Hartnal and the others develop the museum's Position. Even Kruger had been there, a flickering presence on the video screen.

Someone clapped her on the shoulder. Ellen saw Tilda Kraft backing away, smiling, waving. She put the food into her mouth.

The main room of the Feininger Gallery on East 88th Street.

A table had been set for dinner in the middle of the floor, and around it a couple of dozen of the New York art world's best and brightest of a bygone era, were pretending that the accumulation of years had done nothing to dim their capacity for raucous fun. Without the usual clutter of masks, wooden sculptures, beadwork rugs, nailed fetishes, and Joseph Cornell boxes (the boxes were what Feininger was now best known for, even though he'd started out in Pop) the space was a booming echo chamber. Fat altar candles sputtered and twitched along the center of the table, lighting wrinkled, age-spotted faces that fifty years ago would have been as fresh as the Wayne Thiebauds on the walls.

Perry's name was on the little place card that she'd found on her plate. Before they'd sat down to eat, Richard Feininger had asked her if she was 'about to make history' at the Modern.

Flash.

'Of course, Koenig thought it was a joke.'

Ellen blinked. Richard Feininger was leaning into the candlelight, pushing his face at her. Beyond him, her face indistinct in the gloom, Leslie Ann was a smiling, watchful presence.

'What was?'

'Pop Art. Johns, Rauschenberg, Warhol.'

He told her how Koenig had come into the gallery with Newman and some of the others one time and asked him to get rid of the 'pie guy' – the pie guy being Wayne Thiebaud, of course. Feininger had stood his ground and Thiebaud had gone on to make his fortune.

Feininger frowned, and it came to Ellen that she was making a bad impression, being unresponsive. She leaned back, emptying her glass. People were getting up at the other end of the table, but she wasn't going to be able to leave for at least another hour. Looking around at the flickering faces, it occurred to her that a month ago she would have given a year's salary to be in this room with these people. A place at this table was a privilege. When Hartnal had proposed she come along to stand in for Perry, he'd made that perfectly clear.

A camera flashed, and suddenly Hartnal was there, as though she only had to think of him to have him come up out of the ground wreathed in smoke. He leaned across Roland Staunton, breathing cigar into her face.

'Ellen? You okay?' He pointed at her plate. 'You hardly touched your food.'

'No appetite.'

'You're worried about Perry,' said Hartnal, shaking his head.

And it was true. She was. People had been calling her at the museum all day, wanting to know what had happened. The news that Perry had gone awol hadn't hit the newspapers until the afternoon editions, but then there had been a flurry of speculative stories following close on the tail of ArtAttack.com, a rabidly anti-establishment website with a considerable following, which had started the ball rolling by suggesting that Perry had been bumped off by the perpetrators of what would turn out to be a massive fraud. Nothing was known about the tampered catalog. Kruger had succeeded in keeping that inside the walls.

'He'll show up soon enough,' said Hartnal.

'What about Self?'

Someone Ellen couldn't see was yelling from the other side of the table.

'Self?' said Hartnal, looking up.

'That's the *name*!'

'They're talking about this sculpture,' said Staunton. He turned to Ellen. 'You met him, didn't you?' Ellen felt his hand curl in the crook of her elbow. 'Marc Quinn,' he said.

'Yes,' said Ellen, 'yes I did.'

Hartnal moved off, and was quickly lost in the gloom.

'Did you hear about his sculpture melting?' said Staunton.

'Someone said it had been valued at two million dollars.'

'Two and a half.'

People were joining in on all sides.

The Marc Quinn sculpture had just been lost in London. An autoportrait bust made from nine pints of the artist's blood extracted over a period of five months, it had been bought by the Saatchi Gallery in '93. It was displayed in a chilled glass cabinet, had to be kept frozen at all times. Ellen had seen it at the Saatchi when it was first acquired, and had been deeply impressed by its odd totemic power. For reasons that weren't quite clear, Charles Saatchi had been keeping the bust in his refrigerator at home and some builders who had been working on the house had accidentally pulled the plug.

'Apparently, these guys noticed blood running out of the refrigerator,' said Staunton, yelling to make himself heard against the general hubbub. 'It was all over the floor.'

There was a great roar of laughter.

Ellen found herself standing, thought for a second she was going to be sick.

Staunton rose with her, had his hand on her arm again. She pulled herself free. More abruptly than she meant to.

'Are you okay, Ellen?'

'I'm fine,' she said, teetering a little. 'Too much . . . too much caffeine, I think.'

'It's been a rough few days,' said Leslie Ann.

She had come around the table to lend her support.

Ellen looked down at her old friend's wrinkled face, then pushed back her chair. She grabbed her shoulder bag and made her way through the bustling waiters, allowing herself to be guided.

The bathroom was blissfully quiet and cool.

She thumped her bag down on the brushed steel basin and looked at herself in the mirror. She was pale, and sweaty, her dark hair hanging in what her mother would have called rats tails. She splashed cold water on her face, then bent to drink from the faucet, came up gasping. Leslie Ann was standing behind her, her back to the wall.

'You should be more pleased,' she said.

Ellen was patting her face dry with a paper towel.

'About the painting,' said Leslie Ann. 'You were right. You knew you were right and you *were* right.'

'I'm worried about Perry,' said Ellen.

'I'm sure Bruce is fine. God only knows what he's plotting.'

Ellen frowned, pursing her lips, applying some gloss now.

'Do you really think that's what he's doing?'

'After what he did at the museum, nothing would surprise me. I mean there has to be a serious problem there. Don't you think?'

Ellen gazed at herself in the mirror, thought for a second that she had everything wrong.

'You're missing your little boy,' said Leslie Ann.

It was true. She felt drifty, ungrounded without him.

Ellen turned to face her.

'Leslie Ann . . . I'm sorry . . . the other night for lying to you about Bruce. About the phone call.'

Leslie Ann shrugged.

'Lewis explained to me,' she said softly. 'You've been under a lot of strain.'

Ellen considered her old friend's face, would have liked to talk to her about Linda Carey.

'You've been thinking about Dan,' said Leslie Ann.

Ellen smiled, and for a second she thought she was going to cry. Leslie Ann nodded.

'I can always tell,' she said.

'Fifteen years later,' said Ellen. 'You'd think I'd have moved on.'

'Perhaps it's Dan who can't move on.'

She didn't get home until midnight, took a couple of Tylenol, and stood in the kitchen listening to her messages. There was nothing from Perry, a couple of calls from friends asking her what was happening at the museum. Jerry Lloyd left her a message asking her what she had done with the body – *I just hope you buried him deep enough to fool the dogs.*

The last message was from Greg.

—*Weren't you supposed to call this afternoon? You're probably tied up with work. Saw the news about the chief curator guy. What's going on over there? A palace coup? Are they going to give you the job now? Ben says, 'hi' . . . Anyway, I'm just calling to—*

The machine cut him off.

She looked at her watch. Ben was almost certainly in bed by now. She grasped the handle of the freezer door, hesitated for a second then pulled it open. There was no bloody head, of course, and the papers were still jammed in back where she'd put them. She took them out, shaking off flakes of ice.

She called Jerry.

'Can I come over?'

'What?'

'It's only twelve.'

'Can't take it on your own, huh? Can't take it without a guy around the house.'

'I need to talk to you.'

Thirty minutes later he was opening the door to his apartment in boxer shorts and a T-shirt. The apartment stank of Chinese food. He gave her a drink, and they sat in his tiny kitchen, both looking at the battered document wallet on the table. He wanted to know what was going on.

Ellen put a hand on the wallet.

'I can't tell you everything, Jerry. In fact, I almost didn't come over.'

He pushed his glasses up against the bridge of his nose.

'So . . . are you going to open it?'

Ellen took a sip of wine, and considered Jerry's face for a moment. He tilted his head, smiled.

'Ellen? What is it? What are they, photographs? What?'

'Documents,' she said. 'I thought . . . I thought maybe you could show them to your brother.'

'Professor Lloyd,' said Jerry, stiffening up a little. He didn't much like his brother. 'What kind of documents are they?'

'Surveillance reports. I think. From the forties and fifties. Some of them are from the House Un-American Activities Committee.'

'The McCarthy thing.'

'Sort of. Anyway, I wanted an expert to . . . You see, I don't . . .'

'You don't know anything about it, and you want the Professor to give you his expert opinion.' He reached for the wallet. 'Can I at least see the things?'

Ellen held on.

'Jerry. This is going to sound a little nuts, but I'm . . . I'm not sure I should even have them. So . . . I'm not sure – I think maybe they could get you into trouble.'

Jerry eased it out of her hands.

'Where did you get these mysterious documents?'

She shook her head. Jerry sat back on his stool and took a sip of wine.

'Ellen . . . does this have something to with—'

'Koenig. Yes, it does.'

'You're not in any trouble are you?'

She shook her head.

'No. No, I'm not. In fact, just the opposite.'

It was getting ridiculous. It was getting late.

'Just show them to your brother. And not a word on the fruitvine.'

She didn't get home until two, and was still too jazzed to go to bed. She went through to the den and turned on her computer, looked at personal search websites, found one that promised to return a result within twenty-four hours. All it required was a name, a date of birth and thirty dollars.

28

Jay called by early Saturday morning, drove all the way up to White Plains to talk to her and to track mud into her kitchen. He said he believed her about the money, said he was sorry he'd doubted her. He said there was someone he wanted her to find, that he'd keep the money coming the same as with Bissel. When he left, Billy gave him a hug for old time's sake, and watched him go down the path to the front gate.

He didn't want to be going elsewhere. That was her take on it. He didn't want to be talking to anyone else about his precious client. That was why he wasn't talking to her at the office. Something made this job special, and the thing that came to her mind was money. Especially now it looked like they were going after Carey. Jay hadn't said that exactly. He wanted her to find a woman by the name of Rosa May King, a woman who might or might not have been born to Carey in August of 1958. But if they were looking for the daughter it was to find the mother. That was how she saw it. The only thing she didn't really understand was, if it was so important to Jay, why didn't he go find Rosa May King himself? She was going to have to think about that.

There was another aspect to the whole thing, of course, an aspect that came up when she pressed herself against him in the doorway: their relationship. It caused him some confusion, she could tell, put him in the father's role, made her the daughter. A daughter he'd abused. However you wired it, she was back in business, and it felt good to be watching the Carey tape, checking through the data she'd picked up in Wyoming, working the telephone with the blinds down, and the a/c up as high it could go.

She called her contact at DataQuest, a Manhattan-based information provider, and requested a nation-wide Department of Motor Vehicles search for one Rosa May King, born in August of 1958.

'You don't have a D.O.B.?'

'Tyler, if I had a D.O.B. I'd give it to you.'

'King's not exactly an uncommon surname.'

Billy listened to the riffle of keys, her eyes wandering over to the TV where Linda Carey was coming into Bissel's office and sitting down.

'All fifty states?'

'Leave out Hawaii, and Alaska.'

She was watching Linda Carey talk about her health problems when paper started chugging out of the fax.

There were five possible matches. Five driving licenses, complete with grainy photographs. DMV snaps were the worst in the world, especially since they'd gone digital. The Rosa May King licensed in Seattle, D.O.B. 08/11/58 looked Vietnamese, so she scrolled on, and found one that looked promising. She sat looking at it for a while, drawing a cigarette out of the pack with her pretty lips, lighting it, taking a leisurely drag as she picked up the phone.

The DataQuest guy sounded frazzled, like he was having a bad afternoon.

'Can you run a credit check on Rosa May King, D.O.B fourth August 1958. Current address—'

'West Mariposa. You talking about the woman in Phoenix?'

'That's right.'

Now that she was looking at the photograph, Billy thought she could see a vague resemblance to Carey. But maybe that was just wishful thinking.

'You realize that the Fair Credit Reporting Act prohibits –'

'I'm not asking for financials, Tyler. I just want to check the address.'

People didn't always notify DMV of a change of address. Not immediately anyway. But unless they didn't care about their credit score, they always notified creditors. That made the big credit agencies the best source of current addresses. And there was other information on the header too – Social Security number, employer, name of spouse.

'Oh and I need you to pull the details from Vital Records. I need to know where she was born. Who the parents were.'

She went back to watching the tape, not really seeing it now, glancing at the fax in her hand from time to time, scenarios going around and around in her head. In nearly all of them, there was an old woman carrying a suitcase around.

She read the fax as it came chugging through. The hair came up on her arms when she got to the end of the report.

She called Jay at the office.

'Five possible matches. One of them, I like: Rosa May King, born fourth August 1958, Phoenix Arizona. Vital Records lists Linda King as the mother. Linda King . . . Linda Carey? King-Koenig?'

'Uhuh.'

'Father registered as unknown. Rosa May's current address, is in Phoenix. 265 West Mariposa #12. So a condo or apartment. Been at that address two years. Taco Bell manager three years now. About to be forty-five years old. Unmarried.'

She held the fax up to the light. The DMV photograph made Rosa May King look fat.

'I could fly down there,' she said. 'Check the place out. You never know. Maybe she's the one.'

'What's going on, Billy?'

'What?'

'Come on, I can hear it in your voice.'

Billy pushed the cigarette into the side of her mouth.

'I got the credit header. Some other people have been taking an interest in Rosa May. Recently, I mean.'

'Who?'

'There's a Debra Holzer, from a local Toyota dealership. Looks like maybe Rosa May's trying to finance a Corolla, and Holzer ran a check.'

'So?'

'And then there's this other woman.'

She put a flame to the tip of the cigarette drew hard.

'Come on, Billy. Don't mess around.'

Billy blew smoke at the photograph she'd cut out of the magazine and taped to the wall.

'Woman by the name of Ellen Lindz.'

29

Prestige Mailboxes was at Broadway and 32nd, a run-down place with scuffed linoleum on the floor, and a single buzzing strip light for people to find their way to the post office boxes that lined the room. A torn poster advertised services which included an on-premise notary, but as far as Ellen could see it was just numbered boxes and an unmanned Formica-covered counter to the right as you walked in through the battered front door.

She inserted key 731 into the corresponding box. It didn't fit. She jiggled it, got it all the way in. Then turned, and pulled open the metal door. There was an envelope inside.

'Morning.'

Her heart stopped. She turned. There was someone there after all. A red-faced lady with a little dog in her arms. She'd been sitting down behind the counter.

'Anything I can help you with, Miss? Stamps, fax, mail forwarding . . .'

Ellen held up the envelope.

'I'm fine, thanks. Just picking up my mail.'

'Okay, then.'

The woman nodded, smiled, watched her all the way back out to the street.

Thirty minutes later, Ellen was sitting in the kitchen with the envelope on the table in front of her. There was no return address, and the postmark was so badly smeared it was impossible to say when or where it had been mailed. It felt weird to be sitting there with someone else's mail, but she'd called at Perry's apartment that morning and there'd been no answer and she was more than worried about that, and couldn't think of any other way to proceed. Perry had been expecting an important piece of information. Maybe this was it.

She slipped a knife under the flap, and peeled it back.

A copy of a smeared mimeographed report. The by-now familiar HUAC stamp was in the top right hand corner on each page. It started abruptly:

—and entered the Liberty Diner at the corner of Mott and Hester. Benton ordered coffee and a sandwich for Koenig, and they proceeded to discuss the possibility of Koenig producing work for the Egan Gallery show in June of next year. Koenig is extremely knowledgeable about current trends in modern art, particularly non-representational art which he sees as the answer to many of what he perceives to be our society's ills. He talked at length about the Moscow Institute (?) and the work of Constructivists (?) in the Soviet Union and the terrible mistakes being made by Stalin in their regard.

It went on for three closely-typed pages, and was all pretty much in the same vein. A meeting between Koenig and Benton. A discussion about art. It didn't seem very earth shattering. Ellen lifted the hair from the nape of her neck. She had the wrong document. Probably something that had been sent a couple of weeks earlier. She'd go back to the mail receiving agency. She'd keep an eye on box 731.

She was putting the sheets back into the manila envelope when she noticed the handwritten note inside. She held the envelope upside down, shook it, but it wouldn't come out. In the end she had to tug it out with her fingers.

It was a single sheet of paper torn from a spiral bound notebook. There were six words scrawled in shaky cursive handwriting: *Pay particular attention to the date.*

She went back to the report. There was no date. The first page began '—and entered.' There were numbers at the bottom of the pages. The first number was '2'. The first page was missing.

She called Jerry. He picked up the phone on the second ring. She asked if he'd heard back from his brother yet.

'No. But it takes him a quarter of an hour to get a leg in his underpants, so . . . Why?'

'Well, I was wondering if he'd take a look at something else I've got.'

30

Linda Carey sat behind the wheel of the Mercury, coughing weakly, dabbing a Kleenex to her mouth, looking across chain-link fences, and scrubby trees and low-rent suburban nothing at the building where her daughter lived.

265 West Mariposa was a three-story structure standing in the shadow of the 17 freeway. In the Monday morning haze it looked as flimsy as a cracker box. She'd rolled past the front entrance the night before, pulled into one of the badly marked parking bays, and sat there for a couple of minutes, feeling conspicuous, feeling exposed among the pick-ups and the battered economy sedans, before driving off again.

It had taken her three days to drive the four hundred miles from the I-5. She'd picked up the 10 in LA rather than go across open desert, had driven a hundred miles south rather than go anywhere near Joshua Tree. And even then she'd been looking in the mirror the whole journey, and every time she'd pulled into a gas station she'd expected to see him come lurching out of the restroom, that dazed half-frown on his face, a shotgun in his arthritic hands. She didn't know what he might be planning, if he was planning anything at all, but she could see nailing her point-blank with a twelve guage being part of it. He liked the twelve gauge. His idea of winding down at the end of the day was to walk out into the desert and take the heads off a couple of snakes. She flipped down the visor, and squinted into the little vanity mirror, tugging at tufts of hair. Skinny and shorn, she looked like a work camp ghost. They could boil her bones for a bar of soap. That was all she was good for now. She shook her head at the reflection. How she'd stayed with him or put up with their horror-show of a house with its freaky display cabinets and stacked dusty books and moldy papers toppling over every time you tried to open a cupboard door was a mystery to her.

Anyway, armed or not, he was looking for her by now. She'd read about the trouble in New York. She'd read about the gallery owner dying. When she'd seen her picture on the news – they'd been showing it again last night, a picture they'd pulled out of their computers – she'd gone straight into the bathroom, and cut her hair. She'd chopped it short standing over the sink. For years Roy had been telling her to get rid of what he called her 'Jackie Onassis', and now it was done. It had been one of the few things that connected her to the woman she once was. Now she felt sexless. A bag of nerves. Nothing more than that.

It didn't matter now, of course. None of it did. All that mattered was giving the money to Rosa May. Rosa May and her two little girls. That had been a shock. She'd had no idea. And they weren't even babies, had to be at least three and four years old.

After she'd checked out the building, she'd driven over to the mall at Buckeye and 19th Avenue to get something to eat. She'd been sitting in a Taco Bell, wouldn't have recognized Rosa May, but for someone calling out the name. But then, when she'd looked, being discreet about it, naturally, she'd known her straight away. It was the eyes. Not dark like hers but blue like her daddy's, and with his eyebrows too. 'Rosa May' someone called out, and she'd turned and seen this tired-looking, old-looking mother with her two children walking by. One of the staff, a brassy girl with a nose ring, went out to say something – something funny by the way Rosa May had laughed – and she'd been absolutely sure. The father's eyes and the father's laugh. Uncannily, because she had never known her father. She laughed the way he'd laughed that year at the Rio Rancho, before he decided to destroy it all.

She'd read somewhere about a woman who was in a coma for fifty-something years and came around, waking up an old woman, her whole life passed in a dream, and that was what she'd felt like sitting there, the food going cold in her hands. She felt like she'd thrown it all away. On a whim really. Not much more than that. Well she was going to make up for it now.

She tuned out, leaning back, gently grinding her teeth as she got a vision of her Jackie 'O' swirling into the toilet bowl. There had been a moment, just before she'd pushed the flush, when she'd thought about pulling it out again, bagging it up, and keeping it. It had become a habit. There was a room in the house where they kept it all – the nail clippings, and the hair, and the other stuff. It was down there in the dark with the journals and the dossiers, a magnet for rats and mice. He was crazy, of course, a crazy hoarder trapped in the fifties, dreaming of the end of the world.

A plane roared by overhead, jolting her back. She looked around, startled, heart pounding, half-expecting to see him looking in at her. If he was going to show up anywhere, it would be here, and if he was going to show up anytime it would be today. He pretended not to hear when she talked about Rosa May, but he knew when her birthday was, knew it was a time that called for extra vigilance.

She looked at the package on the seat next to her. If you didn't know what it was, you might think a video machine, or a bunch of paperbacks bound together with duct tape. She wondered what Rosa May would say when she opened it. Whatever she said, they'd both be crying, she was sure of that.

She'd seen her leave in the early morning, loading the girls into the back of her beaten up Honda, then climbing in behind the wheel.

There'd been a huge temptation to just get out of the car and say 'hi', to discount fifty years of warnings, to believe that a harmless old woman, a woman with just a few months to live was of no interest to anyone.

Billy in Phoenix

Except for the blue sky hanging over it, the building reminded Billy of the Lafayette Projects in Baltimore. There were the same cement color walls, the same peeling burgundy trim on the windows. Even the people were the same – the colorless single moms with the perms and those lycra leggings, the sullen kids, the scared seniors with the shopping bags.

She was parked in the shade at the back of the parking lot, reading the *New York Times*, and watching a tree shed sticky fluff onto the hood of the pick up. She'd rented the thing in Sun City, picked out something she thought would blend in. The window was down just a little on the passenger side to let the smoke out, and she was drinking coffee to stop herself from crashing – a big temptation after the past few days of running around. She'd flown down on Saturday night, had been on the plane two hours after her conversation with Jay, and since then it had been work, work, work – gaining access to Rosa May's shitty little apartment on Sunday afternoon, putting a wire tap on the junction box at the back of the building, locating the mail boxes, and then setting up her thing with the garbage sacks.

Looking for Ma Carey. That was the deal, had been the deal from the beginning. The client – and Billy figured it had to be the museum, because who else? – wanted the money back. From what she was reading in the press, *Mirror* was staying on the wall despite threats from the Chief Curator to resign. It was playing out just like Bissel had said it would, except, of course, Bissel didn't say the museum would also be trying to recover the money paid to Carey. The fact that the Chief Curator was now, apparently, a missing person, and that Ellen Lindz was taking an interest in Rosa May King didn't change the basic scenario. Billy blew smoke at the paper. She didn't know what to think about Lindz. If she was working for the museum, then who was Jay working for? Of course it was Lindz who had started the ball rolling in the first place. So maybe she felt responsible, maybe she was going it alone. Whatever her reasons, the person she was interested in was Rosa May. And the only reason to be interested in Rosa May was because she might lead to Carey.

Looking for Ma Carey. An old lady with nine million dollars in the bank. Or maybe not in the bank. Maybe under her bed.

Rosa May's apartment had turned out to be a dry well. There were no photographs, or letters or early birthday cards that looked even vaguely promising, and her address book, a horrible desk diary thing in blue vinyl – probably a Christmas gift from the kids, was empty except for a couple of local numbers alphabetized by first name. She'd called them, doing her local government official shtick and heard nothing that sounded even vaguely like the woman who'd walked into Taylor Bissel's gallery. The speed-dialer on Rosa May's telephone was programmed with the same numbers, except for number one which was for a pizza delivery service.

So that had left her listening to the phone, and watching the mail. The problem there was that the mailboxes were in the lobby and people went past all the time. Which was why she'd taken the decision on Sunday night to distribute some garbage sacks. The garbage went into two big Green Tree Garbage Disposal dumpsters by the entrance to the parking lot, with everyone's shit – knotted shopping bags in plastic and paper, old newspapers and magazines, bottles, cans, packaging, chunks of old carpet, different color garbage sacks – everything all mixed up. So, unless she sat there all day, and was lucky enough to actually see Rosa May drop a bag in, there was no way she could know where to look. Also, a stranger hovering around the dumpster was just as suspicious as a stranger hovering around the mailboxes.

So Sunday night she'd taken a clipboard, and gone through the building knocking on doors. At each apartment that opened she'd offered a pack of thirty dark green garbage bags, saying that Green Tree Garbage Disposal was conducting a study in the area, and wanted to see if a new double-seamed garbage sack would cause less spillage when the trucks were unloaded at the plant. She said if the person used the bags for the next seven days, she'd give them another pack for free. At Rosa May King's apartment, she handed over a pack of light green garbage bags with the same story. Rosa May seemed to like the idea that less spillage would lower overall costs.

So far she'd hooked two of the light green bags, one of which offered a torn up bank statement, and a telephone bill. Neither was of any help. But today was Rosa May's birthday, and things could always change.

It was getting really hot now, and she was having trouble keeping her eyes open. She thought about Jay sitting in his nice air conditioned office in Queens and gave a tight little nod. He'd had no hesitation in sending her down to Phoenix, booking the flight and the hotel, paying the doubled up per diem. But if this was all about recovering nine million dollars for the client, there was no reason he shouldn't. He was going to sit up there until she called him with news. That was when he was going to get off his ass. When his bird dog barked.

32

All she had to do was make a phone call. Ellen bit into the silky flesh of an oyster, this thought going around and around in her head, as Leslie Ann, looking withdrawn and disheveled in her burn-spotted black Nehru jacket, watched from the other side of the table. Beyond her head, Manhattan glistened dark as a coal seam under the lowering sky. They were on the deck of the River Café, taking lunch on the prow of a ship that was headed for a storm.

'The *Mirror* sale really broke the ice,' said the man from Sotheby's, a plump, smooth-faced person in his mid-fifties, an expert on post-war art who had been invited to attend what was a very select gathering of museum high-ups and trustees by MAM president Glen Schaeffer, seated today at the head of the table between Lewis Hartnal, pale and tired in an impeccable gray suit, and vice chairman Michael Pauling.

'Until *Mirror* came along I'm not sure the market knew how to price a Koenig. They're so few and far between.'

'How many are going to be in the sale?' said Schaeffer.

'There may be as many as a dozen,' said the Sotheby's man. 'People who have held onto them all these years are being tempted out into the market.'

'Who wouldn't be?' said Hartnal.

There was muttered assent around the table. Leslie Ann cleared her throat, took a sip of wine.

'You're selling, Lewis?'

The questioner, an oriental-looking woman in a dark blue suit who had been something huge in arbitrage in the eighties, gave a bird like twitch to her glossy head.

'Indeed,' said Hartnal, dabbing his napkin to his lips. 'Reluctantly, but yes. I have to think of my family. My sister.'

'There's unprecedented interest in Koenig,' said the auctioneer, hungrily biting into his salad. 'All the excitement at the museum has . . .'

He seemed to become aware of the long faces turned in his direction, and decided to leave the sentence unfinished.

'We would have foregone the excitement,' said Hartnal gloomily.

Thunder rumbled over the city.

'Let's hope it holds off,' said someone to Ellen's left.

'What about you, Leslie Ann?' said the arbitrageur. 'People have been after you to sell for years.'

Leslie Ann shook her head.

'I can't,' she said. 'If I sold my paintings I wouldn't get invited to these lavish lunches anymore.'

There was some polite laughter.

Someone asked what the news was on the Perry front, and Hartnal, looking very bored, set out the official position: it appeared that Bruce Perry had sought to discredit an authentic Koenig. Whatever his reasons, and it had to be admitted that at that point they appeared somewhat obscure, they seemed not to involve a pecuniary interest. For the time being David Kruger was treating it as an internal museum matter. If friends or relatives of Bruce Perry wanted to register him as a missing person, that was another matter, and *their* business.

'But what do you think, Lewis?' said the auctioneer.

Hartnal looked up from his plate, squinting.

'What do I think of what?'

'Of Perry? What do you think he was trying to do?'

'Honestly?' said Hartnal with a sigh. 'I don't know. Attempting to undermine a painting he didn't like?'

'Or didn't trust for some reason,' said Schaeffer.

'Or Ellen,' said Tilda Kraft. She was sitting diagonally opposite, her face partially hidden by a spray of flowers. 'Doesn't that seem more likely?'

Heads turned. Ellen looked down at her plate.

'Well, if that was the reason, thank goodness he didn't succeed,' said Glenn Schaeffer. 'I for one, certainly never doubted the authenticity of Ellen Lindz.'

He raised his glass, and glasses came up all around the table. People were smiling, saying how delighted they were to have her there with them. Ellen raised her own glass, saw flickering lights on the horizon.

'How's your boy doing?' said Tilda Kraft, leaning around the flowers.

'He's away in Los Angeles at the moment,' said Ellen. She had spoken to Ben twice over the weekend. He'd said he wished they lived in California. 'He wants me to go and work at the Getty. He said there's a big white museum on a hill where I could probably get a job.'

Kraft laughed, her surgery-tightened face pulling into odd brackets either side of her blue eyes.

'I hope you're not thinking of leaving us. Especially not now.'

Kraft glanced across at Leslie Ann, making sure she was listening.

'I'm a firm believer that things happen for a reason,' she said. 'This . . . this little convulsion was just what we needed. It's time for a change.'

Leslie Ann inclined her head.

'How do you see the museum post-Perry, Ellen?' said Kraft.

'Post-Perry,' said the arbitrageur, 'I like the sound of that.'

'Can't we just forget Perry,' said Hartnal. 'At least for the time being. How do you see the museum, Ellen?'

Ellen got a flash of Perry standing in the lobby. *In a way you deserve it for being so fucking blind and stupid all these years.* The internet search had come back with a couple of pages on Rosa May King. She was living in Phoenix now. Just a phone call away.

Kraft was frowning at her across the table.

'A white box,' said Ellen. 'A white space.'

'Like a church?' said the arbitrageur.

'What does that make the art?' said Hartnal. 'Reliquaries?'

Ellen shook her head.

'Reliquaries are worshipped for their sanctity. For a kind of magic that's ascribed to them. Like fetishes.'

'That's what I thought about the Marc Quinn piece,' said someone to Ellen's left.

'Self?'

'Yes, Self. I thought it was very close to being a reliquary.'

'You can fetishize the art object.'

'The art object is *always* fetishized.'

People were weighing in from all sides.

'Seeing a cigarette butt trapped in the surface of a Pollock brings a magical charge.'

'But for me,' said Ellen, raising her voice against the tide of talk, 'art, experiencing big art is like being plugged into something. Something I can't normally see. Or sense. Because of my mediocrity.'

You're so fucking stupid.

'Yes,' said Leslie Ann. 'I know exactly what you mean. That's how it always was for me with Koenig.'

'Art lets you see,' said Ellen. 'You come away from it dilated, opened out, turned inside out even. You feel as though you can see into the heart of things.'

'The heart of darkness,' said the arbitrageur.

'Or the heart of light,' said Kraft, her plastic face settling into a deader stillness.

'A state of enlightenment, then.'

'More a state of soul arousal,' said Ellen. 'For me.'

'And *Mirror*?' said the arbitrageur. 'When you first saw it . . . You were what?'

Ellen nodded, frowned.

'Aroused. Yes. Definitely. That's how I knew.'

'Ellen has the eye,' said Leslie Ann.

Everyone around the table was looking at her now.

'Tell them your story, Ellen. Your Harvard story.'

Ellen blushed, and so Leslie Ann took it up, telling them all how her group had once been presented with a series of pre-war bronzes, had been naming the artists, analyzing stylistic characteristics, and then been shown a heavy piece that nobody in the group could recognize.

'They were all really puzzled, coming up with all kinds of interesting theories, including someone saying it was a Picasso. And then the professor handed it to Ellen . . .'

'And she knew,' said Hartnal. 'Knew that it was something industrial. That it had never been meant . . .'

'It was from a cobbler's workshop,' said Leslie Ann. 'A form. Isn't that right, Ellen?'

Ellen nodded, returning Leslie Ann's weary gaze.

'A form. A piece of bronze he'd used when he was repairing the shoes,' she said.

'Nobody knew,' said Leslie Ann. 'But Ellen only had to touch it.'

The rain held off until they'd finished coffee, then came down in an abrupt downpour that drove a smoke off the East River and veiled the Brooklyn Bridge from view. Huddled inside the restaurant lobby, everyone was laughing, clutching at wrists and hands, offering damp clothes to feel, then hugging, kissing. Ellen strained to be responsive, feeling out of it, feeling blank, looking around for Hartnal. They'd shared a limousine coming out to the restaurant, and as far as she knew he was her ride back into town.

'Ellen.'

Up close, Kraft's eyes were much older than her face, milkily rimmed and lusterless. She put hot dry hands on Ellen's cheeks, admiring her as though she were a prize bloom.

'This has all been miserable for you,' she said, cracking her smile, her mouth going a little lopsided. 'But I'm so glad you're not leaving us. The museum needs your eye, Ellen. Now more than ever. I know David thinks so.'

Ellen blushed. Despite herself, despite everything that had happened in the past week, she blushed with pleasure. Kraft pulled her into an embrace that prickled somehow somewhere, then let her go – hands splayed, releasing a dove, the gesture as fake as her face – saying that Ellen must come see her in San Francisco, that a decision would be taken sooner rather than later, and that Ellen should keep up her very good work.

People were moving out through the main entrance in groups of two and three, umbrellas flaring. Ellen watched Kraft cup another face, then felt bony fingers close in the crook of her elbow. Leslie Ann was leaning against her, looking the worse for wear. She'd aged in the past couple of weeks, looked haggard, and a little hunched inside her loose-fitting black clothes. A smell came off her that wasn't good – a mix of sweat and cigarettes, the smell more surprising than anything in her appearance.

'They're going to ask you to stand in for Perry,' she said, slurring her words a little.

'They already did,' said Ellen. 'Lewis asked me on the way out here. It's just a temporary arrangement of course.'

Leslie Ann took a cigarette from her purse, shaking her head.

'No, no. You heard Tilda. It's time for a change. We all . . .' Ellen watched her put a flame to the tip. 'We all think so.'

She snapped her lighter shut and gave Ellen a defiant look.

'It's what you've wanted for a long time,' said Ellen.

Leslie Ann crimped her eyes at that, exhaling smoke.

A dead look came into her eyes.

'I know you have questions about Koenig, Ellen.'

She was holding onto her elbow as though expecting her to bolt. Ellen looked up. The others were running out to the cars, stooped under umbrellas.

Leslie Ann examined her fingernails which looked unhealthily ribbed, mauvish gray against the blue of Ellen's jacket.

'I'm asking you, as a friend, and I hope you still believe I *am* your friend – I'm asking you as a friend . . .'

'What are you asking?'

Leslie Ann blinked, seemed lost for a moment.

'To let me give you my version.'

Ellen looked down and was surprised to see that her legs were splashed with little dabs of grayish mud.

'You feel cheated,' said Leslie Ann. 'I understand that. You want to know why I didn't talk about . . . any of these matters while you were writing your . . .'

'I really don't know what you're talking about.'

Tears came into the old woman's eyes.

'He got to you.' She looked away, dabbing with her sleeve. 'He's lying to you. This is wrong, Ellen. Trusting him. Knowing what he did to you. He is completely and utterly ruthless. He's going to drag us all through the shit now, and for what?'

She took a breath, then pulled on her cigarette.

'All I'm asking is for you to listen to my story. Then . . . well, then you can judge.'

The rain was easing up, but the air stayed cold. Ellen found herself following Leslie Ann to the car, the keys in her hand. There was no way Leslie Ann could drive them back into the city. They were both clear about that.

At the car, Leslie Ann turned.

'I want to go out there.'

She squinted up at her in the fine rain, her old woman's hair showing pale stripes of scalp.

'Where?'

'To Springs,' she said. 'I'd like to see the house.'

33

The windows fogged as soon as she turned on the engine. She tweaked the a/c as they worked their way around to the Brooklyn Queens Expressway, and then they picked up the LIE and headed east. The sky hung low over Brooklyn, with ragged streaks showing silvery white along the horizon. Leslie Ann smoked, slumped against her door, looking out at the sprawl of houses.

She kept saying how much it had all changed since the fifties.

'That night I came out here, it was so *empty,* Ellen. And dark. Not that many street lights even in the towns, and the roads getting worse and worse. Three and a half hours it took. Can you imagine? I mean, it's not much more than a hundred miles.'

She held her hand against her mouth, the cigarette wedged between her middle and ring fingers.

'You were going to tell me your version,' said Ellen.

Sunlight slanted in under the clouds, striking silvery lights off the wet buildings.

'Why are you looking for Rosa May?'

Ellen glanced across. Leslie Ann had her eyes shut against the glare.

'Okay,' she said, exhaling smoke. 'Okay. You want to know the truth. You think Rosa May is going to help you find the truth. I can understand that.'

They drove in silence. It was slow going at first, trucks and cars weaved in and out, trying to make headway.

'Did you ever get to Venice?' said Leslie Ann.

'What?'

'Venice. Did you ever go?'

'Yes.'

'With Greg?'

'Earlier.'

'With Dan, then.'

'Yes.'

They had backpacked around Europe in the summer of '84, before she started her year at art school. He'd been at school in London for a year and was already showing signs of falling apart. Not that she'd seen it at the time. At the time, the craziness was just part of the whole artistic experience. They'd done Amsterdam, then Berlin, then headed south.

'I was there just after the war,' said Leslie Ann. 'With Lewis.'

Ellen checked her rear-view mirror. The sky over Manhattan was black. Ahead of them, the rain pulled streaks in the low cloud.

'Did you know that it's a fake?' said Leslie Ann. 'The city fathers cooked up some documents, forgeries, one in particular – the *Praedestinatio*, where Saint Mark is described having a vision that tells him he'll be buried in San Marco on the Rialto. They inserted this story into the older legends to establish a prehistory of the church.'

It was sedans now, the commercial traffic pretty much behind them. Buildings huddled in clumps, then single houses. A mall. A stretch of muddy-looking agricultural land. Leslie Ann smoked and talked, talking about Venice mostly, how the city had suffered from the lack of a past.

'That was a problem back then,' she said. 'I mean, it still is a problem, of course. It was a huge problem for us after the war. But not to have a past in the Middle Ages was like not having a shadow.

'I remember seeing Saint Mark's in this . . . it was really the most flamboyant Turner dawn. I'd read my Ruskin, of course. I was prepared to have my great religious experience. I was drunk with it. Europe. Not in the way you were with your Dan. We weren't high on anything other than the place itself. This place that we were saving. We'd beaten back the Nazis and now we were holding back the communists.'

She chuckled, looked over at Ellen.

'It's probably hard for you to imagine, how—'

'No, I can imagine.'

Leslie Ann stirred in her seat. Ellen saw cones up ahead, moved across a lane.

'It was Lewis who told me about the *Praedestinatio*. And pointed out the elaborate fakery of the buildings, sections of wall with blind arches where there had never been arches. A fabric that was meant to look ancient from the beginning.'

Ellen glanced over at her.

'Leslie Ann? What does this have to do with Koenig?'

'I'm getting to it.' Leslie Ann sighed, rubbing at her face. 'I met Lewis at Harvard, of course, but we really became friends that summer. The summer of 'forty-seven. Working on the exhibition in Prague. That was how we got to Europe in the first place. The exhibition. "Advancing American Art". It was funded by the State Department. There were seventy or so works – O'Keefe, Gottlieb, Gorky. I don't remember how Lewis and I ended up being invited. Word came around. Some professor taking an interest, I suppose. I remember I jumped at the chance.

'There was an itinerary: Paris, Prague – a clutch of European capitals then Latin America – always Latin America in those days. I was writing pieces for the Partisan Review. I was wiring these pretentious reports about Europe pulling itself out of the ruins of the war, about the Russians staging opera in the rubble.'

She turned in her seat, easing at the belt.

'They did, you know. They staged Gluck's Orpheus at the *Admiralpalast* in Berlin before the city was even cleared of corpses. By the time Lewis and I got there *kulturkampf* was a kind of buzzword.'

'*Kulturkampf*?'

'Culture struggle. With the Marshall Plan we wanted to buy the Europeans' friendship, but Stalin wanted to seduce them with culture. He thought there were converts to be had. The French and Italians were already half way there. They looked down on us. They saw us as gum-chewing morons. Still do, of course.'

They hit another belt of rain coming into Southampton. Ellen slowed to a crawl, listening to Leslie Ann lay it all out: 1947, the Marshall Plan, the National Security Act, the Russians opening the 'House of Culture' on *Unter den Linden*, the government hitting back with the *Amerika-Häuser* – proto-institutes with comfortable reading rooms, film shows, music recitals, talks, art exhibits.

They were close to the sea now, hitting pockets of holiday traffic, RVs that seemed to need the whole of the road. Ellen could smell barbecues through the open window.

'Anyway the exhibition in Prague was part of it all,' said Leslie Ann. 'The *kulturkampf* – our attempt to stake a claim to some high ground. Lewis and I knew nothing about that, of course. For us it was just a rather wonderful exhibition.'

She looked across.

'What?' said Ellen.

'Do you know what happened to that wonderful exhibition?'

Ellen shook her head.

'Congress pulled the plug,' said Leslie Ann. 'They denounced the exhibition as subversive, as un-American. There was this character – Senator Brown, I think it was. He said if there was anyone in Congress who thought that this sort of 'tripe' – he was referring to the paintings of course – that this sort of *tripe* improved foreigners' understanding of American life then they should be sent to the same nuthouse the artists had come from.'

She laughed again, and the laughter became a cough.

'The Prague show was cancelled. They sold off the paintings at a ninety-five percent discount. It was surplus government property, you see. Georgia O'Keefe! Government surplus! I picked up a beautiful little desert landscape for fifty dollars.' She shook her head. 'I don't know what became of that painting . . .'

She cleared her throat, pointed a finger at a sign for East Hampton.

'The State Department issued a directive. No American artist with communist links should be exhibited at government expense. And since most of the New York people – the people of the New York School, as we were starting to call them – had come through the depression and the New Deal pretty much pro-Stalin, if not actual CPA, that was the end of government support for Modern Art. The end.

'But we'd *seen* the exhibition. And without even being aware of the *kulturkampf* thing, we could see the effect it had on the Russians. It was almost funny to watch. They walked around open mouthed, could see something was going on, something important, but their ideology wouldn't let them embrace it. It was like an Islamic fundamentalist looking at Da Vinci's *Virgin of the Rocks*. The Soviets couldn't sell the idea of abstraction to the proletariat. I mean, what was it about? What was it *of*? Like the Nazis, like Hitler I suppose one should say, they considered it degenerate junk. And by then they'd thrown their weight behind Socialist Realism; heroic peasants, harvesting grain, shoveling coal.

'Later on, when I was back in the States, I came to see how much Abstraction was actually about freedom. Coming out of surrealism, out of Jung, automatic writing – all these things that were going to liberate the unconscious, tap into the deepest wells of creativity.

'We came to see, Lewis and I, we both came to see that when Congress pulled that exhibition we lost one of our most powerful weapons. It wasn't until I started working under Frank Wisner that I realized how many people shared that perspective.'

Ellen frowned. She'd read Wisner's name in Perry's papers.

'Wasn't Wisner . . .?'

'He was with something called the OPC. Sorry, the Office of Policy Coordination. In Washington. He ran it. On a shoestring to start with, before the money started to flow. There were some run down buildings near the Capitol. A rambling brick brewery, warehouses. I remember the smell of the place, the sound of the coal barges on the Potomac.'

Ellen turned off the main road just after East Hampton. They were heading north towards Springs now through a flat landscape punctuated here and there by stands of trees.

'This was a government department?' said Ellen, feigning ignorance.

Leslie Ann was peeling varnish from a cuticle.

'In a sense,' she said softly. 'Probably not the sense you mean though.'

Ellen looked at the old woman's face. Then she pulled off the road and drew slowly to a halt. She wound down her window all the way, sucked in a lungful of clean air.

'I'm not sure I follow, Leslie Ann.'

Leslie Ann kept her eyes on the cuticle.

'You don't follow or you don't *want* to follow?'

Ellen looked at the distant horizon.

'I don't really like this game,' she said.

'It's not a game. It's the opposite of a game.' She looked ahead through the windshield. 'I'm not telling you anything that isn't already known,' she said. 'A lot of this came out in the sixties when certain people decided to talk. People have forgotten, that's all. These . . . cultural activities got washed away by all the blood – the Bay of Pigs, Vietnam, El Salvador . . .

'I do understand. Your reaction. Say the fatal initials and immediately everyone is thinking black ops or whatever they call them –

spooks in suits. But back then, back in 1949, the only people wearing suits were the FBI, and they were very suspicious of us. As were the HUAC people, of course. The HUAC people, more so if anything.'

'HUAC?'

'The House Un-American Activities Committee. I'm surprised you've never heard of it.'

'The McCarthy thing.'

Leslie Ann shrugged, gave a nod. She put a hand on Ellen's arm.

'Ellen, this is *me*, remember. Your old friend. And it was me in 1949, a rather idealistic young person with a passion for the arts. Pretty much OPC standard issue in fact. We were all that way – mostly out of Harvard or Yale. A lot of us had spent time in Europe which was, of course, one of the reasons we were distrusted. We were young, liberal, sophisticated, idealistic. We *did* believe in America as a force for good in the world. It was easier to do that back then. We thought the Union of Soviet Socialist Republics was *very* bad news.'

She looked out at the horizon.

'Why have you stopped here?'

Ellen turned the ignition, and pulled back onto the road. A mile further on, she made a right into Old Stone Highway. The land was utterly flat, dotted with houses and scrappy woods. She was looking for the house now. She'd been up here a number of times over the years. The museum financed part of the maintenance costs.

She saw the reconstructed barn first.

She pulled over next to the gate. The house was a stark wooden building, partly hidden by a dip in the ground. A scrappy tree grew against it on the seaward side.

'Shall we get out?' said Leslie Ann.

Ellen turned to look into the old woman's eyes. Leslie Ann looked past her and shook her head.

'Every time I come up here . . .'

Her chin puckered, and trembled and then she was crying. She dabbed at her eyes with a bunched Kleenex.

'I'm sorry. I'm sorry.'

She got out of the car, and went in through the gate. Ellen watched her make her way up to the house. Rain hit the windshield. Three big drops, leaving a dusty trail. The light was going blue. Ellen got out, and stood there for a moment listening to the silence. This was the first thing that hit her whenever she came out here.

She found Leslie Ann opening the front door. It was dark inside the house. Ellen could see appliances, a table. The kitchen. As it would have been the night Koenig killed himself.

'What *were* you doing?' she said. 'In this OPC.'

Leslie Ann turned and looked at her out of the gloom. Her eyes were red from crying.

'Encouraging a point of view. Funding tours in Europe. Orchestras, singers. Exhibitions.'

'Artists.'

Leslie Ann nodded and turned away.

'They didn't know, of course,' she said, 'Pollock, Gorky, Motherwell, de Kooning. There was never any question of complicity.'

She moved on into the house. Ellen crossed the threshold, and stood there blinking in the gloom. The whole house had been restored with Fifties fixtures and appliances. A big Electrolux refrigerator hummed in the corner. She could hear Leslie Ann moving around in the living room, still talking.

'The artist doesn't know what's going on, but he is doing well, better than he might otherwise be doing. He's doing well because he represents a certain world-view.'

Ellen moved into the house, following the woman's voice.

'He can be held up as an example. He is thriving because of the support.'

She found her in the living room, standing by the little window. It was raining again.

'OPC ran a thing called the Congress for Cultural Freedom,' she said. 'It got to be quite big. Funded magazines, held art exhibitions, conferences. Not directly, of course. The money went through foundations. We'd approach some sympathetic millionaire, a credible philanthropist, get him to set up a foundation – the Farfield was one of them; all it required was a signature on a piece of paper, and you were up and running. The black money flowed through the millionaire's account and into the projects. Nobody was any –'

'He found out,' said Ellen.

Leslie Ann fell silent. The only sound was the rain tapping against the glass.

'Koenig found out.'

34

Rosa May King saw the kid push in through the front door, watched him shuffle over to a group of youngsters settled in one of the booths and start handing out the novelty key rings.

'That kid with the dolphins again,' said Stacey Bishop, giving a little shove to her paper hat. Dolphin Boy had been coming in every afternoon at about the same time for the past month, seemed to have decided that the mall was exploitable terrain.

'I feel sorry for him,' said Rosa May.

'Jacob comes on at five. You know what he's going to say.'

Jacob was the other manager, an eager-beaver college graduate who was just passing through on his way up. Jacob treated everyone like shit. He'd threatened to call the cops the last time the kid came in.

The kid was shuffling along the central aisle now, his pants hanging over his sneakers in dirty folds. People turned their backs, pushing the dolphin key rings to the very edge of their tables. A card fell to the floor. An odd high grunting noise came from the back of the boy's throat. If he was faking, he was very good. A card and then a dolphin. Rosa May heard Stacey Bishop say something about Jacob going ballistic, as the kid kept coming, shuffling straight down the center aisle, straight for Rosa May and the cash register, a determined look on his face. He couldn't have been more than twelve years old.

'Maybe he wants to order a taco,' said Stacey Bishop, talking about the kid as though he was deaf as well as dumb.

When he reached the counter, he handed Rosa May a card. It was brown from handling, and creased at the corners. The message looked like it had been hammered out on an old typewriter: **Deaf! Mute!! You help is appreciate!!!** She turned it over, saw something scrawled on the back: *Rosa May. Go to Buckeye and 19th. Use the payphone. Call mom on 625 9898. They're watching you.*

The blood seemed to leave her heart.

Stacey Bishop's voice was buzzing in her ear, saying something about love letters, but Rosa May was watching the dolphin boy now, the boy making his noise, moving away from them, folding a dollar bill into his big vinyl fanny pack. That's where the dolphins lived. The dolphins and the cards.

Someone started yelling. Jacob – arriving just in time for the floorshow, crossing the diner, jabbing a finger at the kid.

'Rosa May?' said Stacey Bishop. 'Are you all right?'

Jacob was trying to steer the dolphin boy towards the door, but the kid wasn't having any, twisting out of his hands, grunting, his face twisted with rage.

'Rosa May?'

Rosa May turned her back on Stacey Bishop, and walked through the back of the diner, through the fire exit and out into the late afternoon sun.

She walked south on 19th Avenue, shaking her head. Then she was at the junction, looking at rush-hour traffic. A jet roared by overhead.

The call boxes were on the other side of the street. She looked at the card in her hand and tried to tell herself that it was just a mistake. Like the words you sometimes saw scribbled on a dollar bill. But her name was there. A number. *Call mom.*

She hadn't seen her mother in thirty years. She'd walked out on her and her step-dad, in the fall of '73, leaving an eight-page letter, explaining about boys and why you couldn't trust them, and how it was important to have dreams, and two hundred dollars in wrinkled bills, her tips for the week. That was it. At the time, she'd felt more shocked than abandoned. She'd always been closer to Vern anyway, and her relationship with her mother had been conflictual at best, full of distrust and rivalry. She remembered her as a dreamy vain person with a dark side that occasionally swallowed her up altogether like with the new moon. Vern was the solid one, the generous one, and of course he was the one who'd taken her leaving the hardest. In fact her most vivid memory of that time was trying to keep Vern from giving up his job and hitting the bottle. He'd driven all over the state trying to find out who'd stolen his love away, but all he could learn was that Linda had been seeing a guy called Roy, some truck driver or similar transient type; not someone from around there anyway.

Six years later, she'd gotten another letter. In this one, posted from Portland, Oregon, her mom apologized for running out like she did, said that she thought about her all the time, and that it was impossible for her to be in touch because her husband had been part of the investigation into the Jimmy Hoffa embezzlement case, and was now in the witness protection program, which meant cutting all ties with the past. This information had neither convinced nor surprised her; her mother couldn't just run off with a guy who had taken her fancy; there had to be a whole drama attached. On top of everything else, having rambled on for three pages about the need for secrecy, she'd enclosed a photograph of herself with her arm around her beau, a handsome middle-aged man with wide set blue eyes.

Another plane swooped in. Sometimes they came in so low it was like they were going to land on the street. In the deafening roar, and the rush of cindery air, she squinted at the handwriting. It was shakier than she remembered it. *They're watching you.* The tone was familiar though. Nutso drama queen. Like the business with the dolphin kid.

Giving him some money maybe to hand her the card so that no one would know she was being contacted? She shook her head. It was elaborate, but kind of slick too. Rosa May looked at the payphones on the other side of the streaming traffic. It was just after five. She needed to get over to Mary Beth's place to collect the girls. But here was her mother back from outer space. Waiting for a call.

She crossed the street. Punched the number, the phone pressed tight against her ear.

'Hello?'

An old woman's voice.

'Rosa May?'

She had to block her ear against the traffic noise.

'Mom?'

There was a gasp at the other end.

'Oh my baby. My birthday girl.'

The voice went hoarse, and then she was sobbing.

'Mom, I've only got a couple of quarters.'

'My baby,' she gasped. 'My sweet girl. I'm so sorry.'

'Sorry for what?' said Rosa May, sounding colder than she'd meant to. Maybe it was her tone, but her mom got a grip then. She said she wanted to meet. She wanted to meet the girls too, her grandchildren.

'So, come over,' said Rosa May. 'Come to the apartment.'

'I can't.'

'Why not?'

'It's not safe.'

Rosa May shook her head.

'Because of the teamster thing?'

'It probably seems crazy.'

'Kinda.'

'I know. I know that. But . . . Listen, I have a plan.'

'Good.'

'You drop the girls at a friend's, right?'

She'd been spying on her. Rosa May looked down, realized she was still wearing her uniform.

'Mary Beth's, yeah. She takes the girls during the vacation.'

'I'm a block from there.'

'Have you been following me around?'

'I have to be real careful, Rosa May.'

'Okay. If you say so.'

'Call your friend. Mary Beth. Tell her I'm coming over. I think, if they're watching, they're watching you, not the kids. Give me ten minutes. I'll be waiting at Mary Beth's when you arrive.'

Rosa May hung up the phone, then punched in the new number.

Twenty minutes later she was pulling up in front of Mary Beth's little bungalow on Sycamore Street. Chain link face surrounded a patch of parched grass at the front. The kids played at the back, Mary Beth's own, and a handful of others. The twenty dollars a day cut into her pay check, but it meant she could keep her job through the summer.

She got out of the car and scanned the parked cars for any sign of out-of-state licenses. She didn't see any, but when Mary Beth opened the door, she knew her mother had arrived.

'She's out back,' said Mary Beth, making big eyes.

Rosa May said it was too long a story to get into right there and went through to the kitchen then out the back door, her heart fluttering under her ribs because it was her mom, after all, crazy or not.

All the other kids had gone home. Her own babies were sitting on a plastic slide, talking to an old woman who had taken a seat on a lawn chair. The girls looked relieved when they saw her, and came running into her arms.

The old woman stood up. She looked like she was dying. She looked like she cut her own hair.

'Rosa May?'

The tears seemed to well out of nowhere. Then they were both crying, awkwardly holding each other while the children, watching her for some sort of clue how to behave, pushed at the parched lawn with their scuffed toes. Rosa May detached herself and knelt down.

'Girls. This is your grandma. Grandma Carey.'

She didn't want to leave the house, said it was too dangerous for them to leave together. So they sat in the backyard talking, while Mary Beth made the kids Pop Tarts in the kitchen. It wasn't easy. It wasn't even very warm. Rosa May could see that her mom was disappointed, could see that she had probably envisioned a reunion full of smiles and forgiveness. But she couldn't help that. They were strangers. That was the truth of it, they hadn't even touched since that first uneasy embrace. And there wasn't much to say until her mom got going about the witness protection program, and how hard it had been all these years. Rosa May did her best to look like she believed it.

They fell silent. The TV was on in the house. Rosa May could hear Mary Beth talking.

'So, why now?' she said. 'Why show up after all this time?'

She watched her mom dab her nose with a Kleenex.

'There's something I wanted to give you,' she said. 'It's in the house.'

Rosa May watched her get to her feet and go in through the kitchen door. Karen appeared at the living room window, and mouthed something like 'I wanna go home'.

The old woman reappeared, carrying a package. Rosa May looked back at the living room window, but Karen had disappeared. TV light flickered on an orange wall.

'Happy birthday.'

Rosa May said she shouldn't have, and took the gift from her. It was heavier than she'd expected, and flexed a little in her hands. It felt like books tied together in a package. The ribbon was wrong for the paper. Rosa May eased it off, then put a finger under a flaps and peeled away the tape.

Money.

'Shit.'

For a second she thought she was going to faint. She took a step back on rubbery legs, then put the package down on a lawn chair.

'You don't have to be afraid,' said her mother. 'It's all legal. And you don't have to tell anyone about it. I mean, probably you should. There's probably rules about gifts. But I don't know what they are, and I don't see why you should give any of it to the government.'

Rosa May opened her mouth but nothing came out.

'There's two million dollars,' said her mom.

Rosa May brought her hands up to her face.

'Mom. What did you do? What have you done?'

'There's more, but I wanted to give it you in a package. Like a nice gift. To make up for being such a bad mother.'

Rosa May realized that she was trembling. She looked at her hands. They were shaking.

'Where did you get it?'

'I sold a picture.'

35

It was getting late. Ellen stood at the window, watching the rain hit the dusty glass, listening to Leslie Ann's ruined voice. She was sitting in the armchair, a massive thing with busted springs, the dusty velour smeared with the orange and black paint of Koenig's last canvases. There was paint on the walls too, smeary fingermarks at waist height. The museum had gone to a lot of trouble to reproduce the interior as it had been when Koenig lived there. The effect was beyond eerie, especially with the light fading outside, and the ticking creaks of the old timbers cooling after the day's heat.

Leslie Ann was talking about the first time she'd met him, the words coming in a cracked monotone. Ellen had heard the story so often, she could anticipate every pause, every catch in the old woman's breath as the memories flowed through her.

'You've seen the photographs, but you had to see him . . . I don't know, talking, frowning. Smiling. He was living in the Bowery. This terrible one-room apartment. I'd met him at the Cedar Tavern, had seen him talking with the others. He was very funny and clever, but so serious at the same time. They loved him. Even before he was anyone. Before he was recognized. He'd sit in a booth with them, jammed in between Reinhardt and Gorky, sit there in this terrible coat, perfectly comfortable in their company. So angular, and starved looking. I mean, he really *looked* the part. I think the others, even a wild man like Pollock, felt almost bourgeois around him. Soft. "Franklin doesn't give a shit." That was the phrase you'd hear all the time. "Franklin could sleep in the gutter. Franklin could eat out of garbage cans."

'They had heat in their lofts. They weren't exactly comfortable, but there was always a corner with a kerosene stove. Somewhere you could huddle. Koenig had nothing. He was like John the Baptist. Clear-eyed. Clean-eyed. John the Baptist in a herringbone overcoat.'

The rain hit the window with a soft dabbing sound. Beyond the glass, the mud flats stretched towards an evening horizon that blurred sea and sky. Ellen turned to face the room. Leslie Ann was sitting forward in the chair, a Kleenex held to her mouth, staring straight ahead of her, lost in thought.

'He had very little money. Then, when the Federal Arts Project was disbanded, he had nothing. He was doing these menial jobs. Washing dishes, mopping floors, just to eat. Just for a meal. He couldn't afford paint or canvas. I remember the first time I went over to his place. There was this terrible stink in the room. He had these big cans of ink he'd pilfered from a printer's workshop on Houston. He was making prints. Woodcuts. He'd find scraps of wood in the street; the sides of packing cases, chunks he'd pulled off billboards, table tops. Anything. Whatever he could find. And he was carving them with a penknife then inking them, laying over a sheet of paper. Wallpaper. The paper the butcher used to wrap the roast. Newsprint – ends of rolls. He'd lay another piece of wood on top and put the whole thing under a leg of the bed. This great iron bed. It was high, the way beds were back then. But, jacked up on these printing blocks, it came up to my chest. When I first saw it, I burst out laughing. But then he showed me one of his prints . . .'

Ellen watched her put the Kleenex to her eyes.

'There's something I don't understand.'

Leslie Ann gazed up at her.

'Why Koenig?' said Ellen. 'You picked him out. He seemed . . . what?'

Leslie Ann was shaking her head.

'Don't try to . . .' She blew her nose. 'You want to make it seem cold, some terrible calculated act.'

'Wasn't it?'

'No. He was remarkable, Ellen. A great painter. I—'

'I *know* that version,' said Ellen, unable to keep the anger out of her voice. 'I helped *write* that version. What I'm trying to establish is what made him a suitable . . . what's the word I'm looking for here? A suitable *target*.'

Leslie Ann contemplated her Kleenex for a moment.

'You feel betrayed, Ellen. I understand that.'

'Duped more than betrayed,' she said, looking out at the muddy fields. 'You encouraged me to write the book, Leslie Ann. You picked me out the same way—'

'Don't even *think* that,' said Leslie Ann stiffening in the chair. 'That is *un*true, and *un*fair.'

There was a creak of boards overhead. Ellen looked up.

'It's just the house,' said Leslie Ann. She looked around at the gloomy interior. 'Just this house.'

She settled in the chair, sighed.

'It was time. That's all. Time to tell the story, and I thought, I knew, that you were the right person to tell it.'

'Because I had a thing about suicides.'

Leslie Ann was gazing at the crumpled Kleenex in her hand.

'Cynicism really isn't your forte,' she said sadly. 'I know how important Dan was for you. I know what a loss that was.'

Tears came into Ellen's eyes. She fixed her gaze on the distant horizon, determined not to cry. It was true, of course. She had never replaced him. Never been able to fill the gap he left.

'And I know you feel guilty about it,' said Leslie Ann.

'You know because I told you.'

'You think you let him fall.'

Ellen leaned forward until her head was touching the glass.

'I did.'

She'd told him he was no good. It was that simple. That childish. She'd wanted to break free of him that was all. His craziness. His extremes. The demands he made of her. So they'd got into the argument on the phone, and he'd said she was headed for mediocrity and babies, and she'd wanted to hurt him, and told him it was the life he loved not the art, and that was why his painting was no good and never had been. He didn't live through the work, didn't even know how to. He'd killed himself a couple of hours later.

Leslie Ann touched her on the arm, making her start.

'That was why I came to you,' she said. 'Because you know how it feels. And the story you told – it's the truth. Franklin, he really was the great artist you described. He didn't *know*. That's what you have to remember.'

'That's not quite true, Leslie Ann. He knew. In the end.'

The old woman put the Kleenex to her mouth.

'In the end,' she gasped. 'Yes. And that's something I have to live with. That's something I've had to live with every day since . . .' She shook her head, swallowed, her eyes streaming. 'But his . . . struggle was his struggle. The paintings are the true record of that.'

Thunder rumbled out to sea.

'You still haven't answered my question,' said Ellen.

Leslie Ann looked out at the flickering storm, and shook her head.

'It's so stupid,' she said. 'It was such a stupid idea.'

She walked away, walked through to the kitchen.

Ellen followed, found her sitting at the scrubbed wooden table.

'It was Wisner. It was OPC. There was so much money after 'forty-nine. Too much. So there were no budgetary constraints. The whole operation was based around projects. That was how you were judged. Projects.'

Ellen sat down at the table.

'Koenig was a project?'

Leslie Ann found her cigarettes. Lit one. Batted away smoke. It was so dark in the kitchen, Ellen could barely see her face.

'Even within the OPC there were critics of what we were trying to do with Abstract Expressionism. The general thrust of the thing was understood, but the Tenth Street people – they were mostly pro-communist. And they were nearly all drunks. Some of them, like Pollock, crazy drunks. So we were channeling money through the foundations, promoting people like Pollock who, for all his talk of the great outdoors and American West, his belief in the possibility of a purely American art, could at any moment have started ranting about the working man being ground under the wheels of capitalism.'

She drew on her cigarette, tore a thin strip of Kleenex.

'It was an issue of control. When Shostakovich stood up and spoke for communism at the Waldorf Astoria, this was in 'forty-nine, he did it knowing that Stalin was listening, and he was *terrified*.' She glanced up at Ellen, and gave her an emphatic nod. 'I was there. I saw it. The poor man was in a muck sweat. At OPC we couldn't exert that kind of pressure.'

'Thank God.'

Leslie Ann inclined her head.

'Sure. But there were people within OPC, Lewis was one of them, who wanted at least some control. Like the control we had at some of the magazines we funded. But what were we going to do? Have a quiet word with Motherwell? Slip Ad Reinhardt a few dollars to toe the party line. Tell Pollock we'd show his work in Paris, publish a glossy catalog, write puff pieces in the specialist press, get him on the cover of *Life*, if he'd just drop his left wing bullshit?'

She was shaking her head.

'Of course not. It would have backfired.

'When I first met Koenig, he was just coming to terms with Stalin the monster. He'd been active in a union, then a member of the Communist Party of America for a while, but he was so shocked by the news coming out of Russia that he . . . He lost faith. Changed tack. It didn't take him that long to equate the Communists with the Nazis. And like I said before, he was popular, eloquent. Well read. Charismatic.'

'A perfect advocate.'

Leslie Ann looked up sharply.

'And a wonderful painter,' she said, setting her jaw.

'But it was his politics you really liked?' Ellen shook her head. It was almost funny. 'You picked him out, and you groomed him. You wrote the piece in the Partisan Review. But . . . he was only one guy in a crowd of commie drunks.'

Leslie Ann nodded, finishing her cigarette.

'He changed the atmosphere. Pollock's position on an American art derived in some way from American-ness, our landscape, our native people. That was all very close to what Franklin thought. "Fuck Picasso" was also very Franklin.'

'So your project was a success.'

Leslie Ann looked down at her empty hands. The Kleenex was confetti now.

'It got the attention of a lot of people. And . . . meanwhile Franklin was growing in confidence, painting wonderful things, and so committed, so vibrant—'

'And then one day you told him he'd be nothing without OPC backing.'

It came out harsher than she'd meant it to.

Ellen bit her tongue, watched the old woman cover her face with her gnarled hands.

'He changed,' she said, crying a little now. 'His reputation grew. He became impossible, totally self-absorbed. They were all like that, of course. I mean they didn't call them 'the irascibles' for nothing. He wouldn't work. He refused to show in exhibitions where he couldn't control the lighting. Or where there were painters he didn't respect. I tried to nudge him along, to encourage him.'

'You needed the work. OPC wanted him on the team.'

'It was hard. Hard for me. I mean I really couldn't understand how he could sit and stare at a canvas all day, and not make a single mark. Not avoiding work, but not doing any either. Just sitting there staring. In a kind of agony. It drove me crazy.'

She looked up at Ellen, eyes glittering in the near darkness.

'This one time . . . I suppose I was out of control,' she said softly. 'I see that now. I was too involved.'

'What did you do?'

'I told him,' she said simply. Then she got to her feet, and walked out of the kitchen. Ellen stayed put. She could hear sobbing. A faucet opened, setting up a knocking in the pipes. Then Leslie Ann reappeared. Her face wet, moisture glistening in the seams and folds.

'It wasn't like Johns or Warhol or Lichtenstein. These men weren't hip, or ironic. They had no distance. None. They thought they were . . . plunging their hand into the bowels of art. They thought they were prophets if not the actual Messiah. When Pollock said "I *am* nature" he was saying, at least in part, "I *am* God". And at the same time, at the *same time*, they were so fragile, stuck up on their crosses feeling forsaken. Rothko, this . . . this *giant* who wanted his work displayed in a chapel, was terrified of his mother's judgment because he felt he was a fraud. And Franklin was no different. On a knife edge every day. So when I told him that the whole enterprise was . . . *funded* by us . . .'

She shook her head, her face twisting in anguish.

'I tried to . . . I talked about patronage, how – how patronage has always been tainted by political-interest, by self-interest. That Velazquez was still Velazquez despite the Hapsburgs, but he went down. Before my eyes, Ellen. Before my eyes. He was out here by then.' She looked around at the kitchen, eyes streaming. 'It was just him and the painting.'

'And the painting was just propaganda.'

Ellen closed her eyes. She felt sick.

'This is what Perry wants to expose,' said Leslie Ann.

Ellen opened her eyes. Leslie Ann came and sat down. She blew her nose again, fumbled for another cigarette.

'That's what happened here,' she said. 'I think. He found something out, or he was *fed* something and now he wants to expose the whole thing.'

Ellen shook her head.

'Ellen?'

Leslie Ann was looking at her.

'Did he say something to you about this?'

Ellen shook her head.

Leslie Ann looked away, lit a cigarette with a trembling hand.

'He wants to drag Franklin through the mud. He wants to make us look, like, Machiavellian—' She sighed. 'When all we were doing—'

'What? What were you doing?'

'Trying to defend ourselves. Trying to—'

'Make the world safe for democracy.'

Leslie Ann glared, her face rigid in defiance.

'And whatever *we* were doing, Franklin was no part of it. He lived his life, lived his work *believing*. Struggling to believe. Like Pollock. Like Rothko. But Perry doesn't care about any of that. All he cares about is his personal . . .' She made a disgusted sound, shook her head. 'They were different times, Ellen. What we did, we did for the best reasons, or at least . . . At least that's how it seemed at the time. And . . .' She covered her face with a hand, rocking back and forth in the chair. 'And it's been hard. God. All these years, to carry this thing with me . . .'

'You say Perry was fed something? Fed by whom?'

She took her hand away, and was quiet for a moment.

'Franklin talked, Ellen. I mean, probably, he talked. That's what he threatened me with. He was going to expose the whole thing. I don't know who he talked to. If he talked to anyone. So . . . And there were people watching. People who knew. People who wanted to trip us up. FBI. HUAC.'

'The man in the gray hat.'

Leslie Ann shrugged.

'I'm assuming there's something on record. Something Perry got hold of.'

'Why?' said Ellen. 'Why would the FBI . . .?'

'They hated us from the beginning. We were Ivy League. Europhile sophisticates. We were channeling money to people they considered commie-loving degenerates. Hoover hated them. McCarthy hated them.'

Ellen thought about it, got a little frisson of cold unease.

'Leslie Ann?'

The old woman looked up. They were in the dark now.

'He did kill himself, right? Koenig? That's what happened?'

Leslie Ann grabbed herself tightly across the shoulders, held herself like that for a moment.

'Leslie Ann?'

'He called me,' she said. 'He said . . . he said he'd hurt his hand.'

'But the stakes were so high. For you. For the people you were with. If any of this had come out at the time . . . In the middle of it all. The Cold War.'

Leslie Ann was looking at her hands now, her mouth set in a grim line. She'd obviously considered this possibility herself.

'When I got there he was dead. That's all I know.'

Ellen stood up, and put on the light. Leslie Ann squinted up at her, a pleading look in her eyes.

'Ellen. Whatever the right and wrong of all that . . . of what happened, you have to believe me when I say that all I wanted was to preserve his memory. That's why I've kept these things from you. These secrets.'

'And now they're coming out.'

'That's right. They're coming out. They're coming out anyway.'

36

Billy saw the Mercury roll in next to the Honda, saw the old woman get out. Couldn't believe it. She dropped her cigarette, down between her feet, plunged for it, came back up just as the woman was going into the building.

She fumbled for her phone, hit one on the speed-dialer.

Jay sounded like he'd been waiting for the call.

'You're not going to believe this,' said Billy. 'Linda Carey just walked into the building.'

'You sure?'

'Carey. She just pulled up in a car, and got out. She cut her hair, but I recognize her from the tape.'

'Shit.'

'What do you want me to do?'

'Stay put.' Jay's voice went tight with adrenaline. 'Stay where you are.'

'She came in with Rosa May and the kids. Just walked in. They all went into the building. What do I do?'

'Okay, okay . . . Don't approach her. Okay? She is not to be approached.' He sounded like he was walking around in circles. 'She . . . what she just rolled up? Is she in a car – what?'

'I just told you, Jay. Mercury Sable. Followed Rosa May into the building.'

'Get the license plate.'

'I already did.'

She read what was scrawled on her notepad.

'Okay.' Jay cleared his throat. 'Look, sit tight. Don't move unless I say so.'

The line went dead.

Billy stared ahead through the windshield, picturing Jay calling the client now, getting instructions. His brief had been to locate Carey. Nothing more than that. Either that or he was getting things set up for phase two. He'd used her to find Carey and now someone else would be brought in. Someone else or maybe Jay himself. Billy hunkered down in her seat, scowling, put a flame to the dead cigarette, sucked smoke.

Using her like a bird dog. Getting her to do all the work. Letting her take the risks.

The Mercury. A new-looking car under a week's worth of crud. Billy checked her watch. It was taking too long. She finished her cigarette, then sat up straight, punched numbers on her cell. Someone picked up at the other end.

'Tyler? Me. I need you to check a license plate.'

She gave him what she had, then killed the signal, sat there, chewing at her fingernails, the idea of the money like a dull ache in her head. Nine million dollars. She knew exactly what it looked like. After a successful bust, they'd always stack money at ATF. Take photographs for the press. Ill-gotten gains.

A senior came out of the building, wobbled over to the dumpster and tossed in a double seamed garbage bag.

The phone buzzed under her hand.

'It's a rental,' said Tyler. 'Budget. Out of San Francisco airport. Lady called Pauline Brook picked it up July fourteenth. Paid cash. Her driving license gives an address in Tucson, Arizona. You want it?'

Billy scribbled notes.

'Put it on my tab,' she said, and killed the signal.

So now she had a false address. False name, false address. It had to be. Carey probably had fake ID out the ass. Someone with backers. Someone with a team.

She fixed on the car again, chewing raw skin. It was fucked up. This old woman. A person who, going by the past few weeks knew all about invisibility. This person goes to see her daughter on her birthday. Did she *want* to get caught? She didn't care. That was the thing. She was dying so she thought, what the hell? Billy could see it. Could see her selling her painting, then going to see her girl with a present. It was easy to see. It was a story she could easily get behind. The cell buzzed again.

Jay spent the next two minutes telling her what she already knew.

'Tucson's gonna be a fake address,' she said.

'I'm checking it out. Meanwhile, I want you to stay close. Can you put a unit on the car?'

He meant a GPS receiver. Jay loved GPS.

'Broad daylight here, Jay. People coming in and out. Later on, maybe. So, is that the deal? I tail her?'

'If she moves, you stay with.'

'Why?'

'What?'

'Come on, Jay. What does the client want? I mean, do you even know? Because I'm not grabbing anyone off the street. We understand that, right?'

'Who said anything about grabbing anyone?'

'Just don't put me in that situation.'

'I'm not putting you in any situation. This is about surveillance now. You stay close to Carey. You call me if she moves.'

The line went dead.

Billy dropped the phone into her pocket, and went back to staring at the car. Jay didn't know what was going down. That was her feeling. He'd been asked to locate Carey, period. The client was probably making other arrangements to collect. If that was what this was about. Some other dick was going to swoop in on a Kawasaki and take the prize. She did all the hard work, and then someone else flew in. Unless Jay was lying to her.

In her mind's eye, she saw him on the phone right now, booking a flight down to Phoenix. It made her face go hot, just thinking about it.

'Fuck this.'

She got out of the truck and strolled over to the Mercury. There was something on the back seat. The old woman had draped a jacket over what looked like a suitcase. That meant there was something else in the trunk. Because if you had room in the trunk you didn't use the back seat, right? Not unless you were stupid.

Another car was turning in off the road.

She went back to the truck.

She scrolled through her address book, breathing light and fast, jazzed now, pumped, ready to roll. She punched a number. An elderly man picked up.

'Sammy.'

'Who's this?'

'Who do you think?'

'Billy, you son of a bitch.'

'Daughter of a bitch, actually, but yeah.'

Samuel Bass was a retired repo man, who Billy had known since her ATF days. He was based in New Jersey now where he did some security consultancy, and grew roses in his front garden. They hadn't talked in a year. Billy promised to go see him next time she was on the turnpike.

'Sam, I need a favor. I'm locked out of my car.'

'What is it?'

'A late model Sable.'

'Yeah, right.'

'Okay, it's not exactly my car.'

'Mercury. Messenger of the gods. Protector of thieves and merchants.'

'Is that right?'

'You're out there in the dark, doing your work.'

'You miss it.'

'I won't lie to you. What are you carrying?'

'A "Z" and a slim jim.'

'Let me have a look at the book.'

He went away to check the Vehicle Index Guide while Billy reached over the back seat for a battered vinyl case. It contained a couple of old fly fishing rods, and a three foot tempered steel rod bent at each end in a series of right angles.

Sam came back on the line.

'Okay Mercury . . . Sable. Forget the slim jim. Hard pawl key cylinder. Secondary lock won't move without the key. The door cavities are guarded on the later models, but there's a one inch linkage exposure at the front passenger door latch. Put a wedge in about ten inches from the button, and use the Z.'

'What about the alarm?'

'I usually divert the guards with an explosion.'

'Sammy.'

'Get under the hood. Disconnect the battery. What can I tell ya?'

Billy thanked him, and rang off. A big Ford truck rolled past. Billy grabbed a couple of wedges, and looked up at the sky. In another hour it would be dark.

Rosa May walked Linda Carey over to the couch and sat her down. Carey pushed back into the cushions, trying to shrug it off, saying it was nothing. She'd collapsed in the entrance, scaring the hell out of Rosa May and the kids. She'd scared herself too. It was as if all the tension of the last few months had been holding her upright, and that now that she'd done what she had to, she could finally relax, go with the flow, die.

Rosa May held a glass of water to her lips.

'Drink.'

Carey did as she was told, did her best to smile.

'I'm getting old,' she said.

The girls were watching her from the other side of the room. Shelly, the younger of the two, was trying not to cry. It was Shelly who had convinced her to come back home with them. She had wanted to show her a picture she'd painted at school. She was good at art. Had a real talent for it, apparently. She had her grandfather's eyes too. Wide set, blue-gray. Rosa May had started to explain why grandma Carey couldn't come home with them, when Carey had put a hand on her arm. 'It's okay,' she'd said. And it had been like breaking a spell. She'd said it was okay, and suddenly it was okay. There was no one outside Mary Beth's house. Not Roy nor anyone else. Or even if there were, it didn't matter, because she was dying anyway, and she had given her daughter the birthday present, and they could all go to hell.

Carey closed her eyes at the touch of her daughter's hand on her forehead. There was a smell in Rosa May's clothes. Taco Bell. That was over now. Grubbing for money in a fast food outlet. Her baby could move out of the apartment, buy a house somewhere, get the kids into a good school.

Shelly ran out of the room, followed by her elder sister.

'Mom?'

Carey opened her eyes, focused on Rosa May's face.

'Mom, you're not sick are you?'

Carey gave a nod.

'It's nothing serious.'

Rosa May pressed her lips into a line. There was a lifetime of lines on her face. A life Carey knew almost nothing about. The girls were laughing in the bedroom. There was a sound of scuffling feet.

'What's this?' said Rosa May.

She had found the dressing in the crook of Carey's left elbow. The place was sensitive to the touch, inflamed, certainly infected.

'I had to give some blood,' she said.

'It shouldn't hurt you.'

'It doesn't, not really.'

'Are you sure you don't want me to—'

Carey put a hand on her daughter's hand, smiled into her eyes.

'The painting,' she said. 'The one I sold. Your father did it. It's important you should know that. Important that you understand this money is yours.'

Rosa May was shaking her head.

'His name was Franklin Koenig,' said Carey. 'He died a long time ago.'

The girls came back into the living room. Shelly was holding up a picture of a house.

Billy sat in the dark, watching the residents return. Then it was quiet for a long time. TV light flickered in the windows, people tuning into fantasies of other lives. Billy allowed herself a moment's contempt, then realized she was no different. She spent most of her time dreaming about the other life, the one she *should* be living. The only difference between her and them was that she had reached out for it once, had tried to touch it. And that was why she was sitting there in the dark on her own instead of having fun somewhere. And things weren't going to change unless she tried to touch it again.

She reached for another cigarette. The pack was empty. She cursed under her breath and fumbled in her pockets for some nicotine gum. No luck there either. There was no question of leaving, though. She just had to sit it out. And for all she knew Carey was going to stay the night. A car rolled past, rap music thumping. The headlights swept over the Mercury.

God of thieves and merchants.

She opened the door.

The air was full of frying smells. Behind her, the freeway was a steady rush. TV light twitched and flickered, the muffled sounds of news anchors mingling with the thump of the rap. The rap stopped. Billy heard a car door close, watched a gangly kid lope into the building.

She made sure the .38 was under her T-shirt, then walked across to the car and took another look, squatting down on the passenger side. She stayed like that for a long time, staring at the grit between her boots. She had to know. That was what it came down to. She had to take a look in the car. Either in the car or in back. In the trunk. If there was nine million dollars in there, she wanted it. She wanted it and Jay could go fuck himself in the ear, and so could the client because she'd be gone. Out of there. Out of the country. People could hunt *her* for a change. She couldn't see the downside. If there was nothing in the trunk, all she'd have done was trip the alarm, and car alarms went off all the time. She'd get back into the truck and eventually Carey would come down to look at the car, or the local PD would swing by or whatever, and she'd be in the pick-up, watching the show, and no worse off than when she'd started. Except that she'd know. Pop the trunk or take a look at whatever that was on the back seat.

She decided on the back seat.

She put the first wedge into the weather stripping at the bottom of the window about ten inches from the vertical lock button. Then she took the Z-Tool and worked the small end down into the cavity, her eyes on the button behind the glass.

Carey helped Rosa May get the girls into their pjs. Karen had the top bunk, up there with her ice-skating posters, and cuddly toys; Shelly was at the bottom with her paintings. She really did have a thing about art, seemed to have adopted it in some way, made it part of her personality. Carey sat at the foot of Shelly's bed for a long time, not wanting to leave now that she'd found them. But eventually Shelly fell asleep, and so did Karen, and it was over.

They left the bedroom door ajar, so that a little light could spill through. Rosa May wanted her to stay, but Carey said she needed to get back to the motel. Her stuff was there, her clothes, her medication.

'What are you taking?'

Carey dismissed it with a flip of her hand.

'Nothing special. Just old timer pills.' She held her daughter close. 'We'll talk tomorrow. We'll have breakfast together.'

'Are you sure you're okay to drive?'

Carey gave a nod.

'Sure I'm sure. It's only a couple of miles.'

'I'll walk you down to the car.'

Carey leaned in close.

'You've hidden it, right?'

Rosa May gave a nod, and something in her face made Carey frown.

'That money is yours, Rosa May. Tomorrow I'll bring more.'

'No.'

'What?'

'Please. No. It scares me.'

Carey patted her on the arm.

'Sleep on it. Tomorrow we'll talk some more.'

Rosa May opened the front door.

Billy backed up a little, then went in again, and this time she felt the vertical linkage, could see the button moving on the other side of the glass. She tweaked the Z-Tool counter clockwise, a quarter turn, and it felt solid. It felt right. She went through what was going to happen next in her head: open the door, grab the case. She took a breath, gripped the shaft of the tool, twisted the handle upwards, at the same time levering up the lock button.

There was an ear-splitting *WHOOOP!* as the headlights started flashing. Then she was inside the car, grabbing for the case. She came back out with it clutched against her, saw Rosa May. Standing there in the flashing light. Rosa May and her mom. No more than three feet away. The gun was pure instinct. Billy had it out in front of her before she could even think. Rosa May put her hands up, staggered backwards, her mouth snapping wide open.

'Get in the car!'

Rosa May kept backing away. Billy brought the gun up. 'Get in the fucking car.'

Rosa May, staggered, turned, ran. Billy pulled the trigger.

Carey was up against her, her screams lost in the whooping of the alarm. Billy fell sideways, saw Rosa May crumple, and go down, felt bony fingers on her fingers, nails digging into her. Carey's face strobed white and red as Billy slammed her up against the car, driving her shorn head back against the door frame. But the old woman wouldn't let go, her fingernails digging deep. Billy yelped, yanking backwards, and the gun popped, muffled this time, muffled by clothes and flesh. There was a burning smell. Carey's eyes went flat. She tried to say something as Billy pulled herself clear, conscious of shouting up above, of lights coming on all over.

37

The secrets were coming out. It was impossible to sleep. At two o'clock in the morning Ellen found herself standing in front of the photographs in the den, holding the printout of the Rosa May King information she'd downloaded from SearchQuest. Koenig gazed back at her out of the gloom, different now – no longer the tortured genius who'd simply lost faith. The picture had been taken just after he returned from Mexico City, a couple of months after Leslie Ann had let the cat out of the bag. In the photograph, he was smiling – a strained smile, Ellen now felt. He'd known. In the picture, he knew. For most people the news would have come as a shock, but for him up there on his cross, who believed *and* doubted so strongly, who could sit for a day in front a canvas unable to make a mark, who could work for months on something before tearing it from the stretcher, it would have been devastating. For Koenig, who didn't 'give a shit', who could 'eat out of garbage cans', creative integrity was the one pure thing. Perhaps the only thing he cared about.

And all Leslie Ann wanted was to preserve his memory, a curatorial task that required the omission of certain inconvenient facts. Perry on the other hand wanted just the facts, wanted everyone to see the museum for what it was, to see Abstract Expressionism for what it was – an expression of personal freedom (as much as you liked), but mainly of political will.

Did that make a difference? Did that make Koenig's personal struggle any less of a struggle? Leslie Ann said Velàzquez was still Velàzquez despite the Hapsburg court. But there was a difference. Felipe IV hadn't invited Velàzquez to play the wild bohemian while secretly paying his rent. And Felipe IV had liked what Velàzquez painted. She wondered how true that had been of Frank Wisner, pulling the strings up there in Washington? The truth was that for most people it was all just squiggles, and for the man in the gray hat, if such a person even existed, it was worse than that: it was a lie perpetrated by an elite that was almost dysfunctional in its appetite for duplicity.

She ran a finger along the bottom of the frame in search of dust, and found herself wishing Perry was around. She'd have liked to talk to him right then. Even if he was an asshole. She would have liked to go over to his place and sit among his piles of books, talk about what the museum really was.

Tuesday morning came in warm and hazy. She ate breakfast in the kitchen with the SearchQuest printout next to her coffee cup. She figured that everyone and his aunt would have been in touch with Rosa May by now. She probably wasn't even answering the phone. But the number was right there and it was hard to resist dialing it. Of course if she was serious about it, she'd get on a plane and go down there, talk with her face to face. But she couldn't just take time off. Especially not now. She was supposed to be running a department.

She sat there sipping coffee and listening to the radio, half-hoping to hear something about Perry on the morning news. But until Perry showed up, or until someone found Linda Carey, the story was going to slip back under the surface of things, too heavy and too complicated for the media to get a handle on.

*

She got into the museum early, and walking into her office with a cup of coffee in her hand, she found two sticky notes on her computer screen from Jil Galen, the person who had been assigned as her assistant while she was filling in for Perry. Apart from being very smart and enthusiastic, Galen happened to be the niece of Kathleen Herzen-Galen, one of the most formidably connected of the trustees. The first message was in Jil's loopy scrawl. A meeting of the board had been scheduled for ten o'clock. The second was in block capitals, and triple-underlined: MIRROR, MIRROR ON THE WALL! COME TAKE A LOOK!

They'd hung the picture.

The door came open and Lewis Hartnal pushed his head through the gap. Ellen met his questioning gaze, wondering if he had heard about her trip out to Springs with Leslie Ann.

'Ellen? You have a stricken look.'

Of course he had.

'You hung it.'

'Naturally. We wanted to get behind it.'

'Aren't you worried about further challenges to its authenticity.'

'From Perry, you mean? Yes. Yes, I am. But I believe that we need to—'

'Get behind it.'

'That's right.'

Ellen took a sip of scalding coffee, winced.

'This is a great day for you, Ellen. This is hard work and perspicacity paying off.'

Ellen did her best to smile.

'Yes,' she said. 'Yes, absolutely.'

Hartnal made a debonair half-turn, holding out a hand as though inviting her to dance. She hadn't seen him so perky in quite a while.

She followed him down to the third floor, nursing her burned palate, listening to him talk in his soft avuncular voice. He was saying how proud, how pleased, how optimistic he was about the museum, about the future.

The usual mix of students, tourists and oddballs had been cordoned off at the entrance to the gallery. Hartnal made excuse-me sounds, effacing himself in a way that made it clear how important he was. Going through the rope, Ellen noticed a young guy with messy blond hair, saw Dan for a moment, Dan almost twenty years earlier. She heard someone say 'that's her' as Hartnal re-hooked the velvet rope.

Mirror, Mirror.

A band of splintered red and black was visible above the mostly balding heads of the assembled board. They were all there, the five vice-chairmen, the heads of departments, the director, the treasurer and his assistant, the secretary. There was no sign of Porter French, and no David Kruger. None of the trustees. Old men, mostly, they were all wearing suits, could have been brokers or bankers.

Familiar faces turned, mouths smiled, heavy hands worked her shoulder pads as Hartnal brought them through the group until there was nothing between her and the painting. They'd hung it between Gorky's *Agony* and Rothko's *Red, Brown, and Black*. On the opposite wall was Pollock's *One*.

All the suicides together.

Harold Rosenau had worked his embalmer's magic; the fine vertical cracks had gone, as had the patina of fifty years. The surface was glossily uniform and, in the stillness of it, the tangled depths loomed darkly through. It was terrific. A great swooning of form and color. It was easy to imagine it newly finished and placed on the wall in Koenig's barn, easy to conjure up the bitter cold of November 27th, 1957.

She hadn't been back inside the boardroom since David Kruger asked her to leave it. It was the same furniture and many of the same people, but unfamiliar somehow. The weirdest thing of all, the dream-like aspect, was sitting there with her own assistant, and being deferred to by people who only a week before had witnessed her expulsion without a word in her defense.

Hartnal was directing things, deferring to Staunton every time he chimed in, and inviting comment from everyone around the table in an affable collegial way, but basically pushing things in the direction he wanted. The talk was all Perry, of course. His resignation, his disappearance. Apparently, his second ex-wife had now reported him missing and the police were reluctantly becoming involved.

'I'm afraid you can expect visits from detectives in the next few days,' said Hartnal, looking around the table.

There was a general shaking of heads.

'Do we have *any* idea why he did it?' said Glenn Schaeffer.

'David is furious,' said Hartnal, as though that answered the question. 'I don't think I've ever heard him quite so upset.'

People started offering outraged comments on all sides of the table. Hartnal shuffled his papers.

'I can only think he felt threatened,' he said.

There was a heavy silence, but Hartnal gave a dignified shake of his head, clearly reluctant to say any more.

Schaeffer put his cup down with a clack.

'All the same, I think everyone would appreciate hearing what you think, Lewis.'

This was seconded, then taken up by someone else. Hartnal settled in his chair, watching the talk go around the table.

'Perry has been under pressure mainly from the media for quite some time,' he said, bringing another silence. 'His incumbency has not been the happiest. Recent speculation about a potential successor may have . . .'

He shrugged again. Ellen became aware of faces turning in her direction. Old men shaking their blue-veined wattles, frowning.

'This was about *infighting*?' said someone, aghast. 'Some sort of internecine . . .'

Hartnal sketched a gesture with his hand.

'That is certainly the view David takes.'

So that was the official line.

'Ellen?'

Ellen blinked, looked for the source of the question, found Michael Pauling's simpering face. He wanted something from her. A handful of soil for Perry's casket. She shrugged, felt a piece of skin detach itself from the roof of her mouth.

'The past few months have been difficult,' she said.

'But is there any proof?' said Schaeffer. 'Actual proof that he tampered with the catalog?'

'A confession,' said Hartnal. 'On Thursday night. I was confronted with some evidence that had been provided to me by Bob Gifford, and he owned up.'

Ellen touched at her hearing aid. The battery was dying.

'Did he say why?' said Pauling.

'There was a great deal of hostility,' said Hartnal. 'Towards Ellen in particular.'

'Despicable.'

Amid muttering assent, Hartnal shuffled papers, wanting to move them on. There were important decisions to take. Perry had walked out, leaving a number of important projects up in the air. One of which, an upcoming Chagall retrospective which had recently run into trouble. Several important paintings were being withheld because of an insurance problem.

'This is all very much on the hoof,' said Hartnal, 'but I want to propose that Ellen take over the department for the time being. All in favor raise your hand.'

It happened so fast. She was given the board's full support. Unanimity of all members present. There were to be no announcements to the press, but for the time being she would be running the department, the first woman to do so in the history of the museum.

Hartnal flushed with pleasure as he turned to congratulate her.

'I think I speak for everyone here, Ellen, when I say how sorry I am for what you have been put through these past few weeks. You have borne it all with remarkable calm and fortitude.'

He gripped her hand, his own hand trembling.

'The annual general meeting will take place in October, and the Perry situation will be reviewed at that time, but as far as I am concerned this business is concluded.'

People were applauding. Ellen looked around at the smiling, nodding faces, and found herself smiling too.

38

She'd blown it. Lost it. Lost everything. She sucked up local cable from the end of the bed, wrapped in a wet towel. Blood spatter on bodywork. Klieg-light flare in smeary windshields. Bystanders gawped behind yellow tape. Phoenix PD had the shootings down as a robbery gone wrong. They'd recovered the Z-Tool from the passenger door, and were calling it professional, somebody stealing to order. There was some stern talk from a starved-looking anchor: Phoenix auto-theft capital of the USA.

No one mentioned millions of dollars in an abandoned suitcase. No one talked about money in the trunk.

She combed her hair flat against her head, pulling it tight as she smoked. Frowned when they described the 'assailant'. Police wanted to interview a white male in his early twenties. A white male with acne scars. She shook her head. It was all too fucking weird. A white male in his early twenties. It made no difference. She was fucked anyway. Jay was going to kill her. She picked yellow hair from the comb as victims' faces flashed up on the screen. A driver's license identified Carey as Pauline Brook, of Tucson Arizona. Rosa May King was a single mother of two young girls, manager of a local Taco Bell. Both victims were now in the John C. Lincoln Hospital.

A Motel 6 on the outskirts of Sun City.

Traffic sounds, and muffled singing – one of the latina maids doing J Lo in the next room. A hoover thumped the baseboard. There was an empty bottle on the vanity table. The first drink she'd had in seven years.

Her hands shook as she smoked. She kept getting flashes of the old woman's face. She'd left town immediately after the shooting, had driven north on the 17, doing a steady sixty-five, her eyes in the rearview mirror. She'd come off the freeway to check her hands and clothes. She was clean apart from a couple of scratches. She'd come away clean.

Whomp – the noise the gun had made up against the old woman's body. Carey's eyes. She'd thought she'd killed her.

She figured the white male description came from Rosa May. Or maybe Carey herself. Several people had seen the pick-up pulling out of the parking lot. Nobody got the license plate. But they were looking for the truck. She'd rented the truck with fake ID, and the worst photograph DMV ever took. But the guy she'd rented it from would remember her face. There was a chance he'd see 'young male with acne scars' and remember her.

She'd scrubbed her hands in the bathroom of a gas station, bought a jogging outfit and sneakers in a Big 5. Her old clothes, the Yankees cap she'd been wearing went into the trash. She'd checked into the motel with a pint of vodka.

Whomp. The woman's body going slack. A smell of burning. Muzzle flash torching clothes.

She had to call Jay. Jay was going to freak, but she didn't see any way around calling him. Anything else would be bullshit. Unprofessional. She combed her hair, stroke after stroke, raking the teeth across her scalp until it was tingling. There had been no mention of the money. The police were keeping certain details to themselves. Either that or there had never been any money.

She got dressed, she checked out. She made the call in the parking lot. Jay started in as soon as he picked up.

'All night I've been calling you!'

'My cell's on the fritz.'

'You *know* the rules, Billy. Every hour *on* the hour. I've got the client breathing down my fucking neck, Billy. She calls me, I have to answer.'

She. She who?

'Jay, something happened.'

'What?'

'You didn't hear what happened.'

'What the fuck are you talking about?'

She told him. She put a little spin on it, said she'd been working on the car, putting a GPS receiver on it like they'd agreed. The women came out of the building.

'The old woman went for me, Jay.'

Silence.

'I think she figured I was trying to boost her car.'

Silence. She could see Jay's colorless face. Could see the vein coming up in his forehead.

'The gun just went off.'

All she could hear was breathing.

'I just wanted her to back off, but she tried to grab the gun.'

Billy closed her eyes, waiting for him to start yelling, but nothing came.

'I didn't kill her,' she said into the silence. 'They're in the hospital.'

'They?'

A small voice. A dead voice.

'Look, Jay, it went wrong, okay? We took a risk and—'

'*You* took the fucking risk.'

'*You* said put a unit on the car. I said, it's risky, Jay. Maybe later on, when it gets—'

'I don't believe this. I do not—'

'The cops think it's car theft. They don't even know it's Carey. The woman had this fake ID. They're looking for a white male. A guy with acne scars. What I'm saying is, nothing's really changed.'

'Nothing's changed?'

'Linda Carey's in the hospital. But other than that . . .'

'Billy?'

'Yeah.'

Jay cleared his throat.

'We're done, Billy. We're through.'

'Jay.'

'I've carried you long enough.'

Billy nodded at her self in the rearview mirror.

'You didn't *carry* me anywhere.'

'I'm coming down there, Billy. And I swear to god, if you're still around . . .'

Despite the heat, Billy went cold. She couldn't be pushed. Nobody could push her.

'Jay? I didn't catch that.'

'I swear on your father's grave. Woman or not.'

'You're . . . you're breaking up on me, Jay. You're breaking . . .'

And she killed the signal dead, holding the button down so hard the phone broke. There was a tight popping sound, and suddenly she was holding two pieces of plastic. She flung it all at the windshield, saw a startled face on the other side. A wetback with a garden hose. She'd screamed, she realized. It just blasted out of her. There was a taste in her mouth now. The wetback looked away.

She yanked the truck into gear, and rolled out onto the highway.

39

Hartnal walked her back to her office, his hand on her arm, reassuring her, telling her she would be given his full support. Being the chief curator wasn't the same thing as being the chief curator's assistant – there was a certain amount of politics involved, but he and Staunton would help her steer between the rocks. And of course the circumstances in which she was taking over were not ideal. There was the Perry situation to consider.

He closed the door behind him, took a moment to smooth his tie, looking around her tiny room.

'I never realized quite how small it is in here.'

Ellen went around to the other side of her desk and sat down. Hartnal stayed by the door. For a moment he stood there, looking uncomfortable now, his head tilted slightly as though listening.

'Leslie Ann said you took a trip out to the house,' he said, his closed mouth twisting in a smile.

'Yes.'

'How was that?'

Ellen touched at her earpiece, took it out.

'I'm sorry, Lewis . . . the battery. I get about a month out of it, and then . . .'

Hartnal came over to the chair opposite and sat down, clutching a sheaf of papers to his chest. Waiting, obviously. For some sort of response. Ellen took a breath. It occurred to her that perhaps Leslie Ann hadn't been entirely open with Hartnal. That he might not realize the extent of the confidences they shared.

'Leslie Ann trusts you,' he said, as though reading her mind.

Ellen nodded at that.

'We've been friends for such a long time.'

'She felt that circumstances demanded a degree of openness.' He looked at the papers he was holding. 'I didn't agree. But then it's in my nature to keep secrets.' He smiled. 'I hope that's something you and I share.'

It wasn't a threat exactly, but it hung in the air nevertheless.

'Look,' he said, returning to something like his usual smoothness, 'there is something I wanted to say. It's by way of a piece of advice really.' He moistened his lips with a little whisk of his tongue. 'Don't take everything Leslie Ann tells you at face value. To hear Leslie Ann tell it, you might get the impression that Koenig was completely in the dark prior to her . . . indiscretion.'

Ellen was shaking her head.

'I'm not sure I . . .'

'I'm not saying it didn't have an effect. I just question the extent to which Franklin was innocent of what was going on. In fact, I question the extent to which any of them were.'

'Them?'

'The artists around him. I may be wrong but I think that the general attitude was "what we are doing is important, and if the government thinks so too, that's swell". I don't think there was any great urge to bite, far less question the hand that was feeding them.'

Ellen put her earpiece back in, nodding, trying to think why he was telling her all this.

He stood up.

'By the way, he's been spotted,' he said. 'Perry. I didn't mention it at the meeting because . . .well, there's been enough Perry talk, and I don't doubt we'll be hearing from the man himself soon enough.'

He was heading for the door now.

'Where?'

'Boston. Yesterday afternoon.'

Ellen shook her head, didn't know what to think now, wanted, above all, to believe him.

'You look surprised,' said Hartnal, his hand on the door handle.

'Do I? No. I'm not. Not at all. I mean, he was bound to show up sooner or later.'

Hartnal opened the door, stood there waiting.

'Are you coming?'

'Where?'

'Ellen, you can't stay in here.'

The blinds were down in Perry's office, and in the diffuse light, Ellen took in the book-crammed shelves, the art work on the walls, the rugs, the furniture. There were a couple of buttery leather armchairs, and a couch in front of one of the big windows. Above and behind the magnificent Frank Lloyd Wright desk, the Edward Hopper drawings glowed softly under their polished glass.

Hartnal crossed the room and raised one of the blinds.

'It was very different when Alfred Faber was in here,' he said. 'Strict International Style. White linoleum floor, pigskin leather furniture, Mies van der Rohe chairs.' He raised another blind. 'Ebony veneer on the walls.'

Ellen stood in the doorway.

'I've seen photographs,' she said softly.

Hartnal turned and smiled at her.

'Faber's father came to visit him when the museum was opened in 'thirty-one. Came in here trying to be positive, trying to like all the austerity. Black *walls* . . .' Hartnal chuckled. 'He asked to make a telephone call. Sat on the edge of a chair, leaned forward to pick up the phone. Sure enough the metal runners of the chair skidded on the linoleum and Faber's father's chin . . .' He was laughing now. 'His chin hit the desk with a tremendous crack.' He dabbed at his eyes. 'Poor man said that was what he liked about modern art – it was so damned functional!'

Ellen was laughing too. She'd heard the story before. It was part of lore in the Modern, but it seemed to bring an intense clamoring humanity into the room, the sense of other years and other people.

And now her.

She walked over to one of the windows, feeling stretched, taut, as though she might burst with pleasure. She tried to picture Perry in Boston. Couldn't do it.

'Lewis. Why do you . . . what made Perry run?'

Hartnal looked over his shoulder at the open door.

'I don't know,' he said. Then, lowering his voice: 'But, between you, me and these erstwhile ebony walls, I suspect that whoever has been feeding him information, has been misrepresenting a certain institution which I hope you won't mind if I don't name.'

Ellen continued to look down at the street.

'I suppose I'm still having trouble taking it all in,' she said.

He set his jaw at that, nodding. Then went across the room and closed the door. He came back to the window, examining his nails, looked out at the road crew that was still working on the pavement.

'There are times when it seems very odd to me too,' he said in the same soft voice. 'That's the comedy of all this, Ellen. We're talking about things that happened a long time ago, and I can assure you that even then, back in the day, the nearest we got to . . . well let's say *that* sort of thing was an unfavorable review. We organized exhibitions, for goodness' sake.'

A backhoe was delving a new trench. Black smoke jetted up from the exhaust. Ellen frowned.

'Perhaps Perry thinks that with all the money invested in Koenig . . .'

Hartnal looked momentarily tired.

'Who knows what Perry thinks.'

'How do you know about the information?'

Hartnal glanced across at her, then went back to his contemplation of the street.

'You said someone was feeding him information,' said Ellen.

'I confronted him with the catalog business. This was last Thursday evening. And he threatened me. He said he had his own personal Deep Throat.' He raised his eyebrows, nodding. 'Yes, that was the term he used, which, I think, of itself, gives you a sense of the rich fantasy world Bruce inhabits.' He tapped a finger on the glass. 'This Deep Throat, some McCarthyite diehard is my guess, has, apparently, been passing him documents.'

'Documents?'

Hartnal shook his head.

'I don't know, Ellen. Files? Surveillance reports? There was an awful lot of that sort of thing going on back then. Anyway, I'm sure, that whatever it is, we'll soon find out. And when we do, it'll be through the ladies and gentlemen of the popular press. Which is one of the reasons I want you to go to Santa Barbara.'

He turned to face her.

'I understand you have vacation plans, but . . .'

'My son is in LA.'

'I'm sure we could organize something, perhaps have him join you at the villa. It is only twenty minutes away by plane.'

Santa Barbara was where the Chagalls were. The Mellon family had an estate in the hills. Perry was booked into a villa on the coast, and was scheduled to meet Lucy Mellon, thirty-year-old daughter of Robert Mellon, and the de facto curator of the collection, to discuss ways around the insurance situation. Hartnal wanted Ellen to go in Perry's place. It would be an interesting first assignment for her, and it would get her away from New York for a few days.

'The villa's very pleasant. I've stayed there myself several times. There's a pool and so forth. Staff to make you at home. I'm sure you and your little boy would be very comfortable.'

He smiled his closed mouth smile, congratulated her again, then went over to the door. He nodded in the direction of the next door office, said he'd already spoken to Grace Hartigan.

'To be honest, I think she's delighted,' he said. And he left the room.

Ellen lifted the blinds one by one, and stood there looking down at the street. A week ago she had been hurrying along it, wondering what had happened to her world. A trembling strip of sunlight touched her feet, and she saw herself in a swimming pool with Ben, saw herself having lunch, discussing Chagall with Lucy Mellon.

Her cell phone was ringing.

It was Jerry.

'Ellen, we need to talk.'

She closed her eyes.

'Did you show the documents to your brother?'

'Okay, listen. I started out by referencing some of the technical stuff myself. I didn't want to look like a *complete* idiot in front of Ken. So . . . there are some initials and stuff. Should I . . .?'

'Just tell me what you've got.'

'Okay.' He cleared his throat. 'OPC. That's the Office of Policy Coordination. It was—'

'I know about OPC.'

'Okay . . . um . . . The FBI documents . . .' There was some more rustling. 'Here we are. Serial numbers at the top of the first document. San Francisco field office. 139 is the code for interceptions. That's wire-taps. And you've got others that came out of New York. Then there's 055. That's counterfeiting. Forgery.'

'Forgery?'

'I thought that might pop out at you. It popped out at me. I put sticky notes on passages that look interesting, but I've got to say it's pretty obscure, and incomplete. I mean what did you, just grab a bunch of stuff?'

'What else, Jerry?'

'One, three, seven – that's informants. What it looks like is some sort of major investigation, Ellen. Into Franklin Koenig.'

Ellen covered her eyes with fluttering fingers.

He was still talking.

'So, I dug up all this stuff, and, well then I showed them to the Prof and . . . I should preface all this by saying that Ken is an incredible stuffed shirt. Anyway, he took a look and . . .'

'What?'

'He gave them straight back to me. He said he wouldn't touch them with a ten-foot pole.'

Ellen stood up.

'And he said that if I said he had touched them, he'd deny it.' Jerry laughed, a nervous laugh. 'He wasn't joking. I think he's worried about losing tenure. There are legality issues. National Security issues.'

'Jerry, you're scaring me.'

'You know what? Me too. I'm sitting with these things in my lap. I mean, have you read some of this stuff? And names are really named. Whoever your source is didn't get them from a university archive.'

'I didn't think he did.'

'Where *did* he get them? And come to that, who the hell is he?'

Ellen got a little tingle. A feeling of exposure.

'Okay,' said Jerry. 'That's your business. But you have to understand they're classified documents, Ellen. Even if they are old. Anything that came out of these agencies through the Freedom of Information Act, anything that came from public or publicly available archives would have been screened and censored to protect people who might still be around. Stuff would be blanked out. Anyway, that's why I called. I think we should destroy them.'

'We?'

'Okay, you.'

'No!' She pushed the hair back from her face, pulled it taut, a good handful. 'I can't.'

Silence. She could hear Jerry's steady breathing.

'Ellen? I think you're in trouble.'

'No.' She shook her head emphatically. '*No*, it's okay, it's just a . . . this is something I needed to be clear about. And . . . the last thing – the *last* thing I wanted to do was bring any trouble to your door.'

'So . . .'

'So drop them off here. Can you do that?'

'Sure.'

'No. At my place. Later.'

'Ellen, wait. There's the other thing.'

'What other thing?'

'The last document you gave me. You wanted to try to date it?'

'Yes.'

'I had a think about it myself, and I talked to some people up here, and the only thing I could come up with was the Liberty Diner.'

'What about it?'

'It was pulled down in the spring of 'forty-eight. Sewers or something like that. So, I mean, at least that gives you a cut off date, right? I don't know if that's any help but . . .'

She lowered herself into Perry's chair.

'Yeah . . . yes, it is.'

'I wish you'd tell me what this is about, Ellen. Maybe I could—'

'Got to go, Jerry.'

She killed the signal, and sat there, seeing everything at once, feeling everything fall into place. Leslie Ann hadn't met Koenig in 1949 at the Cedar Tavern.

She looked out at the street. Burn the documents, she said to herself. Do what Jerry said. Forget you ever saw them. That was all she had to do – forget about the documents, and they would give her this office, and this life. Because Perry was dead. She was sure of that. Perry was dead, and the Koenig, all the Koenigs were worthless. Historical curiosities at best.

For a long time she was completely immobile. Then she took the crumpled printout from her bag, and spread it out on the desk in front of her. She picked up the phone, struggling to control her breathing, punched the keys, sinking, feeling like she was going down, losing everything right there.

A woman picked up, shouted her hello against a background of breakfast TV and yelling kids.

'Rosa May?'

'What?' The TV jumped louder then stopped altogether. 'No. No, I'm Mary Beth, a friend. Who is this?'

'I'm . . . my name's Rebecca – Becky. I'm a friend of hers.'

'Oh yeah? You don't sound like you're from around here.'

'I'm not. I'm based in New York, actually.'

'You a reporter?'

'Pardon me?'

'Because if you are, I'm not talking to you.'

A fluttering started up in Ellen's stomach.

'I'm not a reporter . . . Why would I be a – is everything okay?'

'Look if you really are a friend, you can call Rosa May at the hospital. She's at the John C. Lincoln. Here in Phoenix.'

'Don't hang up! Please. Please tell me what happened.'

'She was shot.' The woman's voice broke. 'Last night. Someone was trying steal her car or – I mean her *mom's* car, and . . . It's terrible. I'm here with the kids.'

'She's dead?'

'No. They're both in the ICU up at the John Lincoln. Rosa May's okay, but her mom's critical.'

'Her mom?'

The door came open again, and Grace Hartigan walked in, beaming. Ellen hung up.

'Ellen? Are you okay?'

'It's my blood sugar,' said Ellen in a weak voice. 'I get a little . . . I get a little fluttery.'

Hartigan had a thick file under one arm. She put out her hand.

'I wanted to congratulate you,' she said.

'Grace?' said, Ellen, squinting. 'Do you think we could talk a little later.'

Hartigan's face dropped, then her hands went up, and she was backing away.

The door closed without a sound.

Ellen sat there staring at the phone, sat there for maybe five minutes before taking the decision. She picked it up, punched in an extension number. Hartnal sounded mildly surprised to hear from her so soon.

'I hope you're settling in okay. I just—'

'There's something I didn't tell you about Perry,' she said.

Silence.

'Something he said to me about the book he was writing. Something he said about his primary sources.'

'Really? Why didn't you—?'

'I wasn't sure I should talk about it. But . . .'

'But now . . .?'

'We should probably meet. I'm tied up until one.'

'One it is then.'

She hung up, and heart pounding thickly, dialed Leslie Ann's home number, praying it wouldn't be engaged. Leslie Ann picked up on the first ring.

'Hello?'

She hit 'conference', then Hartnal's cell number.

'*Hello?*' Leslie Ann, getting impatient.

Hartnal came on.

'Hello?'

'Lewis?'

'Leslie Ann? Is that you?'

'Of course it's me.'

Hartnal mumbled something incoherent, sounded like he was putting something down, then he was right there, clear as a bell.

'Guess who I just spoke to?'

It worked. Ellen stood up, eyes clenched tight.

'Ellen,' said Hartnal. 'She says Perry talked to her about the source.'

There was the snap of a lighter, a sharp inhale.

'And?'

'She wants to talk.'

'I thought you just *did* talk.'

'There's something she didn't say. Something she was unsure about.'

'What?'

'I don't know.'

'Isn't she supposed to be playing chief curator?'

'That's going to unravel pretty quickly.'

'All we need is a couple of days.'

'I already had a call from David. He's been talking to Lyndon Friedman at the Tate. He thinks he can tempt him back over to New York. He was categorical about Ellen, I'm afraid.'

'Just get her on the flight to LA.'

'I'm going to see what she has to say.'

'Fine. But she doesn't know anything about the source.'

'How can you be so sure?'

'Because *Perry* didn't know, and—'

'*Not* on the phone,' hissed Hartnal.

'*You're* the one who called.'

'What?'

Silence. The hair came up on Ellen's neck.

'Hang up,' said Benton, and the line went dead.

III

40

There was plenty of time to cry on the flight from Kennedy to Phoenix, plenty of time to feel sorry for herself, to recall the years of friendship and shared secrets, and endless, *endless* discussions about Dan and Koenig, Koenig and Dan – their supposed similarities, their fragilities and strengths – plenty of time to absorb the simple stark truth that it had all been a lie.

Isn't she supposed to be playing chief curator?

That was the phrase that snagged her. She was yanked back to it again and again – a question so filled with contempt it was difficult to fathom. By the time she touched down in Phoenix she was pretty much cried out, and all that was left was a feeling of hollowness, a lost feeling that was close to the disorienting depression she'd felt in the aftermath of Dan's death.

She was helped from the plane by one of the cabin staff, a young woman who clearly thought she was in danger of pitching head first down the steps. She stumbled through the paperwork required for a rental company to give her a car.

The John C. Lincoln Hospital sprawled like a university campus in the early evening light, but there were no students around, no sign of life at all except for the cars parked out front of the main hospital building. Dehydrated, blinking eyes that were red from crying and lack of sleep, she got as close to the main entrance as she could and parked.

She'd had five hours to think about what she was going to do, and it was pretty simple. All she wanted was for Linda Carey to tell her everything. She flipped down the visor and looked at herself in the little vanity mirror. At least she'd come. At least she'd made the commitment. At least she was doing what no one at the museum, including Perry, had wanted her to do.

Going in through the entrance, she checked her cell. She'd turned it off in Manhattan, hadn't wanted to be taking any calls from Leslie Ann or Hartnal. It wouldn't have taken them very long to work out what had happened with the phone. So now they would be looking for her, probably thinking she was wandering the streets of Manhattan with her face in her hands.

She told the woman behind the desk that she was a close friend of Linda Carey and Rosa May King, that she'd heard about the shootings and had flown down from New York to see them. The woman had glasses hanging around her neck on a chain. She put them on to look at her computer screen.

'Rosa May King checked out.'

'Checked out?'

Ellen leaned over the counter, trying to see the listed names.

'That's not possible. She was only admitted last night.'

'Well, I guess it couldn't have been that serious.'

'She was *shot*.'

The woman removed her glasses, blinked her cold green eyes.

'Maybe they moved her to another hospital,' she said. 'Or maybe she went home. We wouldn't have released her unless she was okay. I'm sorry.'

'What about Linda Carey?'

The glasses went back on. The woman stabbed keys, then shook her head.

'No one by that name.'

Then Ellen remembered. Carey and her fake ID. Another receptionist was sidling over. She dropped a newspaper next to the keyboard, said something Ellen didn't catch.

'I'm sorry?' said Ellen, turning her head to favor her left ear.

There was moment of readjustment, a pause Ellen knew only too well. Her face went hot.

'There were two admissions to the ER last night,' said the woman, raising her voice now as though Ellen were stone deaf. 'Two ladies got shot.'

She held up the newspaper. A headline jumped out: *MIRROR WOMAN SHOT DEAD.*

'That was her mother?' said the lady with the glasses. She was punching keys again, blinking at her screen. 'Mrs Pauline Brook?'

Ellen was backing away from the desk.

'She's dead?'

'Died in the night.'

Ellen's legs went rubbery.

'I'm sorry . . . Miss—'

'Lindz,' said Ellen. 'Ellen Lindz.'

'I'm sorry, Miss Lindz.'

'What . . .?' Ellen was shaking her head, looking around for a chair. 'What happened?'

The women had pitying looks on their faces.

'We can give you a number to call,' said the woman with the glasses.

'And you can have this,' said the other, offering the paper.

Back in the car, Ellen sat for a long time too stirred up to be able to read. In the end she forced herself to focus on the newspaper.

Linda Carey, who came to be known in recent weeks as the 'Mirror Woman' was gunned down last night by an unknown assailant who was in the process of stealing luggage from her car. Carey, a sixty-seven-year-old of indeterminate address, was visiting her daughter, Rosa May King, who was also injured in the attack. King was released from the John C Lincoln Hospital with superficial injuries this afternoon. Carey entered the hospital with fake ID, and was identified by one of the staff. *(Details: turn to page 3.)*

She put the paper aside, then reached over and opened the glove compartment. It took her ten minutes of twisting and turning the little map that came with the rental for her to find Rosa May King's street.

It was a little girl who answered the door, a plain little girl with striking blue eyes. A TV was on somewhere.

'Hi.' Ellen tried a smile. 'Is your Mommy home?'

The little girl turned away.

'Mommy! It's another reporter.'

'Close the door.'

'I'm not a reporter, Mrs King!'

The TV noise stopped. There was a groan and then the sound of shuffling feet. Another little girl bounced into the kitchen, this one wearing jeans and a T-shirt, and holding a pair of paper scissors.

The mother appeared in the doorway. She was in a quilted house coat, and her left arm was in a sling. Her hair was sticking out at the side, looked like she'd slept on it.

'Miss,' she corrected. 'Miss King.'

'Rosa May?' said Ellen.

The woman gave a nod, extending her good arm to gather her little girls.

'My name's Ellen Lindz. I'm from the Modern Art Museum in New York.'

There was a sound of heavy footsteps on concrete. Someone was coming up the stairs behind her.

'Is it about the painting?' said Rosa May, a doomed look on her broad face.

'Yes,' said Ellen. 'That's right.'

'Excuse me.'

Ellen turned. A woman was standing there. Heavy set, breathing through her mouth. She was carrying a Walgreens bag in her bunched fingers. She looked Ellen up and down, a sneer twisting her mouth.

'Ain't you people had enough?'

'She ain't a reporter, Mary Beth.'

'That right?' said Mary Beth, pushing past.

'She's from New York.'

Mary Beth shot her a look.

'You the one who called this morning? Said you was a friend?'

Ellen shook her head.

Mary Beth looked unconvinced, sucked her teeth as she started unloading the bag on the kitchen table. Medication.

'Reporters been calling all day,' said Rosa May, by way of explanation. 'Asking about the shooting.'

'They should pay her for her time,' said Mary Beth.

41

She'd dumped the truck as soon as she'd heard the old woman was dead. She'd set fire to it outside Sun City. There'd been no sign of the Mercury in the parking lot, and she hadn't been able to get into the apartment. Someone was in there – some busybody do-gooder, trying to help out with the kids. She'd stood at the door for as long she'd dared, listening to voices on the other side, then made her way out of the building. Even in the new car, she'd considered it way too risky to be hanging around, so she'd ended up parking on the street, had been sitting there, thinking about driving to a public phone and calling the apartment, pretending she was from the hospital, and telling whoever it was to get over there straight away because Rosa May was dying or whatever, when she'd seen Ellen Lindz drive past in a silver Oldsmobile Olero.

It had brought her upright in her seat. Lindz. She'd recognized her immediately, would have known her stuck-up face anywhere, and knew just as surely that she was there to talk to Rosa May King about the painting. Because why else, for chrissake? Things were moving fast. She'd sat tight for a while, burning to do something, but not knowing what, expecting to see Lindz re-emerge at any moment, but then ten minutes had passed, and the light was starting to fade, and there was no silver Olero . . .

So now she was moving again, pulling into the parking lot, seeing Rosa May's Honda back in its slot. It hadn't been there earlier in the day, and now it was. That didn't mean that Rosa May herself had been discharged, but Billy couldn't see any other reason for Lindz to be sniffing around there. If Rosa May was still at the hospital, Lindz would surely be heading up there. The only way to be certain was to call the hospital. She sat there in the fading light, cursing herself for trashing the cell phone.

Then she remembered the wire tap. All she had to do was listen to the tape. There was bound to be something, a call to whoever the fuck it was that was sitting the kids.

Billy got out of the car, and walked across the parking lot to the main entrance as though she were going inside, then, at the last moment, ducked into the scrappy shrubs that grew between the building and a chain link fence running along the side of the property.

The telephone junction box was located around the back next to a big ventilation outlet that emerged from the basement laundry room. She figured that with any luck there'd have been some back and forth on the phone, and she'd know whether Rosa May had been discharged or not. If she had, and if they were all sitting up there talking about the painting, then the time had come to do something. No one was going to just give her the money. That was guaranteed.

She was unscrewing the front panel on the junction box, when she felt the gun. It came up against the base of her skull. Not hard, just a cold touch of metal that was unmistakable. Then it was pushing. Billy went with it, falling forward a little, until her head was up against the junction box.

'Jay.'

Billy looked at the ground. She had the screwdriver in her right hand.

'What did you think, Billy?'

'About what?'

'Did you think I wouldn't find out about the Z-tool? You were *in* the car, Billy. What were you gonna do? Put the GPS in the suitcase?'

'I thought—'

He jabbed the gun, pushed her face against peeling paint.

'Don't insult me, Billy.'

He breathed for a moment, angry fluttery breaths. It sounded like he was working himself up. Billy blinked sweat out of her eyes, trying to think.

'You thought the money was just gonna fall out of a suitcase. Just like when you were in the A-T-fucking-F. You're just a dumb skank, Billy, and your dad would have been ashamed.'

Billy looked down. Scattered bits of telco wire. A cigarette butt. The screwdriver in her hand.

'Carey's dead, Billy. Did you know that? It's a homicide investigation now.'

Billy closed her eyes, focused on his breathing. It was the only thing she had. He was thinking about his options. He'd only shoot her if he had to. Wouldn't want to risk having people come take a look.

Suddenly the gun was gone.

'Stand up.'

Billy got to her feet.

'Drop the screwdriver.'

She opened her hand, heard the screwdriver hit the dirt.

'Now turn around.'

42

They talked in the living room. Sounds of splashing and subdued voices came from the other side of a frosted glass door. Mary Beth was giving the girls their bath. The living room was tiny, just big enough for the big velveteen couch, the armchairs and the TV. Some sort of reality show was playing without the sound. People were eating bugs.

'My insurance ain't so great, so they patched me up, sent me home with some painkillers.'

Rosa May lifted her arm. The bruise spread past the stubble in her armpit.

'Doctor said the bullet went straight through. Didn't hit any bone or nothing. Didn't even bleed that much. Got a bruise though. Got a bruise to beat the band.'

She peeled back a little of the bandage. Ellen saw blue-green mottled flesh.

'I'm sorry about your mother.'

Rosa May mumbled something and Ellen looked up, meeting her gaze. She was prettier than her girls, a looker who had stopped taking care of herself a long time ago. Thirty pounds lighter, she would have resembled the Linda Carey who was photographed at the edge of the Grand Canyon in 1980.

'They told me at the hospital,' said Ellen.

'He shot her in the chest. Close up. Which was bad anyway, but then the Doctor said there was something wrong with her blood. They couldn't stop her bleeding. She was sick. I could see that. She was dying.'

She sighed, and shook her head, but it wasn't exactly grief in her eyes. She didn't look like someone who had just lost her mother.

'Am I in trouble?' she said, softly.

Ellen frowned.

'You said you were here about the painting,' said Rosa May. 'I know mom was crazy.'

Ellen thought about it for a moment, thought she understood.

'Is that why she came here, Rosa May? Yesterday. To give you a birthday present?'

Rosa May set her chin, rubbed at her small round nose with the back of her good hand.

'She said she wanted to make up for running out on me.'

She got up. Pushed out a sigh and slouched out of the room. Ellen heard voices in the corridor.

When she came back in she was carrying a package, struggling a little with her bad arm. She thumped it down on the coffee table.

She sat back down.

'It's all there,' she said.

Ellen stared. A big square package that might have been a VCR.

'I didn't touch a nickel,' said Rosa May. 'I knew it was wrong when she gave it to me.'

The paper had little cherubs on it. Cherubs and hearts. Rosa May ripped back a flap, pulled a hole in some plastic. Ellen saw the corner of a hundred dollar bill.

'My God.'

Rosa May sat back in her chair.

'She said there was more somewhere. I don't know where, though. I don't even know . . .' Her voice faded and she held herself, tilting back her head, trying not to cry. 'She said it was to make up for not being around.' Then she was shaking her head, touching tears away with the sleeve of her house coat.

'Why wasn't she?' said Ellen.

Rosa May looked at the TV screen, told the story as though she were reading from a text that had nothing to do with her. How her mother had left when she was fifteen, running off with a character named Roy. A trucker. Someone who had been involved in the Hoffa investigation.

'He was in the witness protection program or whatever they call it. That was why mom disappeared. That was why she could never be in touch.'

Ellen tilted her head.

'I know,' said Rosa May. 'That's what I thought. She sent me a letter when I was twenty-one, telling me this whole complicated story.'

She shook her head.

'That was just mom. There had to be *some* kind of story. It couldn't just be ordinary.'

'Ordinary?'

'You know, like this guy didn't want a ready-made family or whatever. Which is probably what it was, because he didn't look like much of a family man.'

'You met him?'

'No. There was a picture with the letter she sent. This guy. Good looking. She dumped me so she could have him.'

Ellen shook her head.

'I know that's not a nice way to talk,' said Rosa May. 'But we didn't really get along, mom and me. She . . . I think she had problems. Anyway.' She brushed hair out of her face, and looked at the package. 'I knew it was all wrong.' She gave herself a little shake, pushed the package across the table.

Ellen pushed it back.

'The money's yours, Rosa May.'

Rosa May put a hand to her hair where it was sticking out at the side.

'Your father painted a picture,' said Ellen.

She nodded.

'She told me. Franklin something.'

'Koenig. He was an Abstract Expressionist.'

'Is that, like, modern art?'

'Yes. He gave the picture to your mother. A long time ago. And your mother, she sold it. Recently. She sold it to a dealer in New York. And he sold it to the museum for twenty-three million dollars.'

Rosa May let out a yelp. It was halfway between a sob and a cry of pain. She brought her good hand up to her mouth.

'She didn't get twenty-three million dollars. The dealer took some of it.'

Rosa May pointed at the package as though it were a bomb.

'She said there's *two* in there.'

They both looked at it. Rosa May couldn't stop shaking her head.

'Congratulations,' said Ellen, but Rosa May wasn't even listening now, mumbling through her fingers, saying 'Oh my God' over and over.

'You're going to need an accountant,' said Ellen.

'Oh my good God.'

The tears came again, and this time she didn't hold them back.

Mary Beth came to the door. The girls wanted their goodnight kiss.

Sitting alone with the package, Ellen told herself that it was over. That was what it felt like anyway. She'd come this far, but the questions she'd wanted to put to Linda Carey would now remain unanswered. The best she could do was return to Manhattan, go see whoever was investigating Perry's disappearance. She could show them the documents she'd taken from his apartment. She could tell them about the San Diego catalog. She didn't see anything coming of it, and it would be bound to put her on the wrong side of Kruger. She was out of a job anyway. That seemed pretty clear. She was out of a career.

There were voices in the kitchen. Rosa May saying goodnight to her friend. The front door opened and closed, then Rosa May came back into the room, a little wild-eyed now, jittery. She was obviously having trouble coming to terms with what was happening.

'Can I get you a drink?' she said. 'Diet Pepsi's about it, unless you want coffee.'

'Pepsi would be great.' Ellen stood up. 'Let me help.'

She followed her into the tiny galley kitchen, wrestled the giant plastic bottle out of the refrigerator. Rosa May put tumblers on a counter top.

'Rosa May, did you – did it occur to you that last night . . .'

Rosa May took her drink, sipped it standing under the kitchen light.

'I thought about it. Thought maybe he was there for mom. For the money. But,' she shrugged, sipped. 'It seemed . . . it was so half-assed, you know? We walk out there and there's this guy with the suitcase in his arms. The alarm's going. The next thing I know is he's got a gun out, yelling at us to . . .' She shook her head. 'I mean I don't even know that I heard him right, I was so scared. But I think he told us to get in the car. I think he was on something is what it was.'

She shrugged, took another sip, then fixed Ellen with a straight look.

'There's something else I don't understand,' she said. 'Why you came here. Why you came down from Manhattan.'

'I wanted to talk to your mother. I wanted to understand something about Franklin Koenig's life.'

43

He didn't say a word, walked her through scrubby bushes to the back of the lot where the fence had been cut. Billy stepped through the gap, and Jay followed close behind. There was a car parked around the back of a building, a Mercedes with maybe ten years on it. Apartment buildings loomed no more than thirty feet away. TV noise drifted down from open windows.

'Don't do this, Jay.'

'You think I'd risk life imprisonment for you?'

He popped the locks, and told her to get in behind the wheel. Then he slotted into the passenger seat and dropped the keys in her lap.

'That's your trouble Billy: you think you're in a bad film.'

Make eye contact.

'Jay.'

He pushed the muzzle into her ribs, eyes on the road.

'Make a right on the street.'

She drove. They were going somewhere quieter. He'd want her out of the car when he did it.

Rush hour was winding down, but there was still traffic. They headed west towards the 17, went under it, came to a stop light behind a Lexus.

'I know I fucked up, Jay.'

'You've got this soundtrack playing in your head.'

Billy checked the rear-view mirror, saw the SUV crawl right up behind them. A Santa Fe. A woman was driving, moving her head around, gabbing on the phone.

'You telling me you're not in it for the drama,' she said, looking at him, wanting him to look at her.

'I'm a professional. Now drive.'

The lights were already changing to amber. She pinched a squeak from the tires, gunning it, her eyes flicking up to the mirror. The Santa Fe was right on her tail.

'And you're an amateur,' he said. 'But don't worry about it. There's plenty of work for people like you.'

They were heading for the suburbs. The city was dissolving into darkness up ahead. Billy saw a cop parked under a street light, a mall, lights, people. The Santa Fe indicated a turn. But then they passed the entrance to the mall and the Santa Fe was still there, good and close, really tailgating, the woman still talking on the phone, throwing her head back to laugh. She was perfect.

'Hope you're wearing comfortable shoes, Billy. You're gonna have a long walk back into town.'

Liar.

Another intersection, another light. The Lexus was slowing down.

'Slow down.'

Billy pumped the brakes.

Thunk.

The impact threw them back against the head rests.

'Shit!'

It was no big deal. A jolt. Nothing more than that. Stuff slid off the back seat. Jay twisted around, cursing and Billy saw the woman getting out of the Santa Fe, *still* talking on the cellphone. She looked at the back of the Merc, was coming around the side of the car. Billy saw her mouth working – *God, I'm soooooo sorry.*

'*Drive*,' spat Jay.

The woman was at Billy's window. There was a little blood on her mouth.

'I need your insur—'

'I said *drive!*'

Billy hit the gas, timing it just right. She slammed on the brakes as a truck flashed through the intersection. A Jeep slewed to a halt. Horns were blaring now, sounding on all sides. They were stuck, committed, blocking traffic. A guy was talking to the woman with the bloody mouth. He came over, squatting down a little to look inside. Jay tucked the gun under his shirt.

'Don't even think about it, Billy.'

Billy turned. Jay's face was flickering with repressed rage, but she didn't see him opening up with the Glock – not stuck there like that. The woman was rapping on her window, her voice coming through the glass.

'You stopped so suddenly.'

Billy rolled down the window.

'I need your details,' said the woman.

'Really?' said Billy. 'It didn't seem too bad to me.'

'There's glass all over the pavement.'

The guy leaned into view.

'You lost a couple of lights, buddy.'

Billy smiled.

'Don't buddy me, you bald fuck.'

The guy's mouth came open.

'You can't just drive away,' said the woman. 'It was at least partly your fault.'

People were yelling at them to get out of the way.

'Pull over to the side of the road.'

'Okay, I'm calling the police,' said the woman.

Billy put up her hands, and taking a breath, she pulled the key out of the ignition. Jay got a hand into her shirt as she was climbing out of the car, but she pulled herself clear and there wasn't a thing he could do.

She was out.

The beefy guy was staring like he was ready to bust her in the mouth.

'Thing is,' said Billy, 'I'm not really insured.'

'It's a *rental*,' yelled Jay, getting out on the other side, and slamming the door hard enough to make the car rock. 'Don't listen to her.'

Billy pointed the fob, and popped the locks. They shut down with an oily clunk. Then she opened it manually. The alarm started up. Jay's eyes snapped wide with understanding as he snatched at the rear passenger door, but it was still locked.

'Look out, he's got a gun!' yelled Billy, ducking inside, and killing the alarm. She jammed the key into the ignition, hearing screams, pulling away in a squeal of tires. The Merc *roared*, fishtailing as she thumped up onto the sidewalk, clipping a mail box, then a car, wrestling to get control. People were leaping in every direction.

And then she was gunning it, streaking down the central divider, laughing like a maniac, glaring at the mirror, *wanting* to see Jay, aching for just one glimpse of his stupid fucking face.

44

'She was such a dreamer,' she said. 'But not happy. She was never happy.'

They were back in the cramped living room, the TV flickering in the corner. More reality. A guy in a tuxedo talking to women in cocktail dresses.

'Your dad died the year you were born,' said Ellen. 'And your mom's husband, I mean the man she was married to when she . . . when she had the affair, he pretty much threw her out. It couldn't have been easy for her.'

Rosa May thought about this, then slowly shook her head.

'Yeah, I don't think it was that. I mean, she never talked about him or anything. This Franklin . . .'

'Koenig.'

'We didn't have pictures of him or anything. The first I ever heard about him was when Mom showed up yesterday, when she told me. And anyway . . . it wasn't that sort of unhappy.'

She was picking at the end of the kitchen roll, rucked up in the housecoat, her hair still on end.

'How do you—'

'She used to hurt herself,' said Rosa May.

Ellen thought she'd misheard. She turned her head a little, sitting forward on the couch. Rosa May was frowning, a piece of tissue in her fingers.

'Rosa May?'

Rosa May blinked.

'She used to cut herself on the legs,' she said in a soft voice. Then she was looking at Ellen with her sad blue eyes. 'There were scars on her legs. At the tops of her thighs.'

She shrugged.

'I never saw her do it but once. But there were other times when I saw blood on the sheets or on her clothes.'

'You saw her . . .'

'This one time. She was on the floor in the bedroom. I was maybe eleven or twelve at the time. I heard her crying. She used to cry like that, and I went to take a look. Anyway, like I say, she was on the floor.'

'You saw her . . . cut herself?'

Rosa May nodded, then peeled another strip off the kitchen roll.

'She did it with a straight razor. Very slow. There was a lot of blood. She just cut her leg, and then she went quiet, like she'd fallen asleep. It really scared me. I thought she'd passed out. I started yelling and she came after me in the bathroom, really lit into me, screaming and yelling and telling me not to say anything to Vern.'

'Vern?'

'My step-daddy. He knew, of course. I remember him yelling at her a lot. I guess he didn't understand it either. She'd come home some times and she'd been to the doctor's and Vern would blow up.'

Ellen frowned. It was difficult to follow.

'The doctor? What? For the cuts?'

'No. She'd bind the cuts herself. She always had bandages. There'd be bandages drying with her panty hose.' She seemed to catch up with herself, with what she was saying. 'I'm sorry,' she said, shaking her head. 'These last two days . . . It's shaken me up. Brought all this stuff back. You probably don't need to hear all this.'

'No, I do. I mean, I'm interested.'

Rosa May looked at her glass. There was no more soda.

'You were saying,' said Ellen. 'About the doctor?'

'It wasn't really the doctor. That's what she called it, but really she was giving blood. Vern used to get mad at her and she'd say she was doing it to save people's lives or whatever, but really it was like the cutting. And she wouldn't wait between times. You're supposed to wait eight weeks or whatever, but sometimes she'd go back – go to a different hospital three weeks later. And then she'd be sick, and fainting and what have you. You know, real anemic. Vern made her eat liver. She took iron and that made her sick too.'

She popped her eyes, faking a big smile.

'Wow, I'm making her sound like a crazy woman.'

Ellen shrugged, nodded.

'But she really wasn't. I mean that was it really. She just had this thing about cutting herself.'

'Rosa May. Last night – the complications, you think it was because of all these years of . . .?'

'I don't know. Sure. Why not? I mean it has to be bad for you, right?'

She shook her head, lost in thought.

A minute passed. The TV flickered blue, green, blue.

'Anyway, with her being so crazy and hard on me all the time, it didn't matter too much when she took off with this Roy character. Now *him* she had photographs of. She hid them from Vern, of course. But I knew where her hiding places were. Where she kept her stuff.'

'So she was seeing him when she was still with Vern?'

'Oh, for a while. A year at least. And I don't think Vern ever knew until it was too late.'

'You didn't tell him.'

She shook her head.

'I thought she'd forget about this other guy. I didn't want to see Vern get hurt.' She was thoughtful for a moment, cradling her arm. 'She was pretty flighty, but it wasn't just stupid or slutty, you know or her needing to know she was attractive all the time. She was pretty clear on *that* score, always combing her hair and what have you. She was just very . . . independent I suppose. Modern really. I kind of looked up to her for it. The fact that she was cheating kind of evened up the score. With the guys, I mean. The way they were in our neighborhood. Even the married ones.'

She shook her head.

'Anyways, she stayed true to this Roy guy. And she didn't forget me.' Abruptly her eyes filled with tears. She dragged a scrap of kitchen towel across her face. Ellen leaned forward, and put a hand on her knee.

'Everything's going to be okay, Rosa May. It's going to be better now.'

Rosa May stared at her over the kitchen towel.

'That's what broke me up,' she said. 'Not when they told me she was dead. A nurse came in this morning to tell me she'd passed away, you know. It was when they gave me her . . . the . . . the pictures she was carrying. They had some personal . . .'

'Effects.'

'Yeah, you know.'

'They thought she was someone else,' said Ellen. 'At the reception desk. Pauline something. She was carrying fake ID.'

Rosa May shook her head, almost smiling.

'You could tell me anything now, and I'd believe it.' She blew her nose. 'No, it wasn't ID. It was this little . . .'

She stood up, went out to the kitchen, came back with a battered leather billfold. It was thickly wadded with paper, receipts, Ellen guessed. There were little plastic windows for photographs.

'This wallet. The nurse said there was a photograph of me in it, a photograph of me when I was a young girl, and she asked me if I wanted it . . . and . . .' She was crying again, as she struggled to remove the photograph with her good hand. 'And I said how do you know it's me? And she said because your name is on the back.'

She finally managed to get the photograph out, and handed it to Ellen – a cheap snapshot, badly creased with years of handling. Rosa May, aged eleven or twelve, maybe. A beautiful young girl with braces on her teeth.

'She carried it around all these years,' said Rosa May, snuffling into her kitchen roll.

Ellen didn't know what to say. That her mother obviously loved her a great deal? In her book, loving someone meant at least sticking around.

'You look pretty,' was the best she could come up with. She handed the picture back. 'That your mom?' she said, pointing at the other picture.

'And Roy.'

Rosa May handed her the billfold.

'She was behind on her book-keeping,' said Ellen. 'Look at all these receipts.'

She held the picture up to the light. An elderly couple: Linda Carey, and Roy, the ruin of a once handsome man. He was in his seventies perhaps, holding himself very stiff. He looked very unhappy about having his picture taken.

Ellen slowly rose.

She stumbled against the coffee table, getting closer to a lamp.

'Are you okay?' said Rosa May.

Ellen pulled the picture from the billfold, and held it underneath the lampshade where the light was brightest. Rosa May said something to her, but she didn't hear it, studying Roy's features now, her face no more than a couple of inches from the picture. A man in his seventies with cropped silver hair. A cleft chin, eyes set wide in his broad face, a notch in the left eyebrow. The resemblance was uncanny.

She shook her head, unable to quite take it in. It wasn't a resemblance.

45

Billy pulled off the road and rolled in behind a billboard that stood back from the highway. She was coming down off the adrenaline now, seeing everything differently. Even the thought of Jay standing in the middle of an intersection, tricked out of his ride, barely raised a smile. She was fucked. She was so fucked she couldn't even count the ways.

She switched off the engine and got out of the car. She lit a cigarette, cupping her hands as if there was a wind, which there wasn't. It was warm in Arizona. A different warmth to the clinging heat of Manhattan. There was a dryness to the air here, even as it cooled. She walked away from the car, kicking at stones and discarded beer cans. She was so fucked, she didn't even know what to do. And she needed a drink. She really needed a drink.

Feeble lights twinkled in the distance. She'd come to some flat nowhere between the suburbs that stretched out into the desert. A truck was coming along the highway, brights up full. She raised her hand, letting the fucker know he was blinding her. The truck slowed down, came to a halt. There was a hiss of air brakes.

'Hey baby!'

The trucker was hanging out the window. A big round-shouldered guy with a beard.

'Go fuck yourself,' said Billy.

The guy laughed, then pulled away.

Billy watched the tail lights until they were out of sight.

She finished her cigarette, and tossed it into the weeds. What she'd have liked to do was go back to the building on South Mariposa. Kick in the door of the apartment, stick a gun in Ellen Lindz's face and ask where the money was. Her or Rosa May. Or both. Maybe grab one of the kids. Get some answers that way. But South Mariposa was where Jay would be heading. He'd grab a cab or boost a car or something. He'd be back there by now, on the job, being professional. He wouldn't stay lost for long.

Thinking about that, she remembered the shit sliding off the back of the seat when they were rear ended, turned and walked back to the car. She opened the back door. There was a bundle of stuff on the floor. Macho special ops gear. A black canvas jacket, a black baseball cap. A pair of black sneakers. There was even a pair of night-vision goggles in a black nylon carry case.

The attaché case was under the passenger seat. She didn't see it at first but then she was groping for the handle, pulling it up onto the back seat. It wasn't an attaché case. It was a laptop. She brought it around to the front and got in behind the wheel. When she opened it up, the screen blinked on and she was looking at a map of Phoenix. There was a tiny black icon in the center of the map. An ace of spades. Very Jay. Billy studied the screen, clicked 'zoom', and the software jumped her in closer. She could see street names now. The ace of spades was at the angle of Buckeye Road, and the 17: South Mariposa Street. Rosa May King's apartment building.

There was a GPS receiver there. That was her guess. Duct-taped to the inside of a fender. A car he wanted to be able to track. She blew out a stream of air, pushing the stiff blond hair back from her forehead. With the system she knew, the GPS unit didn't have enough power to transmit so you had to dial a number, call it the way you would a cell-phone.

She was looking around for dial-up icon now. And there it was, right in the bottom left hand corner of the screen. She put the cursor on it, clicked.

A light came on. There was a series of digital beeps. A box popped up – *connecting*.

The ace disappeared.

'Shit.'

She stared, open mouthed, waiting for something to happen. But the map was frozen now. She re-clicked the dial-up icon.

'Piece of junk.'

The icon reappeared. Blinking on and off now, moving. A car, then, just like she thought, moving incrementally, advancing in little jumps as the GPS unit updated the coordinates, and the cartographic software replenished the screen. Whoever it was, was getting onto the interstate.

46

Ellen drove north to the 10, then headed west, driving with her hands high on the wheel – hanging on more than driving, that was what it felt like – blinking eyes that were raw from fatigue and dehydration. Twentynine Palms was on the other side of the Sonora desert, a two hundred mile drive. She figured it would take four hours at most. She'd get something to eat on the road, maybe stay overnight in a motel, be in Twentynine Palms when the Desert Ranch Store opened.

Linda Carey had carried fake ID, and she'd never used credit cards, but she'd kept records of her expenditure, till receipts she carried in her billfold – had probably kept them until there was a good wad, and then stuffed them into a drawer somewhere; that was what *she* did anyway – it was her way of placating the gods of personal finance. Sometimes she checked them against her credit card statements, but mostly they just sat there until she threw them into the garbage for the identity thieves to go through.

Linda Carey hadn't checked her receipts against anything. The only information they carried was the amounts she spent and, on some of the receipts anyway, where she spent it. The bigger supermarket chains thanked you for shopping with them, and put their address and telephone number at the top of the bill, just in case you wanted to go back.

When she'd told Rosa May who Roy was, Rosa May had barely reacted. It had been too much for her. The whole thing. Her mother, the shooting, the money. Above all, the money. She'd walked out of the living room, gone to be with her little girls, leaving Ellen alone.

There were maybe sixty receipts, some for a couple of bucks, some for a couple of hundred, some too faded to read; a patchy record of her last twelve months. There were receipts from New York and San Francisco, receipts from a motel in Cheyenne, Wyoming, and there were receipts from the Desert Ranch Store in Twentynine Palms. Those receipts went back the furthest – there were three of them spaced at weekly intervals. They were for a couple of hundred dollars each time. And they were itemized. Food and household stuff. They were the only receipts with cleaning products on them. Twentynine Palms was home. That was Ellen's guess anyway. On one of those receipts, razor blades were itemized, as was shaving foam. So either Linda Carey was still shaving her legs, or there was a guy in the picture. A guy called Roy.

It seemed pretty crazy, but once she'd seen it like that, she couldn't see it any other way, and then she'd remembered what Perry had said about the calls he'd received from Arizona and Nevada, and a picture started to form. She'd stood there in the middle of the living room, a wad of paper in her hand, looking at the door Rosa May had just walked through, and she'd come to a decision. If she could find the store, show the photograph of Carey and Roy, there was a chance somebody might recognize them, there was a chance someone might know where they lived.

Her headlights sucked up the 10 which stretched away in front of her, straight and hard as a piano wire, lit here and there by the sparkling reflectors of the big rigs, and the tail lights of an SUV.

Koenig was alive, she was pretty sure of it. He'd met Leslie Ann Benton some time in 1948 before the Liberty Diner was demolished, had met her for a leisurely conversation long before their first official contacts at the Cedar Tavern, or the first supposed epiphany in his Bowery rooms. They'd met to discuss modalities, the way in which things might work – that was her guess anyway. She knew exactly what he looked like, and she had a feeling she'd already heard his voice.

Under the desert

The mercury had hovered just below 110 all day, but now it was almost chilly as the old man made his way up through the clumps of Mojave yucca towards the rock formations that formed a broken rampart on the south side of the property. He was carrying a gun in his right hand, and walked hunched forward, oblivious to the spikes and spears of plants snagging his loose-fitting clothes.

It was incredibly still. So still, you could hear the kangaroo rats foraging in the tinder dry scrub. There were snakes out here too. There were always plenty of snakes. He had seen a mountain lion turd near the house a week earlier, and normally it would have been an exciting thing to think about the creature out there stalking in the dark, but tonight he wouldn't have noticed if it had been waiting for him on his favorite rock.

It wasn't waiting, of course. The desert didn't do that. Desert life had a way of shrinking back like water from a drop of grease, unless there was something wrong with you – you were walking funny, say, or lying face down in the weeds – then it might come take a look. He'd often thought about that, the possibility of keeling over when he was out on one of his rambles. He'd almost hoped for it sometimes as something that would remove the burden of responsibility.

He'd collapse and the buzzards would spot him; then the coyotes. Or maybe a dusty kit fox, padding lightly on fur-covered feet, sniffing lightly. The coyotes watched the buzzards. He'd watched them do it, seen them break into a trot as a buzzard dropped earthwards. They'd be there pretty quick. The coyotes and the buzzards. They'd take him apart like a garbage bag.

The boulder loomed palely in the dark. It was the size of a Buick, and flattened at one end like the bill of a goose. Stumbling a little, he came up against it, brushing the harsh granitic surface with trembling fingers before sitting down in the notch he'd used for more than thirty years.

Shallow old-man breaths in the furtive crackling night. His old squeeze box body. The stone was warm under his hands – bone dry, stone dry stone, warm as a kiln brick and harsh as a cat's tongue. It was funny how he'd come to experience the world through his hands. It was as though they had taken over from his eyes. He brailled the world now, loved the swell and pucker of it under his fingertips, loved to palp the ribbed and wrinkled surfaces. He didn't sculpt, though. Didn't cut. Hated the idea of banging away with a hammer. He molded mostly. Also, he made molds of things. Her face. Negative and positive. Like the inner and outer surface of the Easter egg. That was certainly one of his earliest, happiest memories – discovering the softly dimpled inner shell. Certainly. The equivalent of the first touched breast.

He brought his hands up to his own outer face. He didn't know why he had come here now. It was a thing he did, of course – come up to the rock to sit and think after a day working underground. Sometimes, when his breathing allowed it, he'd smoke a cigarette, or just sit and enjoy the air, maybe fire off a couple of rounds from the Magnum. Firing the gun was always a good idea. The hollow crack and boom of the .357 let the neighbors know you were home. Kept the sons of bitches off his property. But he didn't generally go up there in the dark. The dark was for the creatures that could see in the dark, like that mountain lion or the scorpions with their clever infra eyes. Retinas. Another concave miracle. As for him, he could barely see in the day anymore.

He'd seen her though. He'd seen her on the TV.

He pushed his finger ends against the convex flesh of his eyes. She was dead. He couldn't bring himself to know that her life had stopped. The thought of her heart, stalled in her chest, of the blood turning to black string in her veins almost stopped his breathing.

It was the end of him. The end of work.

The house was strewn with her clothes. They were scattered among the other wreckage. He'd pulled them out of the laundry hamper the day he knew she'd gone, ripping, rending, breaking the mold. They'd been on the floor a year now, were trampled and scattered with the broken glass and china, the torn books and files, the broken mirrors.

They'd killed her in Phoenix. When he'd first heard about the painting, when he'd first realized what she'd done, he had wanted to kill her himself. He hadn't even known about the painting until he saw it on the screen and then, later, in the newspaper. He'd forgotten all about it. It wasn't something they ever talked about. That time. What he'd done back then. But she'd had it rolled up, and tucked away somewhere. A keepsake.

She'd walked out in the middle of his work. He'd lost two months careful preparation because of her. He'd wanted to kill her. In the end, he'd done the next best thing, and tried to kill the painting. But that hadn't worked out either. They'd killed the curator. Also. He was sure of that. And the dealer. Also. He was sure.

He shook his head now, his hands over his eyes. They called her the 'Mirror Woman' on the news. As soon as he'd heard about the sale in New York, he'd known they were going to hunt her down. The press talked about the mystery woman, but he knew she would leave a trail. She'd always left a trail. It didn't matter how often he talked to her about it, she was always writing stuff down, scribbling things on bits of paper, keeping records of expenditure, wanting to have a post office box, wanting to take a photograph – 'just one' – collecting things. She said he was paranoid. Well, now she knew how paranoid he was.

He took his fingers away, and without looking, picked up the Magnum. It was over. She'd brought it to an end long before he was ready. He was only seventy-four years old. There were years in him yet. Years of work, his best work probably. And at the back of his mind, there had always been the thought that people would come; they'd make the trip to see the frozen gallery. That would not happen now. They would come for him, they would kill him, and the gallery would be destroyed.

From this elevation the house made a solid-looking 'L'. The light was on in the kitchen. If you listened really hard, you could hear the generator in the basement. He was connected to the grid, but drew his night-time power from the generator. One of his neighbors used to grow marijuana in his swimming pool – out in the desert everyone was cooking speed or growing grass. The guy had covered the pool with dry wall to beat aerial surveillance, had strung up u.v. lights to fool the plants, but then the local power company noticed he was sucking amps around the clock, and had tipped off the feds. The week the feds had come knocking at his neighbor's door, he'd installed his generator. No one was getting into his swimming pool.

One angle of the 'L' was the house, and the other used to be the rooms. When he'd bought the place back in the seventies, it was already pretty run down; a motel supposedly, although why anyone would drive all the way up there to spend the night, he'd never been able to figure out. There was the army base, of course. So maybe whoever built it thought they could skim a little change from the soldiers looking for off-base kicks.

The swimming pool had been sited in the angle of the 'L'. When he'd arrived it was already falling to pieces from years of neglect. There'd been big cracks in the sides. It was deep at both ends, rectangular. The first thing he'd done, before he even started work on the main building, was rent a backhoe and dig the passage that connected the pool to the house. Then he'd covered the whole thing with concrete. Reinforced. The bunker. Linda's name for it. The refrigeration unit had come from a transit firm in San Bernardino. They'd let him have it cheap, but it had been down to him to get it out of the container. It was a big unit that really sucked the juice, but it got the pool down to zero, put thick ice on the walls, and kept it there.

It was the gallery that had kept them poor. That was what she'd always said, and it was true. But the work was the work. He'd starved to buy paint and canvas in Manhattan, and this was no different to that. Or rather, this *was* different to that, because what he'd achieved here was significant – he had no doubts about that. He'd changed everything long before the others came along. That had been the hardest thing over the years. Not the isolation, not the fear, but the imposed obscurity.

Something big was moving in the brush. Stones trickled into a gully. But he was oblivious, thinking about the work now, thinking about the piece he'd had to abandon. It was the biggest thing he'd attempted, and dramatic in a way he'd always distrusted, but that was part of getting old – you became bolder, stronger. And of course he had never been fettered by commercial pressure or the desire for recognition. He'd suspended the piece, thought of it as his angel, even though there were no wings. It was manneristic in a way, a great altar piece, a secular altar. He hadn't been down there for a week now. Longer perhaps. He was too depressed. There'd be some mold. There always was despite the antibiotics. There'd be insects.

The shooting in the parking lot was just a story. He was sure of that. They'd found her, and they'd asked her where he was, and now it was only a matter of time before they showed up at the house. But he was ready for them. Everything was prepared. And he relished it in a way, relished the idea of confrontation, of seeing her, particularly. Benton. The bent one bent on world domination. He loved the idea of telling her how he'd done it; how he'd acquired the body from the paupers' cemetery on Hart Island (thirty bucks it had cost him, *including* delivery); how he'd knocked out the few remaining teeth, then hacked off the hand; how he'd had his own teeth pulled so they wouldn't be able to identify him. He relished the idea of showing her what he'd achieved, showing her how wrong she'd always been, how sterile, how small. He'd make sure she understood all that before she died.

48

Dan hadn't died immediately. It was his mother who had called her at college to give her the news. They had him in St Mary's on the Marylebone Road, didn't think he was going to make it through the night. She'd taken the train down from Oxford, remembered the journey as a jolting neon-lit nightmare in which she'd stood out by the doors rather than suffer the stares of the other passengers crammed into the compartment, weeping all the way, almost crazy with guilt and grief. She'd reached the hospital after visiting hours, had been taken up to the ICU by an intern, who explained the situation as they went. Dan had sustained injuries to the head, four of the vertebra in his lower back had been smashed in the fall, and the ribs on his right side had been driven inwards causing massive internal injuries. He'd been unconscious on arrival, had regained consciousness briefly and was now heavily sedated. They were not going to operate.

She'd greeted his mother in a dingy corridor. They'd held each other for a moment, saying nothing, and then she'd gone in.

She'd steeled herself to go inside the curtain that had been drawn around the bed, expecting to find him horribly disfigured, but in fact his face was completely unblemished apart from a couple of small cuts on his chin. He looked like he was sleeping, a slight frown puckering the skin of his forehead. She'd taken his hand, sat there weeping quietly, talking to him softly, telling him that everything she'd said on the phone she'd said in anger, that she'd meant none of it, that she'd always loved his work, and him. Minutes passed. An hour. There was paint on his hand, dabs of earth-color pigment on his knuckles, and under the nails. The hand was slack and cool, completely unresponsive. His breathing had become more and more shallow, and then, in the moment that he'd passed, he'd pushed out a soft little cry, almost a cry of pleasure, and he'd come awake, his eyes fully open for a moment. His head rolled over and he saw her there, and frowned. He'd not been strong enough to pull away from her, but that was what he'd wanted to do. She'd opened her fingers, and his hand had dropped onto the sheets. He'd turned away from her and died.

A hotel in the desert.

She woke up once in the night, thought for a moment that she was back at Oxford, alone in her narrow college bed, and then she remembered Leslie Ann, and Koenig, and Perry – the whole history of deceit. She thought of Ben, only two hours away, sleeping in a bed she didn't know, in a room she didn't know. The head of the bed was under the window and she could see the desert dark, prickling with stars. After Manhattan, the quiet was unnerving. She pushed herself up on her elbows and stayed like that for a while, staring stupidly at the fireplace on the other side of the room. There were logs, a couple of twists of paper. The makings of an evening blaze.

The next time she opened her eyes was in dazzling sunlight. Through the window she could see scattered rubble strewn over terrain that rose gently towards a distant bluff. The land was yellow. Blue shadows folded it into purple and blue black. It looked hot.

She showered, and put on the clothes she'd arrived in, feeling dirty, feeling lost. She had a moment of longing for Ben, of wanting to hold him, see him, smell him.

She ate breakfast by the swimming pool, asked the waitress, a rail-thin woman with a weather-beaten face, where the Desert Ranch Store was. It was impossible to miss, apparently. You went down the hill to the highway. You made a left. The store was on the right about two miles along.

Ellen held up a hand, shielding her eyes in the glare.

'Is there somewhere I can buy clothes?' she said. 'T-shirts, jogging pants. That kind of thing.'

The woman stared.

'I had my bag stolen.' Ellen patted the shoulder bag on the seat next to her. 'Luckily they didn't get my purse.'

'They have stuff at the Desert Ranch, or there's a Circle K, a Costco. We got everything here.'

The Twentynine Palms Highway ran east west in a straight line. There were stores set back from the road, and every hundred feet or so bail bonds offices or car dealerships in about equal numbers. The judicial system seemed to have a considerable stake in the local community. A half mile along, she found a clutch of electronics stores in a mall, and picked up a new battery for her hearing aid. The world was stereophonic again.

The Desert Ranch Store was a glass-fronted block set back from the highway, with buckled asphalt for parking in front. There was nothing 'ranchy' about it. She rolled into the shade of a street sign, then went through sliding glass doors into an air-conditioned space that could have been anywhere in the USA. There were ruler-straight aisles, Day-Glo stickers advertising discounts and specials. The a/c thundered through silver-papered ducts. It was cold enough to start her shivering in the refrigerated section.

She bought a couple of bottles of mineral water, then found a T-shirt with a palm tree logo, plain sweat pants, cotton underwear and a pair of sneakers.

At the cash register she took the photograph from her shoulder bag, held it up for the clerk to see, asked him if he'd seen either the man or the woman in the store recently. 'The lady – I know she shopped here a lot,' she said. 'May not have been around for a year or so.'

The clerk, a young guy with big expressive eyes shook his head. Without turning away from her, he yelled to the woman on the next register.

'Edna's been here twenty years,' he said. 'If anybody knows her, Edna will.'

Edna said the woman looked familiar, but beyond that, she couldn't be of any help.

Ellen was on her way out the door, when someone called her back. A woman in a black jogging suit. Stiff-looking blonde hair shelved out from under her Lakers cap, shading intense blue eyes.

'Let me take a look at that,' she said, extending a muscular hand.

Ellen hesitated, then handed over the picture.

'She's from around here, you say?'

'That's right.'

The woman scratched her throat, musing, turning the photograph to catch the light. She had acne scars on her cheeks.

'I'm not sure about her,' she said, 'but *he* looks familiar.'

'He does?'

The woman tapped the photograph with a nicotine-stained finger. 'What name does he go by?'

'Roy. I think.'

'Roy.' The woman stared. 'Just Roy?'

'I'm not really sure.'

'So he's what? Her husband or something?'

'Something like that.'

'And her name's . . .'

'Possibly Pauline. Pauline Brook.'

'So he's Roy Brook. If they're married, I mean.'

'It's not quite as simple as that.'

The woman gave a nod. Apparently, she knew about unsimple.

'What are you, a cop? Parole officer?'

Ellen took the picture back, and looked out at the street.

'It's okay,' said the woman. 'Makes no difference to me.'

She leaned in towards Ellen, getting too close.

'You should put up a flyer.'

'I'm only here . . . I'm only going to be here for a day.'

'So what? Make some copies, put a little note underneath with your cell phone number. Put 'em on every telegraph pole in town. That's what I'd do.' She was moving off now, a hand raised. 'Like I say, somebody's gonna know who she is.'

Ellen looked at the photograph.

'They got a photocopier right here,' said the woman, pausing in the doorway. She pointed at a machine in the corner. 'Do a couple dozen. Get some push pins. Worked for my dog.'

She smiled when she said that, and it was a pleasant smile, surprisingly. Ellen looked over at the photocopier. It wasn't such a bad idea.

'You like dogs?' said the woman.

Ellen shook her head, moving in the direction of the machine now.

'Well, good luck,' said the woman and she was gone.

Ellen made thirty copies. She marked '*Have you seen us?*' under the picture, put her cell phone number under that.

The push pins didn't want to go into the telegraph poles. She got tar all over her hands and a splinter in her thumb. By midday she was about ready to give up. The heat was unbearable, and even with the bandanna she'd bought, she felt like her head was cooking. And Twentynine Palms was a big place. It spread either side of the highway, and ran on pretty much unbroken to Joshua Tree which in turn became Yucca Valley.

On top of everything else, someone was taking her flyers. Coming back east along the highway, working the south side stores, she saw that two had been ripped down, and realized she should put the cellphone number on little tabs along the bottom so that people could rip them off without taking the whole flyer.

She worked Twentynine Palms for two hours, then drove west over the hill towards Joshua Tree, stopping from time to time in a car dealership, or a store, even trying the bail bonds offices because you never knew, handing out flyers and asking her questions. And it got her nowhere.

At five o'clock in the afternoon, with the sun just beginning to lose a little of its intensity, she walked into a mail receiving agency in Yucca Valley, about ten miles west of where she'd started. There was a counter at the back of the room where a fan was turning back and forth, stirring the fetid air.

She didn't see the guy sitting in the lawn chair at first. He was sitting at the end of the counter, reading a paperback.

'Excuse me?'

The guy looked up as another man came in behind her and walked over to the post office boxes that ran the length of one wall.

Ellen showed the guy in the chair the flyer. He looked at the photograph, then looked at Ellen.

'What is it with you people?'

He leaned past her, smiling.

'Hey, Mort. Check this out. Now they send the pretty one.'

Mort, an elderly man, with a palsied tremor to his narrow head, looked Ellen up and down, sucking his teeth.

'Don't tell me,' said the other guy. 'You're the nice cop.'

Ellen shook her head.

'I'm not a cop.'

'I'm sorry,' said the guy, deadpan, 'I meant *special agent*.'

'I'm a reporter,' said Ellen, starting to feel very uneasy.

'Yeah, *right*.'

'With the *New York Times*.'

The guy pointed a stubby finger.

'So what's that in your ear?'

Ellen instinctively reached, covering her ear with a lock of hair. The guy was grinning now, thinking he'd caught her out.

'If you must know, it's a hearing aid. I messed up my ear listening to loud music.'

'Sure,' said the guy, but he wasn't smiling anymore. He was trying to decide whether or not to believe her.

'I'm writing an article about Linda Carey,' Ellen went on. 'She sold a painting in New York a couple of weeks ago.'

'I read about this,' said Mort, pointing a finger. 'The *Mirror* woman.'

'That's right,' said Ellen. 'She was killed in Phoenix yesterday. I'm trying to find her husband. This man.' She held the picture in front of Mort. He stared, slack-mouthed, shook his head. 'She may not have been using her real name. She may have been calling herself Pauline Brook. Or something else altogether. I just wanted to ask if you ever saw her come in here.'

The guy in the chair stood up. He leaned over the counter, putting his weight on his knuckles. He was perspiring heavily despite the fan.

'Lying bitch,' he said.

'Now come on, Nate,' said the old man. 'Maybe she's telling the truth.'

'I'm talking about the other one. Lying bitch. Came in here flashing her fake ID.' He frowned, trying to recall the name. 'Agent . . .'

'Rissoli,' said Ellen, going cold. The FBI agent who'd called on Taylor Bissel. The FBI agent the FBI knew nothing about.

'Rissoli,' said Nate, eyeing her coolly. 'Yeah, that's right. 'How'd you know that?'

Ellen was shaking her head.

'Did you tell her . . .'

Nate threw up his hands.

'What am I going to do? I thought she was a fucking fed.'

'What did you tell her?'

He gestured at the boxes lining the walls.

'I told her the old woman's name – the name she used here anyway, and I gave her the address. This is all mandatory public information since 'ninety-nine anyway.'

'It is?' said Mort, looking at the thick brown envelope in his hands.

Ellen swallowed hard.

'Then you can tell me.'

Nate got a sly look.

'Oh no,' he said, rubbing finger and thumb together under her nose. 'If you're such a big shot reporter, *you* can pay.'

49

Billy bumped the car off the twisting road. Then, working her way around to the back of a big granite outcrop, nosed into the weeds and turned off the engine. She got out. After the air conditioned interior, the desert air came as quite a shock. She stood there, squinting in the late afternoon light, just able to see the top of the house over the slow roll of the stony land. Dotted all over the slope were Joshua trees, primitive-looking things, some of them just straight stalks driven into the ground like raggedy broom handles.

She walked back to the road, then made her way uphill, keeping her eyes on the house. She stepped over a dry ditch onto what she guessed was the property itself, although there was no indication – no mail box or anything like that. Whoever owned this house, valued their privacy. Squatting a little, she worked her way up the slope, keeping a little to the side of the building to avoid being seen. Stuff moved in the undergrowth ahead of her. She saw a lizard on a rock, *knew* there were snakes around. She paused for breath, blinking sweat out of her eyes, then took the gun from her waistband. She had to wipe her right hand on her pants to take the safety off. Snakes, she could not handle. Snakes, she did not like.

She came to a halt within thirty feet of the house. It was a one-story building laid out in an L and very, very rundown. Some of the boards used to patch up an exterior wall had been left unpainted. They'd used roofing felt cut into rectangles instead of real tile on the roof. On the far side of the L, some of the windows were broken. Net drapes hung limply in the baking air. In the angle of the L there was a patch of dirt the size of a tennis court that had been cleared of rocks. Tire tracks led to the front door. There was no sign of a car.

Billy wedged herself between a couple of rocks. The door looked like it was held back with a piece of string or wire. She checked her watch. It was just after six. It had taken her thirty minutes to get up there from the town. With any luck, the Lindz klutz wouldn't even get as far as Yucca Valley, let alone walk into the mail service place, but with the kind of luck she'd been having, there was always a possibility she might.

Whether it was a personal thing or whether she'd been pressured into doing something by the museum, Billy didn't know, but she was sure that Lindz had come to Twentynine Palms to fix something that had gotten unfixed when the painting was bought, and she couldn't see that meaning anything other than recovering the money. The fact that she was driving around with a GPS unit attached to her car was just confirmation. People didn't track art historians. The GPS unit was a worry, of course. Twice in the past twelve hours, she'd used Jay's laptop to dial in, and gotten a busy signal. So either Jay, or someone Jay had set up with the software, was calling too. Either way, it meant that whenever Lindz did get there, if she ever did, the other parties would be able to find it too. She'd considered taking the unit off the Alero, but by that time she'd been talking to the dickhead in the Yucca Valley mail receiving agency, and figured she had all the advantage she needed.

Because how hard could it be? The character in the photograph looked old. Older even than Carey. Old people were easy to intimidate. Of course, nothing said he was even still alive. All she really knew was that this had been Carey's home, and other people, people from the museum, wanted to take a look at it.

She fixed her attention on the front door. She'd been there maybe twenty minutes and seen nothing.

She scudded across the patch of open ground to the door, and came up against the sun-warped, splintered boards. There was nothing. No radio. No television. A smell drifted out from the interior. A bad smell. Blinking perspiration out of her eyes, she edged around the door frame, and peered into what looked like a kitchen.

There was a screen door. She pushed it back on squeaky hinges, then stepped inside. A rat scurried across the floor and under some cupboards. There was food on the floor. Meatballs, it looked like. A big footprint smeared sauce. She looked around, saw open cans, torn packaging, broken crockery. Flies drifted into the air as the refrigerator came on with a shudder. A big yellow thing with rust around the hinges. A piece of seventies junk. Billy wiped her mouth. There was a cold beer in there, she just knew it. She shook her head, and moved deeper in.

A narrow passage, then a living room. The blinds were down. In the gloom she could make out terrible seventies furniture. It was Naugahyde heaven with a couple of rag rugs over a bare wooden floor. She took a step and her foot caught something on the floor. A picture. A canvas half sticking out from under a couch. It looked like it had been slashed and stomped. She pulled it out, lifted it up. A red and black thing. Smeary daubs over darker shapes. Billy gave a nod, looked for a signature, found something, a crude scrawl. The 'K' was unmistakable. So was the last letter, a big looping 'g'. She'd been right all along. Forgeries. Carey and her old man in it together. If it had been genuine, the thing she was holding would have been worth a couple of million dollars with or without the damage. She could have walked away with the thing under her arm. She dropped it on the couch and moved on.

A noise. A footstep it sounded like. Billy tensed up, listening. But there was nothing now. She moved silently through the gloom to an open doorway, stood there, listening. The smell was stronger here. A weird smell. Rotten but not like rotting meat or vegetables. She was going to find the old man dead. That was the next thing – pushing open a bathroom door to find him dead on the shitter with maggots in his eyes. She'd had a few of those in her ATF days. Well, dead was fine as long as she could find the money. She looked back at the fake Koenig. The house was probably full of them. Somewhere or other there'd be a studio, paints, brushes.

The room ahead was even darker, the windows boarded up. On the wall opposite heavy drapes covered what she guessed was a third. She took a step, then twitched the drapes back on the brass rail. Something fell to the floor, and scuttled away into the shadows. She shrank back, sucking in her breath. A scorpion. She'd caught a glimpse of it before it disappeared. The whole house was probably crawling with insects. Insects and rats.

A refrigerator came on.

She turned sharply, the gun out in front of her. That was what it had sounded like – the compressor kicking in. It was humming there in the dark right ahead of her. She went back to the door, looking for a light switch, couldn't see one.

Scuttling sounds. Coming from behind her. In the living room she'd just come through. The place was alive with them. She shuddered, moved across the room in the direction of the humming sound.

She came up against a cabinet. Not wooden. Metal. She ran her hands over the cold surface, found glass. A chilled cabinet. That was what it felt like. The kind of thing you might find in a restaurant. Again she was fumbling for a switch, and again she found nothing. It was starting to annoy her, being in the dark. But then she did find it. A big clunky thing. She flipped it. A blue neon light flickered on.

It was a cold cabinet. A chrome and glass thing that looked like it dated from the fifties. The neon tube produced an eerie blue glow that illuminated a little orange head. There was condensation on the glass, so it was hard to see. But that was what it was – a sculpted head. Made of amber maybe. Creepy.

'Fucking freak show,' she said under her breath.

She looked around at the room in the strange blue light. Here too there was shit all over the floor. Over by one of the windows there was a big scorpion hanging on the wall.

'Terrific.'

Then she heard it.

A thump, then what sounded like a generator coming on. It was very faint, and for a moment she thought it had to be coming from somewhere else. But there weren't any properties near enough, and now that she was listening for it, she could feel a faint vibration in the floor.

She looked down at her feet. Bare boards here, vibrating just the tiniest amount. There was a faint throbbing pulse to it. A generator, definitely. In a basement.

She could see the light switch now. It was over by the door, not far from where she'd been fumbling around in the dark. She went over to it and flipped it on, and now she was seeing marks on some of the walls, dark smears, finger daubings. And something on the floor. In amongst the torn clothes and books. Hair. White hair, in clumps and curls, snagged here and there around the baseboards. She shuddered, backing away into the living room.

Then she was back in the kitchen. She stood at the front door for a moment, breathing the clean desert air. The light was fading fast.

No car. At least none that she could see. No one around. Just that smell. She was going to have to find the source of it. She needed a drink. A drink and maybe a flashlight. She put the gun on the kitchen table and went over to the refrigerator. Opened it.

50

She missed the turn, overshot by a couple of miles before realizing her mistake. At seven o'clock, with the sun starting to set, she spotted an old guy clearing ground behind an ugly cement bungalow, and stopped to ask for directions. He had crosses tattooed on the back of each hand, squinted at her piece of paper as though it were a subpoena.

The track that ran up from the highway twisted between huge rocks before cutting sharply right and climbing through the Joshua trees. If she hadn't been told, she wouldn't even have known the place was there. The building was at the top of a rocky slope, wedged into the hillside under a teetering granite outcrop that ran along the top of the bluff in a broken crest.

The light was changing, the intense blue of the desert sky darkening to violet and indigo.

She sat there with the engine running, feeling fluttery, her hands tight on the steering wheel, picturing herself turning around and pulling away. LA was only a couple of hours further west. That was all she had to do, turn around, go get on with her life as though *Mirror* had never happened, care for her baby boy, take a job in his white museum on the hill.

Of course, that wasn't going to happen. They wouldn't allow it. They would smear her now, like they'd smeared Perry. She hated to think what kind of a reaction her abrupt departure had provoked. There'd be head-shaking in the board room, suggestions that perhaps she wasn't as innocent as they'd all thought. Of course, if they knew where she'd gone, if they knew what she knew, it would get a lot uglier than that.

What she knew. That was the problem. All she had was some assumptions and a bunch of illegally obtained documents. As usual the picture was just a little out of focus. But this time she wasn't going to accept it. She switched off the engine.

Dusk was coming in so fast she could almost feel the planet turning, and, sitting there looking out at the lunar landscape, she remembered Dan walking away from the car the time they'd stopped in the middle of nowhere, no-place, Union County, New Mexico. He'd walked out into the shimmering flatness, his arms held out like wings, laughing. He'd loved the desert so much. That had been in the summer of '86. He'd wanted to sculpt it all in paint, to drag his hog bristle through the rinding layers, plough it up, build pictures.

A light came on in the house. She caught her breath, watched without blinking, hoping to see something – a shadow, or maybe a face, an old man looking out at her. Koenig. He'd been up here incognito for forty years. She imagined rooms stacked with paintings, then pictured empty rooms – a sad old man watching TV sports. An angry old man who couldn't bear to see other people making money out of a lie.

She got out of the car, and looked back down the hill towards the highway. Just thinking about the other woman was enough to make her shudder – so hokey and local-seeming in the supermarket, with her simple advice and talk of dogs and honest blue gaze. There was an ugliness to her that went beyond the acne-scarred skin, a bad impression that you carried away with you like a spore.

It wasn't hard to imagine her being involved in what had happened to Bissel. She shivered, and rubbed at her bare arms. Who the woman was, or who she was working for, she had no idea. Benton, perhaps. Or maybe Kruger. How she'd gotten to Twentynine Palms was another mystery, but Ellen couldn't see the point of the morning's pantomime with the flyers if she'd known where Koenig lived. No, she'd acquired that piece of information at the mail receiving agency.

So where was she now? Ellen looked around, saw only rocks and scrub. She'd missed the turning, perhaps, and was now on her way to Victorville. Unless she'd parked her car somewhere out of sight. She turned on her heels, surveying the stony land. Bristling yucca and ragged broom-stick Joshua Trees. Boulders. Nothing. There were furtive rustlings in the trashy undergrowth that began a few feet from the road, and then, once she'd started up the track that led to the house – faint at first, but increasingly audible as she approached the open front door – a faint rhythmic vibration that seemed to be coming up through the desert floor. There was something down there underground.

The smell drifted out to greet her.

'Hello?'

Her voice sounded cracked and small in the silence. She cleared her throat, called out again. Then rapped on the door frame. Nothing. She pushed back the screen door.

Standing on the threshold, breathing garbage smells, she saw the stuff all over the floor – spilt food, empty cans, a footprint smeared in tomato sauce. And something else. It was in front of the buzzing refrigerator. Something opaque and pinkish yellow. Glossy.

'Hello?'

The refrigerator shuddered, and fell silent.

Stepping over broken crockery, she moved further in, skidding a little in the pinkish yellow stuff. Whatever it was, it was as slippery as chicken grease.

In the open doorway, she froze.

The woman was standing there. Holding a gun. She brought a cigarette to her lips, pulled, exhaled, saying nothing. Then she glanced down at her foot, wiping whatever was on it on the rug.

'I bet you can't guess what you just stepped in,' she said.

Ellen couldn't take her eyes off the gun.

'So,' said Billy. 'What's the deal?'

Ellen shook her head.

'I don't . . .'

Billy smiled, nodded.

'Ellen – it's Ellen, right?' She paused, nodding again, smiling. 'I can't tell you the kind of day I've had. The past couple of days, in fact. I can't tell you how tired I am.'

Ellen became aware of the room, the floor.

Billy stepped over the rubble of broken plates, strewn clothing, torn papers and books, got close enough to touch the gun against Ellen's left nipple.

'Fooled you with those flyers, didn't I? You're not as smart as they say you are. You know what else? You're prettier in the magazines.'

She drew her cigarette to a glowing point, tossed it aside.

'Okay,' she said, wearily, smoke leaking from her mouth. 'I'll put the question a different way. Why are you here? And . . .' She held up her free hand. 'Before you have a stab at that, you'd better think seriously about giving the right answer. Because, I *know* you didn't come all the way here for nothing.'

'I came here to talk to Franklin Koenig.'

The smile died on Billy's lips. She smacked her with her open hand. Not hard – enough to draw a little blood, though. Ellen took a step back, tripping on junk, bringing her hands up to her face.

'You think I'm stupid?' said Billy under her breath. 'Koenig's dead.'

Ellen was shaking her head now.

'I'll knock that smug look right off your face if you try to fuck with me, Miss Lindz.'

'I'm not. It's the truth. He's alive.'

'Talk to me about the money.'

'She got it. Rosa May. Carey gave it to her. On her birthday.'

Billy blinked, knew it was true, and knew how close she'd been. A black bitter feeling swept through her as she drove her fist into the other woman's stomach, watched her go down, rolling on the floor.

'It's the truth,' she groaned. 'Not all the money. Two million she said.'

'Two million,' said Billy, choking on it. 'Two million?'

'It's true,' said Ellen. 'I swear.'

Billy backed away from her, aimed the gun at the tangled head of hair.

'That leaves seven million,' she said. 'Where is it? Is it here?'

'I don't know.'

Billy racked the pistol.

There was a simultaneous flash and bang.

Ellen felt like her head had split down the middle, couldn't hear her own scream, rolled over, pushing up on all fours, ears ringing, breathing smoke, seeing the woman back across the room in a stuttery puppet walk, seeing her sit down hard, her limbs thrown outwards.

There was a horrible croaking sound. The woman was clutching at her throat, eyes staring. Then she made a gargling roaring noise as she struggled to get to her feet.

Boom!

Ellen's head rung like a hammer-split bell and Billy snapped backwards in the chair. Her mouth came open.

Ellen turned and saw smoke twisting under the naked light bulb, then the old man standing underneath, shirtless, mildewed black suspenders hooked over shoulders that were covered with a fuzz of gray hair. He was older even than the man in Linda Carey's snapshot. Gravity had gotten its hook into him, gravity or grief, snagging sallow cheeks, drawing creases into folds on his wattled neck, opening moist red seams under the wide set blue eyes. Only the nose hadn't really changed, spearing out of the thickly tangled eyebrows in a clean ridge that ended in a powerfully spreading tip. His mouth, twisted to one side as it always had, worked in a slow toothless churning above the cleft chin. The ammoniac stink was his – the stink of old urine in older clothes.

He was hurt, drawing tight rasping breaths, fluttering fingers pressed to his distended belly.

'Where is she?'

For a second Ellen thought he must mean the woman on the other side of the room.

'*HEY!*'

His forehead clenched, compressing ridged brows. The voice was extraordinary, seemed to boom out of the depths of him.

He raised the gun.

'Who?' said Ellen, cowering. 'Where's who?'

'One.'

'I don't know who you mean.'

'*Two.*'

'Please.'

He cocked the hammer, and sighted along the barrel. Ellen squeezed her eyes shut, then heard her name through the pounding of the blood in her ears. He was saying her name. She opened her eyes. He was staring at her, a smile twitching in his cheek.

'You're the one she chose. You're the successor.'

Ellen nodded, understanding. That was who he'd been talking about. *Her*. Benton.

'You think I came down here with . . .' She shook her head. 'No. No, Benton doesn't know anything about this.'

'Liar.'

'It's the truth. Nobody knows.'

He pointed the gun at the dead woman in the chair.

'She knew.'

He sighed, and the anger seemed to leave him. Then he was looking down at the wound in his stomach. Blood was pissing out between his fingers.

'She shot me. Can you believe that?'

He wavered for a moment, looking lost.

'They said she was sick,' he said dreamily. 'In the paper. They said they couldn't stop the bleeding. There was something wrong with her blood. I didn't know. How was I supposed to know that, if she never talked to me?'

Ellen looked around the room, saw torn books, smashed pictures, dead house plants, an iron stove. A torn canvas was slanted against the wall under a filthy window. A door led through to another room which was glowing blue. Her eyes came back to the woman. Still now, staring, her tongue pushing out over her bottom lip.

'What did you do to Perry?' said the old man.

'I didn't do anything.'

'Where is he?'

'I don't know.'

He stabbed the gun at her, suddenly angry again. 'You killed him.'

'No.'

'To hide the truth.'

'I *wanted* the truth. I tried to get him to tell me.'

'You were worried about your precious *Mirror*.'

Ellen shook her head.

Koenig looked at the blood on his fingers. There was a neat little hole in his belly, sending out a steady pulsing stream.

'It was you,' said Ellen. 'Who sent the documents to Perry.'

'She shot me,' he said, sounding astonished now.

He worked his lips. 'Trailer trash. Coming in here. Rummaging in my stuff.' Sounding nuts now. A nutty old man. He scratched his chin with a harsh rasping sound, seemed to waver, to tune out. 'What are we going to do now, baby? What are we going to do?'

'You wanted Perry to tell the truth,' said Ellen.

His eyes wandered. He seemed not to have heard, but then he was nodding, looking at the blood on his fingers.

'So let me tell it,' said Ellen. 'Let me get you to a hospital.'

He walked past her, groaning softly, pointed the gun at the other woman. For a second Ellen thought he was going to pull the trigger again. But then he slumped down on the black couch.

'No hospital,' he said. 'They'll find me there.'

'But you've been shot.'

He was still for a long time, sitting there with his hands on his knees. Then his face twisted in grief. Ellen moved toward him, and he stabbed out the gun.

'I only want to help,' said Ellen.

'You can't. Too late. She's gone.'

He closed his eyes, then leaned back against the couch.

'Forty years,' he said softly. 'A life's work.'

Ellen looked around the room. Apart from the battered canvas under the window, she couldn't see anything.

'Some special things,' he said.

Suddenly he was furious. He struggled to his feet, and slouched over to the body.

'Coming in here! Rummaging around! Are you trying to tell me she isn't with you?'

Listening to himself as he talked. Ellen could see it. Listening to himself as though it were someone else talking. He'd been alone for a long time. He jabbed the gun out again.

'Answer me, *goddamnit!*'

Ellen jolted, shook her head, backing away.

'I think she followed me,' she said. 'In Twentynine Palms today . . . she just showed up.'

'She just showed up. And what about you? How did *you* find me?'

'Rosa May.'

That threw him. His mouth came open then snapped shut. He lowered the gun, walked through into the next room.

She was alone.

She looked at the dead body and shuddered. Then looked through the doorway at the kitchen.

'She gave me a photograph,' she called out. 'Of you. And your wife.'

The blue neon flickered in the other room. Through the doorway Ellen saw a recliner. A TV. A small table. There were drawings on the wall. Some of them under glass. She took a step towards the door.

'Your wife; at the hospital, they found some papers on her. This photograph. Some till receipts from . . .'

He was standing in front of a freezer cabinet. A neon tube produced an eerie blue glow. The glass was fogged with condensation.

'Mr Koenig?'

Blood dripped from his overhanging gut. He seemed not to hear her, was gone again, all sense of urgency forgotten. He just stood there gazing into the cabinet. The blood made a tapping sound as it hit the boards.

'Why did you do it?' said Ellen.

He put his head against the glass, singing softly to himself.

'*Icicle Joe the Eskimo lives upon the ice.*'

'That night on Long Island.'

'They were going to kill me,' he said.

'Who?'

'They thought I was gonna talk. *He says it's very nice as he cuts himself a slice.*' Singing again now. 'Getting the body was easy,' he murmured. 'The teeth – that was harder. Mine really weren't too bad.'

Ellen came and stood beside him, peering in through the foggy glass. There was a small bust on a shelf. No plinth or stand of any sort. Just a woman's head. It looked like it was made of a pale cloudy amber.

'What is it?'

'It's what I do.' Koenig stared, dead-eyed. 'You'd think that being shot would hurt more,' he said, dreamily. Then he looked at her, sober, stern. 'This is old. This is nearly thirty years old. I don't do this anymore.'

Ellen looked back at the bust. There was a softness to it, as though it had been modeled rather than carved.

'What is it?'

'Linda. It's always Linda. Linda means beautiful. But Belinda means snake.'

'Is that a resin?'

He shook his head, eyes on the sculpture.

'She had some cosmetic surgery back in the seventies.'

'Oh,' said Ellen, bringing her hand to her mouth. 'Liposuction.'

The bust was made of human fat.

'Clinics, they just throw the stuff out. Bagged up in sachets. Not so nasty. I pulled them out of dumpsters. It's liquid at room temperature. I started out molding, then freezing. Then, later on, modeled it cold.'

Ellen shook her head.

'It's strange. It reminds me of—'

Koenig flinched and put a bloody hand on her arm. For a second Ellen thought it was the wound. But it was the comparison he couldn't bear. He didn't want to hear about what anyone else was doing.

'I did this long before . . . I was doing this long before . . .'

'It's beautiful,' said Ellen.

He seemed to relax again, and went back to looking at the sculpture, and for a moment they stood in silence, gazing at the strange little head in its wash of neon blue.

Neither of them heard the kitchen door open.

'Fat *is* beautiful,' he said. 'Candles. Soap. Ambergris. Not to mention butter, cream, liposomes themselves. Also, what do you think a breast is? Fat was of fundamental importance to the development of life. Membranes and so on. The inside and the out. One of the first tricks the embryo performs when it becomes a little ball. So it's far more precious than gold, say, or lapis lazuli, which I only mention because I was conscious, have become conscious of working in that tradition – the precious substance to represent the precious thing, but not in the conspicuous consumption way of cathedral treasuries –

closer to the shamanistic arts, magical or occult correspondences.'

He stared and stared, lost in the object and its associations, his free hand modeling the air. He didn't even know he was bleeding now, didn't know he was holding the gun.

'And there's a kind of . . . there's an emotional spectrum that makes it . . . that made it interesting to me. From desire to disgust, you know. Crème Chantilly, earwax.'

Staring in at the piece as though he had never seen it before, totally absorbed.

'When I did this it was more of an ironic piece; came out of the relationship we had at that time, Linda's obsession with her looks. But then . . .' He sighed, winced, shifting his weight, 'I got excited about it. I did a big soapy holocaust piece, but I lost that. They're hard to maintain.'

'You have to keep them cold.'

'That's the least of it. There's mold. Fungi. The piece that was in the refrigerator . . . I was cleaning it.'

'The woman . . .'

Koenig nodded.

'She dropped it. I saw her do it. That piece was older,' he said. 'Precious.'

'It's like the . . .' She'd been on the point of mentioning *Self* melting in Charles Saatchi's refrigerator.

'Then there's bacterial infection,' he said, rambling on, oblivious. 'I buy antibiotic sprays in Tijuana. Anti-fungals. Insecticides.'

'You get insects?' Ellen peered in at the head. 'How do they get inside?'

Koenig tapped the glass.

'Not in here. They don't get in here. In the studio. They love the blood pieces.'

'You work in blood.'

He turned to look at her.

'Why did you never denounce them?' she said.

He frowned at that, shaking his head. Then looked down at the pool on the floor.

'And why . . . Perry?' said Ellen. 'Why not just . . .'

'Back then.' He drew his hand across his face, smearing his forehead and nose. 'After I . . . I was scared. I mean, I was looking over my shoulder for a long time. And then, well, I'd betrayed some people. I thought . . . I was concerned they'd be dismissed. I didn't want people trashing Gorky. Or Jackson.'

'Did you ever . . . did you tell Pollock what was going on?'

He shook his head.

'Anyway, it doesn't matter now.'

A floorboard creaked.

Ellen turned, felt the old man's arm go around her neck, felt the gun at her temple.

A small withered ghost was standing there. Her haggard features blurred by blue light. She was holding a small silver pistol.

'I'll kill her too,' said Koenig.

'She doesn't care,' said Ellen watching Leslie Ann take aim, seeing the flash as the little pistol popped, knowing she'd been shot as Koenig pulled her against him. His big gun banged so close it burnt her face, then she was falling, going down, aware of Koenig trying to hold on to her, knowing she'd been shot, thinking – having the time to think before she hit the floor – I'm dead now, then hitting the floor, seeing Koenig stride, seeing in a kind of frozen blur his great jutting belly leaking blood, firing again, striding over and away, still firing, leaving her there in the smoke and glass.

Things blurred. She rolled, thinking I can still roll over, aware of glass on her face and in her hair, pushing herself up on her knees, hearing shouts that made no sense to her. Blood was streaming from her right ear. She saw something on the ground, realized it was her hearing aid, got a flash of Dan, his face up close, concert lights twitching on his sweat-slick face, then she grabbed a big piece of glass, and the feel of the edges in her palm brought her back, and she tried to stand and could stand and walked stiff-legged away from the noise, going deeper into the house, pushing through a door, moving along an unlit passage, getting as far away as she could so that they wouldn't shoot her again.

A musty room.

She was breathing. She could feel her lungs filling, but it was impossible to hear because of the ringing in her head. There was a pain high up on her chest. It felt like she'd been hit with something. Struck with a hammer on her left shoulder. More struck than pierced. She felt at the area with trembling fingers, shrinking from the wound itself. There was a hole there, she was pretty sure of it. There was a hole and she was bleeding, but it made her feel woozy to think about it, so she concentrated on breathing, beginning to think a little more clearly, beginning to take stock.

I'm okay, she said to herself. I'm not dead.

Sounds filtered through. Muffled thumps and shouts. Put pressure on the wound. In her head she was talking to herself. She had to put pressure on the wound, but she couldn't bring herself to touch it. She tried tearing a strip from her T-shirt, biting, pulling, getting desperate. A piece came away. She scrunched it into a pad, held it against the hole.

She was in a storeroom. That was what it looked like. There were boxes around the walls, what looked like mail sacks. A small window opened onto the rising ground behind the house. She could see the rocks out there. That was where she wanted to be. Out there under the stars. She'd been shot. She couldn't believe it, got a flash of the pinched look on Leslie Ann's face in the muzzle flash, then panicked because she wasn't thinking clearly. She needed to think if she didn't want to die.

'Don't want to die.'

The fuzzy sound of her own voice was scary.

Someone was yelling obscenities. Her mouth was unbelievably dry.

For a long time it was quiet.

She didn't recognize the smell at first, but then she knew it. A cigarette. Harsh, slightly peppery. Leslie Ann.

'Ellen?'

The smoke-veiled voice. Close. Ellen caught her breath, pressed back into the mail sacks.

'He was going to kill you, Ellen. I was trying to hit *him*.'

Footsteps, moving softly over wooden boards.

Something moved in the mail sacks. It came to Ellen that she was standing in something soft. Hair. She was standing in human hair.

A creak of floorboards.

'You only have to look at this place to know he's mad,' said Leslie Ann.

She was on the other side of the door.

A snout emerged from one of the mail sacks. Ellen closed her eyes.

The doorknob jiggled, then started to turn. Ellen pushed backwards, and the rat came all the way out, dropping lightly onto her shoulder, then leaping to the floor. The door came open. There was a muffled yelp as the rat skittered out.

'My *God*.'

Ellen could hear the old woman gasping. She was standing there in the open doorway.

'My God, this place. He always was such a pig.' She took a breath, called out: 'You always were a pig, Franklin.'

Stillness. Someone went past the window. Ellen pushed back into the mail sacks. There was someone out there. They came back. There was a face now. Hartnal. He had his hands up, was trying to look in. He rapped on the glass.

Leslie Ann came into the room. She crossed to the window, tried to open it. But it wouldn't open.

'It's nailed *shut*,' she hissed. 'Go around to the front. Go Around To The Front.'

Hartnal disappeared.

Leslie Ann, stood there, head tilted to one side, listening.

'Oh Jesus,' she whispered. 'Sweet Jesus. My sweet Ellen.'

All she had to do was turn around.

Heavy footsteps out in the passage.

Leslie Ann crossed to the door, then stepped outside.

Ellen breathed again, listened to receding footsteps, then moved softly over to the window. Nailed shut. Just like she'd said.

She crossed to the half open door, and put her head out into the passage. Nothing. There were three doors on each side. No windows. At the end of the corridor, an open door. There was blood on the floor and on the walls. Keeping her eyes on the open door, she started to back away along the corridor in what she thought was the direction of the living room. A hinge creaked.

'*Lewis*?'

Ellen froze, turned her head, trying to pinpoint the sound.

Then she was hearing Hartnal's voice. It sounded like he'd just come into the house.

'No sign of her outside. Is he dead?'

'Dying. Bleeding like a pig.'

'What about Ellen?'

'Shot. Hiding.'

'Burn the house.'

'We find her first. We make sure.'

A door opened. Ellen saw blue light on a wall, heard footsteps coming in her direction. She backed away along the corridor, stepping in blood, tried a door handle, turned it, pushed. The door was jammed. She pushed into the gap, saw stacked boxes. She could hear breathing now. It sounded like Hartnal, sounded like he was standing in the corridor.

'I don't know what he told you, Ellen.' His voice boomed, bogus, avuncular. 'But what you have to understand is he was a terrible liar. And a fraud. He let so many people down. He was never even a painter, you know. He'd been a painter, but he'd given it all up.'

Footsteps.

'He *said* he was a painter, but he wasn't.'

'It's true, Ellen. He could never paint.'

Benton now.

Ellen could hear them trying doors. She looked down, saw bloody footprints. Hers.

'He talked and talked, but when it came to sitting down, the poor man just couldn't . . .'

They were whispering. Ellen looked at the footprints, *knew* they were doing the same thing.

She ran.

A gun banged, once, twice, three times. Something hit her in the leg, spinning her round. She clattered into the staircase, and slammed the door shut behind her.

It was cold. It stank.

Bam.

The door jumped under her hand, and suddenly there was a hole in the wood. Fragments floated in a narrow shaft of light.

She moved on down the steps, slipping a little. There was blood here too. In the light coming through the hole, she saw steps going down into the darkness. The walls were roughly gouged, scabbed with red-painted plaster. She could hear the generator more clearly now. There was a smell of diesel mixed in with the other stink.

Muffled urgent talk from the other side of the door.

She took another step, stepped on something hard, kicked at it. A shell casing. They were scattered all over the steps.

Above her, the door cracked open an inch.

She moved on down into the darkness, slipping in blood, dizzy with the pain in her leg. She hit the sandy floor, came up hard against some oil drums, spinning, groping forward into deeper darkness, passing the generator that clattered in the dark.

Then there was a wall. She came up against it, gasping for breath. A dead end. It took her a moment to realize that it wasn't stone, but metal. She felt around, felt rivets, the seam of a weld, a lever. Part of some sort of mechanism. She pulled it. It didn't budge, but the door came back against her as she pulled, spilling freezing air onto her feet. The stink rolled out in a putrid wave. She gagged, set her teeth against her rising gorge, pulled harder and the heavy door rode slowly back.

Freezing blackness.

The stink was too much. Too bad. She couldn't go through it, fell to her knees, choking.

'Ellen?' Benton's voice came from above. 'Ellen it's okay. He won't hurt you now.'

Silence. They were listening at the top of the stairs.

'What *are* you doing down there?' said Hartnal.

'Fuck you, Lewis,' she croaked. 'Fuck the both of you.'

'Oh dear,' said Hartnal.

A round of diffuse light appeared at the bottom of the stairs. They'd found a flashlight. Ellen turned and peered into the darkness, trying to see what the hell it was. A storeroom was her best guess. A place where Koenig had kept his work. But it was too dark to see. There were more drums here. Diesel for the generator.

Footsteps. They were coming down the stairs.

She stepped over the threshold, and pulled the door closed behind her, held her breath for as long as she could, then sucked in air and gagged and retched. The vomit hit the floor with a smack, hot and almost sweet-smelling in the foulness. She heaved and heaved, until she was heaving nothing, then leaned back against the door, gasping.

Muffled voices.

They were on the other side of the door. There was a clank. They'd taken hold of the lever. The door started to move. She turned, fumbling for something to hold on to, scrabbled at the heads of rivets as the door inched open and then in the flashlight beam saw a bolt, two bolts, and grabbed hold of them and yanked the door closed. Clenching her teeth against the searing pain in her shoulder, she shot them across, felt them bang home, collapsed, gasping to the floor.

She must have blacked out.

When she came round she was face down on the floor, and there was a disgusting taste in her mouth. She rolled onto her back lanced by a stabbing pain in her leg. She was shaking convulsively, couldn't stop. She let out a groan, forced herself up onto her knees.

'Ellen?'

They were still there.

She felt at the bolts, made sure they were still in place.

It didn't make sense to her – a refrigerator door that locked from the inside. Then she thought of what Koenig had said about the studio, and she knew where she was.

It was freezing. She lost it for a moment, sobbed, terrified in the overwhelming blackness and the cold. Her leg hurt and it felt like there was a metal spike in her shoulder now, and she was going to black out at some point and then die. She felt around her, trying to orientate herself. There was the door, and then further along . . . ice. Not a frozen wall, or a wall with some frost on it. Ice.

If it was a studio there had to be a light. And it would be near the door. She ran her fingers over the frozen surfaces, but they were so numb she didn't even know if she'd feel a switch sticking out.

The generator stopped working.

She hadn't noticed it for a while, but now that it had stopped there was a new depth to the silence. All she could hear were her own shuddering breaths.

A groan.

Right behind her. Or to her left. It was impossible to tell. She spun round, trying to pinpoint it.

'Koenig?'

She stepped forward, stumbled against something, and went down hard. She came up holding onto what felt like a table leg. She managed to struggle to her feet.

'Mr Koenig?'

The groan came again. Ahead of her. She reached out, touched something cold and slightly wet. Something fell, rolled and dropped to the floor with a thud. She knew exactly what it was, thought for a second she was going to be sick again.

'Oh God, oh God, oh God.'

'Ellen?'

Hartnal. On the other side of the door.

'It must be terribly cold in there.'

A groan came then. Clearer this time. Koenig was coughing weakly. She crouched down, listening, moved on her hands and knees in the direction of his fluttery breaths. She found him jammed in next to a bench. He was shivering, his naked torso was ice cold.

He groaned again, and tried to say something. Ellen put her ear to his mouth.

'Ca . . . ca . . . can't do it,' he said.

'Is there a light?'

'Ge-generator. Off. Ca-candles,' he said, his voice barely a whisper. 'Matches.'

'Where?'

'Other side . . . Cu-cupboard.'

'On the other side of the room?'

Ellen turned around, and fumbled her way across the freezing gritty floor. She could hear Hartnal again.

'I don't suppose there's a body in there with you, is there? Ellen?'

Koenig sucked in a breath.

'G-go to hell,' he managed.

'Gu-go to hell yourself, Franklin. You miserable prick.'

Ellen bumped up against a cupboard door. It took her several minutes of feeling around to find the candles and matches.

But then she had a flame.

She struggled to her feet, her breath condensing in the candlelight. A room. A hall. It was hard to say how big exactly, hard to see beyond the light of the candle. A freezing mist hung in the air. Above her on the wall some sort of frieze was faintly visible under the rind of ice. It looked like a swimming pool. That's where they were. In a pool.

There were tables. and they were covered with heads. The heads were life-size, all facing the same direction. Some had rotted. Some were covered in pale blooms of mold.

Koenig coughed, choked. Ellen shuffled, hunched, freezing in her torn T-shirt to where he was propped against the wall. His pale bulk was streaked with frozen blood. There was frozen blood on his lips and on his chin. His left eye was almost closed.

He pointed a finger. Up above him on the wall was a battered ski jacket. Ellen took it off the wire hangar and tried to get it over his shoulders, but he was shaking his head.

'You,' he whispered. 'I'm a . . .'

But he slumped back against the wall.

'Over,' he said.

Ellen put the jacket on. It was a struggle with her left shoulder, brought the sweat out on her forehead despite the cold. She tried to zip it up, but she couldn't get hold of the tab. She sat down next to him. Then pushed up against him, trying to give him some of her warmth.

'F-forty years,' he said, his voice barely more than a whisper. 'Blood,' he said. 'Heads.'

'I t-talked to Rosa M-May,' said Ellen, pressing herself against his bulk. 'She t-told me what Linda used to do to herself.'

He nodded at that. They sat there watching the candle flame.

'Ge-generator . . .' he said. 'N-no more oil.'

Ellen wiped vomit from her chin with numb fingers.

'Are you having a nice cozy chat in there?'

Hartnal.

'Go to hell,' said Ellen.

'Is he telling you about the exhibition?' said Hartnal.

They were having to shout to be heard.

'There was an exhibition,' said Hartnal. 'In '53, I think. The first one we – I mean the museum – dedicated to the Tenth Street crowd. Twelve Contemporary American Painters and Sculptors.'

'To *hell*!' yelled Koenig, slumping sideways, gasping for breath.

Ellen put the candle on a work bench and helped him upright again. He'd stopped breathing. She tapped his face, slapped him harder. He coughed, spluttered, drew a deep shuddering breath.

They were laughing on the other side of the door.

'It was going to open at the Musée National d'Art Moderne in—'

Ellen slammed her fists against the door.

More laughter.

'M-MAM f-funded it,' said Koenig.

She turned. It was incredible. He looked half dead, but he was still lucid. She squatted down, got close to him.

'Don't talk.'

'Give me . . .'

He pointed at a head that was on the work bench nearest to them. Shrinking with disgust, she picked it up. It was heavy and very cold. She handed it to him, and he clutched it close. 'Want to . . . tell you.' He faded, struggled to stay conscious. 'MAM p-paid and the . . . the Association . . .' He moistened his bloody lips. 'Francaise d'Action . . . d'Action Artistique. The association paid . . . De luxe catalog, posters, publicity. Erlanger r-ran it. Erlanger. He was the . . . the CIA contact at the French Foreign Office.'

'The CIA paid.'

Koenig shrugged, coughed.

'L-Looked like official French money, but really . . . and then—'

'He was supposed to produce six canvases,' said Hartnal. 'We set him up, we promoted him. But he couldn't paint. You couldn't paint, could you, Franklin?'

'I kept going around to his studio and he'd be sitting there, agonizing as though he were a *real* painter,' said Leslie Ann. 'And then he started to have his doubts.'

Ellen shone the candle close to Koenig's face. The wax dripped onto his arm, but he didn't move.

'You met in f-forty se-seven,' said Ellen. 'Before . . . before . . .'

Koenig's lips puckered.

'P-planned it. Planned it. I w-was . . .with them . . .'

'You were with them? From the beginning?'

He shook his head, rolling it slowly back and forth.

'But when she . . . when she came to me . . . I'd already g-given up. Given up.' He gripped her arm, his hand like a frozen claw. 'But then . . . then I was. Again. An artist. And I wanted . . .'

He settled back against the wall.

He'd wanted to grow. And that was what he had done. In the dark.

Leslie Ann was talking again.

'He'd daub away at something for months, looking for the music – that was his phrase. And then he'd get so angry, so frustrated, he'd put the thing aside and start again. So, in the end, I painted them. That's the comedy of it, Ellen. Not all of them, of course. But certainly some of the best. And he didn't even know which were his.'

'All of which made him *very* depressed,' said Hartnal.

And so he'd sought a way out. Ellen knelt on the frozen floor. She couldn't stop shaking. Koenig was still now.

'He spent too much time in their company,' said Benton. 'It turned his head. He came to believe in it all, you see.'

'He had their respect. He had the esteem of the collectors. He loved it.'

Koenig tried to speak, but he could barely form the words.

'Discuss,' he said or maybe it was 'disgust'.

He tried to rally, tried to tell her something, tried to shake his head. Ellen put her ear against his mouth.

'Can't,' he murmured. 'I can't.'

And then he was still.

The candle was burning down to a stump. She lit the next one, letting the wax drip onto her fingers. Then she forced herself to stand, steadying herself against a work bench. She shuffled forward, determined to keep moving.

In the candlelight the heads were powerfully expressive, like some buried emperor's cortege of slaves. There was a central island of tables, then others around the walls. She shuffled along the aisles, letting the wax run on to her hands, holding her finger tips close to the flame, vaguely aware of Benton's voice on the other side of the door, explaining that it was her paintings that had received the accolades at the exhibition in Paris. It was she who had painted the Koenigs in her apartment.

And then there were no candles left, and Ellen was in the dark again.

At some point in the night, she heard Benton and Hartnal trying to get the generator going. But then it was quiet. They were still out there, though. They were just waiting for her to stop moving.

The dark was full of dripping sounds, and the steady crepitation of insects. There was less of an edge to the cold now, and pools were forming on the floor where before it had been dry. Ellen shuffled through the blood, too numb to feel disgust, or the pain of her wounds, too close to death to care. And then she couldn't walk anymore and dropped to her knees. On all fours she made her way back to where Koenig was.

She spoke to Dan. She told him that she knew he hadn't meant it when he'd taken his hand from her that night in the hospital.

She leaned against the stiffening corpse.

On the far side of the room a head slid from a table with a thud and splash. Then another. Koenig's work was dying with him.

'I'm s-sorry,' she whispered to the darkness. 'I didn't m-mean what I s-said.'

She felt for his hand in the darkness, his beautiful soft hand, but it was thick and rigid. It was difficult to get her fingers inside his, but then they were inside and she became aware of the wires.

'Dan?' she said weakly.

He was attached to so many machines. Tethered. And it came to her that it was his panic button, and that if he pressed it the nurse would come and make her go home. She tried to untangle the fingers and the wires, but they ran underneath his body which was bloody now. There was blood everywhere. And somewhere in the frozen layers of her mind, this registered, the wires registered, and she knew she wasn't with Dan at all.

She pushed him, sending his great bulk sideways, and then she was holding the wires, and feeling a switch, then more wire and what felt like a car battery. Everything connected. Everything connected to the switch in her hand. She smiled, and her lips split. A blood taste came into her mouth.

There was another heavy splash in the dark.

He'd planned another firestorm, but this one with no rebirth. Now she understood what he'd meant when he'd said, 'I can't'. He couldn't, but she could. She called out, heard a voice that was not like her voice, croaking in the dark.

'Leslie Ann?'

Dripping silence.

'*Leslie Ann*!'

She heard movement on the other side of the door. They were still out there. Ellen smiled her bloody smile and settled in against the artist, searching for his hand. She found it, gripped it tight. Then she thought of Ben, playing in his swimming pool, and her eyes filled with tears.

'Goodbye, my baby.'

She twisted the switch.

There was a muted thump, and the ground jolted, sending heads to the floor in a thudding cascade. Then there were a series of thick detonations on the other side of the steel door.

They hadn't even screamed.

Ellen opened her eyes, listening to a roaring crackling sound overhead.

It seemed to go on for hours. In the studio there was barely any change except for the door which began to heat up. Even where she was, slumped on the floor, she could feel the heat build, until finally it was too hot to bear, and she had to crawl further into the studio.

The heads were rolling now, sliding from the tables, and splashing into the blood. It seemed incredible that it had all come from one person. Forty years of bleeding.

She expected to hear fire engines at some point. But there was nothing.

She slept. Came sharply awake, feeling dizzy and dehydrated. Her neck and shoulder were fused in one block of pain.

It was silent now. The floor was sticky, scabbed with wrinkled clots. And there was light. Just a little. It was squeezing in around the top of the steel door. Either the heat had distorted the frame or a gasket had burnt away. Something was different. She crawled across to the door, and pulled herself up with the bolts, groaning against the pain. She slid them back, and pushed.

Daylight was streaming in through a hole in the roof, and what she could see of the cellar was just blackened debris. She clambered over what might have been a body, and crawled up the stone stairs to where the house had been. There was nothing now. Just a few jutting spars of wood, and a piece of low brick wall.

The air was so clean it made her head spin. She stumbled away from the house and down the slope in the direction of the highway, alive.

In LA

Mar Vista. March 2004.

The orange trees had been planted too close to the wall. They struggled there; the smallest of the three in particular, shedding leaves, rubbing its hard misshapen fruit against the stucco. The plan was to dig them out, relocate them to another part of the courtyard. But Ben was never around for long enough, and she wanted to do it with him.

Right now she was painting, trying to shut all that out – all her worries about Ben, the book, the goddamn museum; she was pushing a feathery gray into the underside of an almond green leaf that she'd sworn not to go back to until she'd finished the rest of the foliage. She tried to work in one key, starting with the darkest, but the temptation to model, touching in shadow and highlight, always got the better of her, and then things got muddy. She loved it though, despite the frustrations; the oily color, the smearing, scumbling, glazing playfulness, the memories of Dan it evoked. Not the sad ones now. Not so much anyway.

The biggest of the orange trees caught the sun in the late afternoon, and bounced back a green light so strong it tinted the columns of her tacky little dry-wall and stucco courtyard. It was amazing to her how much a dusty little ant-infested fixer on the wrong side of Pico Boulevard could cast a spell. The whole of LA was like that, though. Hockney had called it the most beautiful city in the world, a remark she'd always thought had more to do with naked men by swimming pools than the city itself, but now she saw how true it was. It was the light, the everywhere-present, eye-popping, super-saturated light.

The phone was ringing. It had been ringing all day.

She picked up the cordless from her little Moroccan table. It was Audrey again, her soon-to-be former agent.

'I can't believe you're doing this to yourself, Ellen.'

'Audrey, I know.'

She touched in a shadow at the top of the canvas, and winced. Her shoulder still hurt sometimes, but looked all right apart from the neat round scar. The mark on her thigh was worse, a scooped out puckered welt that drew stares whenever she succumbed to the temptation of a short dress. Cut off cargo pants were fine though, and since that was what she seemed to wear most of the time anyway, she didn't feel too sorry for herself.

'I read the email and I almost fell out of my chair.'

'I'm sorry.'

'You're throwing away a six figure advance, Ellen. *High* six. What happened to buying a house? What happened to getting a swimming pool for your little boy?'

Audrey had a way of sticking the knife right in.

Ellen dabbed in another shadow.

'I just can't bring myself to ...'

She shook her head. It was all too painful.

'To what?'

'Come on Audrey, we've talked about this. You know I had doubts. I just can't ...'

'*What?*'

'Destroy him.'

There was a clunk at the other end. Audrey, standing up. She had a telephone set that she wore on her head. She liked to walk around when she was making a point.

'Ellen, the guy was a *fake*. A spook, for chrissake! And the paintings – you said yourself, I mean it's right here in your proposal, half of them were painted by Benton!'

'More than half.'

The Sotheby's sale was a month away. Eight of the twelve canvases coming up for auction were from the Paris exhibition of 1953, and all but one of those were Bentons.

'The woman who, by the way, manipulated you for ten years and then tried to kill you. Not to mention bumping off the Chief Curator.'

'Unproven,' said Ellen frowning, rubbing gently at her shoulder. 'They still haven't found a body.'

It had only been six months since her night in the freezing dark. She still had nightmares about it.

They'd thought she was the victim of a hit and run. She'd been picked up on the highway, covered in blood and wearing Koenig's battered old ski jacket. And then they'd seen the bullet wounds, and she'd started to be able to talk, and they'd gone up to the place where there used to be a house, and found the bodies and the cellar like something out of Edgar Allen Poe.

'He was an artist,' said Ellen softly.

'*What?*'

'That was how he started out. And then he starved and struggled and he lost his way. Like people do. The irony is, Benton probably gave him back his sense of self-belief.'

'How do you work that out?'

'She was the one writing the articles, establishing him as an artist to watch, connecting him with the right people. She really made him what he was.'

The tip of the brush flexed against the taut canvas, depositing color. Leslie Ann had made her what she was too. Another irony. She'd taken a depressed student of English Literature and turned her into a curator. Without Leslie Ann she would never have achieved what she'd achieved. She often thought about her, and the thoughts weren't all bad. She often remembered the moment standing in a darkened room, pressed back into the mail sacks filled with hair, and hearing the old woman say, *My sweet Ellen*. There had been something like love in that. Even at the very end, there had been something like love.

'But it was all a *lie*,' said Audrey, starting to sound desperate.

'Except the part Koenig believed. There was this germ of belief and it grew. It's a big part of being an artist, don't you think? Believing that's what you are. That's why it was all so searingly painful. There were times when he forgot he wasn't one of those people. A Pollock. A De Kooning.'

'This is terrible. You've dwelt on this too long, reached some kind of sophisticated—'

'There's nothing sophisticated about it, Audrey. The person who painted *Mirror* was an artist. That's really simple. *Mirror*. A huge painting. For me, no less of an achievement than, I don't know, *Guernica*.'

'Come on.'

'I mean it. For me, it's right up there. It absolutely has its rightful place in the museum. And if I told the story, the whole story, they'd take it off the wall, shove it in a warehouse with all their other fakes.'

And it wasn't just a question of *Mirror*. There was the other work to consider, the forty years that had drained into the desert dirt. An artist's life.

'But, Ellen – this story, it's coming out anyway. There've already been leaks.'

Ellen nodded. The leaks had started almost from the moment she'd been admitted to the hospital in Palm Springs. That was where they'd patched her up, rehydrated her, put her back on her feet. Ben and Greg had gone to see her there, but most of her waking time had been spent in the company of the local police, who'd wanted to know what the hell had happened at the house. She'd told them the whole story, from the tampered catalog on, and they'd called Phoenix PD, who'd sent homicide dicks to talk about Linda Carey, and NYPD, who'd sent the guys looking into the Perry disappearance. It had ended up being quite a posse, and in among that posse there had been people with contacts in media. She was pretty sure about that.

By the time the first 'Curator's Night of Terror' stories had started coming out, she'd been in LA, where Greg had insisted she stay at the house. Abigale couldn't have been nicer, although it had been pretty clear she wasn't too keen on having the police parked at the bottom of her drive day after day.

'They only leaked what I told them,' said Ellen. 'And I didn't tell them everything.'

'Sweetheart, I know that. That's why we have a book deal.'

'Everybody thinks he was a painter. No different to Motherwell or any of the others. They think he was a painter who just happened to find out. If anything it raised his standing.'

'That's right. Which is a whole other issue. They're talking about twenty million dollar reserves on the big pieces at the Sotheby's sale. Doesn't that bother you a little?'

'That people are going to be shelling out for Leslie Ann's work? Sure. It does. But, you know. Caveat emptor and all that.'

Audrey pushed out a long sigh.

'God knows what the publisher's going to say. They were excited about this story.'

'Me too, Audrey.'

'And they're probably just going to look for someone else to tell it. That's the pisser.'

'Well whoever it is, they'd better have the proof. Because there are going to be a lot of very angry collectors out there.'

'Oh they'll dig up something.'

'I doubt that somehow.'

'Koenig did.'

'He had his connections. And he was very motivated.'

Audrey put her hand over the phone, said something to her assistant.

'Before I go,' she said, a little steel creeping into her voice now. 'There is one thing I feel I have to ask you.'

'Go ahead.'

'This has nothing to do with David Kruger, right?'

Ellen tightened up. She'd been talking to Kruger people all week, and the conversations had not been very pleasant.

'Why should it?' she said.

'It's just ... well you know, Manhattan is kind of small, and people talk. I know he's been very upset by all the press coverage.'

'Audrey. This is about me being able to sleep at night. It's got nothing to do with David Kruger.'

'Are you saying you haven't talked to him?'

'His attorney. Brokaw. I've had a few conversations with him.'

'Kruger unleashed his pit bull.'

Ellen put the brush down.

'Audrey. I'm telling you, it's got nothing to do with any of that. It's between me and my conscience. Me and ... Koenig.'

'The word is, Brokaw's in LA this weekend.'

'If it was anything like that, I'd have told you.'

Audrey wrapped it up, going brisk on her now. She wished her all the best in LA, and the way she said it, Ellen knew she wouldn't be hearing from her again.

The light was changing. The color was bleeding from the air.

Ben got out of school at four.

He was at a private school in Santa Monica Canyon, about four miles and at least four tax brackets further north. Every afternoon she drove up there in her rusty Volvo to pick him up. His friends' Moms drove Lexus and BMW SUVs. Watching him hunch his shoulders with shame as he climbed in next to her was not her favorite moment of the day.

All that had been very difficult, of course. Just as she'd feared, he had fallen in love with California, and (although this was harder for her to admit) with a house containing a swimming pool. He was a different boy in LA, a boy used to having expensive fun with his ready-made family.

And she'd moved out there so that he could have that fun, and, more importantly, be with his father. She'd come to the end of the line with the museum anyway. Most of the time Ben stayed with her in Mar Vista and only put up with it because it was temporary. At least, that had been the idea up until now. She'd made the mistake of talking to him about the eight hundred thousand dollars the Crucible Press had agreed to pay for her book. It wasn't the kind of money that bought you a house with a pool in the Hollywood Hills but it did get you out of Mar Vista.

Ben was not going to understand. And neither was Abigale. Without ever saying anything to her face, Abigale had let it be known that she should be trying harder, getting on with her book instead of sitting around the house in her paint-spattered clothes, and slowly pissing her savings away.

She grabbed a piece of kitchen towel and wiped her hands, then went into the house. In the bathroom she slipped on a clean T-shirt and checked her face for paint smears in the mirror. She'd cut her hair since Manhattan. Now it stood out in springy curls that made her look slightly crazy – 'edgy' would have been Tilda Kraft's word. She leaned in towards the glass, looking at a tiny broken vein under her left eye, wondering what you said to a little boy about choosing to stay poor. *This man – he was very special, and he really suffered for his art*. She shook her head. 'Suffered for his art'. What did that mean to a seven year old? What did that mean to anyone? It was such a cliché, but it was right there in the core of the truth.

It was between her and Koenig. It was between her and Dan.

The phone was ringing.

She shuddered as the skin came up on her arms, and for a second she was back there in the freezing dark, reaching out in total blackness, touching a head made of a woman's blood.

It was Dan who had saved her. It was Dan who had made her take Koenig's hand. She was sure of that. Since she'd been living in LA, she'd come across a lot of people who claimed to be in touch with the spirit world at one level or another. They talked about their karma and their former lives as though talking about their health insurance. It was part of the general drifty flakiness of the place. It would have been easy to talk about her feelings of connectedness with Dan, but she never did. Instead she painted, and, painting, she felt his presence. Not like a ghost at her shoulder. It was more like, in painting, she was doing something that rhymed with something else, something that was both outside and inside her. She rhymed when she painted. She wasn't alone.

The doorbell was ringing. A silly sitcom chime.

He'd saved her that night. He'd put the idea into her head to take Koenig's frozen hand. She knew that. Without that impulse she would have died there in the dark. And he'd done it because he wanted her to live. Because he forgave her.

The doorbell. She heard it now, blinked, pulled back from the mirror. Pushing aside the cheap cotton drapes, she looked out at the street. There was a Bentley parked in front of the house. Black as a coffin. A security guard type was standing by the driver's door.

'I don't believe it.'

The doorbell rang again. Whoever was out there, was really leaning on it.

She walked around to the front door and opened up. A flunky in a blue suit was standing there, looking her up and down. He asked her if she was Ellen Lindz. He said David Kruger wanted to have a word. Ellen looked past him at the car.

'You know what? I really don't have time.'

The doors opened and Sam Brokaw got out, buttoning his jacket, scoping the street as though expecting to be assaulted; then Kruger, smoother, touching at his hair, looking vaguely amused by the comedy of a neighborhood where people had to park on the street.

*

They talked in the kitchen. Kruger, wearing a beautiful pale blue suit and white shirt, looking a little lost on the Ikea stool she'd provided, Brokaw, short, balding, sly, standing at the sink.

Kruger said he really appreciated her giving him the time.

'Sorry it's only ten minutes,' said Ellen.

Kruger said he understood she'd been talking to Sam about why it was a bad idea to go ahead with her book.

Ellen nodded.

'Listen, if you've come here to talk about *Mirror*—'

'Please, Ellen.' Kruger held up a manicured hand. 'I need to say a few things, and since my time is limited ...' He brushed at his pants. 'First. I want you to know that neither I nor my family knew anything about Koenig. And when I say family, I include my grandfather, Henry. We didn't know about Koenig, and we certainly didn't know about the arrangements Benton and Hartnal seem to have made to keep this thing covered up.'

'You knew about OPC,' said Ellen. 'At least your grandfather did.'

Brokaw shook his head, and gave Kruger an I-told-you-so look.

'He never talked to me about it. Those were different times, Ellen. As I'm sure you appreciate. Now, I have been speaking to friends in the community as they say, and it has come to my attention that Franklin Koenig may not have been all he seemed.'

Ellen nodded.

'You knew,' he said.

'I know, and I have documentary proof.'

'Which, if it has anything to do with the documents recovered from Lewis Hartnal's residence,' hissed Brokaw, 'was obtained illegally and would be inadmissible in court, and which –'

'Sam, Sam please.'

The manicured hand came up again and Brokaw bit his tongue, glaring.

Ellen looked from one to the other, and suddenly she'd had enough of their bullying. She rose from her chair.

'Look if you've come to tell me to keep my mouth shut—'

'To make you an offer,' said Kruger. 'I'm here to make you an offer. Please.'

He waited for her to sit back down.

'You know how much I hate to see museum business discussed outside the museum.'

'You think you can just buy me,' said Ellen.

He shook his head. Nothing was further from his mind, apparently.

'Ellen. You're a person of great integrity. Naturally, you have a desire to see the truth come out. I just wanted to … to put an idea to you. I've been looking into this question of … Koenig's life, and well …'

It took him quite a while to develop the point. In the end it came down to precisely the conclusion she had reached. Koenig had struggled as an artist most of his life. *Mirror* was a remarkable work.

'Not everyone would be able to appreciate this argument,' he said, casting a disparaging glance in Brokaw's direction, 'which is based, at least in part, on a value judgment. A question of connoisseurship. My hope is that you … as the person who first responded to *Mirror*, will be able to see its merits.'

Ellen was shaking her head.

Kruger clicked his fingers, and Brokaw handed him an ostrich hide document wallet. He unzipped it on the table. There was a check book in there. 'Kruger Trust and Banking Corporation' was written in flowing copperplate across the thick ivory paper.

'I believe you have a publishing deal,' he said. 'Somewhere in the order of eight hundred thousand dollars.'

Ellen gave a nod. She could barely breathe.

'I'm willing to double that,' said Kruger. 'In exchange for your silence.'

'And the documentary proof,' said Brokaw, giving her a bullying look.

Ellen took a breath. She could feel the color rising in her cheeks.

'The paintings in the Sotheby's sale,' she said. 'The three you are selling.'

'Yes,' said Kruger, giving a little tug to his collar.

'They're fakes.' She let him sit with that for a moment. 'Wouldn't it be better if you were to withdraw them?'

Kruger swallowed hard, looking suddenly much less smooth. There was a softness to his mouth that had never struck her before.

'What's the reserve?' said Ellen. 'As a matter of curiosity.'

'I'm not entirely ...'

'Thirty million,' said Brokaw, gruffly.

'I can easily check that,' said Ellen, without looking at him.

'Forty,' said Kruger. 'Forty million.'

'So that gives me an idea of what my silence is actually worth to you. But then there's my sense of self-esteem. Self-worth, I suppose would be more appropriate in this context.'

She shot Brokaw a smile.

'Ten,' said Kruger.

Ten million dollars. For the first time Ellen noticed that he'd got a little paint on his sleeve. A little dab of red. She was always trailing it into the house. He saw it at the same time, rubbed at it, made it worse.

'Ten million dollars,' she said.

'You wouldn't be able to talk about it,' said Kruger.

'What do I say to my publisher?'

Kruger frowned.

'You say what *David* just said,' said Brokaw, shaking his head at her.

'Sam.' Kruger frowned, the faintest of lines appearing between his smooth sandy brows. 'If you can't maintain a civil tone ...'

Brokaw stalked out of the house.

Kruger wrote the check right there in front of her. There were a lot of zeros.

'And the documents?' he said.

'I'll give you the documents when the money is safe,' said Ellen.

He handed her the check, and then he was standing, looking around, looking out through the kitchen doorway at her beautiful dry wall courtyard.

'Nice place,' he said, 'Atmospheric.'

'It's all fake,' said Ellen with a shrug, 'but the sun's real and so are the oranges.'

He nodded, backing away. He wanted to get back to the safety of his car. She looked at the check, thought of Dan, thought of Koenig and for a split second it all came flooding back – the darkness, the cold.

'Mr Kruger?'

He stopped, turned.

She held out the piece of paper.

'I'm sorry,' she said. 'This isn't going to work.'

He came back to her, white faced.

'You have to sign 'em,' she said. 'Without a signature they're worthless.'

He signed it against the wall.

And then he was gone. She watched the car pull away, watched it turn the corner and disappear, only then becoming aware of the time. She was late. She was going to have to hurry to go find her little boy.